PASSION TO LIVE

Ron Lee

To Jennie and Peter

Ron Lee

TRAFFORD

Printed in Victoria, Canada

A cataloguing record for this book that includes the U.S. Library of
Congress Classification number, the Library of Congress Call number and the Dewey Decimal cataloguing code is available from the National Library of Canada. The complete cataloguing record can be obtained from the National Library's online database at: www. nlc-bnc.ca/amicus/index-e.html
ISBN: 1-4120-1824-2

TRAFFORD

This book was published *on-demand* in cooperation with Trafford Publishing. On-demand publishing is a unique process and service of making a book available for retail sale to the public taking advantage of on-demand manufacturing and Internet marketing. **On-demand publishing** includes promotions, retail sales, manufacturing, order fulfilment, accounting and collecting royalties on behalf of the author.

Suite 6E, 2333 Government St., Victoria, B.C. V8T 4P4, CANADA
Phone   250-383-6864   Toll-free 1-888-232-4444 (Canada & US)
Fax   250-383-6804   E-mail   sales@trafford.com
Web site www.trafford.com TRAFFORD PUBLISHING IS A DIVISION OF TRAFFORD HOLDINGS LTD.
Trafford Catalogue #03-2201   www.trafford.com/robots/03-2201.html

10   9   8   7   6   5

For Lena with Love

CHAPTER 1

In the murky light of the stormy afternoon, the big car skidded out of control on the rainswept surface of the road, then on the wrong side of the road, it smashed into the guardrail of the bridge. The occupants didn't have a chance. The front of the car folded like an accordion; then, broken and twisted, the car turned slowly end over end in the air on its way to the torrent of water in the swollen river below.

The police, and the newsreporter, while knowing of the victims' involvement with illegal drugs, never suspected that the incident was anything but an accident, which was exactly as Danny had planned. The tragic deaths of his erstwhile friends were in the past, and in the comfort of his first class airline seat, with his face showing no sign of emotion, Danny decided that Maria should never learn of his involvement.

Lying back in the seat of the large sleek jet, Danny closed his eyes and listened to the whine of the jet engines as the plane climbed steeply away from the Vancouver airport. He could relax for the next hour or so until the plane landed in Edmonton.

A brunette flight attendant, her short tight skirt accentuating her long legs, studied the passengers from the far end of the cabin as the plane climbed through the canopy of clouds into the blue sky above. The young stewardess' eyes lingered on Danny, noticing his tall near six foot body, his thick brown hair that was styled to be casual, his well tailored sports suit, together with his tanned handsome face made him appear younger than his thirty years.

Silently Danny cursed his father and his retirement that necessitated he become almost a slave to his work, and prolonged his separation from Maria. His father had become squeamish in his old age, and perhaps the part he had played in the fate of their friend, Doc Ellis, had contributed to his father's illness. The incident involving the death of Doc Ellis had shed some light on traits in his character that even a father found disquieting, traits that were better left to dwell in the dark places where they belong. With his eyes still closed, Danny's mood changed as his thoughts turned to Maria, his mistress ever beautiful, intelligent, with dark shining eyes.

Danny had a beautiful wife in Vancouver, but he had no compassion now, having a mistress was a way of life for him.

And now with his father's recent retirement, Danny had assumed the position of president of the multimillion dollar L.W.C. Import and Export Corporation, which did a large business; importing everything from fruits and vegetables to automobiles, and exporting such items as lumber, wood products, and fish. However, the company's one purpose for Danny, as it had been for his father, was to accumulate wealth and power; and few, if any, scruples were allowed to stand in their way to these ends.

Unlike his father, who was a public celebrity, Danny was relatively unknown in British Columbia. Even so, Danny was making the trip to Edmonton under an assumed name as a safety precaution, and to avoid unnecessary publicity. In Edmonton, Danny intended to visit his sister, Irene, who was attending the University of Alberta, and like himself, she was a partner in the family corporation. Irene lived in an expensive apartment with his mistress, Maria, who doubled as a companion and bodyguard. The young and pretty girl, smaller than Danny's sister, besides being a good friend of Irene's was intelligent, and with her training and experience as a private detective, she could be counted on to protect Irene with skill and efficiency. However, whereas Danny's business discussion with his sister was important, his greatest interest was, by the invitation of his sister, his surprise reunion with Maria, his lover and confidant. They had been separated because of family pressure and the necessity for her to go to Edmonton to assume the role of protector and companion to Irene, and they had been apart for a number of weeks.

Knowing that there were two private detectives on board to insure his safety, Danny could relax in the plane. His life was insured for fifty million dollars and the detectives, who for the most part remained discretely in the background unless danger threatened, were employed by the insurance company to protect their investment.

Danny had long become a friend with the detectives who were assigned to his protection, and they willingly cooperated in blocking the attempts of photographers and reporters to keep track of his movements. Thus, while Danny had in the past considered the detectives unessential, he had found them to be a convenient luxury that enabled him and his friends to enjoy the nightlife of Vancouver and meet people, which for a man in his position would have otherwise been imprudent. Then one such meeting, perhaps ordained from above, had profoundly influenced his life.

In the calm of the cabin, as the plane appeared to glide in space, Danny continued to think of Maria; a trace of a smile on his face as he contemplated the happiness their reunion would bring. While outside, high above the jagged peaks of the Rockies, the cold air, rent by the mighty thrust of the big plane, screamed about the fuselage. Like a merciless juggernaut, it drove on towards its destination, happy thoughts flying before it. However, the turbulence in its wake went unheeded, although a delicate balance was being disturbed, with a potential to create hell on earth. Such turbulence similarly caused in the minds of man and equally unheeded; unleashed fury, ugly in its intent, and terrifying in its consequences.

CHAPTER 2

It was on Friday afternoon, some time before, when Danny first met Maria. Danny and a friend, Tom Balant, after an enjoyable and exhilarating morning of sailing on Howe Sound, relaxed while enjoying a beer at Anne's Lounge in downtown Vancouver. Bert O'Brien the proprietor of the lounge was an old friend of the Lewes family, and as a child, Danny had played with Bert's son Ted although of more recent years, perhaps because of Ted's position as a lieutenant in the police force, they saw little of each other. However, this distance did not extend to Bert, and Danny glanced around the luxurious lounge hoping to see him.

Skillfully decorated, the lounge imparted the mellow and leisurely atmosphere of an old English manor. Heavy wooden beams supported the ceiling, and the dark wood paneling on the walls was decorated with an impressive display of shields, armor, helmets, swords, and lances shining metallic in the dim light. A large and expensive painting of an old English manor surrounded by lawns and trees, dressed in the rustic beauty of their autumn foliage lent richness and affluence to the surroundings, while a log fire flickered in a fieldstone fireplace which cut across one corner of the room. A hardwood floor fronted a low platform for a band, and at a lower level of the room, there was a place for dancing and entertainment, whereas the rest of the floor was covered with a rust colored carpet, which matched the upholstery of the comfortable chairs. The lounge was about half filled with predominantly young people and while some of the patrons leaned across their oak tables in deep conversation, others leaned back in their chairs enjoying, the scene before them. Pretty young waitresses moved gracefully between the tables supplying the food and drinks. The soft lights, and the music, punctuated by male and female laughter of some of the conversants added to the calm and happy atmosphere.

Laughing and talking with a young girl, Bert O'Brien emerged from the larger polished bar, where bottles gleamed and the barman poured and mixed; attending abiding waitresses, their hair swinging, eyes shining, and breasts heaving. Bert, after noticing Danny and Tom, said a few words to the girl by his side, then advanced across the floor towards them. His shoes shining, well tailored suit, white shirt and tie, receding hair, and ruddy face with the lines of sixty years creased into a smile all in keeping with his pride of ownership; as with his robust body swaying only slightly, he walked with dignity. Working hard and saving every penny they could, Bert and his wife, had planned the bar, together but she died before their dream could be realized, and he had given the lounge her name. A cheerful and pretty woman, Anne still lived on in the memory of Bert and influenced his decisions. As for an instance when Bert was contemplating employing topless waitresses in the lounge, he decided against it. Topless waitresses would increase his business he thought, but on the other hand, Anne would not have approved. Therefore, Bert knowing that Anne would have been sporty enough to go along with another plan settled for short skirts, and low cut necklines for the waitresses.

With, a large strong hand, Bert shook Danny's then Tom's hand as they rose to greet him and smiles of pleasure spread across their faces.

"I am glad you came in. There is an old friend of mine here whom I would like you to meet," Bert said. Then while still smiling, he turned towards the bar and beckoned to a dark haired young girl who, while smiling and swinging her hips in time to the soft music, was walking towards them. She was extremely attractive, and the young men, without being rude, studied her carefully. About five foot three inches tall her short blue dress, tied at the waist, revealed a lithe and well proportioned figure. Her shining dark eyes were set in a pretty face with a small turned up nose and a shapely mouth, which showed white even teeth as she smiled shyly. She breathed deeply when Bert introduced her as his niece, Maria Petersen.

"It is a pleasure to meet you," Danny and Tom said in unison, and they all laughed at the obvious enthusiasm of the two men trying to please Maria.

"Please join us," Danny said, as he and Tom pulled out chairs for Maria and Bert to join them at the table.

"Thank you," Maria replied, and smiling happily she accepted Tom's assistance with the chair, but Bert graciously declined the invitation, and after talking for a minute or two with his friends, he returned to the bar.

Examining the cocktail list and chatting with her two new friends, Maria, after some indecision, decided on an Alexandria no. 1. Danny summoned a waitress and ordered two more beers and an Alexandria no. 1, while Tom, who was single, dazzled by Maria, continued the conversation and failed to notice the waitress, as she bent forward attentive to Danny's request.

An hour of animated conversation passed with Danny and Tom describing the events of their sailing trip of that morning, until Tom excused himself.

"I am expecting a shipment of cattle at my ranch this afternoon so I must leave," he said, and addressing Maria, he went on. "I would very much like to see you again," and he smiled as he took a pencil from his pocket to write her telephone number. Smiling happily, Maria gave the telephone number, and then explained that she was staying with her cousin Ted and his wife for the time being. Tom stood and then walked towards the door, and with a wave of farewell, just before he passed through the door Tom excused himself. Then a strange foreboding crossed Tom's mind and silently he cursed his best friend.

Danny ordered another beer and an Alexandria no. 1, and he and Maria continued to talk amicably. Maria was twenty-one, and from Toronto, where her parents lived and she had come West for a change of scene and to look for work.

Later, while enjoying the conversation and when their glasses were almost empty, Maria accepted Danny's invitation to tea at the Bay Tide Hotel. Then on finishing their drinks Maria and Danny went to the bar, talked to Bert for a minute, and told him of their plans before they turned to leave. Absorbed by each other's attention, and happy they took a taxi to the hotel, which was not far away.

The restaurant in the hotel was near empty in the late afternoon, and sitting at a table by a window, Danny told Maria about Vancouver. Relaxed with one another they let the conversation lag and looked out over Burrard Inlet, reflecting the blue of the sky and the white puffy clouds that cast moving shadows on the water. A British freighter, flying the red duster and lying low in the water, was making its way to the sea, as busy deckhands hurried to batten down the hatches. A number of small boats crisscrossed the inlet and a ferry, its rails lined with people, was docking at a nearby wharf. A large Japanese ship, its decks laden with automobiles, moved slowly up the inlet in the company of a tug, and there was the muffled noise of racing winches as the sailors on the large ship raised the derricks in preparation for unloading. Then a blast from the ship's horn resounded a warning along the inlet, and a jet of white steam puffed from the funnel.

"Our yacht is at the club not far from here. I would like you to see her," Danny said, watching Maria as she turned her eyes away from the inlet. Maria smiled and reflected on the invitation. She had enjoyed boating and fishing with her parents on her father's homemade boat, with its three horse power motor, and though she had often admired sailing boats she had never had the opportunity to go sailing. "Have you done much sailing?" Danny asked.

"No," Maria replied, shaking her head slowly, and from the look on her face, one may have concluded that her lack of experience in sailing had been from choice, and not from necessity. In addition, while her face concealed her inward laughter she continued. "My father has a powerboat, which we used for pleasure," and to avoid the inevitable questions for details about the boat, Maria added, "how far is it to the club?"

"About a half hour by taxi, and my car is at the club, so I can drop you off later if you wish."

"That sounds okay, if I can get home before about six as I have promised to go out this evening with Ted and Alice."

The waiter poured them another cup of tea from the teapot he had placed on their table, and Maria finished the English muffin she had been eating. "My first and it is delicious," she said with a coy smile.

Danny smiled, and he wondered about the extent of her experience.

The two large ships they had been watching had disappeared from view and a tug, pulling two barges piled high with fresh cut lumber, was making its way to the mouth of the inlet.

Feeling light hearted, Maria settled back in the taxi that would take them to the yachting club, while the awareness and closeness of Danny stirred her inner emotions. The traffic was getting heavy as they crossed the Lions Gate Bridge heading for West Vancouver, and their driver sounded the horn impatiently to the driver of the car ahead who was driving slowly as his passenger watched the ships riding at anchor in the bay.

"Tourists! It is a wonder they didn't stop to take a picture," the taxi driver said, as the car ahead speeded up and the gray haired lady who was the passenger looked back. "Get a move on!" The driver exclaimed.

"There is no hurry," Danny said as he and Maria noticed the Ontario license plate, and turning to each other, they laughed together.

"Yea I guess you're right. We are all tourists sometimes," the driver said glancing in the rearview mirror.

Turning left off Marine Drive into the grounds of the Regal Yachting Club, the car slowed down to stop on the signal from the commissioner, at the gate, who on recognizing Danny sitting in the back seat waved the taxi on. The taxi drove, along a wide driveway flanked by lawns and trees, towards the large gray stone clubhouse, passed round the side of the building where rows of cars were parked, and stopped at the main entrance facing the sea.

The driver opened the rear door and Maria and Danny alighted from the car, and as Danny paid the driver, Maria her hair and dress catching the breeze, turned and surveyed the scene before her.

At the side of the entrance, rows of large windows faced the sea, and further along glass doors led out onto a terrace where a number of people sat at tables sipping drinks. A Canadian flag, its red and white colors bright in the afternoon sun, fluttered in the breeze atop a flagpole near the main entrance. Well cared for lawns with paved paths and beds of flowers stretched towards the blue sea, which was broken by the occasional white cap further out in the strait. Towards one side of the grounds four young couples were playing tennis on a court, and at an open swimming pool many people mostly children, were enjoying themselves while the sound of their shouts and laughter drifted across the grass.

Taking Maria by the hand as the taxi drove away, Danny pointed to the small cove on their left where rows of yachts were tied up at the wooden piers. A boat was being tied up after coming in from the sea, and an older man stood on deck watching as two bronze youths, clad only in shorts, their hair in disarray, busied themselves to make the boat fast. A boy and a girl were washing the deck of a white yacht, and three young boys sat at the end of a pier, their fishing lines, and their feet dangling in the water.

"The yacht with two masts, is the Bliss-In," Danny said, as they walked hand in hand along the path towards the harbor.

Maria surveyed the forty-six foot ketch in silence as they walked towards the boat. She noticed the boat's graceful lines, the fresh paint, clean teak decks, tall masts, and white sails lashed to the booms. Then as they reached the wooden gangway leading to the harbor below, Maria exclaimed with unconcealed admiration. "She's beautiful." Then going before Danny down the gangway, her short dress catching the breeze, she continued, "Does she belong to you, Danny?"

"In a way, the Bliss-In belongs to the Corporation."

Maria aware of the tax advantages of such an arrangement, thought of her father's meager wages, his home made boat, and the high taxes he paid. Then she laughed at the irony of the situation, and new disrespect for law was born in her mind.

Hand in hand, they walked along the wharf to the yacht, and as Danny climbed aboard, Maria, her long black hair hanging away from her head, looked up at the tall masts swinging gently against the background of a white puffy cloud.

"All aboard," Danny said with a smile, and Maria taking his outstretched hand, and revealing the extent of her long shapely legs, swung easily onto the deck.

"Do you mind if I look around?" Maria asked, smiling into Danny's eyes as she smoothed down her dress.

"Please do," Danny replied with a smile. Then leaning against the rail, he watched Maria moving about the boat gracefully as she inspected it from bow to stern with admiring eyes.

"She's really magnificent," Maria said, returning to Danny' side, her dark eyes shining with pleasure.

"I'm glad you like her," Danny said, visibly pleased that Maria's feelings for the yacht were akin to his own. "She is truly a lady under sail, seaworthy and fast in a good wind." Then as he took Maria's hand to show her below deck, Maria realized that, though she had only known Danny for a few hours, she was falling in love.

At the bottom of the steps to the cabin, Danny turned and put his hand lightly on Maria's waist to help her down the remaining stairs, and obeying her impulse, she leaned forward and kissed him on the forehead before stepping down into the cabin. Slipping his arms about Maria's waist and drawing her close, Danny felt her warm breath on his face as her arms circled his neck. Maria's soft warm body pressed to Danny as their moist lips met, and a surge of excitement gripped them.

"Not now," Maria said, as she gently held Danny's hand resting on her thigh. However, her words belied her feelings; her body yearned for fulfillment, and replacing her arms about Danny's neck, she allowed his exploring hand to find its goal. Her knees felt weak, as Danny, with an arm about her slim waist, led her to the chesterfield, in the stateroom of the boat; where, after unbuckling Danny's belt, Maria, aided by Danny, slipped out of her clothes, then lay back on the chesterfield while Danny undressed. Her pale skin contrasting with her black hair and her bosom heaving with anticipation, Maria with red lips apart, waited for Danny until he eased the weight of his youthful body upon her, and with impatience born of desire they united.

The sun was bright and the breeze felt cool on their cheeks, when Maria and Danny opened the door from the cabin and stepped out on deck. In response to their needs, the two lovers had accepted each other and found harmony. They had laid bare their passions, and the communication had given birth to an understanding that enabled them to be at ease, attune to nature around them, and happy with one another. The sounds of the water lapping on the hull and the wind playing with the rigging above deck came to them clear and beautiful as if life had only just begun.

"Take the wheel," Danny said, as hand in hand they walked the deck, both laughed happily. Maria, taking the wheel in her hands, pretended she was sailing the ketch before a fresh summer breeze. "Tom Balant and I are taking her out the day after tomorrow. Would you like to come along?" Danny asked, and as she looked up into his eyes, he put his arm about her waist.

"I would love to!" Maria exclaimed. Then thinking of the necessity of finding a job, she added, "Although I don't think I will be able to make it."

"We plan on going as far as Victoria," Danny said, frowning with disappointment. "You would enjoy the trip, and I would be delighted to have you on board."

"Okay," Maria said impulsively, having decided, that to hell with the job, or no job, she would go on the trip anyway. Danny's lips parted in a smile, showing his white teeth against the background of his bronze and handsome face, as his arm tightened about her waist.

The three boys at the end of the pier were shouting with excitement as one of them pulled in a small fish, and the seagulls that had been floating lazily overhead, swooped low over the water, as Maria and Danny, talking of the coming trip, walked towards the parking lot.

* * *

The following weeks flew by for Maria. She had accompanied Danny and Tom on sailing trips on five occasions, and she enjoyed and looked forward to the trips as much as her two companions. They were, for the most part, happy and carefree days with only the necessity for Maria to find a new job to mar her peace of mind, as they laughed and talked with abandon; while with the salt spray in their faces, and taking advantage of every breeze they maneuvered the spirited yacht through the sea.

Maria enjoyed sharing the work and the thrill of sailing the Bliss-In with the two men, and while she became a proficient sailor, she assumed the responsibility of cooking the meals. They enjoyed the times when they dropped anchor in a quiet bay, where Maria would show her skill in cooking a delicious meal while the helping hands and the appreciation of the two men made the work a pleasure.

The love that Maria felt for Danny had grown deeper in these past weeks, and with the knowledge that another woman had a prior claim on his love, she refused to let her mind dwell on the future. Life was something to be enjoyed to the utmost here and now; no part of this happiness should be sacrificed by attempting to foresee the future and prepare for possible eventualities that may never occur. It was only her dreams that she broached the subject of the future, and her conscious mind put it aside to let the chips fall as they may.

However, while Danny was preoccupied by the responsibilities to the company and his wife, Maria dated Tom a number of times, and liking his brawny build and generous nature, she grew very fond of him. They enjoyed each other's company in the restaurants they frequented, at the theatre, walking in the park and along the beaches, and on the occasions, they went fishing in a small boat, which Tom rented at Horseshoe Bay. Happy and carefree in Tom's company, Maria had not realized that their relationship was any more than that of good friends, until Tom sent her a bouquet of roses on the day following their first kiss. She was thrilled when she received the flowers and the small card, which read, "With love from Tom." Yet, when later she analyzed her own feelings she found only a reaffirmation of her love for Danny. Then on that same evening when she sat down to relax and read in the company of Ted and Alice, Maria felt sad; her tender feelings for Tom were not true expressions of love, and she was afraid that she might unwittingly hurt him.

Making Maria welcome in their home, Ted, and Alice bid her take time to find a job, and Maria, with her ego stimulated by their friendship and kindness, started her quest for employment with confidence. During her first three weeks in Vancouver, Maria, in spite of the time she had spent with Danny and Tom, used a good deal of time looking for work. Then it was only after a number of unsuccessful interviews and visits to Human Resources that she gave up, at least for the time being, her ambition to obtain work, which required intelligence, education, and initiative. Maria wanted to be self-supporting and independent, and when after buying a new dress and some necessities, she was down to her last ten dollars, she began to worry. Then finally at the beginning of the fourth week, demoralized and feeling that perhaps her three years of university education had been wasted, Maria found a job as a clerk in an office of a large department store. It was the same kind of work that she had done in Toronto, and disliked so much.

Maria hated the nine to five routines and the tedious work of filing and typing. Maria, while disappointed that her university education had not been seen as sufficient to obtain a better job, was aware that with her broad education and success in school, she was capable of doing more creative and responsible work. Thus, Maria, even while disappointed, rationalized her situations, and rebuilding her damaged ego, she was able to look to the future with hope.

Shortly after beginning to work, Maria, eager to be independent, moved into an apartment with two girls from the department store. She was not as comfortable as she had been with Ted and Alice, still; she liked her new friends, and the three of them together would be able to afford the two-bedroom apartment. Tom came to Ted's and Alice's place on the evening she moved and the four of them had a drink together before Tom drove Maria to her new home.

In the space of the next week, Danny telephoned Maria to invite her out for lunch during her noon hour break, and acting on impulses, for which on reflection she could find no reason, Maria while thinking about Danny almost constantly and longing to see him, made excuses to avoid meeting him.

CHAPTER 3

The buzzer sounded on the time clock to signal the start of the noon break and Maria automatically glanced at the clock as she pushed back her chair from the desk where she sat typing for most of the morning. Then she sighed with relief; Monday mornings were always a drag at work, and this one had seemed longer than usual. The rest of the week would not go so badly now. Taking a brown paper bag that contained her lunch from a desk drawer, she placed it on the desk. The room was quickly emptying of the girls, who a few moments before had been sitting behind the double row of desks that were flanked on one side by the private offices of the manager and the department heads. To the right the sun streamed through the Venetian blinds that covered the windows. Maria tucked her white blouse into her red skirt as she looked around the room for her two friends, and seeing Val and Debbie standing by the entrance waiting for her, Maria picked up her lunch bag from the desk and hurried to join them.

The girls were both eighteen and their pretty faces reflected their eagerness for life as they greeted Maria, with lunch bags in hand.

"Hi," Maria said, returning their smiles as she came to a stop in front of them.

"You should have seen Mr. Evans smiling at Debbie this morning," Val said, turning towards the door and putting her arm around Maria's waist.

"It was nothing really," Debbie retorted. "Mr. Evans brushed a pencil from my desk and he picked it up for me. Oh Val! You're exaggerating," she said as the three girls walked through the door into the furniture department.

Danny watched the three young girls as they walked towards him. Maria was prettier than the other two, and more mature. He also noticed Maria's shining dark eyes, her suntan, and red cheeks that contrasted with the other girls' pale complexions.

Then as Maria saw Danny before them, she stopped abruptly and the word, "Danny," escaped her lips.

"I have made reservations for lunch, will you join me?" Danny asked Maria, as the girls came to a stop and Debbie took Maria's lunch bag from her hand.

"Okay," Maria replied her voice almost a whisper. Then while Debbie and Val looked after them, Maria and Danny walked hand in hand through the furniture display towards the escalator.

"We will see you after lunch," Val said. Then Maria, with a backward glance, turned and waved to her two friends before they turned and resumed walking to the staff lunchroom.

"Egg sandwiches," Debbie said, holding up Maria's lunch bag.

"Ugh!" Val responded, pulling a face as Debbie laughed. "Let us eat in a restaurant tomorrow. I am getting sick of sandwiches every day."

* * *

Still hand in hand, Maria and Danny stepped into the busy sunlit street, and Maria realizing that she had left her sunglasses in her purse in the desk turned to Danny. "I hope you are not planning on a Dutch treat as I have forgotten my purse at the store," she said, looking up into Danny's face and smiling, as amid throngs of people and the noise of traffic, they made their way towards the hotel.

"Oh," Danny said, wrinkling his brow in feigned concern. Then with a smile, he continued. "We may end up washing dishes for our meals."

At an intersection, light hearted and happy to be alive, they observed the traffic and the bustle of people around them and waited for the traffic light to turn green before stepping off the sidewalk into the street. Then Maria felt Danny's hand tighten on her hand, and she was yanked back onto the sidewalk as, with screaming wheels, a late model black Ford wheeled around the corner, and after swerving to avoid some other pedestrians to their right, it sped off down the street.

"The idiot!" Maria exclaimed. "He could have killed us."

"Maybe he tried," Danny said his face grim and ruthless as he looked after the vanishing car. Then turning to Maria he smiled and went on. "But we are alive, that's the main thing". A shiver ran through Maria as she grasped the significance of Danny's words, yet she smiled to the thrill of the danger that threatened.

A tall man, dressed in blue slacks and a purple shirt, wrote down the license number of the car in a small notebook, and asked Danny if he noticed what the driver of the car looked like. Danny shrugged, "Dark wavy hair, sallow complexion, sunglasses, medium build, and that's about all."

"Thanks," the redhead replied, glancing up before continuing to write in his notebook.

The traffic light turned green again, and Maria and Danny walked across the street in the company of a crowd of people. Maria glanced in the windows of the dress shops as they hurried on their way, and she might have stopped to examine some of the clothes closer had she not been required to be back to work for one o'clock.

The dining room of the hotel was crowded, and a number of people stood in the entrance waiting for tables to become vacant. The experienced eyes of the maitre d'hotel saw Maria and Danny as soon as they entered, and he beckoned them to him. Then turning, he led them, through the maze of tables filled with people and passed waiters who politely stood aside to let them pass, to a vacant table by the window overlooking the inlet. With a slight bow and one graceful sweep, born of years of practice, the maitre d'hotel removed the reserved sign from the table and pulled out a chair for Maria to be seated.

"Thank you, Charles," Danny said, as he pulled a chair from the table for himself.

The maitre d'hotel smiled, "It's a pleasure, Sir," he replied, and promptly signaled a waiter to take care of them.

It was the same table where they had sat on the first day that they met, and the changing scene on the water, ever beautiful, brought memories of that day flooding back. They smiled across the table to one another. "It is like coming home again," Maria said, her dark eyes shining with happiness. Then after looking at the wide choice of food on the menu, she glanced at her watch; it was twenty minutes after twelve, there would be hardly time for a full course meal. "I will have the salmon and salad please," she said, handing the menu to the waiter. The waiter looked towards Danny.

"I will have the same, and bring us a small bottle of Chateau d'Yquem please."

The food was delicious, and as they sipped their wine, Maria told Danny about her apartment and her two girl friends who were so young and full of fun. "I never knew that housework could be so easy," Maria said, recalling to mind how the three girls pitched in together to clean the apartment and do the cooking. "But I have missed you, Danny." Then with laughter in her eyes she continued. "I am afraid that in a few more weeks I will have lost all my tan."

"Tom and I sailed the Bliss-In to Victoria a couple of days ago, and I missed you, Maria. Things were not the same without you."

Sipping their wine after the meal, Maria noticed Danny's every change of expression and listened while he talked of the Bliss-In and the voyage to Victoria. She could never forget him and sitting opposite each other at the table, she thrilled to see him and hear his voice. While Danny realized that for him, the Bliss-In could never be the same without Maria as part of the crew.

The soft music from the five-piece band filled the room, its members, dressed in purple uniforms, swaying in harmony with the tune. The music was superb and the men looked colorful in their purple suits. Then a frown crossed Maria's face, "Danny!" she exclaimed. "The man with the red hair and the purple shirt, who talked to you on the street, is sitting by the band."

Turning his head, Danny looked at the band. The tall man sat on a high stool and looked for all the world like a vocalist who was waiting to sing. "He is a private detective." Danny said, turning once again to Maria. Then hesitating as if in search of appropriate words, he continued, "He is supposed to see that I am not involved in any serious accidents."

A puzzled look crossed Maria's face, and then her eyes widened and a gasp escaped her lips as she glanced at her watch. "It is ten minutes past one, and I am late for work," she said, alarm evident in her voice, as she stood up.

"I'm sorry, Maria. I should have realized the time," Danny said, at the sound of urgency in Maria's voice. Then while biting back a smile, he signed the cheque for the meal.

"It is not that important really," Maria said, smiling with a show of confidence she did not feel. Allowing herself another white lie as they hurried from the restaurant, she continued. "The manager is a reasonable fellow."

Double-parked outside the department store, Danny watched from the taxi as Maria, her head held high, and her red skirt swinging, disappeared through the revolving doors of the store. A horn sounded behind the taxi and with a smile on his face, Danny instructed the driver to take him back to the Bay Tide Hotel.

Walking into the office as casually as possible, knowing that the eyes of most of the other thirty-five girls were upon her, Maria walked directly to her desk, and avoided looking towards the glass fronted manager's office, while Debbie, standing by a filing cabinet watched her with a broad smile on her face. Sitting down at her desk, Maria used both hands to smooth her black hair back over her shoulders, reached for a customer's, statement as the steady click, click, of key boards returned to normal in the room.

Fifteen minutes later Mr. Evans stood by Maria's desk, "Miss Petersen," he commenced. Maria looked up, the blood draining from, her face. "We start work here promptly at one o'clock, understand?"

"Yes, sir," Maria heard herself reply, although the little respect she had for the man, had drained away as the blood had drained from her face.

"Good," was Mr. Evan's curt rejoin, then wheeling on his heels, he headed back to his glass cage.

Bastard! Maria said to herself without movement of her lips as the color began to return to her face, and she started once again to mechanically type the statement into the computer. There is no reward for excellence, she mused while her fingers moved accurately and effortlessly over the keys. I do twice the work of some of the girls, and because they flatter Mr. Evans and tow the line, they stay out of trouble and are well thought of.

It required mechanical skills and ingenuity to keep the job that Maria, and most of the girls in the office were doing. Mechanical skill was required to do the work in the office, and the ingenuity was required to keep one's head above water on the meager wages the job paid. I will lose a half-hour's pay, Maria thought, as she continued to sum up her position.

Lacking a university education or training for a job, Marie's parents had found life far from easy in the work-a-day world, and she realized now that her father suffered injustices, and humiliation to continue with his jobs so that her mother and she could live a decent life.

However, I have a university education, and I don't intend to take dirt from anyone, Maria thought, while her fingers flew over the keys, and her mind rebelled against the situation in which she found herself.

Maria glanced up to Mr. Evans' office. He was watching her intently with a serious and thoughtful expression on his face. She opened another file on the computer and began to work on it, her pace slowing as her anger subsided. The clock on the wall showed a quarter after two; it would be a lifetime until five o'clock.

The remainder of the week bore on uneventful until a quarter to five on Friday when Mr. Evans asked Maria and eleven other girls to come to his office. Maria turned and looked at the rain through the window, and then with foreboding feelings she got up from behind her desk and crossed the room to the glass enclosed office.

Mr. Evans sat on the corner of his desk and smiled benevolently as the girls arranged themselves in an arc about him. His nose was too long for him to be handsome, although dressed in his business suit, white shirt, dark tie, and his wavy gray hair swept back from the temples, he looked impressive. Maria studied the girls who accompanied her. Some were new to the work and poor typists, and there was Phylis, the girl who always dressed like a hippie. Standing behind her was Doreen who was five months pregnant, and awaiting the return of her boyfriend who had gone up North to earn enough money for them to get married.

"Girls," Mr. Evans said in a loud voice to gain the attention of the girls, who were, for the most part, busy talking, and asking each other why they had been called into the office.

Looking serious now, Mr. Evans moved behind his desk, sat down, and leaned back in the swivel chair in readiness to start his little speech. Who in hell does he think he is? Maria thought, as she waited to hear what he had to say.

"The company has contracted outside help to do the work that you girls have been employed to do until now, and thus they find it necessary to terminate your employment as of five o'clock today. I have discussed this matter with your union representative, and as you are all temporary employees who have been with the company less than six months, he sees no reason to object."

Mr. Evans paused to give the girls time to absorb his messages and to observe their reaction. Most of the girls were dumbfounded by the news and some were angry, and while Doreen could be heard sobbing one of the girls said, "Amen." Clearing his throat, Mr. Evans began where he had left off. "However, I want you all to know that it has been a pleasure working with you. The store will be increasing its hours shortly, and we will need more part-time sales clerks. Therefore if you fill an application for part time employment at the employment desk, I will personally see that your application is given top priority."

"Bull shit!" Phylis exclaimed.

Some of the girls giggled, and Mr. Evans coughed in his hand before continuing. "Your salary cheque, including your holiday pay, can be picked up from the payroll manager right away."

Taking from his desk a small ornamental flag with the inscription, "THE MAPLE LEAF FOREVER, Mr. Evans fingered with it as he watched the girls file out through the door. Then with a worried expression, he considered the insecurity of his own position. It was not inconceivable that the company would require their office managers to have a degree in computer science in the near future.

Maria joined Val and Debbie who were talking to Doreen while they waited for her in the furniture department, Doreen was crying, and Debbie in an attempt to comfort her, placed an arm around her shoulder. "Don't let it worry you Doreen, everything will be okay," she said. "Write a letter to Joe tonight, and explain the situation to him. I'm sure he will think of something." Then as an afterthought, she added. "If you are stuck for a place to stay for a while, you can come and stay with us."

Val and Maria hastily gave approval to this idea, and sobbing anew, Doreen thanked them and declined the offer. "I'm okay for a time," she said. Then after a pause to control her emotions she continued. "If necessary I can go home." The girls paired off, and with the necessity to conserve their pennies, Maria and Doreen walked to the exit, and stepped out into the flood of people on the street to await the buses that would take them to their apartments. While Debbie and Val talking enthusiastically, headed for the ladies' fashions department.

CHAPTER 4

Feeling miserable and lonely, Maria arrived home at the apartment at six p.m., and while thinking about her parents, she put water and coffee into the maker. Then going to the window she looked down to the long lines of cars, buses, and trucks waiting at the intersection for the lights to turn green.

Maria moved her gaze up to the mountains. Rain clouds obscured the peaks so white and beautiful in the sun, and her thoughts turned to Ted and Alice. They had a lovely home and a good life together. Then she looked around the drab apartment, which nevertheless was her home and sanctuary from the world outside. Still, there was no permanency, and she wondered how long she would stay with Val and Debbie.

When the coffee was ready Maria poured herself a cup, put on a pretty red and white checkered apron that belonged to Val, and with her mind preoccupied with thoughts of Danny and the loss of her job, she busied herself preparing a casserole for their supper.

Danny had not been in touch with her since they had lunch together on Monday and because he was going to be busy with his family on the weekend, she would probably not see him until at least next week. The disgrace of being fired from such a crummy job was disconcerting; Maria frowned and wondered what Danny would think as she put the casserole into the oven.

The two girls burst into the apartment at eight-fifteen, hungry, and bubbling with life.

"Mmm, something smells good," Debbie said as she entered the door.

"Do you have enough for three, Maria? We are starved." Val said, while standing on her toes and speaking from behind Debbie.

"I've cooked enough for an army," Maria replied and she smiled as the melancholy mood lifted at the sight and sound of the two girls.

Putting on a bit of a show for her two friends, Val placed a case of beer down just inside the door and straightening up, with her ample breasts pushed against her short white dress, she breathed deeply. "We should drink wine instead of beer. The beer is just too damn heavy to carry," she said pretending to complain. Maria and Debbie smiled as they watched Val kick off her shoes and lay back on the chesterfield with an impish smile on her face, and an exaggerated show of being exhausted. Youthful, healthy, and pretty,

Val's short blond hair stood out against the maroon of the chesterfield, and legs bared to the thighs, she looked taller than her five feet four inches.

"What a show off," Debbie said good naturally before she and Maria went to the kitchen table. Then sitting down at the table, Debbie placed her hands behind her head and adjusted the pink ribbon that tied back her straight brown hair in a ponytail.

Observing Debbie as she laid the table with cutlery, Maria noted her small and slender figure. Although a serious person, Debbie was pretty, and her fitting pink dress showed a youthful figure with small firm breasts. Something was troubling Debbie, and Maria continued with her work and waited, for Debbie to unburden her problem.

Taking her hands from behind her head, Debbie toyed with the fork on the table before her. "Maria, will you and Val let Bill and me have the apartment on Sunday afternoon? I would like to cook dinner for him," she said, watching Maria's reaction carefully.

Smiling, Maria paused before replying, "I think it can be arranged," she replied with a smile, and after a second thought she continued, "I hope, that it won't be raining."

"Oh Maria!" Debbie exclaimed a smile of relief sweeping over her face. Then taking two pairs of panty hose from the bag that she had put on the table, she went on, "I just knew that it would be okay, so I bought you and Val presents."

It was sunny and breezy on Sunday afternoon when Tom took Maria and Val on the ferry to Nanaimo, where they had dinner and did some sight seeing before returning to Vancouver. It was an enjoyable afternoon, and they laughed and talked on the deck of the boat, the breeze blowing their hair about their faces, as with hundreds of others they breathed deeply of the fresh clean air. Tom was concerned when Maria told him that she lost her job, and it was only after she made light of the matter that he was reassured.

After stopping his truck at the girls' apartment, Tom held Maria close and kissed her as Val stepped onto the sidewalk. Then with a final squeeze of her hand before letting her go, he whispered. "You are beautiful, Maria."

Smiling happily, Maria looked into Tom's eyes, and the serious and thoughtful expression on his face changed to a smile before she got down from the truck.

The two girls, color in their cheeks, the wind in their hair, and smiling, waved to Tom as he drove away, then turning they walked in step to the apartment: their long slim legs, pink from the exposure to the wind.

* * *

It was six o'clock when the two girls arrived at the door of their suite, and not knowing whether Bill was in the suite, Maria rang the doorbell and waited for Debbie to let them in.

Looking angelic in her white mini dress Debbie opened the door for her two friends, greeting them with a smile, and asked if they had a nice time.

"Wonderful," Maria replied, as standing aside, Debbie allowed the two girls to enter the room.

"Help yourselves to some Chinese food," Debbie said, after closing the door and following her friends into the room.

"Chinese food!" Maria and Val exclaimed together inquiringly.

"We thought you were going to cook Bill a dinner," Val said, with a puzzled expression on her face.

"Bill said that he would prefer to have some Chinese food," Debbie said, smiling mischievously to her friends. "I phoned the delivery service for four orders as Bill said that he wanted to treat you to a meal also." Then as Val followed Maria to the kitchen Debbie went to her bedroom and started to make up the bed.

In the kitchen, Val sat down by the table and frowned up at Maria who was busy opening a carton of food. Maria returned Val's frown playfully before tousling Val's blond hair with her hand. "Chicken chow mien and flied rice, Miss?" Maria said, trying to imitate the accent of a Chinese waiter.

"Please," Val replied, and the expression on her face changed to a smile.

Maria and Val were enjoying the food when Debbie entered the kitchen, and taking three bottles of beer from the refrigerator, Debbie passed one to each of the girls, and joined them at the table.

The frown returned to Val' face as Debbie sat down by her side. The matter was not over as far as Val was concerned; although, she was not as much offended by Debbie's actions, as she was by being deliberately misled.

"I am sorry." Debbie apologized. "Bill is a nice boy, and I was aching for a man."

"That is not the point," Val said. "Why did you tell us the story about wanting to cook Bill a meal?"

"Did you believe that story?" Debbie replied matching Val's frown. "It was an excuse, I thought you would know that." Debbie turned to Maria. "Did you believe that I wanted the apartment just to cook a meal for Bill?"

"I didn't believe it was your main purpose," Maria replied. "You know what you are doing, and it really didn't matter."

"Forgive me for being naive," Val said. "I took you at your word."

"I'm sorry," Debbie said, repeating her apology, and understanding Val's feelings.

The girls were quiet for a while, each alone with her thoughts, as they continued eating and drinking, until Val, speaking to Debbie after an unusually long drink from her beer, broke the silence. "Does Bill want to marry you?" she asked.

"I don't know, and I am not sure that I want to marry him."

"You make it all seem so casual," Val said. Then turning to Maria she continued, "What do you think?" Not wanting to be involved, Maria shrugged her shoulders, and Val said in a quiet voice, speaking to herself as much as to the other two girls. "I guess I am the only virgin here."

Changing the subject, Maria told Debbie about their trip to Nanaimo, as Val serious and pensive, continued with her meal and contributed little to the conversation.

* * *

Restless and thoughtful, Maria lay in bed wide-awake. She had not slept a wink since retiring at eleven o'clock and it seemed that her whole life, past, present, and prospects for the future had been mulled over in her mind. She would not tell her parents about losing the job; although, she must write and thank them for the fifty dollars, which they enclosed in their last letter. She would visit the Human Resources office tomorrow, and the prospect of standing in line at the office made her wince. Danny would be fast asleep with his wife now. The sound of heavy breathing came from the other bedroom, and Maria switched on the bed lamp; it was two-thirty.

Slipping out of bed, Maria walked quietly into the hallway, and closed the door of the girls' bedroom before going to the kitchen. She poured herself a glass of milk, returned the carton to the refrigerator, then turning a chair sideways to the table; she sat down, brought up one knee, placed a heel on the chair, and hugged her leg to her breasts while she pondered the future.

The floor creaked, and Val crossed to the bathroom. A couple of minutes later Val entered the kitchen, her hair freshly brushed and looking tall and slim in her long flowered nightgown. Maria greeted her with a smile.

"I couldn't sleep either, Debbie's snoring is keeping me awake," Val said in a whisper.

"Would you like some milk?" Maria asked as she removed her foot from the chair. Val nodded in reply, and sat at the table and watched Maria as she walked to the refrigerator.

"Do you always sleep in the nude?" Val asked, as Maria took the milk from the refrigerator.

"I never feel comfortable in night clothes," Maria replied, reaching to the cupboard above the counter and taking out a glass. Maria poured a glass of milk for Val and brought it to the table, and she was conscious of Val as she walked back to the table.

"You have a beautiful figure, and you would be a success as a dancer," Val said, as Maria sat down and faced her at the table.

"I used to take ballet dancing lessons once, and I enjoy any kind of dancing," Maria paused and smiled before continuing. "Perhaps that is my field, as I can't hold a job as a typist."

The two girls drank the milk quietly for a time, until Val broke their silence. "Something has been bothering me since last night, and I hope you don't mind me asking you this?" she said. Then quietly pausing to look directly into Maria's eyes she continued. "Are you a virgin?"

"No." Maria replied, her eyes seeming to look into the past.

"Maybe I have been doing the wrong thing?" Val said, looking down at the table, her face revealing her troubled thoughts. "A number of boys have wanted to, and I have never let even one go all the way," she said. Then while conveying the feeling that she had been betrayed, she went on. "My parents always advised me that I was doing the right thing by remaining a virgin."

Taking Val's hand across the table, Maria looked into her friend's eyes. "The decision to remain a virgin, until a girl falls in love with a man with whom she is sure she will have a lasting relationship, is a personal thing, and is neither right nor wrong. Whether it is a wise decision or not, depends upon the personality of the girl. Your parents know you well, Val, and probably helped you make a wise choice." Maria released Val's hand, and took a drink of milk from her glass, before leaning back in the chair with her hands behind her head, the nipples of her breasts standing out red and firm as she studied Val with a thoughtful expression on her face. "Once a girl gives up her virginity, she arouses desires and emotions that are sometimes hard to control, and although sex is very pleasurable and satisfying it may cause problems for a single girl."

"A girl does not have to become pregnant anymore. Debbie told me last night that she has been on the pill for two years," Val countered.

"There are other problems that can arise; for an instance, venereal diseases, aids, and problems involving changed human relations," Maria said.

"Are you sorry that you gave up your virginity?" Val asked.

"No," Maria replied, smiling at the abruptness of Val's question. "I have to admit that I have enjoyed the excitement and pleasure that intercourse brings."

"Well, where is the harm?" Val asked, smiling now at Maria's frank admission.

"Don't get me wrong," Maria said, as she rubbed her wrists lightly across the nipples of her breasts. "I'm not trying to convince you that you should remain a virgin. That decision is yours alone. Most people, I believe, have sexual relations before marriage these days, and enjoy themselves with no harm being done. But occasionally someone falls in love only to find out later that they have been used, and not all people are strong enough to accept this without receiving long lasting and sometimes permanent psychological scars."

"You don't think I'm that weak-kneed do you?" Val asked, with a serious look on her young and innocent face.

Maria smiled. "Don't take it so seriously. Val I don't think anyone will break your heart, and you may break a few before you are married."

"Ah, you are pulling my leg now," Val said.

"Not really," Maria replied her expression thoughtful. "For an instance. I like Tom very much, and I believe that he has deep feelings for me and I could fall in love. We do a lot of kissing which arouses me sexually, and if he makes the proper advances, I don't think I will be able to resist. If this should happen I am afraid that Tom might be hurt when he finds out that I am in love with someone else. I will never marry him and bear his children. So you see, I am in a dilemma because I treasure Tom's friendship and wish to continue seeing him, and I am afraid I might do him harm because of my hunger for sex."

"It sounds as if sex can be both a reward and a weapon," Val said, and the girls laughed quietly before Val continued, "do you mind if I sleep with you tonight Maria? I don't want to awaken Debbie."

"Okay," Maria replied, and walking carefully so as not to wake Debbie, the two girls retired to bed. Minutes later in twilight between being asleep and awake, Maria felt Val's breasts soft and warm against her back, then she was asleep.

CHAPTER 5

When Maria awoke the sun was streaming in the window, and sitting up in bed, she stretched and looked around the room. It was nine-thirty, Val's nightgown was thrown over a chair, and her houseshoes were close to the door where she had discarded them hastily. Maria slipped out of bed, put on Val's nightgown, and turned in front of the mirror. It looked nice, and she wondered if Danny would like it too.

The kitchen was in a shambles. The breakfast dishes were still on the table, corn flakes were spilled on the table and the floor, and there were two unfinished cups of coffee. The girls had slept in, Maria concluded, and as she began clearing away the dishes, she hoped that they would not be late for work; they couldn't afford to get the axe. After cleaning the sink and table and stacking the dishes neatly, Maria made fresh coffee, and ate some corn flakes with milk before going to the window with a cup of coffee in her hand.

The sky was blue over the mountains and she could see the vapor trail of a jet flying east. She would write a letter to her parents right away in case they started to worry about her, and she would visit Human Resources in the afternoon.

The telephone rang just as Maria finished the letter. It was Danny, and her heart skipped a beat when she heard his voice. Danny asked her out for lunch. The invitation was a happy surprise, and later while they dined at the Bay Tide Hotel, Maria, with expectations of not being able to find work soon, promised to accompany Danny, starting Thursday, on a weekend cruise, on the yacht along the coast to Powell River. Maria chose not to tell Danny about losing her job.

It was two-thirty when Danny dropped Maria off at the front of the apartment, and parking for a minute, he watched her walking away towards the entrance. Maria's short green and white flowered dress showed her figure to perfection, and he regretted having promised his wife that he would take her to the club that afternoon.

The telephone was ringing when Maria entered the suite. "Hello," she said after hurriedly picking up the telephone, her handbag still in her other hand.

"Miss Petersen?"

"Yes," Maria replied.

"This is Steve Bailey, and I think you may know me. I am the redhead, who doesn't play in the band at the Bay Tide Hotel."

"Oh yes, Danny has spoken of you," Maria said, smiling at his novel introduction and realizing that Danny must have told him of her observations.

"I'm in the coffee shop downstairs, and I would like to speak to you regarding Danny. I wonder if you will have coffee with me?" Steve Bailey asked.

"I will be down in about ten minutes," Maria replied, and there was a puzzled look on her face as she replaced the receiver. Maria changed into her red skirt and white blouse to be more presentable for her visit to Human Resources, and being in no hurry to meet Steve Bailey, she lay back on the bed with her feet on the floor. Why did the detective wish to speak with her? Did, he think she was a security risk? Did Danny's wife have something to do with it? Maria waited fifteen minutes, took her raincoat from the rack by the door, and left the suite to take the elevator to the lobby.

It was coffee time at the nearby office buildings and the coffee shop was packed with young men and women laughing, talking, drinking coffee or soft drinks, and enjoying themselves before returning to their jobs for the remainder of their shift. Maria looked around the crowded room; Steve Bailey was seated by the window with his back to the wall; a position which gave him a good view of the coffee shop, the street, and the lobby entrances. Then he stood up and waved to her, and remained standing with one hand on the back of a chair until Maria arrived at the table.

"Miss Petersen?" Steve Bailey asked, as he pulled out a chair for Maria to be seated. Maria nodded in response, and sat down waiting for his introduction. "I'm Steve Bailey," he said, sitting down opposite Maria at the table.

The coffee shop was quickly clearing of people and there was a line at the cash. Maria was tense as she watched the detective signal a waitress. This was the first time that she had a good look at him from close, and though he looked handsome in his white and blue shirt, with a matching tie, and gray pants, he was older than she first thought. His arms were long and sinewy, and she could see a mat of red hair on his chest through his shirt; he was lean and hard, and whatever the reason was for their meeting, she knew, it had nothing to do with Danny's wife.

Steve Bailey pushed his empty cup towards the waitress. "Two coffees please." When the waitress had left, he smiled to Maria " It is the best that they have in the house and as you probably know my taste runs to beer."

"What is it that you want to see me about, Mr. Bailey?"

"Please call me Steve," he said, and he paused as the waitress set the coffee down and wrote out the bill. "I work for a detective agency, and my employer has instructed me to ask you if you will consider working with the agency as a detective."

"Why?" Maria asked. Suspicious of the situation, she continued. "I have no experience in detective work."

"Yes we know. We were in possession of your complete records the day after you met Mr. Lewes, and for instance, we know that you completed two criminology courses at university, and presently you are unemployed."

"You are right, Mr. Bailey," Maria said, smiling at the accuracy of the statement. "I planned to visit Human Resources this afternoon."

"Will you consider a position working for us?"

"I would like to hear more about it," Maria replied cautiously.

"Good," Steve said, smiling good naturedly and obviously happy with her decision. "If you will come back to the office with me, my boss will discuss it with you."

"Okay," Maria agreed, still dubious about the whole situation. While they were in the car, on their way to the downtown office of the detective agency, Steve explained the situation to Maria.

His boss was convinced that the man who had almost run Maria and Danny down a number of days ago had deliberately tried to kill them. The car used was stolen, the driver was an alien with a criminal record, and he had crossed into the United States that same day and disappeared. Further, it was suspected that other attempts would be made to kill Danny, and with training, she could help to prevent this. She would be responsible for Danny's safety while she was with him, and her remaining time would be spent studying and training in detective work. The traffic was getting heavy as they approached the Lions Gate Bridge leading to the city center, and Maria noticed that dark clouds were building up in the west and the waters of the Strait of Georgia appeared black. There would be a storm by the evening.

After alighting from the elevator on the fifteenth floor of a new office building, Maria and Steve walked along the corridor and stopped at a door with a sign; The Plastik Utensils Company printed in gold lettering. Opening the door, Steve allowed Maria to enter ahead of him into a reception office. A tall and attractive woman with dark hair sat behind a desk on their right, and behind her, a glass partition separated them from an inner office where a young man, and three girls were working. The woman behind the desk greeted them with a smile, "Mr. Dolansky is waiting for you inside," she said.

"Thanks," Steve replied, and accompanied by Maria he walked to a door, marked private. Once inside, Steve closed the door carefully while Maria looked about. They were in a large room, which contained five desks and other office equipment, the windows at the far end of the room overlooked English Bay, and to their left there was another small glass partitioned office. Maria and Steve walked to the office door, and a man of about thirty with dark brown hair and a swarthy complexion, who was sitting behind the desk asked them to enter, and rose to come around the side of the desk to meet them.

"Mr. Dolansky, I would like you to meet, Maria Petersen." Steve said.

"It is nice to meet you," Dolansky said. Maria smiled in response, and Dolansky continued, "please be seated," he said, indicating the chairs with his hand, and while Maria and Steve took chairs facing the desk, Dolansky returned to sit behind the desk.

Serious and thoughtful, Dolansky paused for a moment before beginning to speak. He was about five foot eleven inches in height and of muscular build, and in spite of his five o'clock shadow, he looked impressive in his blue slacks and white shirt with expensive cuff links, and his bearing was one of authority. "Steve has told you of your work as a private detective," Dolansky said.

"Yes, and it sounds interesting," Maria replied.

"Good. We have had quite a bit of difficulty keeping close enough to Mr. Lewes where we could really be effective in the event of a serious problem; your assistance will be greatly appreciated. You will have an expense account besides your salary, and to avoid unnecessary questions you can tell your friends that you are working at the Plastic Utensil Company as a typist, and making some deliveries where complaints are involved. Do not tell, even Mr. Lewes, the nature of your actual work," Dolansky said.

The discussion, which followed, lasted for another half an hour with Mr. Dolansky doing most of the talking and Maria agreed to start work the following morning at nine o'clock. When the interview was over, Maria declined Steve's offer to drop her off at her apartment; she wanted to be alone for a while to give her mind time to assimilate the past events.

The air felt cool and refreshing on Maria's cheeks as she stepped out onto the street. She would walk the four blocks to the bus stop by the department store where she used to work, and take the bus to her apartment from there. She glanced at her watch; it was five-thirty p.m.; her friends would already be on their way home, and she frowned as she thought of their disappointment when they would discover that she had not prepared dinner.

It had turned a little colder and the odd drop of rain was falling from the heavy clouds overhead as Maria, gathered the collar of her raincoat about her neck, and hurried along the crowded sidewalk, past the great variety of stores, amid the noise of the traffic on the street.

The rain was falling in sheets before Maria reached the bus stop, and her long black hair was shining and straight when she arrived home at the suite. Debbie and Val, still dressed in their office clothes, leaned back on the chesterfield with their feet resting on the coffee table. Val, holding a half empty bottle of beer in her hand, smiled to Maria as she came in through the door, and Debbie dabbed the ashes from the cigarette into the ashtray, which she held on her lap.

"Any luck?" Debbie asked.

"I found a job with the Plastik Utensil Company, doing typing and handling complaints." Maria took off her raincoat and hung it in the closet.

"I'll get you a beer. You probably need one," Val said, as Maria dropped into the easy chair facing Debbie.

Stretching out on the chair, Maria smoothed back her wet hair with her hands, and kicked off her shoes. "It is pouring with rain, and I got caught in it on the way to the bus. I thought I was being baptized."

Returning to the room, Val handed Maria an open bottle of beer, then going behind the chair where Maria was seated, she used a towel, that she had brought with her, to gently dry the rain from Maria's hair. "We don't want you to catch pneumonia now that you are in the money," she said, and continued. "Have you noticed that Debbie has taken up smoking again?"

"I noticed it as soon as I came through the door," Maria replied. Debbie took a long pull on her cigarette, and tilting her, head back she blew a cloud of smoke towards the ceiling. "It is part of my weight control plan," she said, bringing her head back slowly and smiling. "I gained three pounds in the last two weeks."

"Thanks Val," Maria said, as Val smoothed back her hair and returned to sit besides Debbie on the chesterfield.

"Are you sure that it is not all the fun that you are having with your boyfriend, that is the cause of you gaining weight?" Val asked, holding back her laughter.

"Not likely!" Debbie exclaimed. "I'm on the pill, and Bill is using condoms. If I get pregnant it will be a miracle," and the three girls laughed together.

"Tell us about your job," Debbie said.

After taking a long drink from her bottle of beer and inwardly wincing from the lies she was about to tell, Maria explained that she would be typing, doing general office work, going out to take care of complaints by customers, and delivering warranty replacements.

CHAPTER 6

Getting up early the following morning, Maria brushed her long black hair until it was shining and dressed as far as her slip, before calling the girls for breakfast. The three girls talked little while drinking their coffee and eating their cereal, and after listening to the news and weather forecast on the radio, Debbie and Val, still moving slowly started to dress for work.

Almost ready herself, Maria put on a short yellow dress with red trim then sat by the window while she waited for Val and Debbie to finish dressing. It was cloudy and the streets were wet, although it had stopped raining. In the distance, the mountains were barely visible. Apprehensive about her new career, Maria wondered about the legitimacy of the position. However, the pay was good and it would be a chance to save some money, and maybe visit her parents during Christmas. Dad could use a new shaver and it would be fun to go shopping with Mom.

"Quit day dreaming." Debbie said cheerfully, from the kitchen doorway, where the two girls were standing dressed, and waiting.

"Coming," Maria replied, and she became aware again of the butterflies in her stomach. "It will be sunny by noon," she said to conceal the apprehension about her job that try as she may she couldn't shake off.

"Don't bet on it. You know how dependable the weather is and we should take our raincoats just in case," Debbie said before she turned away and walked towards the outside door.

"If you don't like the job, quit," Val said, while she waited for Maria at the kitchen door. Then as the two girls walked through the living room, Val went on, "with both Debbie and me working, we have enough money to get by and you don't have to take any crap."

"Don't worry, I will be okay," Maria said with more confidence than she felt. Then she put her arm around Val's slim waist as they walked towards the door.

The bus was crowded and the three girls, with their raincoats on, stood crushed together on the way downtown. Then just before the Lions Gate Bridge, a woman, seated near where they were standing, got off the bus. Smiling broadly, Val motioned to Debbie to take the seat. "I think maybe you should sit down, Debbie; you know miracles have been known to happen," she said.

Debbie took the seat and looking up, she smiled to Val and Maria and the girls giggled while the other passengers looked on and wondered about their private joke.

* * *

"Good morning, Miss Petersen," the tall dark haired woman said, greeting Maria and smiling when Maria entered the reception office of the Plastick Utensil Company.

"Good morning," Maria replied, with somewhat less enthusiasm than she had hoped to convey, and she forced a reluctant smile.

The woman, in her early thirties, was well proportioned, and looking attractive in her dark green dress, rose from her chair and came around the desk to meet Maria. "I'm Mrs. Delilah Jonson," she said. "Mr. Dolansky asked me to send you right in when you arrived."

More at ease now, Maria's smile of gratitude came easy, although she was puzzled by Mrs. Jonson. There was something familiar about her that she had not noticed the last time they had met. I have seen her somewhere before in another context, Maria thought; yet, she just couldn't place the event.

"Mr. Dolansky will be in his office," Mrs. Jonson said, opening the door marked private and standing aside for Maria to enter.

"Thank you," Maria replied, smiling pleasantly.

At a desk facing her, and bending over a typewriter, where he typed laboriously with one finger, was a small man dressed in gray pants and a blue sweater. His thin face, hooked nose, and receding hairline combined to give him a gaunt appearance. Then as Maria crossed the room to Mr. Dolansky's office he raised his head, and looked briefly at Maria before returning to his work.

"Good morning. Please come in and take a seat," Mr. Dolansky said.

Maria returned the greeting, and sat down in a chair as Dolansky rearranged some papers on his desk. His expensive brown business suit fitted his solid frame to perfection, and gave him the appearance of a successful sports personality. When the papers were neatly arranged, Dolansky with a thoughtful expression on his face, leaned back in his chair and surveyed Maria with cold blue eyes. Conscious of his surveillance, Maria crossed her slim legs, straightened out her pretty yellow and red dress, and waited for him to begin. Then for the next one and half hours, broken only when a young girl brought them coffee at ten-fifteen, Dolansky talked with Maria in a soft and forceful manner, asking questions, considering her answers carefully, and outlining the techniques, requirements, and importance of her new position. No effort was spared to provide Maria with the necessary knowledge to start her new career, and impress upon her the gravity of the position.

She would be required to take two night courses in criminology at the university, and an afternoon course in physical training. In addition, she would practice with a pistol, which she would carry in her purse whenever she was with Danny, and if the occasion should arise, use it without hesitation in his defense. When Dolansky had finished with this outline at eleven-thirty, he asked. "Do you still want to take the job, Miss Petersen?"

"Yes," Maria replied immediately.

"Good," Dolansky said, and coming around the desk, he gave Maria a book on the work and responsibilities of a detective. "I want you to study this book and discuss it whenever possible, with one of the detectives who will be on duty in this office every morning. I will expect you to have a thorough knowledge of it within a month. Any questions?"

"No, and I will do my best," Maria replied, realizing that although she found Dolansky to be interesting, he had never once smiled, and he was just as formal as when they had first met.

"I will introduce you to the rest of the staff in the office," Dolansky said, and he motioned Maria to precede him through the door.

The man whom Maria had seen in the office when she arrived in the morning was sitting at the same desk. Cecil Banas looked thin, almost to the point of being frail, as he stood and smiled to Maria when they were introduced, and the hook in his nose became more pronounced, while his shining brown eyes indicated an alert and shrewd mind beneath his gaunt exterior. "We are on the same team guarding Danny Lewes, so please call me Cec," he said, and for some unknown reason, Maria felt a closeness and attraction to Cec; it was uncanny, and when they shook hands, their smiles had a quality like that of old friends who had met again after not seeing each other for a long time.

"Mr. Banas will give you a pistol this afternoon, instruct you in shooting at the gun club, and provide you with a company car," Dolansky said. "Mr.

Banas has only one fault as far as I know. He is an atrocious typist. Perhaps, you will give him some help with typing up his report after dinner."

"I would be glad to," Maria replied, as Cec, smiling with relief, let an eraser drop from his hand onto the desk.

A side door led Maria and Dolansky into the adjoining office of the Plastick Utensil Company. A number of girls and a man were working at their desks, and through a glass partition at the far end of the room, Maria could see Mrs. Jonson working with a computer in the reception room. Serious and formal, Dolansky introduced Maria to the persons in the office as a salesperson for the company, before they proceeded to the reception room.

"I believe you two ladies have already met," Mr. Dolansky said, when they stopped by Mrs. Jonson's desk.

"Yes, we met yesterday," Mrs. Jonson, said with a charming smile, and Maria noticed that Dolansky's face remained as serious as ever.

"That will be all for this morning," Dolansky said turning to Maria, "You can see Mr. Banas regarding your duties this afternoon. If you feel like a coffee at any time you will always find a good supply on hand in the outer office."

"Thanks," Maria replied, and she smiled in appreciation as Dolansky excused himself to return to his office.

It was noon and two girls from the outer office said. "Hi," and smiled as they passed by on their way out to lunch.

"You are new to Vancouver," Mrs. Jonson said.

"I have been here for a little over a month and I like it." Maria replied, as Cec Banas came hurrying from the inner office.

"Hold on for a moment please," he said to Maria, before addressing Mrs. Jonson. "Are you ready for me to take over while you go for lunch, Delila."

"I'm famished. I was afraid you may not relieve me today," Mrs. Jonson replied, busying herself putting papers away into the desk drawers. Then speaking to Maria, she asked. "Care to join me for lunch?"

"No thanks, there are a number of things that I want to clear up with Mr. Banas before I eat," Maria replied.

"I'll be in the cafeteria downstairs if you get through early," Mrs. Jonson said, smiling pleasantly. "I usually sit by the window." Then after picking up her purse from the desk, she walked gracefully from the office. Maria watched her go, and tried to recall where she had seen her before. There was still something puzzling about the woman, and the pertinent clarifying information seemed to be fighting to enter her conscious mind.

"I will get us some coffee, Maria," Cec said, breaking into her thoughts. "Would you mind looking over my report and correcting any mistakes you find?"

"Sure, is this it?" Maria asked referring to an envelope that Cec had placed on the desk.

"Yes," Cec replied turning at the door of the glass partition. Then with a wistful look on his face he continued, "I would have got my wife to do the paper work, except that I don't want her to see this one."

Still reading the report and making corrections with a pencil as she went along, Maria didn't look up when Cec returned with two cups of coffee. He placed one on the desk by Maria, and sat down on a chair facing her. Maria's face was grave as she read the report. She could understand why Cec would not want his wife to work on it, and perhaps her new job as a detective was more than she had bargained for. Although, from past experience she knew that she could handle just about anything.

* * *

Cec had intervened to protect Danny's father and mother after a knife wielding man attacked them. The incident had occurred a few days previous, just at dusk as Bill Lewes was leaving his West Vancouver office with his wife.

The assailant, a big man in his early twenties, stood in the doorway of a nearby bar watching the light in the window of Bill Lewes' office, and the door leading into the street. The man's hands were thrust into the pockets of his dark brown windbreaker, pulling it tight about his hunched bony shoulders, while his balding head, pale hollow cheeks, and sunken eyes made him appear older than his twenty-three years.

When the light went out in the window, he moved away from the doorway and walked briskly along the street towards the office, meeting Mr. and Mrs. Lewes as they walked towards their waiting car. Stumbling as he came abreast of them, he pulled a switchblade knife from his pocket and lunged for Mr. Lewes.

Bill Lewes swore as with a big powerful hand be brushed the man's hand away, and using a Judo chop, he knocked him to the ground.

Sitting in his parked car on the opposite side of the street, Cec had signaled the Leweses of possible danger before they came out of the building, and he was racing across the street to aid the Leweses when they were attacked. Cec kicked the knife from the man's hand before he had time to get up, while Mr. and Mrs. Lewes hurried to their parked car to drive away. Cec calmly stepped back from the assailant.

Staring at Cec intently, the man came up from the ground slowly, a look of hatred and contempt on his face for this small, and seemingly frail intruder, then a look of almost disbelief crossed his face and a bullet from Cec's gun slammed into his shoulder.

A police car and an ambulance arrived on the scene shortly afterwards and the man was taken quickly from where he lay bleeding on the sidewalk, but he died on the way to hospital.

The medical stated that the man, whose name was James Helliar, was a heroin addict, and if it was had not been for his poor health, he probably would have survived his wound.

The police report identified Helliar as an exconvict, who had been twice jailed for extortion and the sale of illegal drugs. He had been shot and killed while attempting to assault and rob Cecil Banas. No mention of Mr. and Mrs. Lewes was made in the police report.

With a serious expression on her face, Maria put down the last of the five typed pages, which described the incident in detail, then took the last drink of her coffee.

"Would you like another cup of coffee?" Cec asked.

"No," Maria, replied her mood pensive and troubled as she pondered what she had read. Had Cec shot the man intending to kill him? She didn't know. The witnesses and the police had cleared him of blame. It seemed that there were no questions raised, as to whether or not it had really been necessary to shoot the man. Why hadn't the witnesses intervened in the struggle?

"If you would be kind enough to retype the report for me, there is a computer in the private office," Cec said.

Maria nodded in reply, and picking up the papers from the desk, she walked towards the private office.

"I will join you when Mrs. Jonson gets back." Cec said, as he got up from the chair. Then going behind the desk, he flipped an electronic switch to unlock the door to the inner office.

When she had finished typing the report, Maria went to the window and looked out over the Strait of Georgia. It had turned out to be a beautiful day, the sun shone from a cloudless sky and reflected from the crests of the waves, whipped up by a stiff breeze.

A sailboat with two masts, her white and red sails full with the wind, was making her way towards the mouth of Burrard Inlet, and thinking of Danny, Maria looked across the waves to the horizon, then back to the sailboat. She loved Danny, and in her thoughts, she was by his side at the wheel of the yacht feeling the motion of the boat and the wind on her cheeks. She closed her eyes. How long will our relationship last? She mused sadly. Nevertheless, I will live my life to the full. Maria opened her eyes. The boat had turned away and was proceeding on a new course; running with the wind towards an unknown destination.

The sound of the office door closing aroused Maria from her daydreams, and she turned to face Cec. His off white crew neck sweaters, gray slacks, and black shoes, were all of good quality and expensive, and combined to give him a casual appearance. It would be hard for a stranger to characterize him into an occupation. He might be a sailor on shore leave from one of the freighters in port, and he would not look out of place in one of the bars off Hastings Street. However, by his dress, bearings, and manner of speech, he could just as well be taken for a business man who is prosperous enough to dress in a manner which pleases him, and which others might find a little eccentric. His hooked nose, shining eyes, and lean build, combined to give him a shrewd as well as a gaunt appearance, and in spite of his only average height, he was a man who commanded respect. She couldn't help liking him.

"Have you finished typing the report already?" Cec asked, as he walked across the office towards Maria his feet making no noise on the soft blue carpet.

"Sure, it wasn't very long," and in spite of the nagging thoughts of the gruesome incident described in the report, she smiled at the obvious relief which showed on his face.

Cec joined Maria by the window, and while standing side by side, looking out over the strait, Maria's thoughts returned to the report she had typed.

"Was it absolutely necessary for you to shoot the man?" she asked.

"He was a powerful man and intent on killing me."

"Why didn't some other people intervene?"

"He acted like a raving lunatic and the few people who had come onto the scene wanted nothing to do with him," Cec said turning to Maria as she looked into the distance across the strait. Then looking again to the sea, Cec continued. "Old man Lewes thought that my shooting was bad and Dolansky said that I should have shot to kill so that the man would never have another opportunity to attack the Leweses. The man was sick and out of his mind and he might have succeeded in killing the Lewes if given another opportunity," Cec said with a shrug.

Neither spoke for a while, and each alone with their thoughts, as they looked out to sea. "By the way, Maria," Cec said as he turned back to the room. "The desk alongside the window is yours." Then he walked to the desk, a little to the left of the window. "Steve cleared his stuff out last night. He thought that you would like a desk with a view of the sea."

"He shouldn't have done that," Maria said, joining Cec near the desk.

"You are the first woman to work from this office and we are pleased to have you on our team," Cec said with a smile. Then becoming serious, he continued. "Although I'm not sure that you could class it as women's lib." Then opening a drawer, he took out a pistol and handed it to Maria. "Put it in your purse. It is part of your equipment, and I hope that you will never need to use it in anger."

"Thanks," Maria said, taking the pistol and turning it over in her hands. It was a 9mm caliber of American make. A heavy gun for women. She snapped out the magazine, which was unloaded, then returned it to the butt of the pistol, before placing it in her purse.

"You have had some, experience with a pistol before" Cec said, which was a statement rather than a question.

"Just a little. I belonged to a gun club during my last year at university."

"We will go to the shooting range this afternoon to get some practice, and from then on keep the gun loaded and close at hand." Dolansky entered the far end of the office, and Cec hesitated for a moment while he raised his hand in a gesture of greeting. "Shall we eat at a café on the way to the shooting range?" Cec asked, giving his attention again to Maria.

"It sounds like a good idea," Maria said with a smile, "I was beginning to think that eating didn't go with the job."

"Wait for a minute while I give my report to Dolansky." Cec said and he walked away towards his desk.

Maria sat at her desk and looked through the window. A large ferry was making its way towards the shore, and she thought of the pleasant Sunday she had spent with Val and Tom when they made the trip to Nanaimo. Maria glanced back to Dolansky's office. Both men were standing and Cec was talking earnestly to Dolansky across his desk.

CHAPTER 7

It was six-thirty p.m. when Maria drove into the parking lot behind the apartment where she lived, and after parking the red Ford, she leaned back in the seat of her car and relaxed for a moment to gather her thoughts. The heat radiating from the pavement of the parking lot wafted through the open window, and touched her face as she brushed a lock of dark hair from her forehead. Cars were coming into the parking lot in a steady stream, and some pedestrians in the next lane stood aside to allow a car to pass before continuing on their way. She was bone tired, and at the same time light hearted and at ease with the world.

In the morning, Dolansky had confided with her that he was a friend of Danny's. He felt sure that when Danny learned that she was working as a typist for the Plastick Utensil Company, he would take advantage of their friendship to enable her to take time off from work to be with him; which is what they intended. Dolansky had assured her that Danny had no advance knowledge of her job, and under no circumstance should he learn that she was working as a detective.

On the way to the shooting range in the afternoon, she had enjoyed lunch with Cec at a small café. They lingered over their coffee while Cec told her something about her work as a detective, but talked for the most part about his family of which he was very proud. He and his wife owned a house in one of the better areas of the city; it was expensive and something they could be proud of. Their daughter had just entered college on Vancouver Island, and their son was in his last year of engineering at U.B.C.

At the shooting range, Maria had been amazed at Cec's expertise with a pistol. She had done quite well and he had praised her for her marksmanship, but she knew that she fell far short of his skill, and realized that it was by choice that Cec had not killed the man instantly who had attacked the Leweses.

Alighting from the car, Maria smoothed down her small trim dress, closed the door, and with her raincoat over one arm and her handbag in the other she walked across the parking lot towards the apartment. The extra weight of her handbag made her aware of the gun, and her new responsibility. Her job and her relationship with Danny seemed almost like a dream, and she swung her handbag slowly in rhythm with her hips as she walked to the apartment. Two young men who passed going in the opposite direction, whistled to her after they had gone by and she walked into the building with a smile on her face.

In her own suite, Maria put her purse down carefully, and was hanging her raincoat in the hallway closet when Val, dressed only in a sheer slip, came into the living room with a glass and a bottle of beer.

"It looks as if you are in training for being a nude waitress," Maria greeted her friend jokingly.

"It is training for married life," Val said, happy to see Maria. Then while putting the beer and glass down on the coffee table, she went on. "Take this beer and I will get myself another."

"Thanks," Maria said, and sitting on the chesterfield, she kicked off her shoes and took a drink from the bottle before filling the glass with beer. Leaning back, Maria closed her eyes and relaxed with the glass of beer in her hand and her feet on the coffee table. From the kitchen, she heard the refrigerator door open and close, the top being removed from a bottle, and the tinkle of glass before Val poured the beer into a tumbler.

"Where is Debbie?" Maria inquired, looking up as Val returned with a glass of beer and sat on the chesterfield.

"Bill met her at the office right after work. They said that they were going to eat out and take in a show." Val took a drink from her beer, put her feet up on the coffee table beside Maria's and leaning back; she stretched, with her hands above her head. "How did the day go, Maria?"

"Pretty good really. I have the use of a company car to make my calls, and it appears to be interesting work, with some responsibility and freedom to make decisions."

"Are you allowed to bring the car home with you?"

"Yes, it is mine, I understand, to use as I wish while I am with the company, and there is an expense account to cover the cost of traveling when on company business."

"It sounds like a very good job. What is the men situation there?" Val said straightening up and looking at Maria with mock seriousness, before she smiled.

Maria laughed, and rubbed the nipple of a breast that had been irritated by her nylon slip, and the two girls continued their conversation and drinking their beer.

* * *

The bedroom was dark when Maria awoke, and turning over onto her back, she placed her hands under head, and listened. She knew that it was not time to get up, yet suddenly, after being sound asleep, she was wide awake, and she wondered if anything had happened to awaken her. Val, breathing easily by her side, was fast asleep, and whatever had disturbed her had left Val sleeping peacefully. Maria opened her eyes. The moon shining through the kitchen window lit the hallway outside the bedroom door, and she heard the elevator pass the floor without stopping. She raised herself into a sitting position and glanced around the room; only the outline of the furniture was visible in the dim light; the dressing table, the easy chair, with clothes thrown across it and the night table with the lamp. Everything seemed to be in order, and the clock ticked away steadily on the dressing table, where Val had placed it so that it would be out of reach, its luminous hands showing the time to be ten minutes after one. Maria lay back on the pillow once again with her hands under her head. The noise of running water told her that someone was taking a shower on the floor above, and her thoughts turned to the events of the evening before.

Taking pleasure in each other's company, Maria and Val had spent an enjoyable evening together. Debbie had telephoned at eight o'clock to say that she was not coming home that evening, and she asked Val to bring her lunch to work. Maria had washed a dress and under clothes while Val baked a pie, and later in the evening when the telephone rang, Val answered it, and Maria smiled now as she recalled Val covering the mouthpiece and saying. "It's for you, and it has got to be him." Danny wanted to see her the following day, and as Dolansky had predicted, when Maria told him about her job with the Plastick Utensil Company, he had been both surprised and pleased. He knew Dolansky very well and it would be no problem for her to get time off to meet him. Maria feigned protestation, saying that perhaps this was not the right thing to do. However, Danny had been unmoved by her argument, and he had promised to drop into the office of the Plastick Utensil Company at about ten o'clock the following morning, and if the weather was good they could possibly go to the club for a game of tennis before having dinner together.

Pleased that she would be seeing Danny again in the morning, Maria sang cheerfully while doing her hair and ironing her dress for the coming day. Then at eleven o'clock, she and Val had a cup of tea and a piece of pie in the living room before retiring.

Now over two hours later, Maria lay wide awake with her thoughts, and the eerie feeling that something ominous had aroused her from her sleep. A door closed somewhere down the hallway and the sound of a car horn came from the street below. Why had that young man tried to kill Danny's father? There was no mention of a motive in Cec's report, and this puzzled her, as the report was extensive. It seemed more plausible now, that the driver of the car, which had nearly run Danny and herself down, had made a deliberate attempt to take their lives. Why would anyone want to kill the Leweses? Was this the price that one must pay for being rich and successful?

The clock ticked on relentlessly; Maria sat up in bed, taking care not to awaken Val, and looked about the room; it was two o'clock. Then a shiver ran through Maria's body, as she heard the outside door of their suite open, and stop on the safety chain. She quickly got out of bed; the rattle of the chain still ringing in her ears as she took the gun from her purse and walked cautiously to the living room, the moonlight caressing her body and casting shadows about the room. The outer door was closed now, and the safety chain, still in position, swung gently to and fro as evidence that she had not been dreaming. Opening the door slowly, Maria looked out into the hallway; it was deserted, and the only sound was the whir of the elevator as it descended to the lower floor. She closed the door, replaced the safety chain, and went back to the bedroom; replacing the gun in her purse as Val turned restlessly in her sleep without awakening. Returning to the living room, Maria switched on the light and looked around carefully in case something had been placed or thrown inside. The intruder had left nothing, and Maria was puzzled by the person's reason to gain entry. She switched off the light and went to the window; the moon was full, some small-scattered clouds dotted the sky, and down in the street, a few cars moved quietly along and nothing seemed amiss.

Maria slipped silently into bed, thoughts racing through her mind, who in hell had tried to get into their suite, and had she been awakened by some premonition of danger? It almost seemed as if she had lain awake waiting for the intruder. Val moved closer, as if seeking protection from some unknown danger, and Maria sank into a restless sleep.

* * *

The next day was happy and exciting for Maria. Danny had come to the office as he had promised, and took her to the club for a game of tennis, before they went to the Bay Tide Hotel for lunch. Then as Maria stood on the sidewalk returning Danny's wave as he drove away, her feeling of well being reflected in her appearance, movements, and spirit. With her face flushed from the exercise and fresh air, and looking pretty in her fitting brown checkered slacks and print blouse, which she had changed into after tennis, Maria was carefree and happy. Then with the sun glistening from her long black hair, she walked into the building where the Plastick Utensil Company had its office.

It was twenty-five to two when Maria entered the inner office of the Plastick Utensil Company. Dolansky was busy working in his office, and Cec smiled and beckoned to her from where he was sitting at his desk.

"Did you have a nice morning?" Cec asked, returning Maria's smile as she sat on the corner of the desk.

Maria nodded in reply, "I noticed Steve Bailey was close to us most of the time, although I didn't see him at the club."

"No, and it was a flaw in Danny's protection until you came along, Maria, as we are not allowed in the club."

It had been with happy abandonment and no thoughts of danger, that Maria and Danny made final plans for their voyage to Powell River, while they dined at the Bay Tide Hotel. Although, now because of her new responsibility, and the necessity of security preparations, Maria thought it advisable to inform Cec of their plans. "If the weather is favorable, Danny and I plan to sail the yacht to Powell River, starting on Thursday about eight o'clock in the morning, and returning on Sunday evening or Monday morning."

With a thoughtful look on his face, Cec nodded his head in response to the information. Then recalling a message he had taken, he said. "By the way, Tom Balant phoned for you at five after one. He is at Anne's Lounge, and he wants you to get in touch with him immediately when you get back to the office."

"Thanks, I will give him a ring now before we go to the shooting range."

"Okay, you can use this phone if you wish," Cec said, and getting up from behind the desk he walked towards the window at the far end of the office.

Maria dialed Anne's Lounge, and while she waited for Tom to come to the telephone, she watched Cec as he walked towards the window. "Hello Tom," she said when she heard his voice on the line.

"I would like to see you right away, Maria," Tom said, with a note of urgency in his voice.

"I'm sorry but I am at work now," Maria replied hesitantly, "and I don't think I can get the time off."

"Bullshit you have enough influence at that office to get off any time you wish. Danny telephoned me last night and told me the good news about you working for the Plastick Utensil Company; a company of which he owns more than fifty percent."

Maria frowned; Tom was angry and upset, and she thought too much of him to give him the brush off. "Hold the line a minute, Tom." Maria put her hand over the mouthpiece of the telephone and beckoned to Cec who was leaning on a desk watching her from the far end of the room. "He wants to see me this afternoon," she said, when Cec approached the desk.

"That's okay. Go and meet him, and I will see you in the office tomorrow morning."

"Thanks Cec," Maria said a look of concern still on her face. Then after taking her hand from the mouthpiece, she said, "I will see you there within an hour, Tom."

"Do you have time for a cup of coffee before you go?" Cec asked when Maria put the telephone down.

"Sure," Maria replied forcing a smile. She wasn't looking forward to a possible confrontation with Tom.

After telephoning the relief man and telling him that it wasn't necessary for him to come to the office to take his place that afternoon, Cec and Maria walked towards the other office, where at the door Cec turned and waved to Dolansky before going through.

"Cream and sugar, Cec?" Maria asked, as she poured the coffee, and glancing up while she waited for his reply, she noticed that his attention was on the reception room where Mrs. Jonson was talking to a man and showing him a catalogue of the utensils, which the company sold.

"Both please," Cec said, and with his eyes still on the front office, he took the coffee. "Thanks Maria," he said. Then raising the cup to his lips, he drank some coffee while continuing to watch Mrs. Jonson until she had finished filling out the order form, and the man had left.

"Shall we finish drinking our coffee in the inner office, Maria?"

"Okay," Maria replied, and she and Cec walked to the door.

Dolansky raised his hand and gestured that he would like a coffee as they entered the inner office, and Cec went back to the door and called to one of the girls. "Bring a cup of coffee for Mr. Dolansky."

Cec followed Maria back to her desk, and leaned against it facing the door while drinking his coffee.

"You seemed quite concerned about the man in the reception room, when we were getting our coffee," Maria said, looking up to Cec from where she was sitting.

"Yes, Dolansky wants one of us to be on duty with him in the office at all times, to make sure that no unauthorized person gets into the inner office. He and Mrs. Jonson control the doors electrically, so Mrs. Jonson is the first line of defense. Cec looked down at Maria, her dark eyes were bright and attentive, and the slight frown on her face was almost imperceptible. "You don't think much of that, do you?"

"No," Maria replied, "there is something about Mrs. Jonson that puzzles me and I can't put my finger on it, and I feel uneasy about her. But I didn't think my feelings were that obvious."

"They wouldn't be," Cec said with a smile except that I have been watching for your every reaction when we speak about her, as I am suspicious of Mrs. Jonson too. Only it took me three years to formulate the suspicions, which you have almost duplicated in a few days. Maybe there is something to a woman's intuition, or perhaps we are both wrong."

"I have to be going, Cec, as I don't want to be late meeting Tom," Maria said, standing up.

"Okay, and I'll take care of this," Cec said, taking the cup from Maria's hand, "and I will see you tomorrow."

"Thanks," Maria said. Then she picked up her purse from the desk, and walked from the room.

* * *

On the street, Maria walked briskly along the block to the locksmiths where she had made an appointment to pick up her new keys to her apartment. She had discussed with Cec that morning, the attempted break-in to her suite, and while he had thought that it could be connected with her new job, he had concluded that it was probably an ordinary burglary attempt, which occurs quite frequently. In any event, Maria had taken the precaution to have a locksmith change the tumbler in the lock of the suite door and provide three new keys.

The young man at the counter in the locksmith shop looked up when Maria entered. "Good afternoon, Miss Petersen. You are early."

"Yes. I was handy to the shop at this time, so I thought I would drop in just in case the keys were ready."

"You are in luck, Miss, our repairman just got back from your apartment a few minutes ago and your keys are ready." He took some keys marked with a brown tag from a clipboard behind him, handed them to Maria, and smiled.

Maria put the keys into her purse, and paid for the work. Then as she was leaving the shop on the way to the parking lot, she glanced at her watch. She would have to hurry so as not to be late meeting Tom.

The traffic was not heavy on the way to Anne's Lounge, and the little car, seeming in tune with her anxiety, sped along the streets; with even the traffic lights turning green as it approached, so as not to slow its pace. Maria looked at the speedometer. She was exceeding the speed limit and she eased up on the gas; a ticket now would only delay her further and add to her troubles.

Pausing just inside the entrance of Anne's Lounge, Maria looked around the luxurious and dimly lit room, as a waitress hurried by with a tray of drinks. The place was unusually busy for a Tuesday afternoon, and she became aware of the steady drone of people talking while she looked for Tom. She let her gaze sweep past the bar, where the polished counter shone under the bright lights, and bottles glistened behind the barman. Tom was sitting facing her leaning across the table, in an animated conversation with her uncle, and he had not seen her enter. Maria's heart skipped a beat; were they talking about Danny and her job? She listened carefully to their conversation as she approached the table, and breathed a sigh of relief when she found that they were talking about the price of cattle on the market.

"Hello," Maria said, slipping into the plush chair besides Tom.

"Hi," Tom replied, turning to face her, their expressions sad when their glances met and held for a moment, before Maria turned to her uncle.

"I have been trying to get in touch with you all day," Bert said, smiling broadly, "I received a letter from your parents this morning and they are getting along fine. What would you like to drink, Maria?"

"A beer please." Maria smiled, evidently Tom had not told her uncle about her new job and its relationship to Danny.

"Bring us a beer please," Bert said to a passing waitress.

"Yes, sir." the girl said as she paused and smiled, the light from the bar shining off her light blonde hair.

"Ted has been staying with your parents for the past week," Bert said, turning his attention back to Maria. "He is in Toronto following up an investigation into a narcotics ring, and he should be back sometime during the middle of the week. Your parents said in their letters that they were enjoying Ted's visit, and they took him out fishing to Secret Cove. They said that you would know the place." Bert paused as he noticed the distant look in Maria's eyes, as momentarily she recalled the good times she had spent with her parents at Secret Cove. Then with more feeling, he continued, "They miss you very much, Maria, and they are looking forward to you coming home for Christmas."

"I think about them quite a lot too," Maria said. Then with a note of sadness in her voice, she continued, "I am going to try to go home for Christmas."

"It is good to see you and Tom together," Bert said.

Maria looked at Tom. His face was expressionless, and her uncle, engrossed in his own thoughts, seemed not to notice their strained relationship.

"You heard that Ted and Alice are going to have a baby?"

"No, I hadn't heard. I haven't been in touch with them lately," Maria said, becoming conscious of the dryness that had been growing in her throat.

"The baby is due in seven months, and it will be my first grandchild. I wish Anne could have been alive to see the day." The waitress placed a glass of beer on the table before Maria. "Bring another beer please," Bert, said, noticing that Tom's glass was empty. Then leaning back in his chair, he took a long drink from his glass of scotch. "They are going to name him Bert, if they have a boy."

"How is Alice feeling?" Maria asked.

"Oh fine. I was up to see her this morning. I took up some wool that she wanted for knitting. I tried to get in touch with you too this morning, Maria, and I phoned the store where you used to work. When the girl told me that you had been laid off, I talked to Mr. Evans, the office manager. We belong to the same club and he's a nice fellow, and it was just a matter of having to cut staff. He said that he had no idea that you were my niece, and if you would like to get back on, you should go and see him as they will be needing another girl soon."

"Thanks Uncle, but I have a job with the Plastick Utensil Company."

"Very good. Give it a good try, and if you don't like it, quit and go back to your old job. Mr. Evans was saying that one of the girls on payroll is pregnant, and there would be a good chance for promotion for an intelligent girl like you."

"You are flattering me." Maria said, smiling to her uncle.

"No, Maria, I mean it, and Mr. Evans is sincere in offering you a job." Then turning to Tom he said, "Perhaps you would like something to eat with your beer?"

"No thanks, the beer will be fine." Tom wished to talk with Maria alone and while planning to leave with her after they had finished their drinks, he tried to look more cheerful than he felt.

Bert looked to Maria. "I went up to your apartment this morning, on the way to Alice's and Ted's place." Bert took a sip of his drink, before continuing, "I thought that you wouldn't be working and might be home. A young man was leaving your suite when I got off the elevator, and by the time I rang your door bell and found there was no one home, the man had already gone down in the elevator." Maria caught her breath and Bert seeing her surprised, went on. "Don't you think that was odd?"

Recovering from her initial reaction, Maria smiled. "No, it was Debbie's boyfriend; he delivers groceries for us." Debbie's boyfriend had delivered groceries for them in the past, but Maria knew that they had not bought any groceries to be delivered this day, and she smiled in an attempt to mask her concern. She was puzzled by this latest event; the attempted entry to their suite last night had not been an ordinary burglary attempt, and it was somehow related to the young man who had been in their suite this morning. However, he could have been the man working on the door lock.

There was a pause in the conversation, and Tom appeared to be waiting for Maria to say more. However, Bert, not wishing to embarrass Maria or pry into her personal affairs, picked up the conversation. "How are your two friends getting along anyway?"

"They are fine. Debbie is courting steady, and I wouldn't be surprised if she announces their engagement soon," Maria said, grateful to her uncle for his tact.

"You should go up and visit Alice sometime. She would like to see you," Bert said rising from his chair. Then before he turned to leave he smiled at them. "You two enjoy yourselves, and order anything you wish; it's on the house."

Maria returned her uncle's smile, and Tom thanked him for his kindness.

Then as Bert walked away looking around the lounge, making sure his customers were comfortable, Maria and Tom looked to each other, their expressions, and eyes searching for some understanding. They drank their beer slowly, and talked amiably, both avoiding mention of Danny and the reason for their meeting. Maria questioned Tom about his work on the ranch, and she listened with wonder as he talked enthusiastically about his cattle and the many calves that had been born that spring.

"The price of cattle has gone up recently, and I am auctioning off one hundred head this afternoon," Tom said.

"Don't you always go to the stockyards when you are selling cattle?" Maria asked with surprise and concern.

Looking out over the room, Tom's eyes seemed to focus on more distant things, and he did not see the men and the women sitting, drinking, talking, and laughing amid the babble of other voices in the room. For a moment, Tom thought of the auction. The sun was high in the sky, and there was the noise and odor of cattle in the air as they were driven off the trucks into the stockyards. There would be the usual cheerful greetings and smiles from men he knew and respected, and above it all, the chant of the auctioneer and the sound of his hammer as the cattle were sold. "Yes, I usually go to the stockyards when my cattle are being sold," Tom replied, turning to look again at Maria, "My mother took my place as it was imperative that I see you today."

"Tom, I could have seen you some other day; it didn't have to be this afternoon," Maria said, saddened by the realization that Tom's feelings for her were much deeper than she had realized.

"After Danny telephoned me last night and told me that you were working for his company, I felt that I had to talk to you today. I know of a nice cafe not far from here where we could go for a cup of tea."

"Okay, Tom," Maria said, and although her heart was heavy, she creased her cheeks into a smile. She respected and liked Tom, perhaps more than she realized, and she was unhappy to see the hurt, which was written, on his face.

They stood up together, and Maria waved to her uncle as she and Tom walked from the lounge hand in hand.

Bert watched them as they maneuvered carefully around the tables, still holding each other's hands, as they made their way to the door. His niece was pretty and Tom was in love. True love didn't always run smooth and they would make a nice couple he thought. Then turning away, he walked back towards the bar feeling happy for them.

Outside, Maria and Tom walked through the parking lot to where Tom had parked his pick up truck. "Your car," Tom asked, noticing the red Ford, with the name Plastick Utensil Company on its door, which was parked next to the truck.

"Not really, it belongs to the company and I have the use of it. We could go together in the truck, and you can drop me off here later."

"Maybe we should walk. The cafe is only about five or ten minutes from here and it is a beautiful day."

"Okay," Maria agreed, glad that Tom had decided to walk; he looked strong and healthy in his corduroy slacks and plaid shirt, and she liked the feel of his rough strong hand with a gentle pressure that made her more aware of his closeness and the beauty of the day. Tom pointed out the stores, which he knew well, and exchanged greetings with a few of the people they passed on the street as she took pleasure in his company and the sound of his voice. However, while the warmth of the sun on her back penetrated her thin blouse and her slacks felt tight about her hips, there lurked in the back of Maria's mind an apprehension of their talk to follow.

The cafe was the same cafe where Maria had lunch with Cec only the day before and the waitress smiled a smile of recognition as they sat at a table near the window. The red and white-checkered tablecloths, the maple furniture, and the wall papered walls combined to give the cafe a comfortable and homey atmosphere conducive to enjoying the good food they served. The waitress brought the pot of tea and the teacake that they had ordered. Then she hurried back to the cash register, where some customers were waiting to pay their checks.

Tom studied Maria, as she looked out onto the street busy with traffic. A bus and a number of cars that had stopped at the corner for the lights started to move forward as the lights turned green, and Maria turned her attention back to the table to pour their tea.

"Did Danny get this job for you?" Tom asked quietly.

"No, and he wasn't aware that I had the job until I told him about it myself."

"You are a pretty woman, Maria, and Danny will use his influence to his every advantage," Tom paused to give thought to what he must say. "Don't be blinded, by a smooth tongue, and the good times Danny can afford to show you into believing that your relationship will ever become something more than it is at present. Danny, like his wife, was born rich and in high society, and they revolve with people whose life style, mores, and values are sometimes hard to understand."

Maria took a drink from her cup and reflected on what Tom had said. She couldn't believe Danny had no love for her and the affections he showed were only a pretense. "Don't worry Tom, I think that I can handle the situation. I value your friendship, and there is nothing I would not do for you. However, I have charted a course and I wish to follow it, and I hope that you will understand so that we can remain very good friends."

Noticing and interpreting Maria's every movement and change of expression, Tom said. "Danny is proud of his family, and his wife is going to have a baby soon. She is a beautiful woman, and when she was a girl she won a beauty contest here in Vancouver, although; God knows, you are more beautiful, Maria. Danny's wife is aware of his occasional diversions, and having been brought up to accept this kind of thing, she does not object as long as it does not disrupt their life together, and Danny will make sure his relationship with you will not interfere seriously with his home life. Danny's wife accepts this as a way of life, and I'm afraid that you are going to be hurt, Maria. You will have no problem from Danny's father, as he and Danny are of one mind in this regard." Tom drank some of his tea and went on, "Danny's mother is different. She does not accept this type of life style, and problems will arise if she becomes aware of the situation."

Walking back to the parking lot in silence, Maria and Tom were very much aware of each other's presence, by the gentle pressure of each other's hand, by their glances, and by their thoughts. Maria did not want to hurt Tom, and her mind searching for a solution to her dilemma found none, then out of exasperation, and with some viciousness, her mind gave reason for her actions; damn it! I want to live my life now and enjoy it while I am young, and not scrape for every dollar like my parents, she thought.

On the parking lot they looked into each other's eyes for a moment without smiling, and Tom kissed Maria gently on the forehead before she got into her car, then he pressed his lips together firmly; there was nothing more to say.

CHAPTER 8

Driving out of the parking lot, Maria turned left and waited at the intersection for an opportunity to pull into the lane of traffic. Coming out of the parking lot shortly after Maria, Tom turned his pick up truck the other way, to drive away in the opposite direction, and a feeling of loneliness swept over Maria, as looking into the rearview mirror she saw the truck receding from view.

A car had stopped to allow Maria to enter the line of traffic, and she smiled to the driver, who had stopped for her, before pulling into the line of slow moving traffic. She glanced at her watch. It was twenty-five minutes after four; at the rate, the traffic was moving it would be too late to go back to the office; yet, she should get in touch with Cec concerning the man whom her uncle had seen leaving her suite that morning. The sound of a car horn, somewhere behind her, interrupted her thoughts, and glancing back through the rearview mirror, she saw that a green car, containing two men, was edging into the traffic flow four or five cars behind, much to the annoyance of the car driver behind them.

Pulling into the first service station along her way, Maria asked the attendant to fill the tank with gas, and then she went to the telephone booth at the corner of the lot. The green car with two men pulled into the service station behind her and parked at the pump closest to the building. Maria dialed Cec's number at the office, and while the telephone at the other end rang, she noticed that the attendant was washing the windshield of the green car.

"Hello," Cec said picking the receiver up after the telephone had rung a good number of times.

"This is Maria, what kept you so long?"

"I was sitting at your desk, and looking through the window, while drinking coffee with Dolansky. We were just about to leave."

"Cec, my uncle went to see me at my apartment this morning, and a man left the suite just as he got off the elevator. He wasn't carrying anything with him, so it didn't seem like a burglary, or the man who was sent to work on the door lock."

"There is something strange going on," Cec said.

"Another thing, I think there are two men following me in a green car. They are here now in the service station where I am telephoning from."

"Can you give me the license number of the car?"

"X5362Z5."

The attendant was looking under the hood of the green car, and a tall man in a gray suit, with his back to Maria, stood by his side.

"The car is on our list as a police car, so it will be two plain clothes policemen who are following you. There is something strange going on, of which we are not aware." Cec paused for a moment. "Can you keep your two girl friends out of your suite until about six-thirty?"

"Yes, I will be able to do that. I will telephone and tell them that I will pick them up with the car from work, and we will eat out."

"Good, and if it is okay with you, Dolansky and I will take a look around your suite, before you get home, to see if there is anything amiss."

"Sure. What do you think you might find?"

"I don't know, but in any event, we should check for finger prints and other clues as to the identity of the person who was in your suite this morning."

"Do you want me to come back to the office to give you a key?"

Maria heard Cec laugh on the other end of the line before he replied. "No, and don't worry about it, we won't have any trouble getting in."

"Okay, bye now," Maria said. Then she hung up the telephone and looked around the lot. Two more cars had come into the station, and the attendants were busy servicing them while the green car with the police officers, was still sitting at the pump.

Maria looked up the telephone number of the department store where her friends worked and dialed the number. Rita, the switchboard operator at the store, answered the telephone; she knew her friends quite well and Maria had lunched with her a number of times. "This is Maria, would you give Val and Debbie a message for me before they leave the office tonight?"

"Sure."

"Tell them to wait at the bus stop after work, and I will pick them up with the car."

"Got you."

"Thanks Rita, bye."

The green car had already gone when Maria paid the attendant for the gas. However, after she had driven only about five blocks from the service station she noticed that the car was following her once again. The traffic was heavy, and it was ten minutes after five when Maria pulled into the bus stop in front of the department store. The policemen, seeing her stop, parked their car in a no parking zone in front of a theatre just over a block away. Then a stream of buses pulled in behind Maria and she was blocked from the policemen's view.

With their attentions captured by the dresses on display in the department store window, Debbie and Val did not realize that Maria had driven up until she tooted the horn. The driver of the bus behind Maria's car frowned and was about to give her a blast on the horn; when he was distracted by Val and Debbie hurrying across the sidewalk, through the crowds of people towards the car, their dresses blowing high in the breeze. The driver's frown disappeared from his face, and he eased his bus up to the back of the car and watched the girls as they got in with a display of pretty legs. Meanwhile a stream of buses backed up behind them, with the last bus stopped across the intersection blocking the traffic and causing a minor traffic jam.

"These kids don't give a shit these days," the driver of the green car said, realizing what was happening and gritting his teeth.

With her two friends in the car, Maria drove away from the bus stop, and the stream of buses moved forwards alleviating the traffic jam at the intersection, and the green car pulled back into the traffic and followed.

"I don't feel like cooking today," Maria said, turning the car down the hill towards China Town, "so I am taking you out to dinner."

Neither Debbie nor Val protested, and broad smiles were their only communication. Maria had not seen the policemen since just before she picked up the girls. Now as they sat down at a table in the dimly lit restaurant, she looked up at the large painting of a red dragon with flashing eyes and nostrils breathing fire, she wondered if they were still with her. The place gave her the creeps and she would feel more comfortable with the policemen around. The girls looked at the menu that the waiter had brought, and decided to get the combination plate for three, which would give them the greatest number of different dishes with their order.

Minutes before the policemen changed cars, parked half a block from the restaurant, and watched the girls as they entered.

"Not Chinese food, I hate the crap," the driver said, and his partner dressed in the gray suit leaned back in the seat and laughed, his stomach rising and falling rapidly as he attempted to contain his laughter.

"Not me, I love the stuff," the policeman in the gray suit said, as soon as he was able, "and we had better get moving in case this is the place where she drops the dope."

"She has got to be up to something," the driver agreed as they got out of the car. Then while walking towards the restaurant, he continued, "Tennis in the morning at an exclusive club that didn't even want to let us in; wining and dining at noon in the Bay Tide Hotel, beer at Anne's Lounge in the afternoon, tea at Emma's Cafe, and now Chinese food. Why in hell doesn't she go back to Anne's Lounge for a beer instead of making my life miserable at this joint?"

The two men fell silent as they entered the restaurant and, the waiter showed them to a table directly beneath the pointed tail of the red dragon. They ordered the cheapest meal on the menu, and watched the girls enjoying their food and cocktails as they talked quietly, after what had seemed to the policemen an intense argument. At first Val and Debbie had wanted to pay their share for the meal, and when Maria insisted on paying, they decided to get cocktails and pay for their share that way. The policemen had expected a fight to start at any moment and they wished they could hear what was being said, but they were too far away and there were too many people in the restaurant for them to overhear the conversation. The policeman in the gray suit ate both meals and smiled broadly, while the other complained that he had not eaten since the morning and was as hungry as a bear.

It was a quarter to seven when the girls arrived home at their suite. Maria unlocked the door, unknown to her friends; she examined it carefully for evidence that might show that Cec had problems entering the suite without a key. Evidently, there had been no problems, as the door was unmarked. Inside the suite, everything seemed to be in order. The three girls had barely got settled down in the living room with a beer, and Debbie with elaborate gestures was telling them about her experiences the previous night with her boyfriend, when there was a knock on the door.

"It's probably your boyfriend coming for you again tonight," Val said, walking to the door. Then Val on opening the door, gasped with surprise as two plain-clothes men, a uniformed policeman, and a policewoman brushed past her into the room. The girls stood up and looked on in amazement as the three men quickly fanned out through the rooms, and the policewoman explained in a brisk and businesslike manner that they had a warrant to search the suite.

Taken aback by the speed of the raid, the girls were silent for a time, until

Debbie recovered and called out in a loud voice. "If you find anything, cut me in on it, as I'm broke."

With the tension eased, the girls sat down again on the chesterfield and resumed drinking their beer. "Can I see your identification?" Maria asked the policewoman. The woman reached into her pocket, and without saying a word, handed an identification card to Maria then waited with her hand out for its return. The other two girls leaned over and looked at the card too as Maria looked at it briefly before handing it back. The woman replaced it in her tunic pocket, and then taking a notebook and a pencil from another pocket, she proceeded to ask the girls their names and places of employment and record the information in her book.

The three policemen came back into the living room, and the man in the gray suit nodded to the policewoman. "You can look to the girls now," he said.

"If you will come to the bedroom one at a time I will search you and your purses," the policewoman said.

Annoyed at the prospect of being searched Val and Debbie voiced some objections. However, they only gave in to the wishes of the policewoman when the policeman in the gray suit told them, in no uncertain terms, that the alternative was to return with them to the police station. Even so, the policeman, knowing of Maria's family ties with Ted, was pulling his punches.

Waiting until the last to be searched, Maria was not in the least concerned that they would find anything, watched the policemen as they searched the living room. Cec and Dolansky would, have gone over the place with a fine toothcomb. If the man who had entered the suite in the morning had left anything incriminating, they would have got rid of it. Still, she wondered if the attempts on the lives of the Leweses and now these events in which she was involved were all tied together by some web of intrigue of which she was unaware. Moving to other chairs to allow a policeman to search the chesterfield where they were sitting, Maria and Val watched him with interest as he examined the cushions carefully. Then they looked at each other and smiled when he slipped his hand down into the chesterfield behind the cushions and felt carefully along its length. With their faces expressionless, the policemen went about their work methodically, and Maria wondered exactly what it was that they were looking for. She thought about telephoning Cec later, and decided against it because the girls would be listening and there was a possibility that the telephone was being tapped, and she would have to use caution even with the cellular telephone.

"It is your turn Maria," Debbie said, coming back into the living room.

Maria went into the bedroom where the policewoman was waiting, and as she put her purse down on the dressing table, she thought about the gun that it concealed. The policewoman looked Maria over; her clothes fitted snugly and there were not many places where anything could be hidden. "Take off your dress please," the woman said, and she looked Maria over from head to toe as she undressed. "Now remove your shoes and turn around." Maria kicked off her shoes and turned. The impassive expression on her face concealed her resentment of the demeaning treatment to which she was being subjected, and she wondered what the woman would require her to do next, and just how much of this sort of thing she could take before she rebelled. "Remove your brassiere please." Maria took off her brassiere and handed it to the policewoman, who examined it for a moment before handing it back. "You can get dressed now, Miss Petersen." Maria replaced her clothes. Had the woman finished, with her? "Now if I could see your purse?" Maria picked up the purse, opened it, and took out the gun as she watched the woman's eyes, a flicker of panic for a second before she handed it to the policewoman.

"Just a minute, I have a permit for the gun here." Then after rummaging in the purse, Maria took out the permit and gave it to the policewoman, who examined it carefully before putting the gun and the permit on the dressing table. Then taking Maria's purse, she searched it thoroughly before returning it.

Without a word, Maria replaced the pistol and permit in her purse, and leaving her purse on the dressing table, she followed the policewoman back into the living room. One of the policemen, in answer to a question from Val was saying that their search was part of a routine check.

"Everything is in order," the policewoman said to the waiting policemen, standing together in the middle of the now crowded room. Serious and formal like guests at a come as you are cocktail partly who were still waiting for a drink; while the girls, sitting on the chesterfield, sipped their drinks and observed the proceedings.

The man in the gray suit thanked the girls for their cooperation, and after gestures with his hands to his comrades, the four disappointed members of the police force filed out through the door, and tramped down the hallway to the elevator.

Alone in the elevator, they looked at each other puzzled. "Do you think Mike was wrong?" one of the policemen said to the man in the gray suit.

"I don't know. Mike doesn't often give us misinformation, and I feel that there is something screwy going on."

The elevator had started on its way down when the policewoman said. "That doll you two have been following around all day is packing a pistol."

"What!" exclaimed the man, in the gray suit.

"It is all nice and legal. She has a permit to carry it."

The three men looked to the woman seeking more information, as the elevator came to a stop on the ground floor. The door opened automatically as a number of people in the lobby watched with interest, when without a word the four members of the police force, two abreast, marched out of the elevator. The policewoman failed to tell her comrade that she had almost ruined her pants when Maria took the gun nonchalantly from her purse.

* * *

Back in the suite, the three girls were engaged in a lively discussion about the raid. It seemed obvious that it had something to do with drugs. Why had they been singled out, and to whom did the hand belong that had pointed the finger of suspicion at them? The discussion continued through the evening as the girls cleaned up the apartment, and later when they sat down together in the living room for a bottle of beer before going to bed.

During the time she was attending university, Maria had gone with a friend to a party where a number of illegal drugs were being used, and she had tried marijuana. However, like her friend, she didn't like it, and they decided then that it was not their thing.

Lounging in the living room, dressed in their new nightgowns recently purchased at a sale, Debbie sat on the easy chair facing Maria and Val on the chesterfield as they sipped their beer and enjoyed their conversation.

"Some of the other girls at the store have been involved in drug raids before," Debbie said. "One girl spent nine months in jail for possession of marijuana, though she couldn't see where she had done anything wrong, and she still believes it to be a harmless drug, what do you think, Maria?"

"The government is considering its use for people with some illnesses, but really that is all I know, and I know it is not for me."

"How can you be so sure?" Debbie asked.

"Because I tried it once when I was going to University, and I did not like it."

"Oh! You didn't tell us that you went to University." Val said.

"I see that my life is being shed like an onion. However that was a time in my life when I found out that I don't like marijuana, period."

"I plan to have a family, husband, children, and a house, the whole nine yards. I don't smoke, so why would I get hooked on marijuana?" Debbie said.

"A couple of years ago in high school, I saw a film on speed and heroin and the effects they have on the people who use them, and I was scared to death." Val paused and laughed, and after taking a drink from her bottle on the table in front of her, she continued. "And do you know, even after all that, a few of us tried heroin; just for the hell of it. Now with all this talk about marijuana; I would try it too, if I thought there was a good chance of not getting caught." Val leaned back on the chesterfield and put her feet up on the coffee table, almost knocking her bottle of beer onto the floor, and putting her hand up to her face, she puffed away on an imaginary reefer.

Debbie laughed and said, "You don't need marijuana, you can get high on a bottle of beer."

"Quit smoking that joint, the persons who made it may have laced it with some other dope in order to get you hooked." Maria said, leaning on the chesterfield besides Val and poking her in the ribs with an elbow.

"Ugh," Val said. Then taking the imaginary cigarette from her mouth she pretended to flip it across the room.

"Your cousin is in the police department, and I wonder if he knows about the raid?" Debbie asked.

"I was wondering when someone was going to get around to saying something about that," Maria said with a smile. " I don't think he knows anything about it as he is in Toronto visiting my parents. But even if he was here, I don't think he would have interfered."

"Are you going to tell him about it when he gets back?" Val asked.

"Sure, and I know he will just have a good laugh over it. He maintains that the police are your friends, as long as you are law abiding."

"He is right too," Val said. "Oh, they are a bit of a nuisance once in a while when you get a parking ticket or get caught for jay walking, but it is nice to know that they are around in case something serious happens. Like the other night when we were almost burglarized. If that man had not thought that we could call the police, he would not have taken off like he did."

"I'm glad that I wasn't here last night when that happened," Debbie, said. "I would have been scared to death."

Giving thought to the coming weekend, Maria felt concerned that Val might be left alone at night in the suite; knowing that if anything else like that was to happen again, and Val was alone she would be scared stiff. "By the way, my job will be taking me out of town sometimes, and I may be required to be out of town, and return home on Sunday or Monday," Maria said.

"Oh no!" Val exclaimed. "If your boyfriend wants you to stay out on the same night, Debbie, I will be left here all alone."

"That is why I thought I would mention it," Maria said. "We should try and see that there are at least two of us in the suite during the nights. When I am away, you should be at home overnight Debbie, even if it means bringing your boyfriend home for the night. What do you say, Val?"

"Well I don't know about that," Val said. Then after a pause, she went on. "I guess you are right, as I would not want to stay here alone."

"Oh no, you don't," Debbie retorted. "I'm not bringing my boyfriend home here for you girls to get your hooks on him. Don't worry, Maria, if you are out of town, I will make sure that I get home." Then the three girls laughed heartily.

Val stood up and stretched. "I'm dead beat and just about ready for bed." Then picking up the empty bottles from the coffee table, she took them to the kitchen.

"I should phone Alice before I go to bed," Maria said, crossing the room to sit on the chair by the telephone.

Alice was cheerful, and Maria and Alice talked for some length about Alice's baby-to-be and Ted's visit to Toronto. However, Maria didn't mention the police raid; she would leave that for Ted to tell Alice, if he wanted to. When Maria put down the telephone, Debbie had gone to bed, and Val was sitting on the chesterfield waiting for her.

"I didn't know that your cousin's wife was expecting a baby?"

"I didn't know either until today when my uncle told me he is really thrilled about it."

"Where did you see your uncle?" Val asked, and Maria became aware of Val's growing curiosity.

"At Anne's Lounge. Tom phoned me at noon and I had a free hour so I met him there for a beer, and my uncle joined us." Maria put the safety chain on the outside door. I had better be careful what I am saying she thought, or Val will get wise to what my job really is all about.

Deep in thought, Val remained sitting on the chesterfield, her expression concerned, until Maria, taking her by the hand, pulled her to her feet. "It's time to go to bed," Maria said, as Val stood. Then the two girls walked to their bedroom amid the sound of Debbie snoring in the other room.

* * *

It had started raining sometime in the night, and the rain was coming down in sheets as Maria and her two friends drove to work in the morning. In good spirits, Debbie and Val looked forward to telling the girls at work about the police raid. However, Maria, was dismayed by the weather, and hoped that it would not interfere with her own and Danny's plans to sail to Powell River. The forecast had said that it would clear in the afternoon, and Maria prayed that it would be correct.

The road shone black with the rain and the car's windshield wipers swished back and forth in a vain effort to keep the glass clear as Maria drove across the Lions Gate Bridge, and there was the sound of a ship's foghorn from out on the strait. Then, as she stopped to let the girls off across the road from the store, a patch of blue sky showed between the clouds, maybe, the weather was going to be all right after all. Maria waited for the girls to alight, and then glancing back she looked for a break in the traffic as Val pounded on the side window with her hand. "Just a minute Maria, we forgot our lunches on the back seat." Then opening the door, she reached into the car for the lunch bags. "If you get a chance, drop around to the store for lunch." The door banged shut, and Maria smiled and turned her attention once again to the traffic.

When Maria entered the door of the inner office, Dolansky and Cec were sitting in Dolansky's office talking. She took off her raincoat, hung it in the closet near the door, and walked to Dolansky's office. "We had some excitement at our suite last night," she said, after returning their greetings.

"Tell us about it," Dolansky said, as with a gesture of his hand, he invited Maria to come into his office and take a seat.

"The police raided our suite at seven-thirty last night, made a thorough search, and found nothing."

Dolansky looked at Cec and rubbed his chin with his hand before he spoke. "We found five capsules of heroin in a plastic bag hidden under the sink in your bathroom, and we flushed it down the toilet. In addition, the doorknobs had been wiped of fingerprints. Therefore, it appears that your uncle was right about seeing someone leaving your suite. Any ideas, Miss Petersen?"

"It seems that someone wants to frame me," Maria said, knitting her brow. "Perhaps to get me out of the way."

"Exactly, this is what Cec and I thought, and it could mean that an attempt will be made on Danny's life when he is at the club or on his yacht; where he was most vulnerable before you arrived."

"I don't know how anyone could know that I am working for you as a detective," Maria said.

"Our office here is not a well kept secret," Cec said. "Anyone really interested in learning its whereabouts could do so by following the detectives. Then by watching your activities, they would eventually come to realize that you too are a detective. However, it does seem that someone has come to realize that you are a detective too soon to be from casual observations. It would have been more reasonable to assume that you are working here as a typist and office clerk."

Looking at Maria thoughtfully, his brow furrowed by concern, Dolansky looked older than he had looked even yesterday. The pressure of his work was beginning to show on him, and Maria revised her first estimate of his age; he was closer to thirty-five than thirty. "There appears to be a plot against the Leweses, and we will have to be prepared for any eventuality," Dolansky said. Then after some thought he added, "I will advise both of you to get as much shooting practice in as possible."

"Do you know who it is that could be plotting against the Leweses?" Maria asked.

"We have some suspicions and we are making investigations," Dolansky replied. "When these investigations are completed we will take counter measures."

Cec ran his hand through his receding hair, the expression on his face revealing his troubled thoughts. "When you are out sailing with Danny this weekend, we will not be in a very good position to help if trouble should occur, although we will do what we can to back you up."

"You and Miss Petersen could look over the maps this morning. Arrange some places where she could get in touch with us at Powell River and along the way," Dolansky said. Then speaking to Cec as he stood up behind the desk, "and tell Betty to bring me a cup of coffee."

"Okay," Cec replied, as he and Maria rose to leave. Then while Cec stood up for Maria to precede him through the door, Dolansky sat down again behind his desk, and picking up the telephone, he dialed a number.

"I will just be a minute, Maria, and I will bring the maps over to your desk," Cec said, on his way to the outer office, while Maria crossed the room to her desk.

It had stopped raining, and the sky was clearing, Maria noted as she stood by the window. There was a stiff breeze blowing and whitecaps dotted the strait - good weather for sailing, and Danny's ketch would be at her best in this kind of a wind. In spite of the warnings, Maria took lightly the possibility of someone causing trouble during the trip, and it was with impatience to begin, that she looked forward to the voyage. She had a university class in the evening, and there was a lot to do to prepare for the trip. Val had promised to wash and iron some clothes for Maria while she was at class, and when she got home she would wash and set her hair and pack some things ready for the morning.

"Here you are," Cec said, breaking into Maria's thoughts, and turning away from the window, she went to join him at the desk where he was laying out a chart of the sea route to Powell River.

CHAPTER 9

The morning light was streaming in through the bedroom window as Danny gave up trying to get back to sleep, and rolling over on his back, he put his hands under his head and looked across to his wife Jean, who was fast asleep on the twin bed. The pink flowered bedspread dipped between her long shapely legs, and then bulged over her stomach, full with their baby. She was pretty, and the waves of her long light blond hair, seeming to flow around the delicate features of her face, accentuated the soft red color of her cheeks and sensitive lips.

Pleased with himself, Danny turned his head and looked through the large sliding glass doors, across the terrace and lawn to the distant sea. He was fortunate to have such a beautiful, intelligent, and understanding wife, and now that they were going to have a baby, he felt elated and proud. It was raining outside, and one of the gardeners, who doubled as a security guard, was working in the shelter of a greenhouse. To the left of the garden, his German shepherd dog laying close by, its ears straight, alert to every sound as he followed the movements of his master. Danny wasn't pleased with the weather, although he would start on the holiday to Powell River with Maria tomorrow, even if it was raining, as long as there were no high winds or fog. Some problems that had come up in the business were being taken care of, and it would do him good to get away for a few days; he would discuss it with his father at the office first thing that morning.

Getting up from bed, Danny went quietly about his morning ritual of shaving and getting ready to go to the office. Jean was still sleeping peacefully, her full breasts rising and falling with a steady rhythm, as he left his wing of the house and went into the main living quarters.

Their sheepdog met Danny as soon as he came through the door, and he wagged his tail furiously when Danny said, "Hello Sandy," and bent down and smoothed the fur on the back of his head. There was no one else in the large open beam living room. Danny glanced at his watch; it was seven o'clock, and he was the first up. The wood fire in the fieldstone fireplace had only just been lit and its flames flickered and threatened to go out. The red tile of the patio outside the sliding glass doors was wet with rain, the sun umbrellas had been lowered and tied down, and the rain splashed and made small circular waves on the surface of the swimming pool at one side of the patio. The dog followed Danny as he walked across the living room and through the dining room to the kitchen, from where the noise of running water and the clatter of dishes told him that Megan was washing the dishes that he and his wife had used the night before. Megan had only recently quit school to become a maid and assistant cook in the Lewes' home; her mother was the cook and housekeeper, and her father was a security guard and gardener for the Leweses. The family had been with the Leweses for many years. Danny had known Megan since he was a boy and she was a baby. She was a responsible girl, and for over a year now, starting while she was still attending school, she had prepared the breakfast for the Leweses and the staff of the house.

"Good morning, Megan," Danny said, as he looked over the bat wing doors of the kitchen, to where a small sixteen year old girl, with brown hair and wearing a black and white uniform, was working over the sink.

"Good morning, Danny," Megan said, looking over her shoulder and smiling, while the dog walked on into the kitchen and lay down in the middle of the floor.

"Is the coffee ready?"

"I will have it ready in two or three minutes and I will bring you a cup."

"Thanks, Megan. I will be in the living room."

"Take Sandy with you, Danny. He has been getting under my feet all the morning."

"Come on Sandy." Danny called as he turned and walked towards the living room, and Sandy, scrambling to his feet on the slippery tile of the kitchen floor, ran to join his master.

Sitting on a large upholstered chair facing the fire, Danny played with Sandy for a few minutes until Megan brought his coffee, then he held the dog for a moment to prevent him from following the girl back to the kitchen. The coffee tasted good, and picking up yesterday's newspaper from the table by his side, Danny read the previous day's news while he drank his coffee. A number of young persons had been arrested and charged with trafficking in narcotics, and the police had seized a pound of heroin at the border with the United States when a woman attempted to bring it into Canada. It was the second such seizure that the police had made in the past month, and there had been an increase in the number of people arrested on narcotic charges, the paper reported.

Putting down the newspaper, Danny lay back in the chair; this was part of what he and Dolansky had discussed last evening when he had visited Dolansky and his wife at their home. He had gone to see Dolansky because he suspected that illegal drugs were coming into the West Coast region by channels other than those controlled by the L. W. C. Import and Export Corporation. Dolansky had confirmed his suspicions, and reported to Danny what his detective agency and its associates were doing in an attempt to block the movement of narcotics that were not shipped through the L. W. C. Import and Export Corporations. The newspaper report partly confirmed what Dolansky had said.

* * *

The detective agency, of which Dolansky was the head, was one of five branches of an organization that had been set up twenty-five years before by a group of companies; which, until that time, had competed fiercely for the lucrative business of transporting and selling illegal cigarettes, alcohol, and drugs.

The competition had resulted in a loss to all the companies, because of frequent hijackings and the intrusion of small time operators. Under the agreement, the group of companies divided the territories among the members, took large insurance policies out for all the major executives of the companies, and set up the detective agencies to protect these executives and prevent competition from anyone who was not party to the agreement.

The agreement brought, order, stability, and prosperity, to the industry, which had lasted for many years. Unfortunately, the police too conducted their own investigations, and some shipments had been intercepted. However, the members of the group that were party to the agreement had taken elaborate precautions to insulate themselves from blame when such accidents occurred. Contingency plans were always ready to prevent prolonged interruptions in the traffic.

Also, there was a side benefit to these operations, in that the information provided to the police, to intercept the drug shipments of small time operators, could be channeled in such a way as to insure the success of some police officers. Unfortunately, Ted O'Brien who was a friend of the family was too honest, and would not have gone along with these plans, thus he never was approached to cooperate.

* * *

Still dressed in his pajamas, Bill Lewes sat down on the chesterfield across from Danny. He was a heavyset man with thick gray hair and large facial features. Both men sat and looked at each other for a while without speaking, the faint smile on their faces revealing their contentment with each other and their lives.

"I heard you up and about early, Danny, and I wondered if there were any problems?"

"There are a couple of things that I want to discuss with you at the office this morning." Megan came into the living room and brought Bill Lewes and Danny some coffee, then departed. "Irene telephoned me yesterday from Paris. She is getting along fine at school, but she has run into some difficulty with one of our long standing business associates; he wants a sizeable increase in the price we pay for his product."

Bill Lewes rubbed his unshaven face thoughtfully. "Mother is coming down to the office too, this morning, and so we can get together and discuss it there." Then getting up from the chesterfield, Bill Lewes put another log of wood on the fire and stood for a minute, watching as it took fire, before he returned to his seat. Father and son leaned back and relaxed as they drank their coffee, and watched the fire as it crackled noisily, sending flames shooting up the chimney, while the aroma of bacon frying came from the kitchen.

* * *

As Bill Lewes' two children, Danny and Irene, had matured, he had taken them increasingly into his confidence and given them increasing responsibilities in the corporation's business, especially in the illegal operations, where their involvement lessened the extent to which he depended on outsiders. Then by changing the methods by which the illegal drug trade was carried out, he reduced the knowledge that outsiders had of these operations, and thus reduced their threat to him and his family. Danny now had equal responsibility with his father in conducting the corporation's business, and they consulted each other on all major decisions. Bill Lewes' twenty-two year old daughter, Irene had attended numerous universities abroad and in Canada, and acted as his personal representative in contacting and helping to complete agreements with agents with whom the corporation did business. Irene was an intelligent girl and she had no difficulty with academic work, although she did not overburden herself with difficult courses. The universities, which she attended, were chosen more for the cover they afforded her and their convenience to her work with the business than to advance her education. Thus, she did not take her university work too seriously, and she had time to attend to the corporation's business and to make friends and enjoy life.

Bill Lewes' wife, Emily had come to Canada with him from Britain, and she participated in the business as his chief advisor from its beginning. Mrs. Lewes possessed extensive knowledge of almost all aspects of the corporation's business, and her advice had proved invaluable. Consequently, she was well respected by her family and participated in the corporation's business, having complete freedom to visit the offices, to observe the work being done and peruse documents, and attend executive meetings.

* * *

Finished with his coffee, Bill Lewes put the cup and saucer down on the table by his side. Then while looking again into the dancing flames of the fire, he said. "Are you still planning to take the yacht to Powell River for a few days?"

Danny looked to his father, who continued to look into the fire, deep in thought. Perhaps there were other aspects to their present situation of which his father knew, and of which he was not yet aware.

"Yes, I was hoping to get away, as there will be no important shipments going through during the next few days. However, it depends on what decisions we come to after our discussion this morning."

"Oh, you should be able to get away. If anything that needs your attention comes up, I will get in touch with you on the radio, and you can cut your holiday short."

"Did you tell Mother that I was planning to take the trip?"

"I discussed it with Mother, but she knew about it from Jean already. I told her that Tom was going with you, and don't ever let her know or think different, Danny because there would be hell to play."

It was eight o'clock, and the two men went into the dining room and sat down at the table that had been set for breakfast. Megan came in from the kitchen, set small bowls of oatmeal down in front of Danny and his father, and went back to the kitchen.

"Good morning," Danny said, as his mother entered the dining room and sat down opposite him at the table.

A slim woman, Mrs. Lewes looked neat in her long blue embroidered dressing gown that made her look taller than her five foot two inches. She was alert and pretty, with few lines on her face, and it was her gray hair more than anything that revealed her age. She had brushed her hair until it shone and put on just a little makeup, before leaving her quarters. Then while she smiled and said, "Good morning," two dimples appeared on her cheeks and her green eyes sparkled.

"Would you like your breakfast served now, Madam?" Megan asked, as she placed two dishes covered with silver lids on the table.

"No thanks, Megan. I will wait and have breakfast with Jean when she gets up. Just bring me a cup of coffee please."

Then, after Megan had returned to the kitchen, Mrs. Lewes spoke to Danny.

"Jean told me that you went to visit the Dolanskys last night."

"Yes. A couple of things have come up that I wanted to discuss with him. Dad tells me that you will be coming down to the office this morning; so if we could get together; there are a number of decisions that we should make."

Megan put a cup of coffee down in front of Mrs. Lewes, picked up Danny's and his father's oatmeal dishes, and replaced them with warm plates.

"What time will you be at the office this morning, Emily?" Bill Lewes asked.

"I will be there by noon." Mrs. Lewes took a drink from her cup while Danny and his father served themselves with fried potatoes, bacon, and eggs. "Is there something really urgent to discuss?"

Bill Lewes nodded in reply and took a piece of toast from the rack on the table.

Emily considered the serious expression on the faces of her husband and son, and noting that Megan was not in the room, she asked. "Has Doc Ellis become involved again?"

"Perhaps," Danny replied. Then the conversation on the subject was not continued during the remainder of the meal.

Danny and his father drove to the office together. It was not raining as heavy as it had been earlier in the morning, and they chatted about the weather and the prospects of a strike by the lumber industry employees, saying nothing about the scheduled family meeting.

It was ten after nine when they got to the office, and it was buzzing with activity when Bill Lewes went into his private office and closed the door. Then going directly to his desk, he pressed the button on the intercom and told his secretary that he did not want to be disturbed until after ten o'clock. Out on the street, it was raining heavy again, and people hurried to and fro under their umbrellas and cars splashed through the puddles. Bill Lewes sat down on his swivel chair behind the desk and turned towards the window; the rain, coming down in sheets, obscured the distant mountains, and the tall buildings of the city stood like ghosts in the dim light. There would be some difficult decisions to make that morning and he wanted time to think and go over some events.

CHAPTER 10

Bill Lewes, a cold and calculating man, could be kind or ruthless depending on which would best serve his ends. He had made many friends and enemies as he clawed his way up to his present position as president of a multimillion-dollar corporation. But he had remained true to his friends over the years; lending Bert O'Brien money to open his lounge when it had been a poor risk at the beginning, and employing Doc Ellis as an advisor and chief security officer for the trucking and warehouse division of the corporation.

An old friend of the Lewes family, Doc Ellis wasn't really a doctor, and he had earned the name because of his many remedies, which ranged from cures for common colds to prevention of conception. Doc Ellis, Bert O'Brien, and Bill Lewes had arrived in Canada about the same time, forty-five years ago, and they had worked together as stevedores on the Vancouver docks in those early days and became good friends. Bert O'Brien knew nothing about the illegal operations carried on by the Lewes' corporation. Outside the Lewes family, Doc Ellis knew more than any other person about the illegal drug trade in which the corporation was involved. Thus, while he was a valued friend, he could become a dangerous enemy, and there were some recent signs that Doc Ellis was betraying the trust that Bill Lewes had placed in him.

It had been ten years since Doc Ellis had caused the Leweses a serious problem, and at that time, Emily Lewes had advised quite strongly that they should get rid of him. Bill Lewes had not heeded her advice because the problem had been caused by Doc Ellis' inefficiency rather than a betrayal of trust. In addition, by involving Danny more in the warehouse and trucking aspect of the corporation's business, he had been able to eliminate this inefficiency.

* * *

Bill Lewes was relaxing in his office, when a buzzer sounded on the intercom, and he bent forward and pressed a button to open the communication between himself and his secretary.

"Hello."

"Mr. Reynolds would like to see you, Mr. Lewes."

"Mr. Reynolds?"

"Yes sir. He is the shipper at A Depot and he says that he has a ten-thirty appointment with you."

"Tell him that I am busy now and to make an appointment for another time."

"He says that it is urgent, Sir."

"Okay, send him in."

Bill Lewes was angry and at the same time thoughtful. This Reynolds had a lot of gall to tell lies in order to bypass the formalities that were necessary for an employee to go through to get an interview with him. Nevertheless, Bill Lewes was intrigued by what Reynolds would have to say. He had learned from an informal source that the morale of the men at A Depot was low and there was some pilfering going on there. Bill Lewes had discussed the situation with Doc Ellis. Because of this, security measures had been stepped up and Doc Ellis was looking into the matter with a view of dismissing Reynolds.

Reynolds came into the office and closed the door behind him. "Good morning, Sir," be said, standing just inside the door. He was wearing a new suit and a white shirt and tie, which were not the dress of a shipper, and Bill Lewes concluded that he had not showed up for his job that morning.

"Sit down, Reynolds," Bill Lewes said, pointing to a chair beside the desk. "Now, what can I do for you?"

"I am the shipper at A Depot and I have evidence to show that the corporation has been shipping marijuana through the depot hidden in cases of lettuce."

"That is a very serious charge, Mr. Reynolds. When, and to whom, was this marijuana sent, and what quantity do you think went through?" Bill Lewes knew this charge to be true and his questions were intended to find out how much the man knew; but, he was not alarmed by the situation, and his voice and manner were now cunningly designed to convey a lack of guilt and much concern in the matter.

Reynolds's eyes narrowed and he smoothed back his graying mustache with his left hand. He had intended to blackmail Mr. Lewes, and now he was not sure whether Mr. Lewes had known about the marijuana. "The shipment went through yesterday afternoon to Cass' Intercontinental Fruit and Vegetable Company. There were five hundred cases; I am not sure that all the cases contained marijuana, but the case that I did check contained two pounds of marijuana among the lettuce."

"And you let the shipment through?" Bill Lewes said, with surprise and concern in his voice and on his face.

"Yes, I didn't know until I got home from work that there was marijuana in the shipment, and I wasn't sure that there was anything wrong at the time I took a case of lettuce from the shipment and put it in the trunk of my car. If everything would have been okay, I would have taken the lettuce back to work this morning."

"Where do you have the case of lettuce now?" Bill Lewes asked, as he stubbed out his cigar in an ashtray.

"I still have it at home. I thought that I would see you about it before going to the police."

"Mm, I see, and how did you become suspicious that there was something wrong with this particular shipment?"

"Mr. Ellis seemed over concerned that the shipment go through quickly and he watched it like a hawk - I had one hell of a job to take a case without him seeing me."

"Did any of the other workmen see you take the case?"

"Yes, a number of guys saw me take it."

The bastards, they are robbing me blind, Bill Lewes thought while not letting this realization or his hate for Reynolds show on his face. Then in a tone of voice that did not reveal his feelings he said, "I am not sure that you did the right thing. Perhaps you should have telephoned the police right away, although I do like to know what is going on in my warehouses before anyone else. If you are correct about this being marijuana, Mr. Ellis has something to do with it, and we will need a new warehouse supervisor. I would want someone like yourself, who is honest and lets me know what is going on in my warehouses. Do you think that you could handle the job, Mr. Reynolds?"

"Yes sir," Reynolds replied quickly. The job would pay at least three times the money he was getting; he could buy a new car and maybe a new house and move to a prestigious neighborhood.

The telephone rang as Reynolds continued to dream. Bill Lewes picked up the telephone. "Hello."

"This is Doc, I have got to see you right away."

Bill Lewes looked at Reynolds; he was through day dreaming and watching him closely. "Yes Mr. Sanders," Bill Lewes said into the telephone, "I have given the purchase of the new forklifts some thought, and after I have consulted with my supervisor, I will come to a decision and give you a call."

"I take it that you know what's up and I will wait for you to call," Doc said. Then he listened as the telephone went dead. As white as a sheet, and breathing heavily, Doc scratched his head and hung up the telephone.

While he replaced the telephone into its cradle, Bill Lewes considered his next move. He would have to get rid of Reynolds somehow; he had not completely swallowed the bait and he still seemed somewhat doubtful and suspicious. "I would like to see the marijuana which you found before we call in the police."

"The marijuana is with the case of lettuce, which I left at home with my wife."

"Could we go over to your place to see it?"

"Sure," Reynolds replied, getting up from his chair.

"Good." Bill Lewes glanced at his watch; it was eleven-thirty. "I'm famished. I didn't have breakfast this morning. There is a nice restaurant in the hotel at the end of the block; we will have something to eat there before we go to your place."

"Aye!" Reynolds exclaimed suspiciously.

However, Bill Lewes cut in quickly; "I would like to talk to you about your background and your experience with the company, with reference to the supervisor's job that will be coming vacant."

"Okay," Reynolds said, reluctantly.

Bill Lewes got up from his plush chair, and both men walked to the door. The pretty secretary smiled to them when they came through the door into the outer office.

"Oh," I had better telephone my wife and tell her that I will not be home for dinner," Bill Lewes said. "Take a seat for a minute, Mr. Reynolds, and I will be right with you." Reynolds sat down on a chair and looked around the office and back to the secretary, as Bill Lewes reentered his private office and closed the door.

Walking quickly to his desk, Bill Lewes picked up the telephone and dialed a number.

The telephone rang just once. "Hello," Dolansky said.

"This is Bill. One of my employees has just visited me at my office. He wants some shares in the company and his assets are too good to ignore. I will leave it to you to make the final arrangements, which will have to be made this afternoon."

"Where can I find him?"

"We are going to the restaurant in the hotel at the end of the block for lunch and we will sit close to the window."

"Very good."

"He is storing his assets at home, and if you could make the final arrangements before he arrives home, I will have them picked up. Call me at the restaurant after you have looked over the situation and you can take it from there."

The secretary smiled to Bill Lewes as he came out of his private office and walked to her desk. "Make reservations for two at the restaurant in the hotel and have them reserve a table close to the window. Also, inform Danny that the meeting planned for this morning has been delayed, and I will explain later."

"When shall I say you will be at the hotel, Sir?"

"We are leaving right away."

The manager of the hotel met them at the door to the restaurant. "Good morning gentlemen. Right this way please," he said, ushering them to a table next to the window. Then after seeing that they were comfortable, he motioned to a waitress to look after them.

Cec Banas entered the restaurant behind Bill Lewes and Reynolds and without any fanfare or even notice from the waitress; he took a table at the window next to theirs. Glancing around the restaurant, Cec summed up the situation; the place was third rate and the attention that Bill Lewes and his guest had received was out of character for the place. However, the manager knew that Bill Lewes had a lot of influence in governmental circles, and if he ever opposed his liquor license when it came up for renewal it could mean serious trouble for the hotel and perhaps bankruptcy. It was ten to twelve and the restaurant was filling up; it would be packed in another fifteen minutes, and people would be waiting for tables. I will never get to finish this meal Cec thought. Bill Lewes and his guest were already halfway through their soup and he had not yet received a menu or a glass of water. To hell with the waitress he thought, then he turned his face up and smiled to the waitress as she placed a menu and a glass of water before him. The waitress did not return his smile and it was another ten minutes before Cec got the no choice soup of the day, and by this time he had forgotten about his dinner and was busy studying the people who were sitting at the tables around him. "No thanks," Cec said, as the waitress placed a bowl of soup on the table. "Just bring me the beef dinner please," and he did not notice the scowl he got from the girl as she picked up the bowl of soup or her smile to a customer at another table when she set the soup down in front of him.

* * *

With his face showing no emotion, Dolansky set the telephone down after speaking to Bill Lewes, and sat back in his chair deep in thought for about five minutes until he telephoned his wife and told her that he would not be seeing her for lunch. Then he got up from his swivel chair, took a pistol from his desk, stuck in his belt, and walked out of his office.

Outside, under a partly cloudy sky, and a cold wind off the sea, Dolansky, amid the noise of the traffic and the crush of pedestrians, walked hurriedly the three blocks to a major department store. He entered the brightly lit store along with a number of people, went straight to the parking elevator, and took it down to the third level. A number of people got on to the elevator after he alighted into the dimly lit concrete structure. The level was about two-thirds filled with cars, and it was cold and damp as he walked slowly along the sloping concrete floor. A woman in a mink coat was getting out of a new Chrysler, and Dolansky looked the other way as she went by. Then a few cars further along he stopped and stood aside as a car passed, and looking back, he noticed that the woman in the mink was waiting for the elevator. Dolansky walked alongside, the old Buick; the parking ticket was on its dash and the doors were not locked. He took the ticket, which showed that the car had been parked for an hour and a half, and walked back to the new Chrysler. The woman in the mink coat had gone up in the elevator and a couple was getting into a car on the other side of the level, when Dolansky took a ring of keys from his pocket; and choosing one, he opened the Chrysler door and got in. He waited for a car to pass before he put on a small false beard and mustache, and when he drove out of the car park, he had all the appearances of a university professor.

Driving slowly past the hotel, Dolansky took a long hard look at the man sitting opposite Bill Lewes; he was wearing a navy blue suit and a shirt and tie; about thirty-five, a close cropped balding head, a pale round face, a large mustache, and a small turned up nose. With this mental picture of Reynolds firmly established in his mind, Dolansky turned the Chrysler around, parked where he could observe the front entrance of the hotel, and leaving the car, he walked to a nearby telephone kiosk.

"There is a telephone call for you, Sir," the manager of the hotel said, as he approached Bill Lewes' table. Then when Bill Lewes got up, he smiled and continued, "you can take it in my office."

"Thanks," Bill Lewes replied. Then turning to Reynolds, he feigned a look of displeasure at being interrupted by the telephone call. "Please excuse me for a moment."

Bill Lewes picked up the telephone, and his brow furrowed as he wondered, what preparations were being made to take care of Reynolds. "Hello, this is Bill Lewes."

"I will make the final arrangements for the corporation when your man is on the way home, so you can go ahead and have the assets picked up."

"Very good. Then that should close the deal. Could you and your wife come to dinner at about six o'clock tomorrow evening?"

"Yes, I'm sure we can make it," Dolansky replied.

"Good. We will see you at my place. Bye."

After leaving the telephone kiosk, Dolansky went back to the Chrysler, where unconsciously he put his hand on the heavy caliber automatic pistol that he had stuck in his belt beneath his coat before leaving the office.

In the restaurant, Bill Lewes finished drinking his wine and apologizing to Reynolds, he told him that his secretary had telephoned to say that an important stockholder in the corporation was waiting for him in his office. He would have to go and see the stockholder right away, and he would be at Reynolds' home in one hour. Reynolds hesitated before giving Bill Lewes his address; he wanted to settle the matter right away and not let it drag on. He was more suspicious of Lewes than ever and he felt certain that these delays were a ploy to gain time although he still held all the cards. He considered going to the police immediately, and while still apprehensive, he concluded that he had nothing to lose by waiting another hour, and there was a good possibility that he would get one hell of a good job out of the deal.

Leaving the hotel together, Bill Lewes and Reynolds walked back to the office building, and Dolansky started the Chrysler ready to move. Cec had been quite pleased with his meal, he had time to finish it without hurrying, and it had been a lot better than he expected. Bill Lewes and his guest were talking in the parking lot by the office, and as Cec strolled leisurely down the opposite side of the street, then they separated. Bill Lewes went back into the office and his guest got into an old blue Ford and drove away.

With both side windows rolled down in readiness to shoot, Dolansky drove the Chrysler carefully, never letting the Ford be more than one or two cars ahead of him. He hoped that Reynolds would stop for a packet of cigarettes or something, so that he would have an easy target, otherwise he would pass the Ford and shoot Reynolds through the window.

The Ford passed a police station, turned around the block, and passed the police station again as Reynolds vacillated between reporting the matter to the police immediately or going home. Then a couple of blocks further on he stopped his car at a park; he would walk and decide what to do. Reynolds looked back through the rear view mirror; there was a car approaching slowly a good distance behind, and he would have time to get out and go around the side of his car.

Dolansky watched as Reynolds got out of his car on the driver's side, and with his face expressionless, he gunned the Chrysler as Reynolds squeezed against the car and pulled the door in to allow room for the car he heard approaching to pass. A pedestrian screamed as she witnessed the Chrysler sideswipe the Ford, then she fainted. The Chrysler swerved wildly after the collision until Dolansky regained control, and continuing on, he made a number of turns from the road on which he had been traveling before parking in a shopping center parking lot, where he removed his false beard, mustache, and gloves. It was a damn shame to have had to wreck such a nice car, Dolansky thought as he got out of the car and walked calmly to a bus stop to take a bus downtown.

* * *

After parking the white Ford Fairlane alongside the curb, Rocky Devis turned off the ignition and smiled to his wife Marj who was sitting by his side. She had long legs, a nice figure, and a pretty face marred only by the blemishes of an earlier skin problem, which showed through her suntan and make-up. Her dress was expensive in contrast to Rock's brown windbreaker and blue jeans, although his looks were every bit as good as hers and the first thing that a stranger would notice about him was his dark blue eyes which stood out against his fair complexion and blond curly hair.

"What do we do now?" Marj asked in an impatient voice.

Rocky did not answer for a while; he was looking down the streets. It was an older district, the houses were all two story, and narrow with a small lawn behind a hedge or low wall which separated them from the sidewalk. Most of the houses were well kept, but a number of them looked as if they needed a coat of paint. "Do you see the white house with the green trim; we just wait here until a lady leaves, then I go in, pick up a case of lettuce, and we deliver it to Cases' Intercontinental Fruit and Vegetable Company."

"How much do we get for this, Rocky?"

"I don't know. Bill Lewes always pays enough to make it worthwhile, so I don't ask."

"How do you know that it was Lewes? He never gives his name over the telephone, and you do what you are asked without question."

"That's right, Baby. Don't knock it while we have it good."

"You would never take this kind of crap from anyone when you were boxing in the States."

"Oh, don't bring that up, you know that I couldn't make it as a boxer."

"You were good, Rocky."

" I know, I couldn't take it, and as soon as I got hurt I had to punch the bastards below the belt. You know you went through it with me; it got to be a habit, which I couldn't stop, so I got busted. Why bring that up now? In our three year's of marriage this is the best we have ever had it."

"I'm frightened." What if that creep in the used car lot reports to the police that you stole the car?"

Rocky laughed. "He won't when he sees me coming, he leaves the keys in the car that he wants me to take. He knows that I always bring the car back, and he gets fifty bucks in his pocket for nothing. That's more than the poor bastard makes all day, some days. He can't afford to turn me in."

"Does Lewes know that you left the States to escape going to jail for possession of marijuana?"

"Yes, he questioned me about it one day, and I gave him the old story about being a draft dodger. However, he wasn't buying any of it; so I gave him the story straight. We have got on fine ever since. He pays me almost twice as much as most of the guys in the warehouses earn, and I get to travel around and work in every warehouse. With my education where could I get a job as an inspector and make the kind of money I'm getting?"

"You're not an inspector, Rocky. An inspector doesn't work as a laborer with the other men, and he doesn't make all his reports over the telephone, or be a delivery boy."

"I like the job, the work keeps me in shape, and I get more time off and money than any of the other guys. Shit! What do you want, Marj?"

"You're a fucking spy and at someone's beck and call. That's what I don't like."

"Oh, come on, Marj, Bill Lewes is a square shooter. He pays me well for the job, and if I do anything extra I get a bonus."

"Does Lewes' son know what you are doing"?

"Yes. He is in on just about everything the old man does, and his word is as good as his old man's."

The sun shone in through the windshield of the car, and Marj, feeling the warmth on her slim legs, turned her dress up to expose more of her legs to the sun. Then she looked to Rocky to see if he was watching, and they smiled together as he brought his eyes up from her legs and they looked into each other's eyes.

"Now that we have the time and money, Rocky; I wish that we could go home and visit my parents. They would give us one hell of a welcome and we could take them out and show off a little."

"You can go if you wish, Marj; however, I couldn't. They would grab me as soon as I crossed the border, and put me on trial for that stupid marijuana deal. For the possession of one lousy reefer they might give me more time than if I had committed murder."

"No, I wouldn't go without you. It wouldn't be any fun. Oh well, one of these days they might legalize the shit and we will be free again."

A car had parked across the street from them, and two teenagers got out, put the hood up, and began to do something to the engine as an old couple stopped to watch, while on their side of the street a woman was walking towards them.

"Did she come out of the house?" Marj asked.

"No, she came from around the block. That little black dog that just ran by is with her."

"Oh my God! Here's the police," Marj blurted out, as she turned to Rocky.

"Take it easy. We haven't done anything wrong."

The police car had passed them from behind and parked in front of the white house with the green trim. The officer got out of the car rang the doorbell, and after waiting, a minute or so went inside. Rocky and Marj were quiet as they waited to see what else would happen, and after a tense few minutes went by, the officer came out with a woman. She had pulled a coat over her housedress, and she brushed her graying hair back with her hand as the police officer opened the door for her to get into the car. The two teenagers and the old couple watched the police car drive away, and Rocky looked back through the rearview mirror; the woman with the dog had gone. A car turned the corner, came down the street, and stopped behind them for a moment to let another car go by in the opposite direction.

Rocky and Marj waited another ten-minutes, until the teenagers had driven away and the old couple had walked on, then Rocky got out of the car and walked up to the white house with the green trim. The door was unlocked and Rocky walked in and looked around. He was in a nicely furnished living room, a television, new chesterfield, wall-to-wall carpet, and a stereo set. A picture on the stereo showed a man and the woman who had just left the house, standing with two children. Rocky walked through the living room into the kitchen, the woman had cooked dinner, and there were some dishes in the sink. There was a baseball bat in one corner and under the table was the case of lettuce. Rocky pulled it out, took the baseball glove off the top, and carried the case out to the street. He closed the door behind him, and Marj, looking straight ahead of her, drove the car up, and then waited for Rocky to put the case in the trunk and get into the car beside her before driving away.

"I don't like what we are doing, Rocky," Marj said; concern evident in her voice. "There is something underhanded about the whole deal and it's giving me the creeps."

"Don't worry, Marj everything is going to be all right." Rocky said, reassuringly, as be squeezed her leg just above the knee and smiled.

* * *

Bill Lewes listened to the news on the radio. A man had been killed by a hit and run driver in North Vancouver, and the man's name was being withheld pending notification of next of kin. The police had a description of the car that killed the man from an eyewitness and their investigation was continuing. He turned off the radio as his secretary came in with a cup of tea; she smiled to him as she put down the tea, and when she turned to walk away, he slapped her lightly across her behind.

"Ouch," she said, glancing back and smiling as she continued on to the door.

"Hello," Bill Lewes said, picking the telephone up on the first ring.

"This is Doc," the voice came over the telephone. "Cass just phoned me to say that he got the rest of the shipment and everything is okay."

"Good. From what I gathered this morning, there is quite a bit of pilfering going on in A Depot. Get someone in there you can trust and find a couple of the worst culprits and fire them. Can you come over to my place about eight o'clock tonight, Doc?"

"Sure, I can be there, Bill."

"Okay. We can continue our discussion at that time."

* * *

An employee from another warehouse was brought in to take the job of shipper at A Depot; Rocky Devis was promoted to the position of foreman, and during the next few weeks, five men were fired from the warehouse. Doc had discussed these aspects of the operation, as well as many others, with Bill Lewes and Danny. The pilfering at A Depot had been stopped, the warehouse employees had been given an across the board increase with improved fringe benefits, and the efficiency and morale of the men had improved. In addition, Danny to gain the confidence and the respect of the men; stopped in at the lunchrooms during their coffee breaks and chatted with them about sports, their outside hobbies, their families, and their work at the warehouse.

Through these informal meeting with the men, besides winning their respect, Danny gained much knowledge and insight into the operation of the warehouses, and it was partly due to his suggestions that some aspects of the operation had been changed and efficiency and morale had improved. However, Bill Lewes, through the reports received from Rocky Devis, had become suspicious that Doc Ellis may have some special relationships with one or two of the warehouse employees. He had discussed these suspicions with Danny, and together with the aid of Dolansky they had arranged for a few more men to be hired, who, like Devis, would report back if anything unusual happened in the depots. Thus, through this increased vigilance, it had become apparent that Doc Ellis was using the company's facilities to further his own selfish ends. The only reason that he had not been removed earlier was by the request of Dolansky, who wished to learn more about his clandestine activities and the persons with whom he was engaged. Although, now it seemed that the time was fast approaching when something should be done about Doc Ellis, especially if his activities were somehow linked with the problems that Irene was experiencing in Paris.

Turning from the window when his wife entered the office, Bill Lewes watched her as she hung her coat in the closet and sat down on the chesterfield facing him.

"The clouds are breaking over the strait and the forecast is for good weather for tomorrow," Emily Lewes said. Then she smiled before continuing, "The weather will be good for Danny to take the Bliss-In on his holiday to Powell River."

"Did we get any mail from Irene this morning?" Bill Lewes asked.

"Yes. She said that she was enjoying her stay in Paris and she is still going out with Pierre. It seems something of a record for Irene to be going out with a boy this long."

"I wouldn't take that as being any indication that she is getting serious with him, Emily, and it is more likely that Pierre is tutoring her for her French class."

"You are probably right. Sometimes I wonder if she will ever get married."

"Did Irene say anything in her letter concerning Philip's shipment for this month?"

"She had an appointment with him at his office yesterday morning, and she would telephone to let us know the outcome," Emily replied.

"That would be the phone call that Danny received from her." Bill Lewes pressed the intercom button on his desk. "Ask Mr. Danny Lewes to come to my office please," he told his secretary.

"Danny didn't say anything about the phone call at breakfast this morning," Emily said, wrinkling her brow.

"He mentioned it to me a little earlier and I thought it better that we discuss it at the office."

The Leweses sat quietly while they waited for Danny. Emily felt more troubled than she had for years; she was uneasy about Irene being in a far away country when there was so much unrest in the world and in their business. She would feel much more able to care for her youngest child if she was at home in Canada. Then she checked this line of reasoning. I'm being an overprotective mother she thought; Irene has been raised and educated well, and behind her charm, youth, and enthusiasm there is an alert mind. She is wise to the ways of the world and she is quite capable of looking after herself Emily thought. Nevertheless, her apprehension for her daughter persisted, and she thought; in case of any major problems it would be better, the family was together.

Danny entered the office and the Leweses watched him admiringly as he closed the door and took a comfortable seat close to his mother. "I told your secretary on the way in that we would be in conference and we were not to be disturbed."

"Good," Bill Lewes said. "Now, where shall we begin?"

"Tell us about your conversation with Irene yesterday," Danny's mother said.

"She met with Philip yesterday morning to discuss last month's shipment and the quantities required for this month, and she will be in Switzerland today making arrangements for payment. Irene was disturbed by what Philip had to say; he suggested an alternate way of shipping and selling his products, and he wants an immediate large increase in the amount we pay. He was very evasive to her questions. From what she could get from the conversation, it appeared that a new company to the industry had already shipped his heroin, opium, and hashish for this month to Canada. Irene suggested to him that our company had a record of dependable service, and that he may be taking unnecessary risks with a new company. However, he used the facilities of the new company to ship his products to the United States last month with good results. I checked with Dolansky on this, and he confirmed that the Seattle member of our group experienced the same problems with Philip last month as we are getting now. All branches of the detective agency, including Dolansky, have stepped up their activities, and because of the information they have supplied to the police there has been a rash of minor arrests and confiscation of small amounts of drugs. Philip is evidently aware of these activities too, and he warned Irene that measures have been taken to prevent sabotage of his shipments, and if any interference is encountered, further steps will be taken to punish those responsible and prevent any reoccurrence."

Mrs. Lewes' face had gone white during the time Danny was talking, and turning to her husband, she said. "We should bring Irene home immediately."

The room had become quiet as Danny and his mother looked to Bill Lewes and waited for his reaction. He put down the cigar he had been smoking, and then replied. "Knowing us, Philip would be stupid to do anything to harm Irene, although what he is attempting to do now is not very bright either and perhaps it would be best to bring her back to Canada now." Bill Lewes paused and rubbed his chin with his hand. "Irene still has some business to complete in the next few days with three of our other suppliers in France and Italy, and it is more important than ever that we have personal contact with these suppliers so that we know exactly where we stand. Does Dolansky know if there are any other dissenters besides Philip among the suppliers, Danny?"

"No; as far as he knows, Philip is the only one dealing with the new company. But they will be watching and they will follow his lead if he is successful."

Getting up from the chesterfield, Emily Lewes walked to the window and looked down on the street, then turning abruptly, she said, "Did Dolansky have anything to say regarding Irene's safety in Europe?"

"Yes, he thinks that she is in extreme danger and he sent Steve Bailey to Paris last night to meet her when she arrives there from Switzerland. He is awaiting further instructions from us now as to whether she will be returning immediately or staying on in Europe."

Obviously worried and restless for action, Danny's mother sat down on the chesterfield besides him. "I think we should bring Irene home immediately, and this would give us a free hand to deal effectively with Philip."

"That is one course of action to be considered, Emily," Bill Lewes said. "But I have another. Shall we have some coffee while we are discussing them?" Emily Lewes nodded her head in agreement, and Bill Lewes pressed the button on the intercom and told his secretary to bring them coffee.

"As you know," Danny said, "Philip had delivered a shipment of hashish to our warehouse in Le Havre and it was awaiting shipment to Montreal; and when Irene talked with Phillip about this month's shipment, she told him that he should pick it up. She said that he got quite angry and he picked it up within the hour."

"There is a little bit of you in Irene, Mother," Bill Lewes said, smiling broadly.

"And there is a hell of a lot of Bill Lewes in her," Emily Lewes retorted angrily. "She should be more cautious when she is wide open. If Philip should seek revenge . . ." and her voice trailed off as she threw up her hands in exasperation.

A light knock at the door indicated that the secretary had brought the coffee. "Thank you," Danny said, taking the tray from the waiting girl at the door. "Have there been any messages while we have been in conference?"

"Yes, Mr. Ellis telephoned for your father about a half hour ago, Sir, and he said that he would call back later."

"Thanks," Danny said, and then he closed the door as the girl walked back to her desk.

Turning to the small table besides her, where Danny had placed the tray,

Emily Lewes poured the coffee into the expensive china cups and added the correct amount of cream and sugar before serving her husband and son.

"I asked Irene if she wanted to drop everything and come home immediately," Danny said. She said that there were still a few things to be done, and it would be the beginning of next week, before she could get everything wrapped up. She promised that she would be extra cautious during the next few days, but she would let us assess the situation and decide whether she should stay or take the first plane home. I have a telephone number where we could get in touch with her and let her know our decision."

"Good," Bill Lewes said. "We will decide this afternoon and let her know. The other course of action, which I mentioned, is this. Leave Irene in Europe to finish the business and bring her directly home as soon as it has been completed. In the meantime, we will send another man to Europe to back up Steve Bailey and we will see that Philip's shipments with the new company are not interfered with until Irene is safely back in Canada. I will get in touch with Chris in Seattle too, and get him to stop the agency there from taking actions against the new company for the time being. I'm sure that he will cooperate when I explain the situation as his back is against the wall right now. He lost his shipment from New York last month, and we are his only source of supply of some hard drugs."

"Chris will cooperate," Danny agreed. "The new company is setting up another trafficking system in Seattle in an attempt to drive Chris out of business, and there have been three front end traffickers and one back ender killed during the last month. Dolansky warned me last night that the same sort of thing would happen here, and if Chris loses his business we could be in serious trouble too; so once Irene is safe, we should cooperate with Chris to clean up the mess that the new company is creating."

Bill Lewes nodded his head thoughtfully.

"I don't like it" Emily Lewes said. "We are leaving Irene out on a limb in case the police should intercept some of the new company's shipments."

"Mother is right, Dad," Danny said, and getting up, he put his cup and saucer on the desk before returning to sit on the chesterfield again. "The police have some leads on this new company and Ted O'Brien is in Toronto now in connection with the investigation. If the police seize any large quantities of drugs, Philip could be hurt badly, and he may think that we tipped them off."

Bill Lewes got up from his chair and walked to the window; the streets below were drying up after the rain, and the traffic was getting heavy again.

Then among the many pedestrians, Bill Lewes picked out the detective who had taken Steve Bailey's place; he was waiting to cross at the lights to the Lewes Tower. Mother and son watched and waited, as Bill Lewes turned from the window, walked slowly back to the desk and sat down and ran a heavy hand through his thick gray hair.

"How close is Dolansky to having something concrete against this new company, so that the police can make some major drug seizures?"

"He says that he should have information in two or three days, that when passed along to the police will enable them to put the finger on a number of the new company's operations. But he warns that there will be repercussions and we should be prepared for any eventuality."

"What does Dolansky say of Mother's theory, that Doc Ellis is working with the new company and passing along information?"

"His investigations indicate that Mother is probably correct, and he thinks we should take him out as soon as possible."

"Well that makes things more serious than I thought," Bill Lewes said. "Do you have any other ideas, Mother?"

"Yes, Doc Ellis will try something real stupid one of these days, and we should get rid of him now."

"Mother is right, Dad, and as soon as Irene is back, we should make the necessary arrangements."

"Yes, we will have to get rid of him," Bill Lewes conceded. "The bastard is doing well; he's never had it so good, and why he should decide to rock the boat I will never understand."

"I told you thirty-five years ago that he was not to be trusted," Emily Lewes said. "He is too ambitious, and he will never be satisfied. His jovial and friendly manner is just a front to cover his real self. You would have been better off to have given his job to Bert O'Brien in the beginning."

"I don't think you are right on that, Emily, Bert O'Brien would never have gone for the kind of stuff we are in now."

"What!" Emily exclaimed, "Anyone who runs a place like Anne's Lounge would do anything for a dollar."

"Christ, you two talk about thirty-five years ago as if it was yesterday," Danny said, breaking into their conversation. Both Mother and Father fell quiet and looked to their son. However, their look was not one of reproach, their minds were again busy grappling with their problem; assessing their present position, weighing the alternative courses of action that were open to them, and considering the possible eventualities. "Perhaps I should go to

Europe," Danny said. "I could take over from Irene and she could fly directly home."

"That would not change anything," Danny's mother said, "it would only be jumping from the frying pan into the fire if something should go wrong with Philip's shipments. On the other hand, if we do as your father suggested and keep things running smoothly for the next few days, because the actions of the new company are unpredictable, Irene will be safer in Europe than here. Chris has been hitting them in Seattle and they know that we will join forces with him and they may decide to strike first."

Leaning back in his swivel chair, Bill Lewes' eyes narrowed and the biceps of his muscular arms stood out as he put his hands behind his head. "Okay, we will try to keep the lid on things for the next few days to give Irene a chance to finish her business in Europe. Then she can fly back to Canada and go into hiding in Edmonton under an assumed name, until Chris and we can clear up this business of the new company. There is a group meeting coming up in a couple of weeks, and we can depend on the other members of the group to lend their support to clean up the whole business. What do you say?"

Emily Lewes nodded her head. In addition, Danny said, "It sounds good to me, and I will pass it along to Irene; although if anything should go wrong I will tell her to drop everything and fly directly to Edmonton. There is one more thing; Mother should go to Edmonton too and take cover with Irene until this whole thing has blown over."

"No," was Emily Lewes' immediate retort, "I will stay here, with you and see it through. Bill, when you speak to Doc Ellis, drop a hint that we are thinking of selling the business and retiring. It will give him something else to think about and perhaps interrupt his stupid schemes."

"I'm going to have dinner with Bert O'Brien," Bill Lewes said. "How about us all going to see him; he would like that?"

"I am sorry Billy," Emily Lewes said. "I can't make it, I promised Jean that I would be home for dinner." Then turning to Danny, she continued, "You should come home too; Jean needs lots of reassuring now that she is close to having her baby."

"I will go home for dinner." Danny said, getting up from the chesterfield. "I hardly spoke with Jean yesterday as we spent most of the evening with Dolansky. You don't mind do you, Dad?"

"No, you are right, you should spend more time with Jean." Bill Lewes paused, and as an afterthought he said. "Since you are going home, you could drive with your mother and leave me your car."

"Okay," Danny agreed, and taking the car keys from his pocket, he threw them into his father's outstretched hands before walking to the door, where he stopped and smiled to his mother. "I'll wait for you in my office, Mom."

"I will just be a couple of minutes, Danny," Emily Lewes replied with a smile.

* * *

Standing by the window, Bill Lewes watched as Danny drove out of the parking lot with his mother sitting by his side. The black Jaguar swung out onto the street, then stopped to let a young couple run across the road hand in hand as the sun broke through the clouds and shone off the top of the black car. Bill Lewes turned away from the window, and crossed the room to a wall cabinet where he took out a bottle of champagne and two wineglasses. Why did Emily want such a sporty car he mused? She is a careful driver and she never uses its full power; there are some things that I will never understand about my wife. He put the bottle and glasses on the desk, before sitting and pressing the button on the intercom. "Would you come to my office, Elizabeth?"

"I will be right there, Sir." Elizabeth rolled her chair away from the desk where she had been typing, smoothed her cream colored skirt down over her slender legs, and picked up a pad and pencil before going into the private office. Her thin face was serious, but she smiled when Bill Lewes asked her to join him in a drink, and going around the desk, she stood by his side and took the glass of champagne from his hand. Her waved auburn hair hung loose on her shoulders as she put the glass to her lips, and while she let the champagne bubble in her mouth before she swallowed, she watched her employer drink down his champagne.

"Were there any other messages for me, Elizabeth?"

"No, there was just the phone call from Mr. Ellis, and he will call back after dinner."

Bill Lewes poured the glasses full from the bottle, and as they raised them to their lips, he turned his chair to face the girl. Their lips were wet with champagne as he put his large hand under her skirt, and her legs opened to accommodate him. They finished their drinks slowly, and the buzzer sounded for lunch as Elizabeth removed her blouse and brassiere - she appeared frail in Bill Lewes' strong arms as he carried her to the chesterfield, while in the outer office the clerks were quickly vacating their desks. Then all was still, and only the noise of the air conditioner disturbed the peace, as appetites were being satisfied.

CHAPTER 11

Standing at the wheel of the yacht in the warm sun, Danny checked the gauges before him and listened to the purr of the powerful diesel engine. His blue jeans and sweater emphasized his lithe figure, and as he lifted his head to look to Maria, standing on the wharf, his wavy brown hair caught the breeze and blew about his head.

Relaxed and at peace with the world, Maria, after a signal from Danny, began her task of setting the boat free, her black hair shining in the morning sun and contrasting with her white sailor suit, as under Danny's gaze she went gracefully about her work. Then, when the last rope was untied, she climbed aboard, the collar of her suit and her hair blowing free in the wind.

With the diesel engine running at quarter speed, Danny eased the ketch away from the wharf, turned her bow towards the harbor mouth, and headed for the Strait of Georgia. Meanwhile, Maria coiled and stowed away the ropes that she had thrown aboard. Then walking to the bow she stood at the rail, her eyes on the splendor of the distant mountains and white drifting clouds, set in the background of the blue sky, as the boat, rolling gently moved out of the harbor.

Her two friends would be on the bus, and on their way to spend another day at the office, Maria thought. Then, she turned her eyes from the mountains to scan the distant horizon. It felt good to be free, and she looked up as seagulls screamed and wheeled towards the stern of the boat. Val had been serious and thoughtful when she helped to get ready for the trip, and Maria sensed that Val knew more than she had let on. Val was aware that her job was not all that it had been made out to be - the clothes, the car, the expense account, and the freedom to come and go as she pleased, had come too quickly, and while Val had said nothing of these things she had been quieter than usual throughout the evening. Then in the morning when Val got up early to have breakfast with her and see her off, Maria wished that she could have taken Val into her confidence. Maria had felt sad when they parted, and it was only when she saw Danny standing on the deck of the boat waiting, her buoyant spirit rebounded. Maria turned and looked back to Danny standing at the wheel; she felt exhilarated and thirsty for the good things of life.

As soon as they were out in the open channel and away from the small boats, Danny shut down the engine and together they unlashed the sails and hoisted them into position on the masts. The white sails snapped open in the wind, and Maria and Danny laughed as the boat heeled to starboard and its bow plunged into the light swell as gathering speed they turned the Bliss-In into her first tack. They changed tack twice during the morning and with time to relax; Maria and Danny observed the passing boats, the islands, and the mountains while they planned where they might anchor for the night. Meanwhile the bow of the Bliss-In cut a V through the water that moved out and behind the boat in two long lines as they traveled up the strait.

They ate their lunch on deck, and basked in the warm sun, but by two o'clock, the wind had risen and the seas were mounting. The weather forecast had changed, and with a small craft warning in effect for the Strait of Georgia, they decided to head for Joseph's Island, ten miles away over their bow. There was a deep and sheltered anchorage at Joseph's Island and they would be comfortable for the night. The big diesel motor roared to life when Danny pressed the starter, then it settled back into a quiet purr as he reduced the throttle; and putting the motor at slow ahead, he eased the boat into the sea.

The storm broke on them sudden and ferocious. A big wave smashed over the bow, and the deck was awash with water as Danny, clinging to the wheel with water swirling about his legs, looked towards Maria. Tight lipped, her white bell-bottom sailor slacks tight against her skin, Maria held onto a rail, which protruded from the bulkhead of the cabin. Another wave broke over the deck and threatened to tear her loose from the rail, but she was strong and unafraid, in spite of the danger.

Danny, with water splashing around him, set the automatic pilot to keep the boat into the wind, while the sails flapped noisily and the riggings delivered a baleful mourn as if to pronounce the urgency of their position. The sea that was calm thirty minutes before was now a boiling foam, and the sails cracked like whips in the rising wind as if urging Maria and Danny to make haste. Glancing up as he tied a lifeline about his waist, Danny smiled to reassure Maria as his own heart pounded in his chest. Then as the boat pitched heavily into the oncoming sea and the waves broke on the deck with alarming regularity, Danny made his way along the deck to Maria and fastened a lifeline around her small waist. Once secure, they went to work to lower the sails, stopping only momentarily when the water swirled about their waists and made it necessary for them to hang on, knowing that a sudden gust of wind across their beam could capsize their little ship. They were a serious couple, as they worked resolutely lowering the sails, making the booms fast and lashing down the sails while the wind and the waves drove them ever closer to the land.

After securing the mainsail, they were working their way forward along the deck when there was a loud crash; Maria felt the deck beneath her feet shudder, and looking forward she saw a huge green wave rushing along the deck towards them. Stopping with his hand on the rail, Danny watched Maria ahead of him take a firm grip on the rail, lower her head, and brace herself before she disappeared beneath the oncoming surge of water. Then gritting his teeth, Danny hung on for his life as the water engulfed him and threatened to tear him loose, and silently he prayed that Maria would endure the storm that was testing his own strength. Then when the rogue wave had passed, Maria was still on board, clinging to the rail just a few feet ahead of him; her black hair plastered close to her head, and her sailor suit tight against her body. They smiled to one another with relief as the boat rose, and as if in anger shook itself free of the water on its deck. Then once again they resumed their work while Danny cast furtive glances past the stern; where an arm of land, its rocks white with foam, appeared to reach towards them.

Their every move fraught with danger, Maria and Danny worked painfully slow as they braced themselves against the fury of the wind and the sea. Then at last, they had finished lashing down the sails, and they worked their way back to the stern where Danny once again took the wheel. While with the wind blowing her hair about her face, Maria untied the lifeline from around her waist, opening the cabin door, and went below deck.

Standing for a moment at the bottom of the stairs with one hand on the rail, Maria brushed her hair back from her face. Her lipstick and make-up had been washed away and her unblemished skin was soft and her cheeks red. With the salt water, dripping from her hair and clothes, forming a pool about her feet, Maria bowed her head as if baptized to a new faith. The two cups and plates that they had used for lunch were on the floor of the stateroom where they had fallen, broken like wine glasses hurled against the hearth, although all else was well below deck. Maria listened to the yacht creaking and groaning as she pitched and rolled in the rough sea. They were not alone with an inanimate thing; the Bliss-In was alive, her sleek hull strong, and with Danny and herself they would endure the storm. At that moment,

Maria's affection for the Bliss-In became akin to love, and she smiled when the motor that had been purring, resounded a deep throaty roar, then the Bliss-In shuddered as if struck by a mighty hand. However, above the noise and the motion of the boat, there was the steady throb of the engine as the propeller bit into the sea and drove them forward, and Maria knew that all was well.

On deck, Danny steered the boat so that the waves quartered the port bow. Then he pushed down on the throttle until the boat was making headway through the sea and moving slowly away from the peninsula of land. Moments before it had seemed like a hand with outstretched fingers, that had for a time seemed to be grasping for the stern. Holding the same course for another hour, Danny inched the yacht up the coast until they were abreast of a broad bay with Joseph's Island jutting into the sea. Danny changed course to starboard and they entered the calmer waters of the bay. Danny opened the throttle further and the Bliss-In surged through the water, and within an hour, they were moving through a narrow channel between Joseph's Island and the mainland, into the calm waters of the anchorage beyond.

There were three yachts tied up at the buoys, and they stood silhouetted against the background of the sandy beach of the island, where people could be seen walking and a number of children were playing. Further back, cottages, their lights burning, nestled among the trees behind the beach.

With his clothes still wet and his hair in disarray, Danny steered the boat towards the other yachts and glanced to Maria as she came on deck. She looked delicate and pretty, dressed in a pale yellow coat tied about her middle, her loose black hair shining in the dying light of the sun. In the shelter of the island, it was another world, like heaven compared to the storm in the open waters of the strait. Leaning against the rail, Maria watched Danny tie the Bliss-In up to a buoy, before she looked at the scene around her, as the boat drifted slowly back the length of the rope and lined herself up parallel to the other yachts.

Taking Maria's hand and drawing her close, Danny kissed her lightly, and then together they looked at the scene before them.

"Pretty," Danny said, with an impish smile. Maria, laughing at the intended double meaning, took Danny's hand to go below deck.

Feeling refreshed after taking a shower and changing into dry jeans and a blue shirt, Danny sat on one of the fawn colored chesterfields in the stateroom and closed his eyes. The soft lights from the brass lamps reflected on the teak walls and shone from the gold of the carpet and drapes. In the galley, Maria busied herself preparing their dinner, and the aroma of cooking steaks filled the cabin. Danny opened his eyes as Maria entered the room. Wearing a pink flowered mini-dress that emphasized her long slim legs, Maria walked carefully so as not to spill the drinks she carried, and Danny, cognizant of her beauty, smiled as the lights reflected from her hair and outlined the soft curves of her breasts through the sheer dress.

"We'll splice the main brace," Maria said, handing Danny a drink and smiling into his searching eyes.

"To a happy voyage," Danny said. Then standing close together, they clinked their glasses, and took long drinks from their rums. Maria could feel the warmth of the rum enter her stomach. Then after setting their glasses down on the table, Danny gathered her into his arms and with her breasts soft and warm against his chest, she returned his fierce kisses until they parted to sit on the chesterfield and savor their drinks once more. The steaks sizzled in the pan and their aroma filled the cabin as Maria, with her body tingling with excitement, put her head back and closed her eyes.

The ship's call signal sounded through the cabin, and a red light flashed on and off on the radio placed in the wall between the forward sleeping quarters and the stateroom. Danny picked up the headphones as Maria returned to the galley.

"You're all right?" Danny's father asked.

"Yes, everything is okay."

Then Danny's father continued. "A number of small boats have reported trouble in the strait because of the storm and two boats are missing. We were worried about you until just over an hour ago when Doc Ellis telephoned to say that he had sighted you down the bay, and you were making your way towards the island."

"Oh!" Danny exclaimed. "I didn't know that Doc was here at his cottage."

"Yes, you recall that he asked me last weekend if he could get away for a few days, and he left yesterday afternoon. Jean sends her love and Mother told me to tell you not to leave the anchorage before the storm blows itself out."

"We will stay here until it is calm outside, even if it means being delayed getting back to Vancouver."

"Good, I will call you again before you get home. Have a nice time and go and see Doc Ellis before you leave the island."

"Okay, bye."

Danny was deep in thought as he took off the headphones, replaced them on the radio, and returned to the chesterfield. Why had it been necessary for Doc Ellis to get away from Vancouver? His father had told him that Doc Ellis had asked for a few days off. Still, there had been no mention of him coming here, and he never visited his cabin on the island without letting his father know in advance, where he would be so that he could be reached in case of an emergency. Danny recalled his mother's warning, "Doc Ellis will do something real stupid one of these days," and he mulled over his father's words. "Go and see Doc Ellis before you leave the island." He had not made the statement in an authoritative way; nevertheless, Danny knew his father well enough to know that it was tantamount to an order. His father would have recalled Mother's warning too - his father wished to avoid any actions with Doc that would lead him to learn that they were aware of his betrayal, and induce him to behave irrationally during the next few days. He would go ashore with Maria tomorrow and pay his respects as if all was well. There was no necessity to be warned to be careful; the family knew of the dangers inherent to the business in which they were involved, and all their actions took this into consideration.

Aware of Danny's pensive mood following the radio conversation, Maria placed a white cloth over the stateroom table, laid out the cutlery and plates for dinner, and returned to the galley; all the time speculating that perhaps some danger was threatening.

Getting up from the chesterfield as the noise of pots being placed on the stove filled the air, Danny took a key from his pocket and opened a stateroom locker; he checked the high-powered rifle that stood in the rack, and picking a pistol, he made sure that it was loaded. He would take the pistol ashore with him tomorrow just in case it was needed. With things all set now, and ready for action, Danny's apprehension left him, and feeling ready to enjoy the holiday, he went into the galley and put an arm around Maria's waist as she finished dishing out the meal.

The dim light, from the lamps in the stateroom, cast shadows on the teak walls and shone from Maria's black hair as sitting opposite each other at the table they laughed and talked while eating their dinner. Then they cleared the table and washed the dishes together while they sipped the champagne that Danny had poured.

"Was that your father on the radio, Danny?"

"Yes, he was worried about us in the storm and he was checking to see that we were alright. A family friend, Doc Ellis, has a cabin on the island,

and my father wants us to go and visit him tomorrow. He is a very jovial fellow and you will like him."

A soft warm breeze rustled the curtains on the portholes while they made up the bed in the stateroom, and a woman called to her children on the beach as Danny took Maria into his strong arms and held her gently. Then Maria, moved by some invisible force, pressed her soft bosom against him as their warm moist lips met. Loving hands fondled, and removed clothing fell to the floor as passions mounted. Then reclining on the bed, with her slender hands beneath her head and her soft hair framing a pretty face, Maria's eyes followed her lover as his bare feet trod the carpet towards her. The lights caressed the smooth lines of her figure, revealing the rise and fall of her level stomach and shining black hair, while with bent knees she waited.

Their lips met and Maria's body arched to receive Danny as they slipped into another world. The bow of the yacht dipped into the swell of the sea and pulled on the mooring cable as rising and falling gently, the yacht rode the waves. A wave splashed noisily against the ship and the sound of music came across the water from a nearby boat, but these sounds went unheard until passions were spent and as time began again with the tick of the stateroom clock. The lovers withdrew from the other world, covered themselves with bedclothes and feeling warm and satisfied slept peacefully.

Danny awoke with a start. The gray light of dawn filled the cabin, and the boat rolled lazily in the swell as the water gurgled about the hull. Then while laying still, he heard the sound that had awakened him - the dull muffled thud of a boat's propeller as a nearby boat got under way. Maria was still sleeping when Danny slipped out of bed, moved quietly across the cabin, and looked out of the porthole. A thirty-five foot cruiser moved slowly out of the anchorage leaving ripples and swirls in its wake; ghostly forms moved about her deck and the name, "Evader 111" was barely visible on her stern. She moved slowly through the harbor mouth against the background of the dark shore and quickly gathered speed as she entered the bay, white foam boiling at her stern as she ploughed through the heavy swell towards Vancouver.

The wind had gone down over night and only the heavy swell was left to remind one of the storms that had lashed the coast the day before. A mist was rising from the calm waters of the harbor, and the sound of a small boat being dragged down the beach on Joseph's Island could be heard as the lights went out in Doc Ellis' cabin. Invisible on the dark shore, two fishermen loaded their fishing tackle into an aluminum boat, and their voices and laughter drifted across the water.

"What do you see, Danny?" Maria asked, joining him at the porthole. Circling his waist with her arm, together they looked out over the water, her soft warm body pressing close against him.

"One of the yachts just left the harbor and it aroused me, and now some fishermen are preparing to leave the beach."

The light was improving, and they could make out the outlines of the two men on the beach as the noise of a boat being pushed into the water accompanied their voices. There was the sound of an oar splashing in the water as the fishermen took their boat clear of the beach, an outboard motor roared to life, then died.

"Give her hell this time, Jack," the fisherman sitting in the bow of the boat called to his friend, and his voice carried over the harbor like the peal of a bell.

Maria and Danny looked at each other and laughed, and the outboard motor once again roared to life, coughed, then caught again, and the little boat turned sharply and headed for the bay.

Laying on his back with an arm around Maria, laying by his side, Danny breathed easily; his thoughts still on the yacht that had left the harbor, he was oblivious to Maria's inner excitement, until overcoming her shyness she slipped her hand lightly over his chest and stomach. While outside the sun rose over the peninsula, at the far end of the bay, bathing the island and the ships that lay at anchor in its golden light, and the tall fir trees on the hill, kissed by the soft breeze, moved gently to and fro. The breeze stirred the curtains over the portholes and the boat rolled lazily in the swell. Then under the gentle direction of Danny's hands, Maria knelt with her face down on the pillow, and as Danny gently fondled her nipples and breasts from his position above, while Maria's slender hands guided him home.

Further, along the shore of the bay, two fishermen pushed the bow of their boat through the waves towards their favorite fishing hole, where the dark brush on a mound at the shore came down to the water's edge. The man in the stern shut off the motor and tilted it forward, as close inshore they approached a gap in the rocks. The second fisherman kneeling on a cushion amidships facing the bow slipped his oars deep into the water to push forward as the boat rose on the crest of a wave. Then rowing with strong steady strokes that were in harmony with the rise and fall of the sea, he maneuvered the boat towards the shelter of the cove as it twisted and turned beneath him. Then with a final surge of energy, the fisherman sent the boat gliding forward into the serenity of the calm deep water.

"I love you, Maria," Danny whispered. When after a final rush of emotion, they satisfied their turbulent passions, then breathing deeply they lay down on the bed, and while clasping each other's hands, they slipped quietly to sleep.

CHAPTER 12

The sun was streaming in through the portholes and a warm breeze billowed the curtains into the cabin when Maria awoke. Then she closed her eyes and Danny's words of love came back to her. A new bond had been welded between them and she felt at home with him on the yacht - their relationship had grown from their initial infatuation with each other into a love that was profound and enduring. Feeling warm and contented, Maria listened to the sound of children playing on the beach, until a seagull cried shrill and clear close by and recalling Tom's warning about Danny, a feeling of uneasiness swept over her, like a cold breaker on some far away shore. However, Maria's mind rebelled against the emotion that swept over her; she could not accept Tom's warning without question, and now lying close to Danny, it seemed unduly exaggerated and her uneasiness diminished. The feelings that Danny had shown for her were not a sham; they were expressions of his heart. Still there was a lingering doubt. However, she had committed her heart and there could be no retreat from her love for Danny. What of the future? She dispelled the thought from her mind as it surfaced; she would live for the present and regardless of the future, thank God that she had lived for a little while. Maria got up from the bed and went to the shower located in the bow of the boat; her secret hopes relegated to a recess of the mind.

She lathered herself with soap and as she let the warm water flow over her body, it washed away what remained of her doubts, and she felt happy, refreshed, and alert.

"Good morning," Danny greeted Maria cheerfully when she returned from the shower.

"Good morning. Is there anything special you would like for breakfast?" Maria asked, tying back her hair into a ponytail as she watched Danny sit up in bed, put his arms behind his head, and tense his muscles.

"Fried potatoes and bacon and eggs, if it isn't too much trouble," Danny replied, perceiving again Maria's beauty as she was, dressed in her pink and white terry towel shorts and blouse.

"It won't be any trouble. I'm hungry myself and I would like a good breakfast," and slipping her feet into her white sandals, Maria continued, "I will have coffee ready in about five minutes."

While making the coffee and preparing the breakfast, Maria could hear the shower running in the forward bathroom. She enjoyed cooking; and looking forward to spending another day with her lover, she felt invigorated and took special pleasure in her work. It was good to be alive, healthy, free, and in love. Maria looked up at the clock; it was a quarter to ten; Val and Debbie would be in the office, typing and waiting for their first coffee break at ten-thirty. Perhaps I should have confided in Val, Maria mused; Val was suspicious anyway and she could be depended on to keep a secret so there was no need to make her unhappy. I will tell her the truth when I get back to Vancouver, Maria thought.

The aroma of frying bacon filled the boat, and Maria caught a glimpse of Danny in the storeroom as he dressed in his brown sports shirt and blue jeans; his brown wavy hair tousled by rubbing with the towel and his cheeks pink from the warm water.

"Mm, everything smells good," Danny said sitting at the bar type table in the galley that Maria had set for breakfast. His hair had been combed neatly into place and the muscles on his arms were visible beneath his thin shirt as he poured the coffee.

Still holding a fork in one hand, Maria poured some cream into her coffee. "Everything is just about ready and I'm starving," she said, putting the cream back on the table. "I was just thinking about how lucky we are to be enjoying ourselves instead of being cooped up in a building somewhere. Do you have anything planned for after breakfast, Danny?"

"No, I thought we would just relax on deck this morning, and go ashore in the afternoon. Is there anything special that you would like to do?"

"I wouldn't mind to go swimming a little later."

"Sounds good to me. Did you bring a bathing suit?" Danny asked, struggling to hold back a smile.

"Danny!" Maria exclaimed, putting her hands on her hips and feigning a look of indignation. "Would I want to go swimming if I didn't have a bathing suit?"

Smiling now without restraint, Danny watched Maria's reaction; her pretty legs, set apart and her breasts pushed forward under the terry towel blouse. She looked as untouched and fresh as a lily. "I don't know," he replied. He became serious reflecting on the mystery and beauty of womanhood. He got up from his chair, put his arm around Maria's waist, and pulled her to him.

They enjoyed their breakfast; and in a more serious mood than previously, Danny told Maria of Doc Ellis, his cottage, and his mistress, Laura. Some time later, they drank a second cup of coffee in the stateroom, and then went on deck into the warm sun. Going to the rail in the stern of the boat, Maria looked at the beauty of the scene around her. Danny, standing for a moment at the entrance to the stateroom watched Maria; her long black hair falling around her shoulders and shining in the sun, and her profile showing smooth features, a small turned up nose, and a shapely figure. Then while Maria continued to drink in the beauty of their surroundings, Danny, preparing to relax on deck, took out two multicolored canvas and aluminum deck chairs from a locker, set them on the deck facing aft, and sat down and reclined back. The sky was clear, and as Danny's body absorbed the warm rays of the sun, the boat rolled gently in the slight swell, and the tip of the masts cut small circles in the blue sky.

The small group of luxury yachts rode at anchor on the calm blue water of the harbor, and Maria closed her eyes then opened them again; it was almost unbelievable that she was a part of this beautiful scene. People were moving around on the yachts, and Maria exchanged a wave and a smile with a young woman on the boat next to them. A blue power boat with a white convertible top sped towards the entrance to the bay; the water curling white at its bow and stern, while circles of foam marked its wake, and the drone of its motor disturbed the quiet of the scene. Maria turned her attention to the island; its gray rocks, dotted with evergreens, stood high above the sea and some adults and children could be seen ascending the path from the beach, through the trees and rocks, to the summit of the island. Her eyes swept back to the half mile of beach, shining white in the sun, where a number of people, dressed in a wide variety of colors, were enjoying themselves. Some children were playing in the water on the beach close to the yacht, and Maria smiled as she listened to their laughter and recalled her own happy childhood. Then lifting her gaze she looked at the luxurious cottages, that stood far apart, nestling among the trees and rocks behind the beach, and noted their sharp contrast to her parents' modest home in Toronto.

* * *

Deep in thought, Maria reflected on the past, and recalled the weekend camping trips to the lakes that she had enjoyed with her parents. They, like the people she saw around her, took pleasure in the activities of fishing, swimming, boating, and walking along forest trails in the freedom of the outdoors. It wasn't until she was in her teens that she had discovered that the camping trips, for herself and her parents, were more than just an ordinary holiday. They were an escape from the drab life in the city, and for her father at least, a chance to renew one's soul after working at a demeaning job from which he received small remuneration.

Andrew Petersen - Maria felt pride and sadness as she thought about her father. A warehouse worker, who worked hard for every cent he received; working long hours to bring in the money for their home, their short holidays, and her college education. She had watched her father come home from work year after year, tired, and sometimes depressed; and she recalled her mother using her beauty and her love for her father. Perhaps feigning more happiness than she felt, revive him to face another day at the warehouse. Maria recalled too, how her mother had pinched their pennies and went to work herself to save money for the holidays that they all enjoyed so much, but had been so short.

With only elementary education, and trapped in poverty, her parents were determined that she would not tread the same path. Maria had enjoyed her rewarding years in school, but her arts degree from the university had not enabled her to find the success, which she sought. The low paying job in the office of a large department store in Toronto, which she found after she graduated, did nothing to relieve her family's poverty, and it had still been necessary for her parents to subsidize her living by providing free board and room. Maria had tried to get a better job, but with no success; then when it seemed that her every avenue was blocked, she borrowed five hundred dollars from her father to supplement her savings, and came West to seek her fortune. That had been over a month ago, and she recalled her parents saying goodbye on the station. Her father had taken a half-day off from work, so that he could drive her mother and herself to the station, then avoided saying goodbye until it was necessary.

There were kisses and tears as they wished her good luck, told her not to forget to write, and visit Uncle Bert in Vancouver. Then after the final kisses and goodbye, she pulled her raincoat around her to ward off the cold that she felt in her body, and taking the old suitcase from her father's hand, she turned away, and boarded the train. Moving quickly to her seat, Maria opened the window as the train moved away. There were tears in her eyes when she waved and watched her parents recede, as they stood hand in hand alongside the tracks waving goodbye; until just before they disappeared from view, they became one as her mother placed her head on her father's chest.

* * *

Brushing a tear away from her cheek, Maria turned her attention once again to the children playing on the beach, and her happy mood returned as she focused on their play. When she turned to face Danny, she smiled spontaneously on realizing that he had been watching her closely with a serious and thoughtful expression on his face.

Sitting down on the chair by Danny's side, Maria kicked off her sandals and lay back with her eyes closed and her face into the sun.

"How old are you, Maria?"

"Twenty-one. Why do you ask?"

"There are times when you don't look more than seventeen. I'm sure that they would ask for you I.D., if you tried to buy liquor in the liquor store."

"They did at first, although they are getting to know us now at the liquor store close to our apartment. I usually buy the beer for my friends too, so we are in the store at least once a week."

"Beer, is that what you girls like?"

"No, we prefer champagne, but we are on a beer budget."

Danny laughed, "I'm not that keen on champagne, and I enjoy a beer at your uncle's lounge more than any other drink."

The noisy roar of an outboard motor could be heard, and the small boat carrying two fishermen entered the harbor and headed for the beach on Joseph's Island. "It's the two fishermen we saw leaving this morning," Danny said. "Do you think they caught anything?"

"Let's see," Maria replied. Then getting up, they went to the rail and watched as the small boat progressed towards the beach.

The boat was now the center of attraction in the small harbor, and people on the beach stopped to watch the boat, while the people on the yachts lined the rails. The man at the tiller in a plaid shirt and blue jeans guided the boat carefully towards the beach. The man standing amidships, in a yellow shirt and blue jeans, put away the fishing rods, near their jacket, which had been thrown into the bow and partly covered a beer case. Both men appeared to be in their forties, and their balding heads shone in the bright sun. The man at the tiller shut off the motor as the boat approached the beach, and when the boat slowed, the second man jumped over the side, only to sink up to his neck in deep water. A ripple of laughter sounded across the small harbor, and Maria and Danny looked to each other and laughed. In shallower water now, the man at the tiller jumped from the boat, and with the aid of the helping hands of many laughing and talking children, the two men pulled the boat from the water. Once on the beach, with the children and some adults gathering around the two men, laughing themselves, dipped into the bottom of the boat and held up, for everyone to see, the three salmon they had caught. Then the two men, renowned in the eyes of the children, with the help of many willing hands, carried the boat up the beach and into the trees.

"Do you still want to go swimming, Maria?" Danny asked, turning to her at the rail.

"Sure," Maria replied with a smile. Then leaving the rail together, they went below deck. It felt cool in the cabin after being in the sun.

Dressed in their bathing suits they came out of the cabin to sit on deck chairs to relax for a while.

The sun was warm on Maria's body as she walked to the rail to join Danny. He was muscular and sun tanned, and dressed in bathing trunks decorated with the swimming awards, which he had won in high school. Maria admired him, then as she looked down into the deep water that surrounded the boat; her light blue bikini bathing suit, that she bought especially for the occasion showed her figure to perfection.

"I would like to go under and look at the boat down to her keel," Maria said. "Is she as pretty below the water as she is above?"

"She is very deep, and her lines are smooth and beautiful. She was built to be quite fast and stable in rough seas. We might have had a lot more trouble yesterday if she had been a lesser boat."

Working together, they put a Jacob's ladder over the side. Then Maria slipped under the rail, poised on the edge of the boat, and then dived gracefully into the water. Danny waved to Maria when she surfaced, then he dived from the rail to join her as she tread water waiting for him.

"It is lovely and warm," Maria said, as Danny surfaced close by her side. Then she dived deep, and Danny breathed in and followed. Maria's long black hair streamed out behind her as she continued her dive. Then with her long shapely legs moving rhythmically, her feet kicking the water, and her arms moving in a breast stroke she glided down to the keel, where leveling out she examined the length of the boat.

Stopping his descent about six feet beneath the surface, Danny watched Maria with keen interest as she moved about the hull of the boat a good distance below him. The grace and ease with which Maria moved through the water had taken a lot of training and years of practice, and he was curious about her earlier life - she had told him very little about herself.

Danny was glad when Maria started to ascend; more at home in a swimming pool, he felt ill at ease in this strange and hostile environment beneath the waves, and he was anxious to return to the surface. Nevertheless, he waited for Maria to come abreast of him, and they surfaced together.

"She is beautiful," Maria, said her words serious and sincere.

"I think you have fallen in love with the boat, Maria."

"I have. It was love at first sight. I fell in love the first day that you brought me aboard." Then they laughed in unison, as they recalled the day to memory.

"I will race you around the boat," Danny said.

"No, I don't want to race," Maria replied. However, Danny didn't hear, he had already put his face into the water, and doing the crawl, he was moving quickly towards the stern. Maria looked after him, and then using the same stroke, she followed and kept pace.

Glancing back to Maria as he rounded the stern, Danny was amazed by the ease with which Maria cut through the water. Although Danny was still ahead when they had circled the boat, he had the feeling that she could have passed him if she had wished, and she had been holding back so as not to damage his male ego.

They did a backstroke away from the boat, and treading water together, they looked at the boat from a distance.

Observing the boat carefully from stem to stern, Maria was awed by her beauty, and conscious that her claim to the vessel and all she stood for was dependent on the whims of Danny's love. Where was the happiness and contentment which she expected to experience, instead she was engulfed by a wave of sadness; she felt cheated, and anger rose within her - God willing, one day she would be given the opportunity to grab enough loot to insure independence and dignity of her own. The muscles of Maria's body tensed, and turning away from Danny lest he see the troubled expression on her face, she swam quickly towards the boat leaving a trail of foam in her wake. Then diving deep, she swam beneath the yacht and surfaced on the far side.

Exhausted, but with her anger vented, Maria floated on her back for a minute or two, watching the seagulls, and the Bliss-In's tall masts swinging lazily and unconcerned against the background of the sky. Then turning once more onto her stomach, she swam leisurely around the side of the boat and returned Danny's smile as he backed away from the ladder to allow her to board the boat ahead of him.

Laying face down in the stern, Maria spread-eagled herself on the deck and rested. Meanwhile Danny busied himself erecting an awning over the stern, and putting an apron of canvas about the stern rail to shelter them from the wind and give them privacy.

"You would get along well with my sister," Danny said with a smile. "She is a blond and likes swimming, and like you, she is for the most part, easy going and enjoys life."

"Will I get to meet your sister?" Maria asked, looking up to Danny, as kneeling on the deck he took off his bathing trunks and dried himself with a towel.

"I think so. She is in Paris attending university, and she should be coming home soon." Danny finished drying himself and gave a towel to Maria as she removed her bikini.

Then taking care not to show herself above the canvas apron, Maria dried herself, while Danny lay on his back with his arms beneath his head. Maria smiled when Danny opened his eyes to look up at her, and after spreading out the towel, she lay down by his side. She felt relaxed and warm, her mood had changed, and she was amused when she recalled her anger, then in the shelter of an awning above them she drifted off to sleep.

The noise of an approaching outboard motor boat aroused them, and Danny, putting a towel about his neck to give him some semblance of dress, raised himself onto his knees and watched a small boat approach the yacht.

"Mr. Lewes," the boy of about seventeen, standing at the wheel, called as he stopped the boat some distance away.

"Yes," Danny replied.

"Mr. Ellis asks if you would like to come ashore for lunch at twelve-thirty?"

"What do you think?" Danny said, looking down to Maria.

"It sounds okay."

Danny turned back to the boy in the boat. "Tell Mr. Ellis we will be pleased to join him for lunch."

"I will pick you up at twelve-thirty, Sir."

Taking Danny's hand, Maria glanced at his watch as the boat headed back to the wharf; it was eleven-fifteen, and they would have lots of time to shower and dress to go ashore.

CHAPTER 13

The cottage which Doc Ellis owned was elegant; its rustic exterior blended with the trees and rocks, among which it was set, and the large sundeck, which extended across the front, enabled one to view the beach and the bay beyond the inlet. Behind the cottage, a paved road ran through the trees to a bridge, which connected the island to the mainland. This provided a convenient access to the owners of the cottages and the people who came in to spend the day on the beach or wander among the trees and the rocks. Doc Ellis had the cottage built five years before as a weekend and a holiday retreat from his work in Vancouver, and he had fallen in love with it. Mrs. Sanders, the architect who designed and supervised its building had been twenty-six at the time, and after completing the cottage, she had given up her career as an architect and her husband, to become the mistress of Doc Ellis.

As Maria and Danny approached the cottage, Doc Ellis came out to meet them, and they paused for a moment to view the front of the cottage, while they boy who had brought them ashore continued on to enter the house by a side door. Smiling broadly, Doc Ellis shook Danny's hand vigorously, and when Danny introduced him to Maria, he took both of her hands in his. "Your presence is like a warm summer breeze to our island. Please come onto the sundeck and meet my wife, Laura."

Maria and Danny preceded Doc Ellis to the sundeck where Laura, a tall slender redhead, waited to greet them. Danny introduced the two women to one another, and Laura's warm smile expressed her welcome, while she appraised Maria carefully. Maria smiled; she knew what the other woman would be thinking of her, and because Danny had already told her about Laura and her relationship with Doc Ellis, she saw the humor of the situation.

"Do make yourself at home," Laura said.

In addition, Maria noted a slight hint of resentment in her voice that escaped the two men. She was glad that she had bought the red dress that she was wearing; it was of good quality material, extremely well made, and showed off her figure to perfection, and to think that she had well-nigh not purchased it, because at the time she considered it too expensive. Maria felt pleased in knowing that among other things, Laura would take into consideration the quality of her clothes in forming the first impression of this other member of her sex. Just as she had formed an opinion of Laura, based partly on what Danny had said about her. Laura's choice of clothes as well as indicating some wealth, showed good taste. Except for the hint of undercurrent that Maria had noticed in Laura's initial reaction towards herself and Danny, Laura conducted herself with grace and charm. Maria's initial opinion of Laura was favorable, and in spite of their differences in appearance, Maria had the feeling that in some aspect they were as alike as if they had been cast from the same mold.

"Please be seated. We have time for a drink while Mrs. Harret and Bobby are finishing the preparations for lunch," Laura said, indicating by a gesture a number of deck chairs.

"Would you like me to get the drinks, Laura?" Doc Ellis asked, as he sat down alongside Danny, facing Maria.

"I will get them," Laura replied. "It will only take a minute," and looking attractive and just a little stork like in her high heeled shoes and short russet dress, Laura walked into the cottage through the sliding glass door.

Maria, conscious of the admiring glances of the two men, chatted with them about the storm of the previous day.

Laura returned with a tray of four glasses and a bottle of champagne, and after serving the drinks, she took a chair alongside Maria. A breeze came in from the sea and ruffled the awning that partially covered the deck, and sipping their champagne, they smiled and exchanged glances as Doc Ellis told a ribald joke. Then as he unfolded the punch line, they all laughed freely, and Laura watched Maria closely for any reaction that might tell her more about the character that lay behind the pretty face and dark shining eyes.

A telephone was ringing somewhere in the cottage and the boy who had brought Maria and Danny ashore, came to the glass door of the sundeck. "Telephone, Mr. Ellis."

"Thanks, Bobby." Then getting up from his chair and addressing his company he continued, "I will just be a minute".

Leaning back in his chair, Danny looked out over the anchorage. The boat that had been tied up next to them was leaving, and two boys were sailing a small boat close to the beach - it was years ago since he and Tom Balant had done the same thing. He recalled to mind the times that they had deliberately turned the boat over for the fun of it. Tom was sticking his nose to the grindstone these days and taking life far too serious, and the last time he had spoken with him, he seemed to have a chip on his shoulder. The two women had complimented each other on their wearing apparel and were discussing the current fashions. Danny drank the rest of his champagne down with one draft - God damn it anyway, they could have been halfway to Powell River by now. Doc Ellis was in his usual form. What the hell did a good-looking broad like Laura want with him?

"Your father is on the telephone, Danny," Doc Ellis said, coming back onto the sundeck and sitting in his chair. "He telephoned to ask if you could come back to Vancouver today. I told him that you could borrow my car as Laura has her car here too, so it wouldn't inconvenience us at all. The yacht will be okay tied up at the buoy, and I could have Bobby sleep aboard to make sure that everything will be all right. Your dad wishes to talk to you too, and he is holding the line."

"Thanks," Danny said. Then getting up, he went into the cottage. The aroma of cooking meat greeted him when he entered the door. It seemed like Doc was preparing a banquet rather than a lunch.

Danny picked up the telephone. "Hello."

"Danny," Bill Lewis said, "I talked to Doc, and he said that you could borrow his car to travel back to Vancouver today."

"Yes, we could do that, Dad. What's up?"

"The police seized five pounds of heroin from a boat; the Evader 111, when she was off Vancouver this morning. It seems that Doc might be involved."

Danny closed his eyes momentarily. "Did you tell Doc?"

"No," Bill Lewes replied, "and it hasn't been reported by the news media yet."

"Good. We are going to have lunch with Doc Ellis and Laura right away, and we will leave immediately afterwards. Have you been able to get in touch with Irene?"

"Yes, I talked to your sister this morning, and she should be aboard a plane now, on her way back to Canada. I told Doc that your wife was not feeling well."

"Okay, and I will see you tonight, Dad."

Danny went back onto the sundeck and sat down on a chair besides Maria, and Laura moved to sit besides Doc Ellis. "I hope you don't mind if we go back to Vancouver today?"

"No, I don't mind, and I hope there is nothing seriously wrong." Doc said.

"My dad would like me to come home and it's nothing serious." Danny said, knowing that the excuse was hardly satisfactory, and later he would have some explaining to do to Maria.

Then speaking to Doc Ellis, "I will take you up on your offer to lend us your car, and we will leave for Vancouver right after lunch. I will make arrangements for someone to come up from the yachting club to take the Bliss-In back to Vancouver, although it may be here for a few days."

"Don't worry about a thing here Danny," Doc Ellis said, and taking the car keys from a pocket, he threw them to Danny. "The car is in the driveway and all gassed up and ready to go."

"Thanks, Doc."

Mrs. Harret, a stout woman with graying hair who was about thirty-five years of age, had come onto the sundeck, and as she wiped her hands in her apron she told them that their lunch was ready.

The lunch was as Danny expected, a banquet, and although they ate heartily and chatted amicably, there was just a little too much talk for it to be natural. Danny realized that Doc Ellis was suspicious of the sudden necessity for him to return to Vancouver. The excuse, about his wife being ill, had not been convincing, and his getting away could prove to be more difficult than he had anticipated.

Maria was aware of the tension too, and recalling the hard look that Doc Ellis and Laura exchanged when Danny had left the sundeck to speak with his father on the telephone, she realized that there was something strange about the whole situation.

Nevertheless, Maria felt at ease, and mentally she examined the surroundings and explored the various possibilities. Doc Ellis' cottage was far too lavish to have been purchased by someone drawing a salary. Also, Laura appeared to be a woman who enjoyed living high, wide, and handsome. Doc Ellis must have another source of income that Danny had not mentioned, and she had the feeling that there was something illegal about the source. She had nothing to go on at present, other than her own observations, but she was suspicious. There was something strange about the Lewes family and the present situation, and she would have some questions to ask of Cec later. Intuition told her that Danny was in some kind of danger, and with her curiosity sparked, she was alert and ready for any eventuality. She felt no apprehension about her ability to defend Danny, and the gun in her purse and her willingness to use it would be a surprise to any would-be attacker. Laura and Doc Ellis had taken her to be nothing more than a pretty girl;

having a fling with a rich man, thus; she was beyond suspicion of taking any decisive action on Danny's behalf. Maria's smile in response to a remark by Doc Ellis was genuine; she was earning her wages for the first time and enjoying it.

"Thanks very much for your hospitality," Danny said. "We are really enjoying the visit and it is too bad that we have to leave so soon."

"You don't have enough time now, Danny, to catch the three o'clock ferry from Langdale," Doc Ellis said glancing at his watch, "and you have lots of time to catch the four o'clock ferry." Doc Ellis smiled, and taking the bottle of champagne from the silver ice bucket, he poured each of their glasses full. "You have time to have one for the road," he continued. "It is really too bad that you can't stay. I'm sure we would have had a very interesting evening." Doc Ellis placed the champagne bottle back in the ice bucket. "Excuse me for a moment please," he said. Then he walked unhurriedly from the sundeck.

"I do hope that you both will be able to visit us again at the cottage," Laura said, picking up the conversation. "This is really a very interesting island, and there are some nice walks and beautiful scenery that makes it well worth exploring."

A door closed in another part of the cottage and Maria had the distinct feeling that Doc Ellis was making a telephone call to someone, although as she continued to listen there was no sound to indicate this.

"I have enjoyed previous visits to the island," Danny said. "But I haven't explored it fully, and it would be nice to return when we will have more time."

"Yes, I recall the time you and Tom Balant brought the yacht into the anchorage to visit Doc and me at the cottage, and we all went swimming off the beach." Laura smiled, seeming to enjoy the recollection.

In a hurry to get away, Danny took a long drink from his champagne, and Maria put her glass to her lips and let the champagne bubble in her mouth for a moment before swallowing. The conversation and congeniality were a pretense to veil the suspicion and intrigue that lay just beneath the surface.

Laura sipped her champagne nervously while they waited for Doc Ellis to return, and Danny, looking out over the bay, made no effort to continue the conversation.

Could the Lewes family and Doc Ellis somehow be involved with illegal drugs? A glimmer of this realization flickered in Maria's mind. There is no evidence of anyone using it. Still, a drug addict had tried to kill Danny's father, and some heroin had been planted in her suite. Doc Ellis could be heard talking in a low voice to Mrs. Harret in another room. Maria listened for a moment. However, the conversation was not loud enough to be understood, and her thoughts once more returned to drugs. Illegal drugs could account for Doc Ellis' wealth.

"I was complimenting Mrs. Harret on her fine cooking," Doc Ellis said, coming back into the room and smiling. "We are quite fortunate to have her working for us. Her husband works at a marina just a few miles away on the mainland, and they have a comfortable home nearby."

"We really have to be going Doc," Danny said as he stood up. "There could be a lineup for the four o'clock ferry, and we don't want to miss it."

Maria stood up, and Doc and Laura followed. "You are quite right," Doc Ellis said. "They are quite busy this time of the year."

"It has been very nice meeting you both," Maria said in the carport, at the back of the cottage, where Doc Ellis' dark green Cadillac was parked.

"It has been very nice meeting you too," Laura replied, "and we would like to get to know you better. Please come back again sometime with Danny, and we will all explore the island together."

Parting as good friends, Maria and Danny got into the car, smiled to Laura and Doc, and Maria waved as Danny drove the car slowly out of the driveway and onto the road. However, the smile disappeared from Danny's face when they were out on the road and away from the cottage, and there were furrows on his brow as the car gathered speed.

The road was rough and winding, and Danny slowed down to take a turn. Ahead of them, there was a stop sign at the intersection to highway 101, and Danny braked as they neared the stop sign. Highway 101 was deserted in either direction. Then without stopping, Danny accelerated the car, and with screaming tires, they turned left away from Langdale and Vancouver.

Obviously troubled, Danny was serious and deep in thought, as Maria looked back at the road behind them. A truck camper had turned from the road, which they had just left and was following them along the highway.

"Maria," Danny began, and she turned to face him. "My father telephoned, to tell me to return to Vancouver immediately, because he thinks we may be in some kind of danger. Attempts have been made on our lives before, and he has received word from the detective agency that other such attempts are imminent. I turned away from Vancouver because, I feel that to head directly back to Vancouver in this vehicle would invite trouble."

While thinking of their next move, Danny slowed down to the speed limit, and a line of traffic, which included cars, trailers, and trucks, came up close behind them. A car pulling a tent trailer pulled out from the line and passed, then slammed on its brakes to negotiate a dangerous turn. Moments later, a long line of traffic rounded the turn approaching fast from the opposite direction, and a car behind, that had pulled out to pass, pulled quickly back into the line.

At a wide section in the road, where slow moving vehicles could pull off, Danny drove the car off the highway to allow the line of traffic to pass, and the truck camper that had been following them pulled off the highway behind them. When the line of traffic had passed, Danny drove the car back onto the highway, and the truck camper followed close behind.

"I noticed that there was some tension between yourself, and Doc Ellis and Laura, after your father's telephone call," Maria said. "Do Laura and Doc know of the danger you are in?"

"My father told Doc that he wanted me to return to Vancouver immediately, because my wife was ill; but I noticed the tension after my father's telephone call too."

The truck camper was following too close behind for safety and Danny slowed the car to let it pass, and glanced to Maria knowing that her inquisitiveness had not been satisfied. The truck slowed too and kept close behind, and Maria, noticing Danny's renewed attention to the rearview mirror, looked back to the man driving the truck behind them. A cap pulled down over his eyes, to shelter him from the sun, partly concealed his face; still there was something familiar about him. Then Maria laughed and turned back to Danny, "One of your detective friends is driving the truck behind us."

Taking a good look at the man through the rearview mirror, Danny's serious expression turned to a smile as he recognized Cec Banas. "We will get this car off the road and keep it hidden for a while, Maria, just in case someone is on the lookout for it, and we can ride with Cec, it will be safer."

Pulling into the next service station along the road, Danny drove into an empty stall in the garage, and Cec stopped his truck camper at the pumps. A middle-aged man, wearing greasy overalls, came around the side of the car. "What can I do for you, Sir?"

"Give her a complete tune-up; she is not running right for a new car," Danny said, sounding annoyed.

The man, in the greasy overalls, put his hand to his chin, in a gesture of thoughtfulness and contemplated the money he was about to make. "The new cars are more complicated than the old ones, a lot better machine mind you, but they don't spend the necessary time at the factories these days to give them the fine tuning they require. It will purr like a kitten when I have finished with it, Sir."

"Good," Danny said, as he and Maria got out of the car. Then following the man into the office, Danny continued, "We have only had the thing a few weeks, and it runs like a tractor."

"Your name, Sir?" the man asked, beginning to fill out the work order.

"Mr. Ellis," Danny replied, "I am staying on Joseph's Island. Give her a complete tune up." Maria looked out of the window. Cec was standing by the truck camper talking to an attendant who was filling the truck with gas, and Danny continued. "What time do you close?"

"Seven-thirty, Sir."

"Have the car ready by about seven, and I will pick her up. We will get a lift back to the island with a friend of ours."

"Very good, Sir. I will have the car ready for you promptly at seven."

The mechanic put his hands in his pockets and watched Maria and Danny walk towards the truck camper, giving Maria most of his attention. He felt pleased with himself, right on top of the situation. "A nice couple," he said to the attendant, who was ringing up in the till the money Cec had paid for the gas.

The attendant finished what he was doing, then with one hand on the till and the other scratching his head, he looked out of the window as Danny helped Maria up into the camper. Danny and Cec stood at the back of the camper for a while and talked. The mechanic and the attendant saw Cec nod his head in response to what Danny had said, and after waiting until Danny was in the camper, Cec got into the cab and drove away.

The attendant followed the mechanic into the shop and kicked a tire of the Caddy. "What is wrong with her?" he asked.

"Nothing," the mechanic replied. "That guy is just too damn fussy." The attendant came around and looked at the engine as the mechanic lifted the hood. "I'll take a look at it," the mechanic continued. "But there won't be a fucking thing wrong, and when the fellow comes to pick it up, I will give him some bull shit along with his bill to make him happy."

About a mile down the highway, Cec stopped the truck camper on a side road and pasted a sign on each side of the camper body, which read in bold red letters, Jiffee Electric Co. Then using his cellular phone, he booked passage on the four o'clock ferry to the mainland. Driving the truck camper back onto the highway, Cec traveled slowly for a white until a line of traffic had built up behind him. Then, after a number of vehicles had passed, he increased speed to keep his place in the line.

Barreling along the highway at a good clip, Cec was relaxed, and he pressed a button on the intercom to speak to Maria and Danny. "If you would like to make yourselves at home, you will find some beer in the refrigerator and some potato chips in the cupboard below the sink. Sorry I have nothing better to offer you. If things go well, we will be at Langdale in about half an hour and in time to catch the four o'clock ferry to Vancouver."

The curtains were still drawn in the camper, and in the semi darkness Maria and Danny smiled to one another across the table as they drank their beers. Then their smiles were gone, and hanging on to their beers, they lurched forward when Cec slammed on the brakes to avoid hitting the car ahead, and Cec's emphatic voice came to them over the intercom. "Son-of-a-bitch, shake your ass and get a move on." Danny switched off the intercom, and Cec didn't hear Maria and Danny laughing aloud.

"What's up Cec?" Danny asked after a while.

"Oh, it is some donkey up ahead; he's traveling so slowly we will be lucky if we catch the five o'clock ferry. I will have to wait my turn in the line and go by him when I get an opportunity."

"By the way, thanks for the beer," Danny said.

"You're welcome," Cec replied cheerfully, having recovered from his sudden outburst, - which would never have occurred, had he known that the intercom was still open.

Cec switched off the intercom and gave his full attention to passing the slow moving car, directly ahead of him. The drivers behind were impatient to pass, and some cars were already across the white center line, with their drivers craning their necks to see if the road ahead was clear to pass. The driver of the car behind the truck camper, not wanting to be outdone by anyone behind, pulled out to pass, then swerved quickly in again as a bus flew by, going in the opposite direction. The road ahead was clear now, and Cec pulled the truck camper out over the centerline and tramped on the gas, with three cars and a trailer following close behind. In front of the slow moving car, Cec pulled the truck camper back to the right side of the road.

One of the cars passed him with its motor roaring while the other car pulled in behind, and the car pulling the trailer dropped back into the line of traffic behind the slow moving car as a stream of vehicles approached quickly from the other direction.

After finishing their beers, Maria and Danny climbed up onto the bunk over the cab to lie on their stomachs watching the road through the thin curtain that covered the front window. They were traveling quite fast, and the camper swayed heavily on the turns as Cec went heavy on the gas to keep his place in the line.

"Why would anyone want to do you and your family harm?" Maria asked, while they looked out over the road, winding up a steep hill lined by fir trees and other evergreens, and through a break in the trees on their right, they caught sight of the blue waters of the Strait of Georgia.

"Because we are successful," Danny replied, putting his arm around Maria's waist. "The import and export business is very competitive, and we have had to cut prices and streamline our operation in order to make it more efficient to compete with the other companies in the business. Unfortunately, we have not been able to do this without making enemies, and some companies have been forced out of business because they have been unable to compete, while others are on the verge of bankruptcy. Our company is not the only successful one, but we are ranked as one of the leaders in the field. A number of the less successful companies have tried to negotiate with our company and others to fix prices so that they can remain in business, and we have refused because it is unethical. Thus, we have made enemies. In addition, in our business organization itself, we found it necessary to cut down on the number of staff we employ, and at the same time increase the services we offer. We laid off the least efficient people on our staff, and demoted some people from positions in which we thought they were not competent. This practice brought us in conflict with quite a number of employees and the union, and it would have been a serious problem except that through negotiation with the union and raising wages we were able to come to a working agreement with the company maintaining complete control over hiring practices. At present, the morale of our employees is high, they are well paid, and the most competent in the import and export business, and this has enabled us to compete successfully with the other businesses in the field. However, once again we have made enemies." Danny paused to give thought to what he had to say. "Doc Ellis was demoted because we found that he was less efficient than he should have been, and in spite of the fact that he has been treated fairly and is well paid, we feel that he is resentful. Also, his wages do not cover the luxurious style in which he lives, and my family has concluded that Doc Ellis is living far beyond his means, and he must have another source of income?"

"What other source of income could he have?" Maria asked, while looking at the road ahead and the traffic.

"The knowledge that he possesses as a result of his position in the corporation, could be very valuable to our competitors. He has knowledge of the services we offer, and the amount of money involved in our bids on contracts to purchase goods and to carry freight. Then by selling this information, Doc Ellis could make a lot of money and we would lose contracts. We have reason to believe that he has been doing this, and more; he has become a partner in a competing company."

"If this is the case?" Maria interjected. "Why would he want to do you harm now? It would be to his advantage to continue in the same manner; at least until he is found out and fired."

"There are two reasons," Danny replied, "Doc Ellis still bears a grudge against us for his demotion. Also, the company with which we think he has been involved, has lost a large shipment of goods which will do it considerable harm, and I believe Doc Ellis found out about the loss this afternoon, right after my father phoned. If this is the case, he will think that my family was responsible, and he may do something stupid to seek revenge. This is what my father phoned to warn me about, and why we are taking precautions to keep out of sight."

"What kind of a loss was involved?" Maria asked.

Danny looked at Maria, her dark hair falling about her face, as she lay by his side. She was more beautiful and exciting than any woman he had ever known; he was in love as he had never been before, and the warmth of her body electrified his senses. He had already told her more than he intended, but he could trust Maria; their love for each other went beyond sexual passions, and she would remain faithful, come what may. "The company, in which Doc Ellis is probably a partner, is involved with the illegal drug trade, and, if our information is correct, the company has lost a large shipment of drugs."

The truck camper slowed down and stopped. Maria and Danny could see about ten vehicles stopped ahead of them, and there were probably more than this in the line behind. A few car lengths ahead, a sign at the side of the road warned the drivers to be prepared to stop, a flagman was talking to the driver of a large truck at the head of the line, and further ahead some men worked repairing the road.

Maria felt Danny's arm tighten about her as he became tense; a line of traffic passed them going in the opposite direction, and three men, seated in a car parked off the road, were carefully scrutinizing the line of vehicles of which they were a part. The flagman stepped back from the truck where he had been talking and turned his sign to go, and soon they were rolling by the workers and the car parked off the road. However, it wasn't until Cec had the truck camper bowling along again at about ninety km, that Maria felt Danny relax and she thought again about what Danny had said.

The information that Danny had given her was plausible, and while Maria knew that, it was the truth; it had been conveyed in terms, which implicated only Doc Ellis and some obscure company. Many unanswered questions arose in Maria's mind, and she puzzled about the mystery surrounding Doc Ellis, the company that Danny spoke of, and the danger that threatened them for a while at the roadblock. Turning to face Maria, Danny put his arm about her waist, and a new excitement was aroused in Maria's mind and body, which interrupted her previous thoughts. The information and questions that had occupied Maria's mind were relegated to her subconscious, to be assiduously digested by the mental faculties, and combined with previous knowledge to increase her understanding and reason, then resurface at another time.

The large truck at the head of the line moved around a series of hairpin turns, and the vehicles behind followed in a long stream, like a serpent, as Danny slid his hand down over Maria's buttocks. Closing her eyes, Maria felt her excitement rise within her, and changing her position, she allowed Danny's hand to pass between her legs and fondle her gently. The truck camper sped along the road keeping its place in the line, and Maria and Danny, in response to their emotions, moved to lay lengthwise on the bed and remove their excess clothing. Maria pulled her small red dress up about her waist revealing her flat stomach and mons vereris, and Danny, bending in the restricted height, came forward between her wide-open legs. In tune only to each other; their moist and warm lips soft to each other's, the two lovers clung together while the camper swayed along the winding road.

The truck camper slowed down and stopped, and the lovers became aware once more of the world around them. Danny raised himself on his elbows and looked through the side window while Maria put her arms about his waist and waited. "We are at the ferry terminal and waiting to go through the gate," Danny said, lowering his head and easing his chest once more onto Maria's soft warm breasts. Then laying still, and moving only slightly when the urge to do so became overpowering, they listened to the activities outside as the truck camper moved with frequent stops towards the ticket office.

"Any passengers?" The man in the ticket office asked. Cec shook his head, and with a bored expression on his face, he took some bills from his wallet and handed them to the man.

"A commercial vehicle?" the man asked, noticing the sign on the side of the camper.

"Yes," Cec replied. "I am booked for this ferry and I hope to get back to the shop before it closes."

Sounds of the cash register being used came to Maria and Danny, and then there was the voice of the man in the ticket office. "Pull into the line behind the freight truck, and you will get on the next ferry," he said, handing Cec a receipt and the change.

The truck camper rolled forward slowly towards its place in the line behind the freight truck, and Maria and Danny, obedient to the demands of their bodies and hearts, moved forcefully until the truck camper stopped again, and they lay still and listened.

The four o'clock ferry was in dock, and a long line of vehicles was driving away from the ship. Outside the camper, people walked to and fro; some carrying coffee and sandwiches bought at the restaurant. The driver, from the truck ahead, came back and leaned on the camper; his head not two feet away from Maria and Danny, remaining quiet, while he talked to Cec.

At last, the ferry was unloaded, and as the truck camper moved with the line of trucks and buses towards the ferry, Maria and Danny once again moved in unison, obeying their hearts' commands. Then as the truck camper lurched over the ramp and onto the ferry, their pent up emotions were satisfied, and they lay still while an officer on the ferry directed Cec to a parking spot near the bow.

The big ferry slipped easily through the calm water on the way to Horseshoe Bay, and the passengers crowded the decks to enjoy the warm sun and view the many small pleasure craft and the rocky coast lines they passed. Below deck, Maria and Danny, deeming it expedient to stay in the safety of the camper, rested for a time before getting up to sit by the table and enjoy another of Cec's beers, while Cec, stayed in the cab of the truck.

* * *

Traveling along the Upper Levels Highway away from Horseshoe Bay, Maria and Danny pulled back the curtains of the camper and watched the ships riding at anchor in English Bay. "What about the yacht?" Maria asked, their eyes still scanning the scene on the sea below. "If your suspicions about Doc Ellis are correct, he could sabotage it."

"He could," Danny agreed, "but I don't think he will. The boat is fully covered by insurance, and other than causing us some inconvenience it would do us no harm."

On the sea below, one of the large freighters was being prepared to go into Vancouver harbor, and there was a bustle of activity on deck, as hatch covers were removed and derricks raised, ready for unloading. They saw an anchor break from the water, to lie against the side of the ship, and they imagined they could hear the noise of the windlass and the clank of the anchor chain. Then the water at her stern suddenly became turbulent as the propeller began to turn, and with a long blast from the hooter, the ship got under way.

"It will probably be a few days before we get together again. It will depend on the accuracy of our suspicions about Doc Ellis, and the precautions we will take to insure my family's safety."

"Take good care of yourself, and don't take any unnecessary chances," Maria said, taking Danny's hands in her own across the table. "I will be waiting to hear from you," Maria continued, and Danny squeezed Maria's hands and smiled in response to her concern.

The truck camper turned down towards West Vancouver, and Danny, more cautious now that they were approaching the apartment where Maria lived, closed the curtains across the windows. The truck camper was traveling slower, and Maria and Danny, standing in the narrow passageway, embraced and kissed. Maria felt sad at the prospect of not seeing Danny for some time. However, life would go on; Danny ever on her mind, longing to see him, hear his voice, and feel his touch; not knowing where he was and what he was doing, while all the time danger threatened; gladly she would have stayed by his side to face the danger together.

However, Danny spoke first to lay bare his feelings. Still embracing after their kiss, and feeling Maria soft and warm against his body, he would miss her while they were apart, having no one with whom he could confide to share his dreams, fears, and passions. Mixed with these emotions there was a tinge of jealousy, lest she find someone else with whom to share her love while he was away. This was a new experience for Danny. Never had anyone had the power to hurt him in this way before, and in the tenderness of their embrace; their hearts beating in unison; Danny spoke quietly. "I wish that we had met a number of years ago, it would have made things a lot easier for us."

"Seven years ago would have been the time, Danny," Maria said, thinking about the seven years that he had been married. Then with laughter in her eyes she continued, "I was only fourteen years of age, and I'm afraid you wouldn't have given me a second glance."

"I hadn't thought of it that way," Danny said, smiling in response to the coy smile on Maria's face. Then their warm breath mingled and their lips met in a kiss as Cec slowed the truck camper and stopped in front of the apartment.

"We are home," Cec's voice came to them over the intercom.

"Okay," Danny replied. Opening the door and taking Maria's hand, he helped her down from the camper. "Goodbye, Maria." Danny said, and their hands remained together for a moment before she stepped onto the street; a gesture that said more than words could convey, they parted.

A picture of vitality, beauty, and youth; Maria stood in front of the apartment amid the many people walking to and fro, her long black hair lying loose over the shoulders of her red dress and her cheeks fresh with color, she watched the truck camper join the busy traffic and drive away. Then turning, she walked slowly towards the apartment entrance swinging her handbag and thinking of Danny.

CHAPTER 14

Glancing at her watch, Maria noted that it was six-thirty as she rode the elevator up to her suite. The girls would have just arrived home from work, or perhaps they decided to eat out and do some shopping before coming home. She had only been away from the apartment for two days and one night, but so much had happened during that time that it seemed like an age, and in the confines of the elevator, she felt hemmed in and ill at ease. Maria let herself into the suite; it seemed desolate, cushions were scattered around on the floor, the ashtrays were full, empty beer bottles were on the floor and the tables, and the smell of stale beer and marijuana hung heavy in the air. No effort had been made to clean up, leaving the untouched evidence of a wild party, and the life that had been. Then as she walked across the living room, the sound of her footsteps echoed in the stillness of the suite. In the kitchen, dirty dishes were strewn around on the counter, the table, and in the sink, and everywhere there were beer bottles and partly eaten sandwiches.

The girls must have had one hell of a party last night, and now they were eating out before coming home to face the mess they had left behind. Maria opened the kitchen window and sat down on a chair, away from the table, deep in thought. It was not like the girls to have a wild party when they had to go to work the next day. She was not angry, the suite was, as much the girls' as her own, and it would have probably all been cleaned up before she came home had her trip not been cut short. Standing up, Maria started tidying dishes from the table, and stacking them near the sink ready for washing. Then she stopped and listened. The faint sound of someone sobbing was coming from one of the bedrooms, and before she had time to investigate; Val, her streaky blond hair in disarray, her face drawn, with shadows around her bloodshot eyes, and wearing a night gown shuffled from the bedroom in her slippers and stood in the doorway to the kitchen. She dabbed her eyes with a tissue.

Remaining where she was with her hands full of dirty dishes, Maria studied Val, who, upon seeing her, started crying once more. Maria looked at her friend carefully, to give reason to what she was experiencing. It was not like Val to be so unkempt; she was usually very particular about her appearance, and it was evident that she had not been to work. More than ever, the drug and beer party, the mess in the suite, the state Val was in, and her absence from work was inexplicable.

"Why are you home so soon?" Val asked between sobs.

Realizing that she had been appraising Val cruelly, Maria turned away to put the dishes she was holding down by the sink. Then deliberately softening her expression and reserving her judgment, Maria turned to face Val. "My boss found it unnecessary for me to go all the way to Powell River, and it cut my work in half; enabling me to come home early."

Coming into the kitchen, Val sat down by the table and dried her eyes. Her sobbing had ceased, although she was still very upset, and not wanting to look directly into Maria's eyes, she inclined her head.

"Where is Debbie?" Maria asked.

"Debbie decided to meet her boyfriend after work, and he said she would be home later," Val replied in a dejected voice as she raised her eyes to look at Maria.

"It was quite a party you had last night."

Val only nodded in reply, and getting up she crossed to the refrigerator and took out two bottles of beer. "Would you like a bottle of beer? My throat is parched."

"Okay," Maria replied, as she joined Val at the kitchen table and waited for an explanation about the party. Val put the bottle to her lips and drank some beer before putting the bottle on the table. Then breathing heavily, she started to tell Maria about the party.

"We had a few people over after work last night. It wasn't going to be much to start with, then after a few beers and some marijuana, the party became a little wild. Debbie was bringing her boyfriend over, so we decided to ask some other people over to have a couple of beers, and just for the hell of it, I decided I would like a few drags on a reefer. I asked Glenda to come over and bring some marijuana, and although she wanted to come to the party and bring a friend, she said she wouldn't be able to get any marijuana, and she suggested I ask Phylis - you know the girl who works in the toy department." Maria nodded, and Val, after some thought, continued, "It is strange; before Glenda said she would come to the party, she asked if you were home. I had the feeling that she would not have come if you were home, although I don't know why, because she hardly knows you. Anyway, I phoned Phylis and asked her and her boyfriend too, and I enquired if she could bring some marijuana, and she said that she would try to get some.

Glenda and her friend Charlie got here about seven o'clock." Val put her head down, rubbed her forehead with her hand, and took another drink of beer before continuing. "I had met Charlie before, and I had gone out with him a couple of times about a month ago. I knew that Glenda was a friend of Charlie's because she introduced me to him when she stayed here with Debbie and me." Maria raised her eyebrows, and a look of surprise registered on her face.

"You didn't know?" Val asked.

"It is the first I've heard of it," Maria replied.

"Glenda lived with us for a little while, and she moved about a month before you arrived. She got into pushing marijuana, made herself a bit of money, and decided she could afford an apartment of her own. Glenda bought herself a new car too, quit her job at the office, and didn't work for about a month until she came back to the department store to work in the beauty department."

"Perhaps she gave up pushing drugs," Maria interjected, as Val paused to take a drink of beer.

"I don't think so. The job at the beauty counter pays next to nothing, and she still drives her car, has her own apartment, and dresses well - the money must come from somewhere, but it isn't from her job in the store; a person could starve to death on her wages." Val got up, went to the refrigerator, and stopped for a moment with one hand on the handle and the other on her forehead. "Oh!" she exclaimed. "Have I ever got a headache?" Then she got herself another beer and rejoined Maria at the table.

"If Glenda doesn't need the money, why the unnecessary toil?" Maria asked.

"She said that she felt empty and needed to feel a sense of accomplishment, otherwise she would go crazy." Maria's expression conveyed her feeling of disbelief. Then Val went on, "I don't see where a job at the beauty counter can give anyone a sense of accomplishment. However, one can't believe everything Glenda says, she has always been known for her BS, and cunning like you wouldn't believe. Her latest story is that she has washed her hands of anything to do with drugs."

Having seen Glenda once or twice in the store, Maria recalled that she was young and pretty and quite pleasant, although the picture that she was formulating of Glenda now was anything put pretty, and if Val was correct, Glenda was using her job in the store as a cover for something underhanded.

"How does Glenda explain the money?" Maria asked.

"She said, an uncle of hers died and left her some money; which to me, if not to the others, sounds like something from Ripley. I believe Glenda is still pushing drugs, and she has established a clientele of people whom she trusts, and she doesn't sell to anyone else."

"Did Phylis and her boyfriend bring the marijuana?" Maria asked.

"Yes, they came about seven-thirty and brought the grass with them."

"Do you think Phylis and her boyfriend are Glenda's customers?" Maria asked.

"I don't know," Val replied, shaking her head. "Phylis and her boyfriend don't touch the stuff, and she wouldn't take any money for the marijuana she brought."

Val laid her head on the table and sighed. She was still suffering the effects of the night before, and the beer she was drinking didn't seem to help. She looked rough, and Maria had the feeling that Val's low mental distress was even greater than her physical discomfort, and there was still a lot to be told about what went on in the suite the night before.

"Do Glenda and Charlie smoke marijuana?" Maria asked, prompting Val to continue telling what had gone on at the party.

"Yes, they both smoke marijuana," Val replied, raising her head and pushing her hair back from the sides of her face. "Although Glenda didn't have any last night, and after having a beer she left before Phylis and her boyfriend arrived."

There was moment's silence while Maria took a drink from her beer. Then when it became apparent that Val was not going to continue, Maria, still fishing said. "So Charlie became your date for the night?"

"Yes," Val replied, looking down at the table, her voice barely audible, a dejected look on her face, and aware that Maria was watching her closely. Val stood up, drained her almost empty bottle, and crossed to the refrigerator to get another beer. "Are you ready for another beer?" she asked, opening the refrigerator.

"No thanks," Maria replied, her face showing her concern for her friend.

"The party wasn't as bad as it seems from the mess everyone left," Val said, bringing the beer back to the table and sitting down. Then after pausing to drink some of her beer, she went on. "There weren't many people; just Debbie and her boyfriend, Phylis and her boyfriend, Glenda, Charlie, and three girls from work with their boyfriends. Phylis and her boyfriend, left about eleven-thirty, after we all had a bite to eat, and just about everyone else left soon afterwards, and Debbie and Bill went to bed."

The party seemed innocent enough the way Val explained it, and Maria was puzzled why Val should be upset. Had something happened of which Val was keeping quiet? Maria felt cold, and she shivered as she got up to close the window. "What time did Charlie leave?" Maria asked, sitting down by the table again. She had not meant to pry into Val's personal affairs, but the pain evident on Val's face told Maria that she had touched on a sensitive subject, and she hastily added. "It is none of my business really." Then to change the subject, Maria continued with a smile and some enthusiasm. "Come on, Val; we will clean the place up a bit before Debbie comes home."

"No, I want to tell you, Maria," Val said, and while closing her eyes, she put her hand to her forehead. "I didn't go to work because I was too upset and nervous, and I'm glad that you came back early." Val opened her eyes and took a drink of her beer. "I went to bed shortly after twelve and Charlie said he would sleep on the chesterfield." Val stopped abruptly, put her head on the table, and started to sob.

Feeling sorry for her young friend, Maria watched Val's shoulders and breasts heave with her sobs. She was eager to be successful and well liked, and exposed for the first time to the world without the psychological support of her family and close friends. Val did not know the fragility of her own defenses; that, as yet, were too immature to face the realities of the world, and lacking in that innate shrewdness which is more apparent in some than others; she could be quickly hurt and an easy prey to unscrupulous persons. Nevertheless, Val would learn; learn to take care of herself and be happy at the same time, as most people do.

"I'm all mixed up," Val said, after a minute or two when her crying had subsided.

Getting up, Maria put her arm around her friend's shoulder, "Come on Val, you will feel better in a little while," she said encouragingly.

"No," Val said, through her now infrequent sobs, "I'm not a virgin any more."

Taking some tissue from a box, Maria handed them to Val to dry the tears from her eyes and cheeks.

"It wasn't Charlie's fault," Val continued, "I asked him to come to bed with me." Then taking Maria's hands she bent her head and sobbed anew. "He was so rough, I never want to see another man."

Maria pulled Val gently to her feet, and then put her hands on her waist.

"You are going to be all right Val. It will just take you a little time to get used to the idea that you are not a virgin any more."

Putting her arms around Maria's neck, Val hugged her friend closely. "No, Maria," she said quietly through her sobs. "I don't want to ever see Charlie again."

Pushing Val gently away, Maria put her hands on Val's shoulders as she bent her head. "Look at me," Maria said, and when Val raised her head she continued, "I promise you that you will feel better about it in a little while." Then noticing the small round scar in Val's arm, Maria's eyes narrowed with suspicion and concern. "Val, you have taken heroin," she said.

Val nodded sheepishly in reply.

"Who gave it to you?"

"Charlie," Val replied. "He only gave it to help me. I was broken up after we had sexual intercourse, and he suggested I take some to help me relax and feel better."

"Carry on, and you will get yourself fucked up yet," Maria said angrily. "You knew Charlie pushed heroin, previous to his showing up at the party." Maria said her words more a statement than a question.

"Yes," Val replied, "I knew from the first time I met him, I guess."

"If you knew he pushed heroin you should not have allowed him to stay at the party," Maria said, her mood changing from one of anger to despair. While the expression on Val's face was one of surprise, like she didn't understand why, and Maria continued emphatically. "You had a responsibility to your guests, that they would not be exposed to scum like Charlie in your home."

"I have known Charlie for quite some time," Val pleaded. "He is not a pusher in the true sense of the word; he never forces the stuff on anyone; if you want it he can get it for you, and that's all there is to it. Heroin is not as bad as it is made out to be; I took it a couple of times before, and I can take it or leave it."

"My God!" Maria exclaimed. "Smarten up. If you get hooked on heroin you've had it."

"I'm sorry," Val said. Then sitting down and laying her head on the table, she began to cry once more. "I've had it anyway," she choked in despair. "This intercourse thing, there was so much promise, and I don't like it. I always thought that one day I would get married, and now it is hopeless." Val turned to Maria, put her arms about her waist, and laid her head on Maria's breasts to cry silently.

Standing motionless, looking down on the figure bent before her, feeling Val's face lying warm on her breast and her arms gentle about her waist, a wave of pity swept over Maria. Then putting her hands on Val's head, she ran her fingers softly through her blond hair. "Come on Val," Maria said sympathetically. "You have got to snap out of it. Go and get yourself cleaned up, and I will start tidying up the suite. Debbie is liable to bring Bill home with her, and won't you look silly if he sees you looking like this?"

Val got up slowly, and taking her bottle of beer with her, she went to the bathroom to take a bath.

Maria started again to clean up the suite. Later, when with the help of Val, the suite was cleaned; Maria took a bath, then as the two girls drank a cup of tea, they took turns brushing one another's hair and talked about Debbie and her boyfriend while the radio played in the background.

The shrill ring of the telephone sounded through the suite, and Maria, putting down the brush she was using on Val's hair, went to answer the telephone.

"Hello."

"Maria," Debbie said with surprise.

"Yes, I got home earlier than I expected."

"Oh good, and how is Val?" Debbie asked.

"Just a minute, and I will ask her," Maria said, then turning to Val, she said, "Debbie wants to know how you are feeling?"

Val smiled, but didn't reply, and speaking to Debbie once again, Maria said. "She is smiling, so I guess she is okay."

"That's good. I was worried about her this morning when she couldn't come to work, and if she was still ill tonight I was going to call a doctor," Debbie said, making it evident to Maria that she didn't know Val had taken heroin. "I guess you will have found out by now that there are no groceries left," Debbie continued. "Bill and I are doing some shopping, and I won't be getting home until late tonight. Do you think you can manage?"

"Sure," Maria replied, "Val and I will step out and have something to eat. It will be a nice break from cooking."

"Do you cook when you're out of town?" Debbie asked.

"Oh my, someone's thinking," Maria replied, and both girls laughed.

"Okay, I will see you later," Debbie said, before hanging up the telephone.

"We are out of groceries, and Debbie says she will bring some home later," Maria said, turning to Val. "What do you say we eat out, Val?"

"It sounds okay to me. Let's go to the restaurant in the shopping center close to the bridge."

"Do you mean the one where the handsome guy shows you to the table?" Maria asked, smiling spontaneously, as she recalled that Val had previously commented on the young fellow's good looks.

"That is the one, but the food is good too you know," Val replied, smiling in response.

The decision made. The girls hurried to dress and put their make-up on while they talked about the restaurant's specialty.

* * *

After waving goodbye to Cec, Danny walked to the house from the camper that had brought Maria and him safely away from the Sunshine Coast. The trip had not been all Danny planned it to be, and while he would have liked to complete their voyage to Powell River and back; under the circumstances, things had turned out well. The two days and a night he had spent with Maria had been delightful, and even the intrigue and danger, surrounding their unscheduled meeting with Doc Ellis and Laura, had failed to spoil their pleasure. The L.W.C. Import and Export Corporation was seeing troubled times, of which Doc Ellis was partly responsible, and Danny was confident and eager to tackle the problems that confronted the family business. Calm and able, the Lewes' managed their affairs with ruthless determination to survive, and they had more than survived; success and wealth had been their reward.

Reclining in their luxurious easy chairs in the large open beamed living room, happy to be reunited with their son, Emily and Bill Lewes listened as Danny recounted what had happened on the Sunshine Coast, and his suspicion that Doc Ellis had planned and failed to intercept him on the road to Langdale. When Danny's recount of what had happened was finished, they sat in silence for a time; a tribunal meditating what course justice would take. Bill Lewes took a drink from the whisky that he had poured for the occasion; visibly hurt now by Doc Ellis' latest act of betrayal, he looked past Danny, through the sliding glass doors to the terrace, where a German Shepherd dog patrolled the grounds between the swimming pool and the fence. He had been suspicious for some time that Doc Ellis was working to the detriment of the company. He had delayed getting rid of him, but this final act by a nigh life-long friend against a member of his family was unforgivable. Bill Lewes blamed himself; he should have acted with dispatch long before, as his wife had advised, and not allowed his sentiment to endanger the family.

"Doc Ellis is a fool," Emily Lewes said.

Danny, restless for action got up to pour himself a drink. He dropped the ice into his glass then turned to face his parents, "Doc Ellis is a pawn of a powerful organization, headed by Mr. Perrelli, which is attempting to take over the drug trade on the West Coast." Emily and Bill Lewes were silent and deep in thought as Danny finished pouring his drink and walked back to his chair. "We must get rid of Doc Ellis immediately," Danny continued, "but what about Laura?"

"She will have to go too, she knows as much as Doc, and she is probably the more dangerous of the two," Bill Lewes replied.

"We should wait until Dolansky has had time to negotiate with Perrelli," Emily Lewes said, looking to her husband for support. However, Bill Lewes was silent, and Danny disagreed.

"No, to delay would be interpreted as weakness by our competitors, and worsen our position with our business associates."

"Danny is right," Bill Lewes said, speaking to his wife, "any delay could hamper possible negotiations with Perrelli. I will see to the job myself."

Emily Lewes smiled; she was proud of her husband; he had built the business from nothing when times were rough. Still, times and men change, and it was Danny and their daughter Irene, whom the family depended on now. "If one of us is to get rid of Doc Ellis and Laura, then it is Danny who should do the job," she said. "Although we should still consider the possibility that Dolansky can be made available to take care of them."

Getting up, Bill Lewes walked to the window while he considered the situation He didn't feel any different than he had thirty-five years ago. Nevertheless, he knew that his wife was right. Danny was more efficient, and less likely to make mistakes. "All right," he said. Then turning to Danny, "Will you take it, if Dolansky is unavailable?"

"Sure," Danny replied, and he wondered if he would have as much spirit as his father when he would be his age.

The telephone started to ring, and Emily Lewes went to the desk, and picked it up. Danny got up to consult with his father at the bar, and they were still talking when Mrs. Lewes hung up the telephone. "It was Dolansky," she announced. "A representative of the new company, headed by Mr. Perrelli of New York, has contacted Dolansky to initiate negotiations for a cut in the west coast drug trade, and Doc Ellis and Laura have entered the United States at Blaine."

"God damn it!" Bill Lewes exploded.

"It may be for the best," Danny said calmly. "The negotiations may stall new actions by Perrelli for a time, and with Doc Ellis and Laura in the States; it will be less likely that the police will connect their death with us."

The Leweses refreshed their drinks at the bar, and sat down again to reassess their position and prepare a plan of strategy.

The branch of the detective agency in Seattle that was associated with them was contacted, and the names and addresses of Doc Ellis' business associates and friends were acquired. In spite of the recent setback caused by the seizure of heroin, Doc Ellis was too valuable to them to be dismissed out of hand; he knew all the ropes of the trade, plus he possessed a wide knowledge of the Lewes' operation, and he could be used by them, or more precisely by Perrelli, to influence the negotiations.

By the use of corruption and power, Perrelli's company in Seattle had been very successful in the past months; virtually eliminating the Lewes' counterpart in that city, and now was disrupting the Lewes' European business connections and threatening to branch out in Vancouver on a large scale, unless a negotiated settlement could be transacted. Such a settlement would be beneficial to both parties, Perrelli had promised, by eliminating the threat of competition in Vancouver and giving the Leweses an opportunity to branch out into the United States market. The negotiations would be delicate and Perrelli's representative tough to deal with, thus Dolansky was necessary to act as a go between.

It was probable that Doc Ellis had business associates in Vancouver also, although Dolansky's detective agency, in spite of an intensive investigation, had been unable to uncover any of his connections, and even the three men who had waited in ambush for Danny and Maria at the road block on the Sunshine Coast had dropped out of sight. With this in mind, it was a puzzle why Doc Ellis had chosen to bypass his Vancouver associates, and had entered the United States.

After a lengthy discussion, and with much misgiving by Danny's parents, it was finally agreed that Danny, using an alias to protect his identity, would slip quietly out of the country to eliminate Doc Ellis and Laura.

That same evening, Danny wearing a false mustache and horn rimmed glasses, took a plane to Seattle to await the arrival of Doc Ellis and Laura. Using the alias, Danny booked into a large modern hotel in which one of

Doc Ellis' business associates owned a substantial share. While it was possible, that Doc Ellis would not stay at this particular hotel, or even come to Seattle for that matter. Danny gambled that he would.

CHAPTER 15

On Saturday morning, Maria, along with Val and Debbie, got up at nine o'clock, and after eating a hearty breakfast, they packed a lunch and drove to Stanley Park. The three girls enjoyed their walk through the park, among the trees and many colorful flowers, and a stroll along the sea front. Then clad only in their bathing suits, their eyes covered with large sunglasses, the girls lay on towels spread on the grass, their clothes neatly folded by their sides, as they soaked up the warm sun.

There were many people in the park, who like the girls had come to walk, sunbathe, and picnic in the fresh air and warm sun. However, the girls, lying close together, were almost oblivious to the people around them, and they politely discouraged the boys who tried to strike up a conversation; engrossed as they were in discussing the events of the past days.

They could laugh now about the party of Thursday night, and talked freely of some of the incidents that had taken place. Phylis' common law husband, John, had told a great number of jokes, most of them now forgotten and unrepeatable. The boys had consumed an enormous amount of beer and really enjoyed themselves, except Charlie, who drank little and remained extremely serious, and even John's ribald jokes had seemed to be either above or beneath his intellect. Nevertheless, the other fellows had respect for Charlie; he was too big and potentially mean to be trifled with, and it was only Val who had dared to chide him for his apparent aloofness, and evoke his smiles. The girls laughed when Debbie recalled how everyone, except Phylis, John, Bill, and herself, sat in a circle to smoke the pot, and how one of the girls from work had burnt her fingers when the reefer had burnt too short. But throughout the conversation, Val, although laughing readily with her two friends, was timerous of any mention of Charlie, and Maria noticed, that as if by consent, Debbie and Val said nothing further about Glenda. It was obvious that the girls, because of their friendship, were covering for Glenda as they had covered for her when the police had raided their suite in search of drugs, and the suspicion arose in Maria's mind that Glenda was connected to the police raid, and possibly she was the architect of the plot to have heroin found in their possession.

Later, while the three girls sat and ate their lunch, Maria learned that the girl on the payroll, in the office where her friends worked, was pregnant and would be quitting work to have her baby. Maria's smile went unnoticed as she reflected about the job and her uncle's advice; just a telephone call to Mr. Evans and the job could be hers.

The girls applied suntan lotion to their bodies before lying down again in the sun, and Val untied the strap on her halter to get a more even tan as the girls continued their conversation. Debbie was getting married in July, and Val planned to go home for a week to Prince Rupert when she got her holidays.

In the evening Debbie went out with Bill, and Maria, and Val went to a movie then came home to watch the late news on television and enjoy a cup of tea. Debbie and Bill came in before the news was finished and joined Maria and Val with their tea. Bill would stay over for the night as had been prearranged during the afternoon while the girls sunbathed in the park. Then after talking for a time with Maria and Val as they drank their tea, Debbie and Bill retired to Debbie's room, leaving Maria and Val talking and drinking their second cup. With all the strange happenings of the past days, Maria and Val felt comforted by Bill's presence in the suite. They liked Bill for his quiet and pleasant disposition, and even though they had only spoken with him for a few minutes over a cup of tea, they were keenly aware of his presence. They had freshened up their make-up before Debbie brought him home, and their short conversation with him about the news was alive and interesting, and now before they retired to bed, Val remarked that it felt good to have a man around the place.

In bed Maria slept fitfully; she heard Bill and Debbie whispering together before they went to sleep, and Val slept peacefully by her side, while Maria's mind pondered the problem that Charlie presented. As a trafficker in heroin, Charlie was a threat to Val; a threat that Val didn't seem to appreciate, and while Maria knew that she should do something about Charlie, she didn't know what to do. To report him to the police would implicate Val and the girls, friend Glenda, although Maria felt no sympathy for her; she had deliberately brought Charlie to the party, and there was something sinister about her. Phylis and her boyfriend would also be implicated for supplying the marijuana, and innocent people like Debbie and Bill would also be involved, and who knows, the chain of events that she would set in motion might even embrace Danny. Maria considered approaching Charlie and warning him to keep away from Val, then thought better of it; from what she had heard about him, she was liable to get his fist in her mouth for her troubles. It seemed that it was best to do nothing. Val didn't like Charlie anyway, and it was quite likely that she would never see him again.

In the morning, it was Val who arose first, and quietly put on her housecoat and applied make-up before going to the kitchen; where through the window, the snow on the mountains stood out, stark white, against the blue of the sky; while in the street below, the traffic was quiet as people went to church and the birds sang from the trees along the road. Maria awoke to the sound of pots being used on the stove, and the aroma of coffee, pancakes, and bacon filled the air as Val busied herself preparing breakfast, and in the background the radio was playing a hit tune.

It was a happy little group that sat down to breakfast, and it was evident from the superb taste of everything that Val had cooked, that her mother had done her job well in preparing Val for her future role as a homemaker. Observing Val's confidence in the work she did well, Maria shared her happiness for the compliments and appreciation which she, Debbie, and Bill bestowed upon her; and Val's happiness was complete; when noting Bill's appetite, Debbie asked Val for the pancake recipe. Then while enjoying their second cup of coffee and laughing at Bill's insistence that he and Debbie wash the dishes, the door bell rang. The girls looked at each other askant; who would be calling on them on a Sunday morning?

"You answer it, Bill," Debbie said, and the girls waited apprehensively as Bill went through the living room to open the door.

"Oh, excuse me," Tom Balant said with surprise, as Bill opened the door. Then recovering, he continued, "I'm looking for Maria Petersen."

"Come on in, Tom," Maria called, as Bill turned and looked towards the kitchen.

Tom entered the suite, and Bill closed the door behind him before leading the way into the kitchen where the three girls, still dressed in their colorful dressing gowns sat at the table.

Standing for a moment in the doorway, Tom looked lean and hard in his new blue jeans and short sleeved purple shirt, his smile revealing his even white teeth as his brown eyes met Maria's. Smiling with pleasure herself, Maria stood up to make room for him at the table.

"Come, take a seat, Tom," Maria said, beckoning him towards her.

"I will get you some breakfast," Val volunteered.

"No thanks, I have already had breakfast," Tom replied. Then turning back to Maria and moving towards her, he continued, "I was passing by, so I dropped in to see how you were getting along."

Taking Tom's hand, Maria pulled him gently to the chair she had just vacated, her smile adding to her gesture of welcome. She knew that Tom had not been just passing by, and he had driven at least fifty miles to see her. "I'm going to change," she said, "I will only be a minute."

"I'll get you a cup of coffee," Val said to Tom, and he nodded in reply, and smiled when Val got up from the table to go to the stove. Debbie got up from the table at the same time, and followed Maria from the kitchen, leaving the two men to talk while Val prepared a fresh pot of coffee.

In her bedroom, Maria was thoughtful as she dressed, applied her make-up, and brushed her long black hair until it shone. Her thoughts of the night before came flooding back to her, and mentally she compared Tom with what she had heard about Charlie. Tom was big too, and she wondered if Charlie would be belligerent with him if they ever crossed paths. Charlie would be foolhardy to tackle Tom she thought; recalling Tom's large hands, brawny arms, and strength born of hard manual work. She would not be afraid to confront Charlie, and warn him to stay away from Val with his drugs if Tom was present. However, this was out of the question; Tom would insist on going to the police.

Debbie was already back in the kitchen, when Maria returned, dressed in her blue jeans and a print flowered blouse that was colorful and pretty. Tom saw Maria as she entered the room; her face flushed, and eyes shining; their glances met and lingered, a trace of a smile on their faces, as if sharing some knowledge that was unknown to the others.

"Break it up you two, this is family entertainment," Debbie said, as Maria sat down at Tom's side. Then they all laughed together, at the remark, before continuing the discussion of the prospects for the Lions in the coming season. Then after a short while, Tom thanked Val for the coffee, and without any prearranged plan, Maria and Tom, after a few words of goodbye to the others, left the suite together.

* * *

A fresh breeze stirred the warm air on Burnaby Mountain, and Maria and Tom, laughing and talking, walked leisurely over the grass, stopping now and then to admire the beds of flowers and watch the birds. Their conversation flowed easily and almost uninterrupted; of the ranch, of Maria's parents, her home in Toronto, and the sailing trips that they had taken on the yacht in the company of Danny. Then with an arm about each other's waists they looked at the spectacular scene of Burrard Inlet and Indian Arm far below, the ships and boats plying the blue waters, appearing like toys to the spectators on the mountain. Maria and Tom, their senses in harmony, happy with each other's company; ignored a bench overlooking the water, and lay down on the soft grass; Maria's delicate hand clasping Tom's, as they watched the hazy white clouds drifting high above their heads in the vast blue of the sky. Quiet, and now intensely aware of each other and the closeness and beauty of nature of which they were a part; breathing deep of the same air, alone with their thoughts; their future or futures shrouded in the mystery of time, they were both keenly aware that their relationship had changed to something deeper and more profound than had existed before. Tom leaned over Maria and kissed her lightly consummating the new bond of relationship and understanding that existed between them.

The sailing trips spent with Danny and Tom had been filled with the thrill of adventure and the pleasure of their company, and while at first, Maria had enjoyed and was flattered by their competition for her attention; as the time went on, she was saddened by the rift she saw develop between the two men who had been good friends. There had been no outward display of anger; only a growing subtle resentment; until their paths separated, never to see one another again, and seldom allow each other's names cross their lips. Maria realized now that as much as she loved Danny, she had missed Tom. Both men had found their way to her heart and her love, still it was Danny who had stirred her passions and satisfied her desires. Tom knew of the relationship that existed between Danny and her, and Maria was grateful for Tom's discretion and thoughtfulness, accepting her as she was and making no demands. Maria confessed to Tom how much she had missed him and her pleasure of seeing him again that morning. They laughed together about Tom's lame excuse of just dropping in to visit her while he happened to be passing by; when in reality, after a restless night, he had left his morning chores untouched to see her again.

They kissed on the grass once more before leaving; the tender and passionate kiss of lovers who must part; comforted only by the knowledge that their love, come what may, would endure. The brakes of the old pick-up seemed to squeal in protest to their parting as they descended the mountain, and while laughing at the symbolized concern they took pleasure in the contentment of their companionship. Tom dropped Maria off at the apartment, where he saw her wave from the sidewalk, and he began to whistle a popular tune as he drove away.

Feeling desolate and alone when Debbie and Bill left, Val busied herself ironing clothes in the kitchen. Then hearing a noise at the entrance she called, "Is that you, Maria?" Val called, pausing with her work to listen when she heard the door of the suite open and close.

"Yes," Maria replied without enthusiasm. Then she walked to the kitchen to join Val.

"By the way," Val said. "What happened to your suitcase and clothes?"

"I left them behind on the Sunshine Coast, near Joseph's Island." Maria stood in the doorway and watched her friend skillfully press a blouse. "They will be sent on in a couple of days, and in the meantime I will have to dig up some clothes appropriate to wear to the office."

"I looked through your things," Val said, "and picked out what I thought was the best, and ironed a skirt and blouse."

"Thanks Val, but you shouldn't be waiting on me."

"Really it's no trouble," Val replied, glancing up from her work and noticing the dejected look on Maria's face. "I'm glad to be able to give you a hand."

Going into the bedroom, Maria lay face down on the bed, and tears welled up in her eyes. Why was it so difficult to make a decision? She loved Danny, and yet Tom meant so much to her and what of the future?

"Can I help?" Val asked, laying down on the bed beside Maria and putting an arm around her.

"No," Maria replied, not wanting to talk of her problems, although feeling comforted by Val's presence and concern. Maria dried her eyes with the tissue Val handed her. "It was nice of you to cook breakfast this morning and make fresh coffee for Tom."

"I did it for you Maria. I'm not interested in men anymore."

"That will last for a couple of days," Maria said, getting up to sit on the edge of the bed and smile sadly down at Val. "Come on, let's get on with our ironing." Then getting up from the bed, she walked into the kitchen with Val following. However, it was Val who picked up the iron and resumed the work, as Maria sat on a chair by the window, to think again about Danny, and wonder where he was and what he was doing. Down in the street, the neon sign on the restaurant opposite flashed on and off, bathing the passersby in its red glow.

* * *

Sipping a beer in the lounge of a Seattle hotel, just off the main lobby, Danny waited for Doc Ellis and Laura to arrive. But they did not show up that evening, and on that Saturday morning when Maria with Val and Debbie lay sunbathing on the grass in Stanley Park, Danny renewed his vigil. It was possible that Doc Ellis had not driven directly to Seattle, and he and Laura had stayed elsewhere for the night. Danny ordered a coffee.

At eleven o'clock on Saturday morning, Danny's patience and vigilance was rewarded, and Doc Ellis and Laura were ushered into the hotel by two well-dressed men in their early forties. They by-passed the formalities at the desk, and with a porter following with two small suitcases, the party boarded an elevator and ascended to the fifteenth floor. Feeling pleased that his long vigil was rewarded, Danny drank up his coffee, and going to the hotel restaurant, he ordered a T-bone steak for dinner. He lingered over desert, and a fruit drink as he waited for his erstwhile friends, but Doc Ellis and Laura did not show up; evidently dinner had been served for them in their suite. Danny went for a walk in the street outside the hotel; it was unlikely that Doc Ellis would leave the hotel immediately, and it was too dangerous for him to go snooping around the fifteenth floor. If his identity was discovered, he would be extremely lucky to escape with his life.

The weather was calm, perhaps too calm, as Danny walked leisurely along the street, looking into the store windows, and taking an interest in the scenic attraction of the girls he saw along his way. Circling back to the hotel, Danny walked around the parking area; Doc Ellis' green cadillac was in stall 1506 - the fifteenth floor, room six. Going to his room, Danny lay down to rest; there wasn't anything that he could do at the present, and he would relax for a time. He awoke with a start and looked at his watch. It was four-thirty, and he had been asleep for over two hours. After examining his disguise in the mirror, Danny put on his jacket and went back to the lobby.

The lobby was busy with people coming into the city for the weekend, and the hotel was quickly filling up. Danny went out to the car park; Doc Ellis' car was gone. Damn it, Danny thought; he had slept too long, and he should have stayed in the lounge and waited. There was nothing to do now, but to wait and see if Doc Ellis would return. Going back to the lounge where he could watch the lobby, Danny ordered a beer, and sipping it slowly, he renewed his vigil somewhat depressed that he might have let his quarries slip through his fingers.

"Are you lonely, Sir?" a woman asked, smiling confidently as she sat down across the table from Danny.

"Beat it," Danny hissed out of the corner of his mouth, and the woman, alarmed and angry, quickly got up and walked back to the bar muttering something about him not having the decency to pass the time of day.

His face masking his feelings, Danny watched the woman with disgust as she walked away; her dress so tight, it looked as if she had been poured into it; and as she walked, she moved her hips back and forth to an extent that was vulgar. He hated whores, and he would have liked nothing better than to give her a good swift kick in the butt. She sat down on a seat at the bar, draped herself over the counter, and looked up at the barman; her breasts almost falling out of her low cut dress. The barman looked down at her and laughed, and she said something and gestured back across the lounge.

Getting up and leaving his beer unfinished on the table, Danny walked out to the car park; there was a white Lincoln with California license plates in stall 1506. "Hell!" Danny exclaimed aloud; he should have seen Doc Ellis and Laura leave instead of wasting his time sleeping in his room. He walked slowly back to the lounge, his face ashen white with anger; the tables were all taken, the beer he had left behind had been removed, and his table occupied by two couples, laughing and talking, oblivious to their intrusion. Danny crossed to the bar and sat on a seat on the turn of the counter, across from the whore, where he could watch the lobby, although there seemed to be little hope of seeing Doc Ellis now.

The whore looked into Danny's eyes with scorn, but what she saw were two slits that glinted like blue steel, then she shivered when Danny's eyes caught hers, and getting up, she walked from the bar and out of the lounge; her self-confidence had deserted her and she was afraid.

The two men whom Danny had seen with Doc Ellis the day before came into the hotel with two women. They were talking and laughing, as if a joke had passed between them, and one of the men waved to the clerk at the desk as they walked towards the elevator. Danny watched the elevator ascend to the fifteenth floor, and then stop; and he turned back to the bar and took a drink from his beer. Doc Ellis was still in the hotel, and it seemed that they were going to have a bit of a celebration. Danny went out into the car park, wrote down the license number of the white Lincoln that was parked in Doc's parking space, and then returned to the lounge. Doc Ellis' and Laura's guests left the hotel at a quarter to twelve in the evening; they had obviously consumed a good quantity of liquor, and Danny was satisfied that he could retire to his room and rest; Doc Ellis and Laura would not leave the hotel before morning light.

* * *

The gray light of dawn was creeping over the quiet city when Danny awoke. He was fully awake immediately, and was dressing when the telephone rang; it would be the desk clerk; he had asked to be called at five-thirty.

"Hello," Danny said, answering the telephone.

"It is five-thirty, sir."

"Thanks."

Danny put down the telephone and continued dressing; the sun had come up, and was casting its golden light about the room. The noise of a jet plane crossing the city broke the stillness of the morning, and then rapidly decreased as the plane flew on its way. A black cloud covered the sun, and the room became dark as Danny stepped out into the deserted hallway and quietly closed the door behind him.

It was five after six when Danny alighted from the elevator into the lobby. There were only a few people around; the desk clerk was talking to a man and a woman with a young boy their suitcases on the floor by their sides, and the doorman was walking towards them from the entrance. It seemed strangely silent and barren in comparison to the lively activity it had seen on Saturday night. Danny crossed to the door to the car park, as the doorman picked up the suitcases by the desk and started for the front entrance. The white Lincoln was still in its stall, and Danny passed and continued on into the street.

The streets, thronged with traffic the night before, were now almost empty, and a strong westerly wind had cleaned the city air. Five taxis stood in front of the hotel, with most of the drivers standing together talking, and one was asleep in his cab. Two girls hurried along the opposite side of the street, their coats blowing open, showing their black and white waitresses' uniforms, and a bus went by carrying only three passengers, as Danny walked along the street towards the long distance bus terminal. There were a good number of people moving around in the terminal, and a black porter was sweeping the floor, when Danny entered a telephone booth and reversing the charges he telephoned his father.

"It appears that Doc will be driving to California," Danny said, "and I will need a large truck. Could you make arrangements for me to pick one up here in Seattle, with bills of lading and everything complete, to pick up a cargo of fruit and vegetables in California?"

"I will get on to it right away," Bill Lewes replied, "and you can walk into the truck terminal and pick up the truck any time."

"Okay, Dad, I will see you in a few days."

The sun had come out again from behind a black cloud; bathing the streets in its light. "I think it will rain," an old man said to his wife, as he looked at the sky, while she continued to look into a jeweler's window neither glanced to Danny, passing on the way back to the hotel.

The dining room of the hotel was already about one third full, when Danny sat down at a table, covered with a white linen cloth and set for breakfast. Danny ordered a coffee from the smiling waiter who remembered the tip he received the day before. Relaxing, while reading the newspaper and drinking his coffee, Danny waited until eight o'clock before ordering breakfast, he had almost finished eating, when Doc Ellis and Laura walked into the dining room and sat down with three men who had arrived a few minutes earlier. Folding the paper, Danny got up from the chair, and with the paper under his arm he walked from the room, and returned to his suite.

The big truck was parked on a roadside lay by; it was fairly new with lots of power, it came with air, of course, a CD player, and a place behind the cab where Danny could sleep. Now it was just after one o'clock and in the cab of the truck Danny waited impatiently for Doc and Laura to pass on their way to California. At one-thirty the blue Cadillac went by and Danny pulled out and followed. It was evident that Doc and Laura were in no hurry as later in the day the Cadillac turned off highway 5 onto highway 101 to travel along the coast of Oregon.

A storm had broken out during the day and huge waves broke onto the beaches and rocks along the coast as Danny gave thought to how he would get rid of Doc Ellis and Laura. He had many options; shoot them in a drive by, or preferably cause what would look like an accident where he would push their car into the side of an overpass or off the side of a cliff.

Early next morning, Danny passed the Cadillac and saw that Doc was driving and Laura was in the passenger seat. Further along highway 101, he stopped at the side of the road and Doc Ellis and Laura passed. Then shortly afterwards they stopped at a roadside lay by and in the company of a number of other people went to watch the huge waves breaking onto the rocks.

Later in the day Danny pulled up close behind Doc's car, and Laura told Doc that he should slow down and let the fool driving the truck pass. When Doc slowed down, Danny pulled the big truck alongside the car. Ahead on the now deserted highway, there was a bridge over a creek where the water rushed to the sea. Laura was fully aware now that something was wrong and taking a pistol from her purse, she took a shot at the driver. The bullet passed through the side window of the cab close to Danny's head and it went out of the windshield.

There was no more time to wait. Danny pulled the big truck over and the huge wheels of the rig pushed the car off the bridge. In the murky light of the stormy afternoon the big car skidded out of control on the rainswept surface of the road, then it smashed into the guardrail of the bridge. The occupants didn't have a chance. The front of the car folded like an accordion, then, broken and twisted, the car turned slowly end over end in the air on its way to the torrent of water in the swollen river below. The truck swerved and almost jacknifed but Danny tramped on the gas, straightened the truck out, and drove on.

The police and the newsreporters, while knowing of the victims' involvement with illegal drugs, never suspected that the incident was anything but an accident.

Later Danny stopped and examined the damage; scuff marks on the tires and two bullet holes. Taking a stone from the side of the road, Danny ground it into the glass until the holes appeared to look like rocks damaged them. In the heavy rain that was faling and the strong wind the marks on the tires would soon be gone. Then Danny put some tape over the holes in the windows. The job Danny had come to do was now done and he could relax and drive on to California. In a few days he would be back in Canada and at home.

CHAPTER 16

The sky was a patchy gray on Monday morning, and the rain was falling in a light drizzle as Maria drove her two friends to work. The news on the radio reported the seizure by the police of a large quantity of heroin aboard a private yacht off Vancouver on Friday. It was believed the drug was to be smuggled from Canada into the United States. Four Americans, three men and a woman, had been arrested, and the police were continuing their investigation. The girls talked very little; preferring to listen to the radio and look through the windows at the rain, the traffic on the road, and the pedestrians on the sidewalks huddling under their umbrellas - perhaps it was the weather and the fact that it was a Monday morning that put them in a melancholy mood.

At the office, Dolansky and Cec were waiting for Maria, and Cec smiled and beckoned her to join them in Dolansky's office, as she took off her raincoat. Dolansky leaned back in his swivel chair behind the desk, the oak paneled wall behind him adding to the integrity and dignity of his appearance. But it was all a sham, the tape recorder hidden in the desk, would record all she said in response to the carefully worded questions asked by Dolansky and Cec.

After exchanging greetings with Dolansky and Cec, Maria sat on a chair facing the desk, and on the invitation of Dolansky, she began to relate her impression of what had happened to endanger Danny and herself when they visited Doc Ellis and Laura on Joseph's Island. Maria told them of the tension that had been apparent at Doc Ellis' cabin after Danny's father had telephoned, and of Danny's decision to leave the yacht and all their belongings and hurry back to Vancouver. She mentioned too, her suspicions that Doc Ellis was involved in the smuggling of drugs and that the yacht seized by the police off Vancouver was probably the Evader 111, which Danny had seen leaving the anchorage at Joseph's Island early Friday morning. However, Maria said nothing of her discussion with Danny concerning these matters, or of her suspicion that the Leweses were also involved in smuggling drugs, and she skillfully worded her statements to avoid any implication of the true extent of her knowledge.

Undeceived, Dolansky switched the tape recorder off with a movement of his foot beneath the desk, and said in a voice cold and hard, "Miss Petersen, we are aware of the knowledge you possess concerning the Leweses, and your secrecy with Mr. Bonas and myself is unnecessary." Dolansky paused, to give Maria time to think about what he had said, as he surveyed her coldly. Maria glanced momentarily at Cec; his expression was as cold and hard as Dolansky's, but she showed no indication, by word or expression, that what Dolansky had said had any basis in fact. "A word of warning," Dolansky continued in the same tone of voice. "Don't breathe a word of what you know about the Leweses or Doc Ellis to anyone."

"I understand," Maria said flatly. Deliberately omitting the words Mr. Dolansky that would have acknowledged deference. She was being threatened to keep her mouth shut, or else, not just to save the Lewes' necks, but their own as well. She had nothing to fear, they would have to trust her as long as Danny would protect her, but if she lost Danny's love, what then? She refused to speculate on what Dolansky and Cec Bonas might do to eliminate her as a potential danger. Maria turned to Cec and smiled, as much as to say. "Knock it off, you bastards."

"We can trust Maria," Cec said to Dolansky, his voice full of sincerity.

"I know." Dolansky replied, and there was just a hint that it was otherwise before he continued. "I wanted to make it clear how important it is that she remain silent on these matters. I'm sure Miss Petersen will continue to do her work efficiently."

Things were not working out exactly as they planned. She had become more involved than they had anticipated, and Dolansky hadn't taken kindly to her attempted deception. She knew now that the Leweses were somehow involved in the illegal drug trade. How much there was to know, or exactly what Dolansky thought she knew, Maria had no idea, and in spite of her outward appearance of arrogant unconcern, she was disturbed to learn that she was not trusted. The words of the two men to gloss over this distrust seemed empty of sincere feelings, and the threat for her to remain silent was undiminished.

"Is it likely that the police will discover Doc Ellis' involvement in the drug shipment that was seized?" Maria addressed her question to Dolansky, and by a movement of his eyes, he instructed Cec to reply.

"Doc Ellis and Laura crossed the border into the United States late Saturday," Cec said, "and he has probably covered himself well against being implicated with the heroin." Cec paused, "of course there is always the possibility that something will go wrong and the police will pick him up,

and if this happens he may implicate a number of people - including you."
Maria smiled, the web they were weaving was artful. "You were there at
Joseph's Island with Danny that night, and Doc Ellis would stop at nothing
to hurt the Leweses."

It was little wonder that Doc Ellis had left the country. He was running
for his life. Dolansky kept a careful watch on people, and Maria reflected on
whether he knew of her meeting with Tom.

"You see how important it is that we keep our own counsel, and discuss
none of these things with outsiders?" Dolansky said, his eyes studying Maria
carefully.

Maria got the message all right. It was coming through loud and clear. "I
understand, Mr. Dolansky." Maria said condescendingly. She would be foolish
to antagonize Dolansky, merely to satisfy her pride; better she would cultivate
some trust for the time when Danny's love might wane. She had neither the
resources or the know how of Doc Ellis to escape, if she were to become a
detriment to the safety of the Leweses and Dolansky. Perhaps Cec, for that
matter too, was not as gentle and good-natured as he appeared to be on the
surface, and he could be a good friend or a dangerous enemy.

"We will type up a full report of what happened on Friday," Cec said,
getting up from his chair. "If there is anything important that we think of
that we have not mentioned, we will include it in the report."

"Very good," Dolansky replied.

"Can I get Betty to bring you a cup of coffee?" Cec asked Dolansky.
Maria, on her way to the door, looked back; Dolansky, serious and thoughtful,
shook his head in reply; the expensive wood paneling and shining glass of
the room imparted an intangible quality of affluence and power to its
occupant.

In the outer office, Maria poured the coffee and let Cec help himself to
the cream and sugar. Two men walked into the reception room, past Mrs.
Jonson, and went directly into the inner office. Cec grabbed his gun from
his shoulder holster, and he was running towards the door where the men
had disappeared, when the rattle of automatic weapons came to their ears.
Everyone in the outer office took cover at the sound of the shots, and crouched
or lay behind the desks away from the door to the inner office.

"Cover the inside door and don't let anyone through, and I will keep my
eye on the front," Cec said, glancing back to Maria, his eyes ablaze with
excitement.

Mrs. Jonson got up from her chair behind the desk and walked unhurriedly towards the door to the hallway. Cec's trigger finger went white on the pistol, and anger was written over his face. "Hold it right there, Mrs. Jonson," he shouted. But she kept on walking, out of the office and into the hallway, leaving the door open behind her. "God damn her," Cec muttered.

The inside door, that Maria was watching, suddenly opened, and the barrel of the gun that was thrust through the small opening sprayed the room with bullets and was quickly withdrawn. One of the girls laying on the floor behind a desk in the rear of the office began to sob, and outside of this sound, Maria heard only the thump of her own heart.

"Don't let him do that again," Cec, said, his voice tense with excitement.

"No way," Maria replied through clenched teeth, as she watched the door intently over the barrel of her pistol resting on the desk before her.

"They are reloading, and they will have to make a break for it pretty quick," Cec advised; his voice almost a whisper.

Suddenly the door was kicked open; revealing a man with a short-barreled gun, leveled at the room ahead of him.

Maria's pistol kicked three times in her hand as she pulled the trigger rapidly, and the bullets from the man's gun went harmlessly into the ceiling as he crumpled to the floor, the gun falling away from him, and sliding on into the room. Maria turned to Cec, standing now, his smoking pistol pointing to the floor. She had been dimly aware of the shots behind her, as Cec shot down the man who had attempted to run from the front door of the inner office. Conscious of the acrid smell of burnt powder and breathing heavily, Maria looked back to the man she had shot, and Cec closed the door to the hallway. Then with his gun still in his hand, Cec returned to the man whom he had gunned down; turned him over onto his back, and looked at him carefully before raising his eyes to Maria. "How is the other one?" Cec asked, his voice calm, and his face expressionless.

"I think he is dead," Maria replied slowly, feeling nauseated, her mind reflecting on what she had done.

The other girls, and Mr. Watson, the office manager, came forward to where Maria was standing; puzzled and dismayed by what had occurred, their faces pale from their experience, and they looked inquiringly about the room.

"Telephone the police, Betty," Cec said to the young girl standing by Maria's side. "Tell them what has happened, and ask them to send two ambulances." Then Cec walked into the inner office and Maria followed.

Dolansky was slumped back in his chair dead, amid broken glass and bullet torn woodwork. Cec picked up a small notebook from the desk and placed it carefully into the inside pocket of his jacket, and opening a desk drawer, he removed the tape from the concealed recorder and placed it in his pocket. Maria looked with pity at Dolansky; his eyes were directed at the ceiling, his face showing no sign of surprise, pain, or anger; he had died as he had lived, expressionless. Pale and feeling upset from her experience, Maria walked out of the small office and back into the outer office, and Cec, staying back, telephoned Mrs. Dolansky.

In the outer office, the girls and Mr. Watson stood together in a small group conferring with each other in whispers. The police arrived shortly afterwards, and to Maria's surprise, Mrs. Dolansky came in almost right behind them, she must have broken every traffic violation in the book to arrive that soon. She identified herself quickly to a police officer in the reception room, and then hurried through to the inner office and her dead husband. Tall and thin with graying hair, her sparse figure was revealed by the blue and white house dress she had been wearing when Cec telephoned, and her eyes, red from crying, seemed to contradict the stern and authoritative manner in which she conducted herself. The police took statements from everyone, and photographed, the offices and the bodies from a number of different angles before they sealed off the area with yellow ribbon. Shortly afterwards the ambulance men carried the bodies away on stretchers.

Then it was all over, and after some advice from Cec, Mr. Watson told the office girls to return to their desks and their work. "Even if they do very little, it will help them to settle down," Maria overheard Cec, reason with Mr. Watson. Then continuing to talk with Mr. Watson after the girls had gone back to their work, Cec went on, "give them a cup of coffee at their desks."

* * *

It was after three o'clock in the afternoon when Maria, feeling tired and dejected by the events of the day, arrived home at her suite. Mrs. Dolansky, Cec, and herself, had returned to the police station with the police for further questioning after the investigation at the office had been completed. Lawyers were summoned by Cec before they left the office, and were at the police station waiting to represent them when they arrived. The statement Maria made at the police station was brief. Pointed questions concerning the Leweses, and a possible relationship between what had happened at the office and illegal drugs, had been asked, and Maria, heeding the advice she had received from Dolansky just that morning and coached by her lawyer, added very little to what she had already said at the office. A warrant had been issued for the arrest of Mrs. Jonson, but no motive had been established by the police for the murder of Mr. Dolansky. Maria, knowing more than the police of Dolansky's involvement with the Leweses and perhaps illegal drugs was equally at a loss to find a reason for the killing. However, she felt certain that Mrs. Dolansky and Cec did not share her ignorance.

As a last resort by the police, or perhaps by his own request, Maria's cousin Ted had been brought into the case. Then disregarding the advice of her lawyer, she had talked with him in private. In her talk with Ted, Maria added nothing to what she had already said in her previous statements, and later when she conferred with her lawyer, Maria smiled just briefly when she noted his relief when he learned that no new statement had been made. But there was no joy in her smile; the interview with Ted had unnerved her more than the questioning by the other policemen. Ted had not, as she expected, reiterated the questions asked previously; rather it had been a heart to heart talk by two members of the same family; friends, on divergent paths. There had been praise for the part she played in foiling the escape of the murderers and of preventing injury to other innocent members of the office staff, and scathing criticism for her supposed position as a detective with the Plastick Utensil Company.

What did he know, about the difficulties of even a well educated young girl to find work that would satisfy her need to feel she was achieving something worthwhile, and pay enough to live with independence and dignity? She had silently reasoned; before to herself acknowledging, that Ted probably knew this and more, and especially her involvement with Danny and a possible connection with drugs.

"Get out now, Maria, while the going is good," he advised. Then she had merely shrugged, neither acknowledging or denying the accuracy of his information - he didn't know that she already knew too much and was in too deep to get out.

Maria and Cec drove back to the office building with the lawyers, who wanted to examine for themselves the scene of the crime and confer further with Cec and herself. Then after a late lunch with Cec, in the restaurant in the building, she learned that Mrs. Dolansky would take her late husband's job in the office next day.

Maria left the office early and stopped off at a liquor store to get a bottle. She needed a drink.

* * *

When Val arrived home from work, Maria was fast asleep on the chesterfield, her body having succumbed to exhaustion after only one drink from the bottle of gin. But she awoke immediately she heard Val's key in the lock, and sat up, swinging her feet onto the floor as Val closed the door behind her.

"What happened to you?" Val asked, while taking off her raincoat. Then noticing Maria had been sleeping, and her pallid complexion, she went on, "Are you not feeling well?"

"I'm okay," Maria replied, then emphatically, "although it has been one bastard of a day. A day I never want to see another one like."

"Are you in some sort of trouble, Maria?"

"I don't think so; that is nothing I could get arrested for, or anything like that."

Val sat down on a chair, opposite the chesterfield, with a puzzled expression on her face, and Maria told her briefly what happened during the day; leaving out many of the details, and her own part in the shooting, depicting the murder of Dolansky as inexplicable and bizarre. Then to avoid the inevitable questions, Maria asked Val to pour some drinks from the bottle of gin she had left in the kitchen.

"Where did Debbie go tonight?" Maria asked, as Val went into the kitchen.

"She met Bill after work. They are going suite hunting." Val took two glasses from the cupboard, poured two stiff shots of gin, and went to the refrigerator for the mix. "If they find a suitable suite, they plan to move in before they get married." Coming back into the living room carrying the two drinks, Val gave one to Maria, and then sat down opposite her on the easy chair. "Debbie asked for a refund on her rent, if she moves before the end of the month."

"What did you tell her?" Maria asked.

"Bull shit," Val replied.

"What did you really tell Debbie?" Maria insisted.

Val smiled. "That is what I said."

Maria returned Val's smile. "We will have to give Debbie something back on her rent if she moves out before the end of the month. She will need every cent she can get for her wedding. Her parents are poor and they will not be able to help very much with the expenses."

"I know," Val said. Then she went on, "I thought I would tease her a little by giving her a bit of a hard time."

"Was she angry?" Maria asked.

"No. It didn't fizz on her, and she told me she was going to ask you anyway."

"About the murder at the office. Were you at work?" Val said, changing the subject. "Why would this Cec fellow be carrying a gun?"

"How the hell should I know, and it's none of your business anyway." Maria retorted angrily.

Getting up abruptly, Val left the room, and taking a tissue from a box in the kitchen she wiped the tears from her eyes. She didn't deserve that sort of treatment from Maria, and with Debbie leaving; Maria was the only friend she had. Val bent her head and closed her eyes, and the tears welled up in her eyes and ran down her cheeks.

In the living room, Maria drank down her gin. She was being angry without reason, and there wasn't anything she could do about it, her nerves were on edge, and she hoped the gin would calm her down.

Going to the kitchen window, Val leaned on the wall and looked down to the street. It was growing dark outside, and the cars had their lights on. She had no right to speak to me in that manner, and I will give her a piece of my mind Val thought; hostility growing within her. But she couldn't do it, and instead she went into the bedroom, took a tranquilizer, and sat on the bed until she felt calm.

Laying her head back on the chesterfield, Maria tried to relax while regretting having spoken sharply to Val. She heard Val go to the bedroom, then return to the kitchen. There was the sound of pots and pans being used, and the aroma of hamburgers frying, and when Val asked if she would like something to eat, Maria replied. "No thanks."

"I will put your supper in the refrigerator, and you can have it later if you wish."

"Thanks, Val," Maria said without opening her eyes, and she was aware of Val taking her empty glass and bringing her another drink of gin. Maria drank her gin slowly while Val was in the kitchen having her supper; too tired to apologize, she felt like a heel, but she would make it up to Val later. Exhausted and perplexed, Maria retired to the bedroom, undressed, and slipped between the cool sheets; to think about the man who fell before her gun, Ted's censure for the way she lived, the threat and the advantages of her work, her growing distrust of Cec as she learned more of the business, the action of Mrs. Jonson, who had opened the door to let the two men into the inner office, and enabled the murder of Dolansky.

Was Doc Ellis involved with the murder and running for his life? Was Danny in imminent danger? She longed to see him, confide in him, and feel the comfort and security of his embrace. But through it all, mingled with every thought, there was the specter of drugs as darkness crept slowly over the world outside. Debbie came home and joined Val in the kitchen, talking enthusiastically; sometimes aloud and then in whispers, a world apart from her own, as she turned from one position to another, restless, and attempting to sleep.

"We found a beautiful suite, and we are renting it from the middle of the month," Debbie was saying.

"Did you eat out?" Val asked.

"Yes, we had fish and chips downtown. The suite is really beautiful, and you should see it." Debbie's voice was alive with excitement.

"Is it as big as this one?" Val asked.

"Not quite, and it doesn't cost near as much, and we will be able to save money for a house. It is almost completely furnished." Debbie's voice became soft. Then after a while Maria heard her going to the refrigerator. "I'm going to have a bottle of beer."

"Perhaps you would like some gin," Val said, "Maria bought a bottle."

"Oh!" Debbie said, sounding surprised.

There was the sound of a chair being pushed back, and of gin gurgling into glasses. Maria felt good that her friends were helping themselves to the bottle.

"Did you hear about the murders at the office where Maria works? She is quite upset about it." Val's voice trailed off in a whisper as the girls put their heads together across the table.

Turning to another position in bed, Maria thought about the coming day. Mrs. Dolansky would be in charge of the office; Maria sighed. Who would take Mrs. Jonson's place? She sure as hell didn't want that job. Thank God her parents didn't know what had happened. Would Ted telephone and tell them? If he did, her father was liable to come to Vancouver.

Maria was still restless and awake; when after what seemed like hours, Val crept into bed. "You are still awake," Val whispered. "Everything is going to be okay." Then Val was asleep. But Maria, lay awake, still thinking of the day's events, of Danny, and for some unknown reason of Tom. Sleep escaped her for a long time, and while Val slept peacefully by her side, Maria lay awake and alone with her thoughts, until exhausted from the events of the day she slipped into a restless sleep.

The radio was playing in the kitchen when Maria awoke, and there was the aroma of coffee and bread toasting as Val prepared breakfast. Then getting out of bed and going to the mirror, Maria brushed her hair, and put on her dressing gown before going to the kitchen.

CHAPTER 17

Val came home alone, and after a brief greeting, she took a beer from the refrigerator, and came to sit alongside Maria on the chesterfield. Debbie had gone to Bill's place to cook supper for him coming home from work, Val explained. Then after downing some beer, Val continued. "Did you hear from Danny yet?"

"No," Maria replied, laying back on the chesterfield, "he told me when I saw him last that he wouldn't be in touch with me for a little while."

Val ran the tip of her tongue around her upper lip as she watched Maria, her breasts rising and falling, as she lay back on the chesterfield with her head tilted back. "Your suitcase and clothes, did you get them back?"

Sensing Val's suspicions, Maria shook her head slowly and continued to look at the ceiling. Her story about traveling for the company on the weekend, and leaving her suitcase at a hotel, had gone over like a lead balloon, and now it was as good a time as any to tell Val that she had been away with, Danny. Sitting up, Maria picked her cup of tea and took a drink before looking to Val. Both girls smiled knowingly as their eyes met. "Would you believe that I was out with Danny on the yacht, and my suitcase is still on the yacht?" Maria asked. Val nodded her head and smiled in reply. Maria, while neglecting to say anything about the mystery and intrigue that surrounded the trip, told her friend about her holiday with Danny, and her leaving her suitcase behind on the yacht when Danny had been recalled home by his father.

"Will the yacht be back In Vancouver by now?" Val asked.

"Probably," Maria replied.

"Then you can pick your suitcase up if you want to?" Val said inquiringly.

"I guess so."

"Since you need the clothes, why don't you go and get them?" Val asked. Maria shrugged.

"I will come with you", Val volunteered enthusiastically. "I would like to see the yacht, now that I have heard so much about it."

"Okay," Maria agreed with a smile. "We will freshen up a bit and drive over to the yachting club, and we can eat out afterwards instead of cooking."

* * *

It was hot and humid as the two girls drove to the club, the wind that had been blowing off the sea earlier in the day had died down, and a haze hung over the city. With some apprehension that they may not be allowed into the club, Maria drove slowly towards their destination. The man at the gate flagged their car down, and after hesitating for a moment before he recognized Maria, and reassured by her smile, he waved them on through the gate. Maria parked her car alongside the blue Cadillac that she recognized as belonging to the Leweses, and she thought of the possibility that Danny was in the club. The girls could see the masts of the boats moving to and fro against the background of a rocky shore as they walked towards the steps leading to the wharf. An elderly man, backing his car out of the parking lot, stopped and admired the long shapely legs of the two girls and their swinging hips, before he put his car into forward gear and drove away.

A young man leaned on the rail close to the gangway leading to the wharf, and Maria recognized him as a detective from the agency with whom she worked.

She smiled in response to the gesture of recognition that he made with his hand, although she was troubled by the thought that she was no longer the only detective who was allowed into the club. There must have been a new ruling since Dolansky's murder. The two girls stopped and looked down at the yachts tied up at the wharf. The Bliss-In rolled gently in the swell, and the sun shimmered from its masts, as the young woman lying on the deck chair in the shade of an awning put aside her book and looked up at the two girls. Realizing that this was Danny's wife, Maria noticed her pretty face, the whiteness of her skin, the platinum blond hair falling around her shoulders, her long slim legs, full breasts, and her stomach that was full with Danny's baby. A surge of jealousy swept through Maria, and she felt her face become hot as the woman returned to reading her book. In the next few weeks the baby would be born, and the slim delicate figure of the woman would return. Danny must have had the choice of many women to choose one with such beauty. Having no desire to meet the woman and at the same time wanting to get her suitcase, Maria felt angry.

"We can come back another day," Val said, turning away from the rail.

"Would you mind bringing the suitcase for me?" Maria asked, while she looked down on the yacht, to which without Danny she possessed no claim.

"If that is what you want, Maria?" Val replied.

"Danny's wife will have seen my clothing in the boat, so there is really nothing to hide. You could tell her that you are a friend of mine."

"Okay," Val said, adjusting the belt about the waist of her dress. Then with some apprehension, she went carefully down the steps to the wharf.

Mrs. Lewes put down her book as Val approached, and stood up as Val, stopped on the wharf alongside the boat. Looking up to Danny's wife, Val brushed back her hair with her hands, and explained her mission. Mrs. Lewes smiled and replied, while to Maria there were no voices; only the screech of the seagulls, the wash of the sea, and the rattle of the lines against the masts. Reaching out her hand, Mrs. Lewes helped Val aboard the boat, then after standing and talking for a few minutes the two women went below deck.

Turning away from the rail, Maria walked back to the car, and as she sat down behind the steering wheel an anger swept over her the like she had never felt before. She glanced at the man at the gate through the rearview mirror and tried to concentrate on his activities. He had stopped a car at the gate and was using the telephone in the small office; possibly to check whether he should allow the car to enter. Involuntarily, Maria's thoughts returned to Danny's wife as her anger continued unabaited, and even while she tried to reason that Danny's wife was not responsible for the dilemma, thoughts of violence welled up out of her subconscious.

The detective, who minutes before had been looking out over the wharf, was walking towards her car, with a concerned expression on his face, Maria's heart leaped within her; the expression on her face would betray her anger and he would know that there was something amiss.

"Hello," the detective said, as he came up to the car door.

"Hello," Maria replied, smiling reassuringly to the man, her calm composure and happy smile belied her inner anger. She realized that she, like her father, could appear self-possessed and calm under most any circumstances and conceal the turmoil within.

"Your friend," the detective said, with a note of concern in his voice; "she knows Mrs. Lewes?"

"Of course, they are friends", Maria replied lightheartedly, while her shining eyes and upturned face reassured the detective that nothing was amiss.

"This is my first time at the club," the detective said, returning Maria's smile. "They really have a lay out." Then he shook his head, before turning and walking leisurely back to his post overlooking the wharf.

After waiting a few more minutes for her anger to subside, Maria got out of the car and walked around the side of the club house to the lounge overlooking the wharf; she would have a drink while she waited for Val to return.

It was still hot and close outside as Maria sat down in the airconditioned lounge, and the shadows of the trees on the lawn outside were long in the evening sun. Most of the ten other people who saw her enter the lounge, noted her youth and slender figure, while Maria, engrossed in her own thoughts, chose a table close to a window.

"What can I bring you, Miss Petersen?" the waiter asked.

"A Pommery champagne please," Maria replied, looking up and smiling, upon being recognized, and because there were no cash registers in the club, she realized that the cost of the drink would be put on the Lewes' bill.

Fingering the stem of the glass, Maria sipped the champagne slowly. She was more like her father than she had realized. The trait which she had observed in her father, of a cold and sometimes, what seemed an irrational anger and the ability to conceal one's inner emotions had been passed on to her. She could understand her father and mother better now, and she recalled an incident that had happened years before when her father, dejected by a his job, had come home from work and told her mother that he would be the warehouse supervisor in one month while his casual manner had concealed from his daughter the boiling anger within.

"You will end up in jail, if you are not careful," Maria recalled her mother's words, which at the time seemed to be out of context.

"No Cathy, there will be nothing to tie me in," her father said, shaking his head and smiling. "A phone call to my brother in New York will start the ball rolling, and within a month the boss will be kissing my ass to become supervisor."

"No, Andrew. This is Canada and these things of which you talk should not take place here."

" They are giving me a raw deal," her father had reasoned, "we would be happy with the money the new job would bring, and you could visit your family in Ireland."

Her mother had cried, and Maria feeling unhappy and confused, hung to her mother's skirt.

"Andrew, I am happy; I have you and we have a fine daughter, and I want nothing else."

Maria had felt relieved when her father put his arms about her mother and said, "It is all right, Cathy, and there is nothing to be afraid of."

"Promise, Andrew that you won't do anything of what you are suggesting," her mother insisted. Then, and it was only after her father had promised, that her mother had dried her tears, and things returned to normal.

Maria sipped her drink. She could see the Bliss-In from where she was sitting, and Val and Danny's wife were still below deck. Away to the left the detective leaned on the rail overlooking the water, and out beyond the harbor wall, a motorboat pitched heavily into the swell, sending white spray high above its bow to fall on its deck, while foam bubbled in its wake. The air was still, and the sea would have been like a sheet of glass if it were not for the swell.

Once again Maria's mind drifted back in time, and she was a little girl again; she and her father had gone fishing early one Saturday morning and like today it was warm and humid. They had arrived at their favorite fishing spot on Lake Ontario early in the morning, and together they took the boat from the top of the car and launched it in the lake. She had thought at the time that her help was indispensable, although she knew now that this was not so, and her father was exceptionally strong. He kept himself fit by exercise and the necessity of hard manual work. He had unloaded their boat virtually alone, and it was her presence and willingness to help that had been his reward. They had been carefree and happy when they loaded the boat with the camping equipment and the fishing rods. Powered by their small outboard motor they headed for a small peninsula that was inaccessible except by boat, where they would set up camp, and be ready for Mother to join them when she got off work in the drug store where she worked. They pitched their tent on the tongue of land, and fished from the shore for a while without success, until a school of perch passed by and they caught six during the next half hour. They laughed and hugged each other in their excitement, then set about cleaning the fish and preparing dinner. They would have everything ready for a fish and chip dinner for Mother when she arrived. The bus was due at one o'clock and Father had gone to fetch her long before time. He had pulled his boat up the beach and was standing by the side of the road when the bus arrived. Maria watched through the binoculars as her mother alighted from the bus still wearing her white drug store uniform looking youthful and pretty. Father had said that she was the prettiest girl in the store and it was no lie. They came down the beach hand in hand, until her father picked her up in his arms and carried her the last few feet, as he waded into the water, and put her in the boat, before pushing it out stern first and climbing into the bow. Her mother started the motor, turned the boat around, and headed for their small camp. Then knowing that she would be watching them through the binoculars, her mother had waved when they were about half way across.

The noise of a motorboat filled Maria's ears, and a large inboard-outboard motorboat containing two young men and a young woman, swept into the bay. It turned abruptly around the small boat, and as the two boats drew alongside, the dark haired young woman in a bathing suit sitting on the motor cover, shouted something to her parents, before the boat turned abruptly once more and sped out of the bay. Maria shifted the binoculars back to her parents' boat. Her mother had throttled down the engine, and turned the small boat so that the bow would meet the waves left by the boat that had sped around them. A large wave broke over the bow and spilled water into the boat. She could see the muscles of her father's arms standing out under his thin cotton shirt as he gripped the gunwhale of the boat, as her mother tight lipped steered the boat as it tossed and turned in the turbulent waters. Then they were through and approaching the shore, and Maria ran to meet them as her mother shut off the motor and tilted it, before her father stepped into the shallow water and pulled the boat up onto the beach.

* * *

Focusing now on the present Maria, sipped her champagne, and looked across the harbor wall as a motorboat sped noisily into the harbor. Then turning her head she looked around the lounge and the waiter, watching her intently, smiled when their eyes met. Maria looked out to sea, and her mind went back in time.

Her mother's face was white when she stepped out of the boat, and Father hugged her close, and as they walked up to the camp hand in hand. Later, her mother gave her a small drink from her beer as they sat around the campfire, and it tasted like champagne.

"I will teach those kids a lesson that they will never forget," her father said.

"They are from Chatwell Marina," Maria recalled saying, "I saw the name on the boat."

"They were just kids having some fun, and they didn't know that what they were doing was dangerous," her mother said with concern.

"You could have drowned, Cathy," her father said, as he threw a stick of wood on the fire.

"Not with my lifeguard along," her mother countered with a smile.

"I know them, Dad. They are old Chatwell's kids, and they are always hanging around the marina."

"You would make a blood thirsty pair," her mother said, laughing at their desire for revenge. "It is a good thing that you have me to guide you along the straight and narrow path."

The straight and narrow path, Maria thought, as she looked around the room cautiously, wondering whether she had said these words aloud. The other patrons were busy with their own discussions, and only the waiter looked up from the counter that he was polishing as she looked towards him.

"Another drink, Miss Petersen?" He asked.

"No thanks," Maria replied, with a smile, and for the first time she noticed that her glass was empty. Then a shudder ran through her, and for a moment it felt as if the hair on her head was bristling, and she turned her head away from the waiter as he resumed polishing the counter. The young girl on the back of the boat, who had shouted something to her parents, was Mrs. Jonson. Maria closed her eyes, the woman had been a lot younger; still there was no doubt about it, and Mrs. Jonson was old Chatwell's daughter. Maria leaned back in the chair, and looked out to sea. There was a breeze off the water now, and some dark clouds in the west.

Val and Danny's wife had come on deck, and standing close and smiling as they talked, the breeze caught Mrs. Lewes' soft blond hair, shining bright in the dying sun. It looks bleached Maria thought; yet, somehow she knew that it was natural. There was no denying her beauty, and the anger that she had suppressed previously rose within her. Mrs. Lewes gave Val her hand, and helped her down onto the wharf before handing her the suitcase; and after a smile, a few words, and a wave Val walked away from the yacht, innocent gestures that would have meant nothing under different circumstances. But for a woman to behave so warmly and friendly when returning the clothes of her husband's lover went beyond an expression of tolerance and understanding, and Maria was suspicious that there was no love between Danny and his wife. Maria's anger left as quickly as it came, and she could have laughed aloud as she stood and straightened her soft blue dress. She glanced at her watch before leaving the lounge; the two women had been together for over an hour.

Changing their minds about wanting to eat out, Maria and Val drove directly home, and it was bacon and eggs for supper and a long talk while they drank their tea. After showing Val about the boat, Mrs. Lewes put Maria's clothes together and she talked with Val about her baby to be. Then while Val told Maria how charming Mrs. Lewes was, Maria's suspicion was confirmed; Danny was hers, to love, honor and cherish. Maria's happiness was complete, when Danny telephoned at nine o'clock and talked with her for about half an hour. He bad been ill for a time, and he would get in touch with her in a few days.

Debbie came home with her hair wet and her face flushed red, just as Maria hung up the telephone. The weather had changed, and it was raining cats and dogs. The girls voted whether they should have a cup of tea, or a bottle of beer before going to bed, and beer was voted in three to zero. Later while in their night attire and drinking their beers, Debbie divulged her secret.

"I'm going to have a baby," she announced.

"What!" Val exclaimed. "We might have thought as much, with the weight you have bean gaining, except that with all the precautions you said you were taking this was supposed to be impossible."

"Oh, that was before Bill and I knew each other very well," Debbie said, smiling in response to Val's surprise. "Now that we have fallen in love, Bill wants a baby, so I threw caution to the wind."

"How long have you been pregnant?" Maria asked.

Debbie wrinkled her brow with exaggerated contemplation before replying, "three or four days."

The three girls laughed together, and their conversation continued in another vein until it was time to retire. However, when Debbie was alone in bed she thought seriously about the baby, that she and Bill were planning for, and she was happy.

Chapter 18

Standing close to the hotel, Maria watched the traffic go by on the busy street. A bus stopped at the curb and the crowd of people disembarked. Should she go home to the dark apartment on such a beautiful day? And what of the assignment to recall something about Mrs. Jonson? Cec had withheld his fire; she would do the same and say nothing. She would like to see Danny, and she wondered what he was doing while the Leweses were keeping out of sight. Suddenly, her mind made up, she went into the hotel lobby and telephoned Tom's home. His mother answered; Tom had gone to the city to get the tractor generator repaired, and Maria might reach him at the Conten Tractor Repair Shop. Maria was thoughtful of the fact that Mrs. Balant had been pleasant and sounded like a very nice woman. Sitting on an easy chair with a cellular telephone still in her hand, Maria telephoned the number that Mrs. Balant had given her.

"Hello," Tom said, when after a few minutes, he came to the telephone in response to a call by the man who had answered the telephone.

"This is Maria. I thought I would call to see how you are doing?"

Tom was surprised, he was expecting it to be his mother wanting him to pick up some groceries on the way home, and he was happy when he heard Maria's voice. "I'm waiting for a generator to be repaired and it is taking longer than I expected. What are you doing, Maria?"

"Nothing really important as I have the afternoon off."

"Can I take you out to dinner?" Tom asked.

"I have just had dinner," Maria replied, "but we could meet somewhere if you wish?"

"How about a walk on the beach?"

"Okay," Maria replied, trying to sound reluctant, while in fact she was happy. She knew that Tom was smiling too. The game had been played too many times before to be convincing.

"Good. I will be at Kitsilano Beach in about half an hour, and I will wait for you there," Tom said, with unconcealed happiness.

Maria put the telephone into her purse, happy that what she had expected to be only a telephone conversation with Tom had culminated into a date.

* * *

Tom was sprawled out on the seat of his pickup truck, with his back against the door, when Maria parked her car alongside. Tom got down from the truck smiling, came to the car door, opened it, and kissed Maria lightly on the lips.

"This is a lot better than a dinner date," Maria said, laughing as she got out of the car.

"What did my mother have to say?" Tom asked.

"She explained why you were in the city and gave me the telephone number where I could reach you. She was very pleasant and not at all like I had expected. I thought all mothers would be over protective of their sons."

"They usually are," Tom said, smiling as he agreed with Maria. Then becoming serious, he continued. "I have talked a lot about you, and she wants to meet you." Tom paused before continuing, "I think you two would get along well."

Hand in hand, Maria and Tom walked to the front of the car and looked out over the park and the beach. A good number of families were picnicking while the parents sat in the shade of the trees while the children, oblivious to the heat, ran around playing on the grass.

"Just a minute," a little girl shouted, as her friends waited for her to return the ball.

Then with her hand she put the last piece of a bun in her mouth before continuing with the game, and Maria and Tom turned to each other and laughed. The beach was crowded. Color and action everywhere; the blue sky, the sea, the sand, sun hats, bathing suits, beach balls being thrown to and fro, and children and youths running and splashing at the water's edge.

"There are more people than I had hoped for," Tom said, turning to Maria. "There is another beach a little way from here, where we would have more privacy if you don't mind the steep walk in from the road."

"It sounds exciting," Maria said, smiling as she looked into Tom's eyes.

"We will go in the truck," Tom said. and together they turned to leave.

Then with her blue mini dress tight about her thighs, Maria, holding Tom's hand, stepped high to get into the cab.

* * *

Emerging from the trees after a long steep walk along the path to the beach, Maria and Tom took each other's hands and stood looking out over the deserted beach, where large logs, bleached white with sun, were strewn close against the trees. Large waves rolled in from the sea, shone white in the sun as they broke and swept up onto the sand, sending the water high up onto the beach before receding to meet incoming waves. In the sky, seagulls soared in the wind blowing off the water

The sun was high in the sky as they sat down on a log bleached nearly white by the sun, and removed their shoes, then went down to the sea, with their shoes in their hands, they let the cool water wash over their feet. Tom removed his shirt, exposing his bronze body to the warm sun, and a little further out a wave swirled around Maria's legs.

"I'll race you to the points" Maria said. And she ran along the water's edge with her black hair trailing and blowing in the wind .

Tom gave chase, until out of breath, they turned up onto the beach, threw their shoes on the sand, and sat down behind a barricade of logs to shelter themselves from the wind. Maria closed her eyes as Tom kissed her, and taking his lips into her mouth she bit him gently, while he cupped a breast in his hand. Then pushing Tom lightly away, Maria stood up and looked out over the beach. "Let's go for a swim before some other people come," she said, as Tom stood up beside her.

The water felt cold to their warm and naked bodies as they ran into the sea, and dived into an oncoming wave. Then close together, they did a backstroke away from the beach, rising and falling in the swell as they moved their limbs rhythmically through the water. "They must be having rough weather on the outside for the waves to be this big here," Tom said. Then a large wave broke over them, and when they surfaced, they laughed before turning and swimming slowly back to the beach, where they ran over the sand to their shelter of logs.

Maria felt fresh and alive, as Tom dried the water from her body with his shirt. Then she put her jeans and blouse under her and the sand was soft and warm on her back as she lay down behind some logs and, out of the wind. Still standing, Tom dried himself and put his shirt over the logs to dry, then closing her eyes Maria listened to the sound of the wind in the trees and the waves breaking on the beach. Tom's lips were warm on her stomach, as holding his head gently between her hands he lay face down between her legs. Then all sound was gone, and only her sense of touch remained, as Tom's tongue, incessant in its movements, glided between her legs. Coupled with this sensation was the warmth of the sun on her face and breasts as with his hands around her buttocks, Tom moved her up to meet him. Then as Tom kissed her stomach, breasts, and lips; Maria, with her, passions in full flower, arched her body to meet him, for a while to become one. While a short distance away, the sea rose and fell as the waves traveled to the beach, where, with a tremendous release of energy, they crashed white upon the sand. Sheltered from the wind, Maria and Tom parted and lay side-by-side and rested. The warm sun caressed their bodies and the sound of the surf was a background to their thoughts.

Later, with an arm about each other, their clothes in a bundle under Tom's arm, they walked slowly back along the beach. Then they stopped and listened; the sound of voices was coming to them over the sound of the waves rolling onto the beach. And as they looked along the tree line above the driftwood in the direction of the voices, the sound faded and became lost amid the trees. Alone once more with only the soaring seagulls to witness their kiss before they slipped on their clothes, then with an arm about each other's waists they continued their leisurely walk along the beach.

After a while the sound of voices came to them again, and two young couples emerged from the trees, at the path leading back through the trees, to stand for a time looking out over the beach. Stripped to the waist and wearing blue jeans, they returned Maria's and Tom's waves without hesitation or embarrassment. One of the boys put a case of beer down on the sand, and his girlfriend, fingered the gold cross that hung between her budding breasts. The other girl threw a red and blue beach ball away from her, and with cries and laughter they all ran after it, rushing to retrieve it before it reached the sea.

With the wind blowing their hair loose about their heads, Maria and Tom stopped to kiss and hold each other in their arms. While the four young persons kicked the ball, and as happy and as free as the gulls that drifted high above their heads, ran by them close to the sea.

CHAPTER 19

Looking forward to seeing her two friends when they came home from work, Maria busied herself cooking supper. Tom had left the suite at four-thirty, and since that time she had taken a bath, brushed her hair, applied makeup, and put on a fresh red dress before starting to cook. Maria possessed a whole new outlook to life compared to the way she had felt before seeing Tom. Unaware of the drama unfolding on the coast of Oregon, Maria's thoughts involuntarily returned to Danny, and as she put the cutlery on the table, she shivered as if from the cold.

* * *

Debbie closed the outer door of the suite as Val did a pirouette in the middle of the room, then stopping abruptly, her blond hair, swung about her face. "I'm going to work on the payroll tomorrow," she announced happily.

"You're going up in the world," Maria said, smiling in response to Val's happy mood.

"Why not, she is always flirting with Mr. Evans," Debbie said seriously, with just the hint of wink to Maria.

"It's not true," Val, replied. Then with concern in her voice, she looked to Maria for support.

"He has always given you preferential treatment for some reason," Maria said.

Then after seeing a smile pass between her two friends, Val realized that they were happy for her advancement, and she smiled. "It will mean a raise you know," she said happily.

"When?" Maria asked, continuing to smile with Debbie, because of the sheer delight on Val's face.

"Oh, I don't know yet," Val replied. "When I have learned the work I suppose. Mr. Evans asked me to come to his office after work, and he told me then that I would be starting on the payroll tomorrow to learn the work." However, Val didn't tell her two friends everything, although it came to her mind.

* * *

"Come in," Mr. Evans said. Val felt afraid as she entered the office. Perhaps she was being laid off. "Take a seat," Mr. Evans continued, indicating a chair to Val, as he got up from behind his desk to close the door. Then still apprehensive that she would lose her job, Val sat down facing the desk while the girls in the outer office were leaving for home. Mr. Evans put his hands on the back of Val's chair and looked down at her neatly groomed hair. "I'm putting you to work on the payroll tomorrow," he said. Val felt a flood of relief, then happiness, and leaning back in the chair she tilted her head back to smile up at Mr. Evans. Then as he returned her smile, he cupped her breasts in his hands from behind. "You will like the work Val," he said, as he went back behind his desk to explain that she would be learning the work for a while, before she took over the job on a regular basis.

Val felt more secure now that her boss was taking a personal interest in her, and the nipples of her breasts were still hard and tingling when the interview ended.

"Thank you Sir," Val said smiling as Mr. Evans showed her to the door.

* * *

On learning that their friend was not getting an immediate raise with her new job, Maria and Debbie became serious, and Val, feeling sheepish, was glad they did not know the full story.

"The payroll clerk is quitting to have her baby in a week's time, so you will be on your own in a week. How long did Mr. Evans say it would be before you get the raise?" Debbie asked pointedly.

"Mr. Evans will be helping me for a while after the payroll clerk quits," Val said, preparing her defense, "and it will be about a month or so before I get a raise."

Anger rose quickly in Debbie. "Holy suffering." Then she stopped the edge taken off her anger. Whatever else there was to the oath was beyond repeating; perhaps in recollection of when she had heard the oath before, or perhaps she recalled the words of a high school teacher, who told his class that violent outbursts were the mark of the gutter. "If you are not going to be paid for the work, Val, you should tell Mr. Evans to stick the job up his ass."

"He would fire me?" Val reasoned.

Debbie frowned, she wouldn't want Val to lose her job, but there was a limit to what one could take. "You should get in touch with the union," she said.

"That wouldn't do any good either," Maria said, "Val is still on temporary staff and she is not covered by the union." Maria could see there was something more to the situation than met the eye. Did Mr. Evans see some promise in Val that was not evident in another girl who had worked with the company for a long time, and who did the payroll when the regular girl was on holiday? "Mr. Evans is a creep," Maria said, shifting the blame for Val's predicament to where it belonged.

"I wouldn't do a job that I am not being paid for," Debbie insisted. "I would starve first."

Her two friends were up tight, however Maria could not help herself from smiling. It wasn't likely that Debbie would ever starve; she was shrewd and well able to take care of herself.

"It is easy to talk, and a hell of a sight harder to act." Val said, almost in tears.

"I know," Debbie conceded, "and I'm sorry."

"No, I'm glad you brought it up. Don't think I didn't consider quitting, because I did. Then suppose I had quit. Do you think I would be as lucky as Maria to get another job right away? I haven't worked long enough to go on unemployment insurance. I don't have a cent saved so I could accept handouts from you and Maria, or go on welfare." Val was angry now and the tears ran down her face as she continued. "I would not go back home to my parents; they think that I am well set, and have it made. Besides, I didn't come all the way to Vancouver to quit. I came here to work." Val had become emotional and she broke down and sobbed as Maria and Debbie looked on in dismay. "But if you both think I should quit, I will quit anyway," Val continued through her sobs. "Well Maria, if you think I should quit too, I will tell Mr. Evans where he can stick his fucking job."

Realizing that Val would follow her advice, and with the eyes of both girls upon her, and not knowing the full story, Maria backed away from saying anything that would cause more hardships for Val; even while knowing that in spite of the certainty of being fired and looking for another job without a recommendation, and under the same circumstances she would not have accepted the position. The recollection of the trauma she had felt when she was fired was too fresh in her mind to subject Val to the same experience. "You don't have much choice Val," Maria said, "it's a better job than typing, and if you stick it out for a while you will gain some good experience. Then if Mr. Evans doesn't come through with the raise you can see what the union can do. Then even if you do get fired, you will have enough time in to get on the unemployment insurance."

"Why didn't Evans give the job to Lorraine?" Debbie asked, not willing to let the matter drop, and deliberately dropping out the Mr. to show her disrespect for the office manager. "Lorraine has more seniority, and the talk has been that she would probably get the job. Evans would have had to give her the raise."

"That is probably why she didn't get the job," Val said, having partly recovered her composure.

"The bastard!" Debbie exclaimed. "You would think the money was coming out of his own pocket."

"I have supper ready," Maria said, "so let's eat. I have a university class tonight, and I don't have any time to spare."

The three girls went into the kitchen, wiser, and serious. "Are you mad at me, Debbie?" Val asked.

"No, I'm not mad at you," Debbie said, with sincerity, and she forced a smile as she sat down at the table opposite Val and Maria.

Maria was glad the confrontation between her two friends was over; Debbie would stand by Val in the office in the coming days, when the other girls would see fit to attack her. Mr. Evans? Debbie would treat him like a king as long as he didn't cross her; and if he did, she would stand her ground and be a rebel like none he had ever known. Maria had an idea that Mr. Evans knew this too, and the relationship between Debbie and Mr. Evans, would be one of quiet diplomacy. The girls in the office knew Debbie also, and they would let many things slide with Val, rather than risk confrontation with Debbie. With a tendency to be quiet and serious, Debbie was popular with the girls, although there was something about her that commanded their respect.

* * *

The following afternoon, Maria parked the car in the parkade of the store where her friends worked. It was a beautiful day outside, with the temperature in the eighties, while in the parkade it was dark and damp, and the low ceilings gave her the feeling of being trapped. However, it wasn't just the parkade; Mrs. Dolansky had been a perfect bitch all the morning, and in her own sly way she had badgered Maria to recall further information about

Mrs. Jonson. Although Maria had told her first thing in the morning that she hadn't come up with anything new. It was almost as if Mrs. Dolansky was aware that she knew Mrs. Jonson, but she would not tell her anything, although she would discuss her knowledge of Mrs. Jonson with Cec later. Maria had noticed Mrs. Dolansky watching her closely on a number of occasions during the morning, while she and Cec were busy preparing a statement of what had occurred for their lawyers, during the day Mr. Dolansky was murdered. Mrs. Dolansky had the knack of making one feel uneasy. Then at one time she had come up to the desk where Maria was typing, and when Maria looked up, she smiled weakly and meaningfully, telling Maria without words that if she didn't remember something soon, then she wouldn't be needed at the office.

Sitting in the parked car, Maria felt depressed and angry. Her job was to protect Danny Lewes, and now it was almost a week since she had heard from him. Mrs. Dolansky had reminded her of this fact before she told her to take another afternoon off to try to recall something about Mrs. Jonson, but she had no intention of telling her anything about Mrs. Jonson. However, it was her final statement that disturbed Maria the most. "Perhaps if you were alone for a while you would find it more opportune to recall the information we need," Mrs. Dolansky said, and Maria was suspicious that she was being kept under surveillance and she had been seen with Tom. If Danny did not get in touch with her soon, she would have to quit.

Had the car that followed her into the parkade been with her since she drove away from the office? Maria didn't know, and she waited in her car to see who it was that drove in behind her. A man and woman got out of their car and went into the store. If it wasn't for the fact that she had promised to meet with Phylis during the dinner hour, and help her with the arrangements for Debbie's shower party, Maria would have driven out of the parkade. It was supposed to have been a surprise party, but, since Debbie and Bill had already been living together in their apartment. Phylis thought it might be a good idea to have the party there, as most of the girls at the office said that they would like to see the place where Debbie and Bill were living. Debbie had no objections, and she had cried when Phylis told her about the plans.

The noise of the car door slamming echoed through the parkade as Maria vented her frustrations on the car. Methodically, she pulled on the door handle to make sure it was locked, dropped the keys into her purse, and went into the store. The man and woman she had seen in the parkade were nowhere in sight. She wished she had one of Val's tranquilizers with her.

She was jumpy, and in no mood to see Phylis. In the store a man, walking with the aid of a cane, was in front of her as Maria hurried towards the escalator to take her down to the ground floor. She tried to pass, but he seemed to monopolize the whole aisle and blocked her way. Annoyed, she waited behind him as he paused in front of the escalator, put his cane cautiously onto a stair, and shuffled forward dragging one leg behind as he took hold of the moving rail, then he was off balance and teetering forward on the descending stairs. Startled, the adrenaline flowed into Maria's blood, and her hands grabbed instinctively his shabby coat to prevent him from falling, but it was unnecessary. The man's cane shot out ahead of him, found a grip on a lower stair, and held. Then bending forward almost double, he steadied himself and with an awkward lurch pulled his cane back to a higher stair and straightened his body. An old man, he turned to Maria and smiled; a silent tribute for her gesture of help. She returned his smile, glad that an accident had been averted and admiring his mental fortitude that carried him on without a trace of bitterness in his face. He got off the escalator easily, and with his cane going before him to steady his body as he dragged one leg behind, he shuffled away. Turning towards the toy department, Maria caught the reflection of herself in a mirror; the blue mini dress she had borrowed from Val looked nice. She was happy again and how the old man's smile of gratitude had helped.

In the toy department, Phylis was showing two small boys how to operate a battery run tractor. The embroidered band of cloth about her forehead, the long string of beads about her neck, and the colorful dress gave her a hippy like appearance that was appealing to the children. "I will be getting off for dinner in a few mlnutes," Phylis said, as Maria came up to the counter. Then obviously enjoying her work, she tousled the hair of the two boys and showed them again, how the tractor could be made to climb over small obstacles.

"There is no hurry," Maria said with a smile. "I am going to buy some lipstick, and I will be back in a few minutes."

At the beauty counter, Maria looked at the lipstick display, until a young girl came to assist her, and pushed the tray of lipsticks across the counter towards Maria. "We have some other brands too, if you would like to see them, Miss," the girl said.

"No thanks," Maria replied, noticing the girl's slender hands, painted fingernails, expensive bangle, and diamond ring. "I will take this one," Maria continued, and after choosing a lipstick from the display, she raised her eyes, and looked at the girl. Her clothes, like her jewelry, were expensive, and Maria knew immediately that she was speaking to Glenda.

"You are Maria Petersen," the girl said in a pleasant and friendly voice. Maria nodded and smiled. "I'm Glenda," the girl said. "Perhaps Debbie and Val have told you about me. I stayed with them at the suite for a while."

"Yes, they told me about you," Maria said, returning the girl's smile. "They said that you had come back to work at the store after quitting."

"I tried to find a better job, and I discovered it wasn't easy, so I came back to this work to make ends meet."

This was a different story than Debbie and Val had told, still; a girl wasn't likely to admit that she was making money pushing drugs. "I recognized you when you were talking to Phylis," Glenda said. Maria raised her eyebrows, and Glenda continued, "I see Debbie and Val quite often and they are always talking about you and they said that you were pretty."

"I'm right out of quarters, Glenda."

Glenda smiled then looked down to the other end of the counters, the other girl was serving a customer, and two more customers were waiting. Glenda took the lipstick from the display and pretended to be showing it to Maria. "I don't mind this job really as I get to meet a lot of nice people, and I get to see the world going by." A customer advanced along the counter towards them, and Glenda held the lipstick up a little higher. "This shade would suit you; it goes nicely with your complexion." The customer turned and went back to the other end of the counter.

"You have heard about Debbie's shower?" Maria asked.

"Yes", Glenda replied enthusiastically, "and I am really looking forward to going." Maria didn't want to keep Phylis waiting and handed Glenda the money for the lipstick.

"You are working for ... ?" Glenda's question trailed off, and she waited for Maria to reply.

"The Plastick Utensil Company," Maria replied. "Office work and some selling. It gives me more freedom than when I worked here."

"It must be a good position. Val tells me they supply you with a car."

"It is not too bad," Maria said smiling. Why was Glenda prying for more information, when Val and Debbie had told her everything they knew?

The girl at the other end of the counter had finished serving the customers who had been waiting, "I'm going for lunch now," Glenda, she said. Then with a wave as she was leaving, she continued, "I will see you."

Glenda rang the money up in the till and put the lipstick in a bag as a customer came along and stood close to them. "I will be getting off in an hour," Glenda said. "Perhaps we could have lunch together?"

"Thanks Glenda, but I have promised to have lunch with Phylis, and she should be getting off any minute now."

"Oh well, I will see you at the party then."

"Okay," Maria replied, and turning she walked away towards the toy department. Was Glenda suspicious that she might be checking on her drug activities? She seemed to make a point of saying that she needed to work for the money, when everything she wore indicated otherwise.

Maria threaded her way through the crowded store towards the toy department. Glenda had found out all she could from Val and that had been enough to arouse her suspicions and want more information.

"I'm sorry to have kept you waiting," Phylis said, as she came out from behind the counter, where the toys were arranged skillfully along its length to attract the attention of children.

"That's all right," Maria, said pleasantly, "I talked to Glenda for a while."

"There is a nice hotel down the street a couple of blocks, where they serve damn good hamburgers in the bar. That's if you don't have someplace else in mind?" Phylis said.

"The hamburger sounds okay."

"This way," Phylis said, and the two girls, in single file because of the crowd, walked towards the exit. Glenda watched them go, Phylis holding the door for Maria to go through first, and with a frown on her face, Glenda went to the other end of the counter where a customer was looking at some perfume.

The noise of the traffic and the warm sun, reflecting its bright light from the pavement greeted Maria and Phylis as they emerged from the store. They put on their sunglasses as they walked past a lineup waiting at a bus stop, and then walking together, they fell into step with one another.

"Did you sell the tractor afterwards?" Maria asked.

"Weren't those two boys cute?" Phylis said, glancing to Maria and smiling. "They loved that tractor, and their mother bought them one each."

"You have everything it takes to have boys like that yourself, Phylis."

The two girls looked at each other and smiled. "I have been thinking about it seriously, and I am planning for the day. How about you, Maria?"

"No plans," Maria said, cheerfully, and then after a pause she continued. "I am living from day to day and making the most of it."

Walking with the agility and ease of youth, Maria and Phylis continued without haste as they drank in the pleasure of living; happiness on their faces, laughter in their eyes, and their minds reveling in the power of nature which was theirs. The seeds of life, the destiny of the species, entrusted to them and their kind to do with what they may. No wine as heady or bouquet as fragrant as this power bestowed by nature; but with it there was a responsibility, the gravity of which stirred their thoughts to contemplate the future.

The two girls entered the hotel, took off their sunglasses, and peered around in the dim light of the barroom. Then, as their eyes became accustomed to the darkness, they spotted a vacant table across the room. Noticing the lingering glances of some men as they moved slowly among the tables, they made their way to the table and sat down, with their backs against a dark wood paneled wall. The waiter took their order, and returned with their beer promptly. The waitress would bring the hamburgers and chips in a few minutes. There were a lot of arrangements to be made for Debbie's shower, and the girls made a list of the things that they would need for the party before deciding on the games that would be played.

"What about the beer?" Phylis asked, as she returned her glass to the table.

"Two or three cases should be enough, and maybe a bottle of wine in case some of the girls don't like beer," Maria replied, and Phylis agreed with a nod of her head. Maria added the cost of the necessary things they would have to buy, and together, after some further calculations and considerations. Maria and Phylis decided that they would charge the girls coming to the party ten dollars each, and they would be responsible for bringing their own presents. Maria picked up the list from the table and put it in her purse. She would purchase the groceries and liquor and deliver them to Debbie's new suite. Their beers were half finished, and as they started on the hamburger and chips that the waitress had left a few minutes before, they relaxed and enjoyed their meal while drinking the beer. Enjoying each other's company the, girls continued to converse.

"Three of the girls, I contacted about the shower, asked if we could have marijuana at the party," Phylis said, as soon as the waiter was out of earshot.

"I don't think so, Phylis. Debbie wouldn't want it, and it may get her into trouble just at the time when she should be happy."

"I have already told them no," Phylis said, "but I thought I should see what your reaction would be."

Thoughtful of what Phylis had asked, Maria looked around the dimly lit room. The room was filled with patrons, and four or five couples waited for tables. "Was one of the girls who asked about marijuana, Glenda?" Maria asked, as she turned back to Phylis.

"No," Phylis replied, perhaps too quickly, "Glenda wouldn't stay at a party if drugs were being used."

"Why?" Maria asked, lifting her glass of beer from the table.

"Because she used to be a pusher, and now she doesn't want to get involved," Phylis replied.

"It was Glenda who asked you to get my opinion after you had turned the other girls down."

"What are you trying to get at?" Phylis asked, her eyes narrow with suspicion.

"I think Glenda is still pushing drugs," Maria replied, as Phylis, her face serious and thoughtful looked into her eyes, "and she is using you to help ply her trade."

"Because she asked me to get your opinion?" Phylis asked, confirming Maria's suspicion.

"Partly", Maria said, and because the conversation was becoming unpleasant, she did not continue.

"What do you mean?" Phylis asked, prompting Maria to go on.

"Do you or your boyfriend use drugs?" Maria asked. "We don' t have any use for them," Phylis replied. Then while smiling, she continued. "My boyfriend, I guess you could call him my husband as we have been living together for over a year."

Maria smiled at Phylis' frank exposure, then Phylis went on. "We love each other very much and we have a near perfect relationship, but John just has a thing against marriage, and I haven't pressed the issue. My parents are not very happy about it, and it does cloud their relationship with us."

"You do know where to obtain drugs if you did want them?" Maria asked, "and you tell your friends where they can be bought if they ask?"

Phylis nodded. "Our friends think we are a bit hippy, and they ask us where they can get drugs."

"Can't they always be obtained from the same persons?" Maria enquired.

"No. Glenda quit selling, and the man who took over from her is serving a year in jail for pushing marijuana. Now there are two new chaps who have taken over from him."

"How do you find out who the pushers are?"

"Oh I don't know," Phylis, replied, "I suppose I ask around. I know that my friends are going to expect me to know, so I make a point of finding out who they are."

"Does Glenda know where drugs can be purchased?" Maria asked getting closer to the point; she was trying to make.

"I believe so, because she knew all these people when she was a pusher herself."

"If someone asks Glenda where they can purchase drugs she always refers them to you?"

"I don't know," Phylis replied. "Although, Glenda has referred some people to me."

Pausing in their conversation, Maria and Phylis looked at each other thoughtfully. "I see what you mean." Phylis said, "Glenda is still pushing drugs, except that other people make the actual contacts and sales for her."

"Exactly," Maria said. "Unwittingly, you have been helping her by telling your friends who her front end men are. Glenda has taken a cut on the money she would make on a sale in order to insulate herself from arrest. However, it seems that she has increased her business as she hires at least two men to work for her."

"Perhaps you are right," Phylis conceded. "But it won't continue, as I don't want to be party to any of her schemes." Then after a thoughtful pause, Phylis continued. "Did you tell anyone else of your suspicions?"

"No," Maria replied.

Phylis picked up her glass to take a drink, then changing her mind, she put the glass down on the table again. "I won't mention it to anyone either; because if you are correct, it could be dangerous. This friend of Glenda's, you know he is the one who used to go out with Val?"

Maria nodded and said, "You mean Charlie?"

And Phylis went on, "I think he is somehow involved in the drug trade, and he would beat you to a pulp if you happened to be right about it."

"Thanks for warning me," Maria said. "I didn't think it was that rough, and I don't think Glenda trusts me even now."

"Then don't do anything to arouse her suspicions Maria, as I don't want to see you come to any harm."

"I'm going to be innocent from here on in," Maria said, smiling to cover up the shiver she felt in her spine and the ominous feeling that she knew she shared with Phylis.

The two girls left the hotel, and standing for a minute or two in the sun on the crowded sidewalk outside, they talked about the wedding shower until Phylis went back to the store.

CHAPTER 20

Looking up from the column of figures she was checking, Betty smiled when Maria entered the outer office of the Plastick Utensils Company, their cheerful exchange of morning greetings in sharp contrast to the weather outside.

"The dress you are wearing suits you, Maria. Is it new?"

"No, I brought it from Toronto with me, and it is one of my favorites," Maria replied, returning Betty's smile.

"We have some new faces inside, this morning," Betty said.

"Oh," Maria said, raising her eyebrows.

"Mrs. Dolansky, Cec, and two other guys came in about eight-fifteen. Cec asked me to make coffee, and told me to ask you to bring it in when you arrived."

"Would you like a cup of coffee too?" Maria asked, taking the raincoat from over her arm and hanging it on the clothes hanger beside Betty's.

"Please," Betty replied, and then she turned as a customer came through the outer door, and Maria went into the office.

While carrying the tray of coffee, Maria thought about Mrs. Jonson. She wasn't sure, whether she should tell Mrs. Dolansky what she had remembered. It seemed that the decision was coupled with the decision of whether or not Mrs. Jonson was an accomplice to Dolansky's murder.

The customer had left when Maria returned to the reception room, set a coffee down by Betty's side, and waited while Betty helped herself to cream and sugar. "The styrofoam cups are going like hot cakes," Betty said. "That's the second batch of a thousand that I have sold this morning."

"Oh, that reminds me," Maria said. "A friend of mine is having a party on Saturday. Could you get me thirty or so styrofoam cups and plates?"

"Sure. I will put them in your car for you when I go out for lunch, and I will wangle it through the books."

"That's all right, Betty, I don't mind paying for them."

Betty put an elbow on the desk and with a hand under her chin she looked up to Maria. "That's the first time that anyone has offered to pay for anything around here. There is no necessity for you to pay, Maria. It is one of the benefits that come with the job. Everyone gets their plastic utensils free - even Dolansky got these benefits."

"Fair enough," Maria said with a smile, and she waited while Betty spoke on the intercom to the inner office.

Moments later, Cec opened the door for Maria to enter the private office, then he took the tray and together they walked to his desk; around which, Mrs. Dolansky and two men were seated. It struck Maria as odd that they would not be sitting in Dolansky's office, and it was not until after the introductions had been completed, and Cec had explained, that she understood. The two men were new detectives who had been sent up to the agency from the head office in New York to bolster their ranks. Cec was taking over Dolansky's job of running the agency, and Mrs. Dolansky was retiring on her husband's pension. Mrs. Dolansky, still pale and drawn from the shock of her husband's death, had known of the situation for a couple of days, and it was apparent that she was not happy. They had just finished their coffees, when the detective whom Maria had seen at the yachting club some days before, entered the office and after being introduced to the two new men, all three left the office together on some prearranged tasks. Then without saying a word, Mrs. Dolansky went to her late husband's office and started to clean out the desk in preparation for leaving.

"Congratulations Cec," Maria said, now that she and Cec were alone, and she started to put the coffee cups back onto the tray.

"Thanks," Cec said with a smile, as standing with Maria, he helped her with the cups. "Would you like another coffee?"

"Okay," Maria replied, and picking up the tray, she led the way to the outer office.

"I felt quite insecure when Mrs. Dolansky was the manager;" Maria began, when she and Cec had sat down with their coffees at a vacant desk in the outer office. "Were these feeling groundless or justified?"

"Your feelings were more than justified." Cec replied, the click, click of a typewriter and their distance from the other people in the office, giving privacy to his words. "Mrs. Dolansky wanted to get rid of you, immediately after her husband was killed, and that was one of the reasons that she and I quarreled violently on the morning after his death."

"She considered me to be incompetent?" Maria asked raising her eyebrows.

"On the contrary, she considered you to be extremely, competent. This she had learned from her husband, a few days before he died," Cec paused before going on. "About a week ago Mr. Dolansky asked me for a full report on the progress you were making in becoming a detective, and my opinion of your usefulness to the agency. It was a verbal report and we discussed your merits as a detective with the agency in some length. Your competence was beyond Dolansky's expectations, and he agreed that you could be a very valuable employee, but he was concerned that you had learned more about our operations than he had intended you to know, and he had uncovered some additional information about your background, which for some reason had not turned up in our previous enquiries. It was because of this, that Dolansky was extremely interested in my opinion of whether you could be trusted with the information you had gained, and was sincere in wanting to see that the Leweses came to no harm." Cec took a drink of his coffee, then continued, "frankly he was considering terminating your employment; nevertheless, he went along with my opinion that your motives for working with us, while not being altruistic, were not deceitful. This together with your relationship with Danny, and your usefulness to his protection, convinced Dolansky that you should stay."

Their conversation was not the casual exchange over a cup of coffee that Maria thought it was going to be. She had been unaware of any considerations of terminating her employment, and how could they terminate the employment of someone like herself, who already knew too much. The train of Cec's statements had underlined the danger of her position and gave emphasis to the part he had played in convincing the Dolanskys of her trustworthiness. Then there was the additional information in her background, which Dolansky had uncovered. Was this at least in part the reason why consideration had been given to getting rid of her?

"Why did Mrs. Dolansky wish to get rid of me?" Maria asked, as the click, click, of the typewriters continued, and the work in the office went on uninterrupted.

"She was deeply disturbed by the loss of her husband, and the mystery surrounding his death made her distrustful of your motives for working with the agency, and your loyalty to the Leweses." Cec smiled, relieving the gravity of their conversation before he went on. "But she has no influence in your career now."

"In your opinion, Cec, what were the motives for my accepting the job?" Maria asked, relieved now that Mrs. Dolansky no longer had any power over her.

Cec showed his bright even teeth in a broad smile. "Okay," he said, "let's see if our views coincide. Basically, you have a fear of being poor, and you like to live high off the hog. However, you have a tendency to be lazy, and this, together with your self concept and your background, makes it impossible for you to be happy in the kind of menial work that most young girls, because of social conditions, must do to earn a living. In the beginning you saw this job as an escape from the necessity of a nine to five routine, and at the same time a chance to enjoy yourself with Danny. Also, there were good wages, a car, and the convenience and prestige that go along with these." Maria was about to speak, but Cec held up his hand. "That was in the beginning Maria, since then you have learned that there are dangers in the job which you had not anticipated, and you continue with the work because you love Danny."

They sipped their coffees quietly for a time, while Maria gave thought to Cec's analysis; over simplified, and only partly correct, Maria concluded. In a self-analysis, she would have emphasized a passion to live while she was still young and her love for Danny as reasons for taking the job. Maria was aware that Cec had deliberately neglected to shed more light on the new information that had turned up in her past, and why Mr. Dolansky had considered getting rid of her. Now that Cec was in charge, what was his consideration for her future? As far as possible, she would avoid trouble, but if there was an attempt to bring her harm, she would unleash fury like the organization wouldn't believe. Mr. Watson, the office manager, was walking towards them across the office, and Maria postponing her questions smiled and asked, partly in jest. "Are we still friends, Cec?"

"On the condition that, you don't analyze my motives," Cec replied. And they both laughed together as Mr. Watson, followed by three office girls, came to the coffee maker to get some coffee.

"Another cup of coffee?" Mr. Watson asked, turning to Maria and Cec. Maria looked to Cec, and he nodded accepting for both of them.

"Pour a cup for Betty too," Maria said, and getting up she walked to where Mr. Watson was pouring the coffee.

When Maria returned after taking the coffee to Betty, the three girls and the two men were sitting at the table, drinking their coffee and talking about the weather.

"Did you tell them about your promotion, Cec?" Maria asked, sitting by him at the table.

"No, I thought that you would make the announcement."

The interest of the three girls and Mr. Watson quickened, and they turned their eyes to Maria and waited for her to speak.

"Cec has taken over the position of manager from Mrs. Dolansky," she announced with a smile.

The girls and Mr. Watson were happy. Cec accepted their congratulations politely, and asked one of the girls to take a cup of coffee to Mrs. Dolansky. Then the conversation continued with Mr. Watson telling them about his holiday to the Caribou country.

When Cec and Maria had finished drinking their coffees, they stood up to go back to the inner offices, and Watson and the girls returned to their desks.

"You were saying that Mr. Dolansky had uncovered some additional information about my background," Maria said as they walked to the door.

"Yes, and I was thinking that we should discuss it as soon as Mrs. Dolansky has left."

"There is one other thing," Maria said, as Cec took a key from his pocket to open the door to the inner office. "I remembered something about Mrs. Jonson, and I was considering whether I should tell Mrs. Dolansky?" Pausing before the door, Cec fingered the key in his hand thoughtfully as he studied Maria carefully, then Maria continued. "Mrs. Jonson's maiden name was Chatwell. Her father had a marina on Lake Ontario, and I saw her around a few times when I was a little girl. Her brother still runs the marina."

"I will leave the decision to you, but be careful," Cec replied before opening the door to the inner office.

Mrs. Dolansky had filled a suitcase with the belongings of her late husband, and she was looking through the files in the filing cabinet. "Come and sit down for a few minutes," she said; a pathetic figure now to those who only a few short days before held her in high regard for the power she possessed. "I packed the suitcase and that seems to be everything."

"If there is anything that I see you have forgotten, I will send it to you," Cec said, as he and Maria, foregoing the offer to sit down, remained standing. "Or if you will be staying in Vancouver for a while, I will give you a call and bring it over."

"I'm sorry, Mrs. Dolansky." Maria said, feeling genuine sympathy, as Mrs. Dolansky, with tears in her eyes, took the suitcase from the desk and put it on the floor.

Straightening up, Mrs. Dolansky looked at Maria with eyes shining as black as coal, and Maria became aware during the long pause that Mrs. Dolansky was suspicious that she was somehow involved in her husband's murder. "Thank you, Miss Petersen," she said, in a voice flat and toneless.

"I will carry the suitcase down to the car for you," Cec said, moving forward.

"I recalled something about Mrs. Jonson that may help you to find her," Maria said.

"Yes," Mrs. Dolansky said, and her eyes moved quickly to Cec, as if questioning the information she was about to receive, before she once again turned her attention to Maria.

"Mrs. Jonson's maiden name was Chatwell. Her two brothers run a marina on Lake Ontario, near Toronto."

"Did she know you too?" Mrs. Dolansky asked.

"I don't think so," Maria replied, "I was a very young girl when she would have last seen me in Ontario, and I have changed quite a bit."

Cec picked up the suitcase as the two women said goodbye. Then Mrs. Dolansky followed him to the door.

Going to her desk, Maria sat down and looked out over the strait. The sky was clouded, and the calm sea showed no evidence of the storms of bygone days. It was the beginning of a new era.

CHAPTER 21

The following morning in the office, Cec was waiting for Maria.

"You were aware that Mrs. Dolasnky thinks that you were involved in her husband's murder?"

"I realized that yesterday, but that is preposterous." Maria said, her eyes narrowing as she spoke. "I was lucky to escape with my own life the day Dolansky was killed. If we had been in the office when those two men burst in, none of us would have had a chance."

"You are right, Maria." Then with emphasis Cec continued. "But we were not in the room."

"What are you getting at, Cec?"

"Mrs. Dolansky's suspicions, although unfounded are not without some justification, and because of her present state of mind you could be in extreme danger. However, my wife has asked me to invite you to dinner, and we could continue our discussion at our home, and perhaps clear up some of the uncertainties that have arisen."

Cec spoke on the intercom, and let Steve Bailey in from the outer office, as Maria picked up her purse and walked towards the outer door. She could feel the weight of the pistol in her purse, and it gave her comfort, as she thought about Mrs. Dolansky. God, she hoped that the woman would not try anything stupid.

Cec waved to Steve when he came through the door. "Look through Dolansky's files and pull out anything that appears unusual. I will take a look at them later. Maria and I will be at my home if you want to get in touch with us."

"Okay," Steve said, and he went into Cec's office as Maria and Cec went out.

* * *

The forenoon traffic was heavy, and Maria and Cec, each alone with their thoughts, drove in silence. A good driver, Cec maneuvered the big car smoothly in the traffic.

Maria pondered the motives that Cec had given for her taking the job.

While substantially correct, they were a gross over simplification of what was complex. Did the laziness that, Cec spoke of, stem from the need to live one's life to the full instead of wasting one's time doing tedious tasks for money that would buy little more than one's bread. And if so, from whence did it spring? She had been brought up to work hard and save; perhaps inflation, in a materialistic and hedonistic society, had helped erode the values of industry and thrift. A fear of poverty? Yes. Although poverty in North America with its systems of welfare, is not the same as poverty in Asia. Her love for Danny? What of this reason?

She had forsaken lovers before for far lesser reasons than the risking of losing one's life. However with Danny and herself there was a difference, to be separated, besides the risk to her life, she had also accepted the fact that Danny and the Lewes family were involved in smuggling drugs, and by this acceptance she had become an accessory to the fact. Were these the reasons Cec saw sufficient to cover this acceptance? Only a short time ago she had attended church religiously, and still said her prayers occasionally before she went to sleep at night? She didn't know; perhaps she was in the grip of something biological, which separated from Danny now would rob her of her rightful destiny. Cec had failed to mention this. The knowledge of the Lewes's illegal activities had not come to her as a sudden disclosure; it had been a gradual process that had evolved as her mind sifted through the information presented to her, the rags to riches success story of the Lewes family, the attempts on the lives of the family members, the elaborate system of protection, the drug seizure off the coast, Danny's, and her flight from Doc Ellis, and Danny's incomplete explanation. All these had contributed to her knowledge.

The car eased to a stop at a red light as Cec applied the brakes, and they both looked up as the sun broke through the clouds. Its brilliance edging the dark clouds with silver, like gigantic halos, and sending bright shafts of light across the sky - a proclamation to those in tune with the universe. The traffic lights turned green and they were moving again, faster now that they were away from the downtown area. Their eyes seeing only the road ahead, while their minds dwelled on self-centered fears and dreams, blind as they were to the wide spectra of the universe, and the power to which they would ultimately atone.

Cec was aware of the knowledge she possessed and its inherent danger to himself and the Leweses; a far greater danger to her safety than the threat posed by Mrs. Dolansky, and a threat which Cec had chosen not to mention.

"Have you heard from Danny?" Cec asked, breaking into Maria's thoughts.

"Yes, I spoke to him on the telephone for a while last night."

They both fell silent for a while, and once again they were alone with their thoughts as Cec increased their speed on entering the 75 km zone.

"Doc Ellis and Laura were killed in a traffic accident in Oregon, a couple of days ago." Maria glanced at Cec, his eyes never left the road, and he continued. "Their car smashed through a guard rail of a bridge and plunged into a creek."

Seeming to fix their eyes on some unseen object far ahead, Maria and Cec looked straight along the road; they both knew that Doc Ellis and Laura had not died accidentally, and that Danny was responsible.

Cec turned the car off the main road into a maze of quiet streets with large expensive houses, and Maria recalled the Sunday drives with her parents to the more prosperous districts of Toronto; where they would pick out a house they particularly liked, then drive by a number of times trying to determine what it would be like inside, and plan that one day they would build a house just like it. They had enjoyed many Sunday afternoons this way, building castles in the sky, and always stopping for an ice cream on the way home.

The car slowed down, and Cec wheeled it into the driveway of a large low-lying house, set back on a long sloping lawn. The garage door opened automatically as they approached, and as they alighted from the car, the door closed quietly behind them.

Cec introduced Maria to his wife Eve, who was a small trim woman in her early forties with an easy smile, who was waiting for them when they entered the kitchen from the garage. "I'm very happy you could come, Miss Petersen," she said, taking Maria's hand, and leading her into the middle of the room.

"It is a pleasure to be here," Maria replied.

Large, and furnished with good taste; the house was the like of which Maria's family had viewed from their car on their Sunday afternoon drives. She thought about her parents and wondered whether their dreams of owning such a home, had long ago been abandoned when; with the passing of youth and the advent of accelerating inflation, the reality of their position became more apparent.

"You have a wonderful home," Maria commented, as they arrived back in the living room after the tour of the house. But she was not envious; her own dreams for material wealth, no matter how impractical, had not been abandoned. "Did you have it built to your specifications?" Maria asked.

"Yes, Cec and I thought about it and discussed it for years before we finally consulted an architect to make the drawings and incorporate our ideas into the plan, and here it is," Mrs. Bonas said, smiling and raising her hands in a gesture that exhibited her pleasure and pride of ownership. Maria smiled. "Please be seated," Mrs. Bonas, said, with a flourish towards the chesterfield, "Cec will bring us a glass of champagne before we have dinner." There was the aroma of a turkey cooking, and it reminded Maria of her last Christmas at home. Maria was curious as to how Cec had done so well. Stocks and bonds, a rich uncle, or more likely, he was a crook.

Cec came into the room carrying a tray of glasses and a bottle of champagne. He poured the champagne, and passed the glasses to Maria and his wife before sitting down opposite the two women with a glass of champagne in his hand. " Terrisa is not staying for dinner," he said. "Her mother has come to pick her up, and she is leaving right away." They heard the front door open, and Terrisa called goodbye before she left. "Terrisa is my niece and she comes in to help Eve three or four days a week."

The food was already on the dining room table, and after a couple of sips of champagne, Maria, together with Cec and his wife, retired to the dining room to eat. The meal was delicious, and their conversation flowed easily of Vancouver, its nightclubs, and some of the places of interest along the coast. Then after dinner Maria helped Mrs. Bonas clear away the dishes and put them in the dishwasher, while Cec was on the telephone. A slight breeze was rippling the water in the swimming pool, when they returned back into the living room, where Cec served them once again with champagne, and all the while the feeling that something was amiss, was growing in Maria; the luxury of Cec's home and the royal welcome she was receiving were beyond her expectations.

"Do you know that you have an uncle in New York who is very rich and powerful?" Cec asked, with an air of casualness, as with his champagne glass in his hand he paused before taking a drink.

"Is this the something extra in my background which has been uncovered?" Maria asked, without answering the question. Cec nodded, and Maria laughed. "I'm afraid there has been some mistake. My father has a brother in New York, but he doesn't have two pennies to rub together."

"Did you ever meet him?" Cec asked.

Maria shook her head. "My mother met him when she and my dad went to New York for a visit before I was born, and he has never come to Toronto. My mother didn't approve of him."

No one spoke for a time, and everything was quiet except for the faint sound of a radio playing in the kitchen. "Are you trying to say that I really do have a rich uncle in New York?"

"Rich and influential," Cec replied, "and, as of recent, we find that he is involved in our business here. His name is Perrelli; evidently your father changed his name when he came to Canada."

"That's right," Maria agreed. It had been no secret in her home, and she was proud of her Italian blood. "It is interesting to know that my uncle is involved in the business here, but he doesn't know that I exist."

"I think he does," Cec said. "But let me tell you a little more first, and I think you will agree."

Taking the glass of champagne in her hand, Maria leaned back on the chesterfield, and listened to Cec as he related her uncle's involvement in the business. Evidently her uncle had become very rich when he was young, and although he was never convicted of selling contraband liquor, it was thought that this was the source of his wealth. Later he became involved in selling drugs, in New York, where his interests were centered. By an agreement with another company there, he had not trafficked in drugs in Canada on a large scale. However, recently he had set up a new company, and had become active in importing and selling drugs in the West. He had successfully taken some trade away from an associate of the Leweses in Seattle, and with the aid of Doc Ellis he had been attempting to compete with the Leweses in Western Canada. Cec paused in his explanation, and took a drink before continuing. "The Leweses and their associates in Seattle are opposing your uncle's intrusion into their business. They combined forces in an attempt to stop his activities, and as a consequence, a trade war developed, resulting in a serious disruption in the Lewes' business, and at the same time preventing the success of the new company. With business at a near standstill in Seattle and a threat of the same thing happening in Vancouver, a representative of Perrelli, and Mr. Dolansky got together to try to negotiate a settlement. However, your uncle is holding out for a share in the Lewes' company and a stalemate had developed in which Dolansky flatly refused to have any more dealings with Perrelli's representative. Two days after that abortive meeting Dolansky was killed, and since that time it was learned that Mrs. Jonson was a divorced wife of Perrelli, and she had come to work for the detective agency a number of years ago in anticipation of what is happening now."

"So you think Mrs. Jonson knew of my identity?" Maria asked.

"Not only did she know your identity; Maria, she made certain that you were out of the inner office before she allowed the two goons who killed Dolansky to enter." Cec smiled, "I was just fortunate enough to be with you."

"Don't you think it is possible that I, like Mrs. Jonson, was planted here to aid in Perrelli's take over bid?" Maria asked.

"It is possible," Cec replied slowly, "but I believe it is not true, and your involvement is a mere coincidence." Both Cec and his wife watched Maria carefully, and then Cec continued. "Am I correct?"

"Yes."

"Now that you are involved, Maria, you could be of assistance to Danny your uncle, and myself." Cec and Eve sipped their drinks while they waited patiently for Maria to speak, and when it became evident that she was going to remain silent. "It would mean a substantial increase in your salary," Cec said. Then he went on to explain how this increase would be paid.

"A part of your salary will be paid in cash, and the remainder will be deposited for you in a Swiss bank account. Thus, you would avoid paying taxes, and avoid drawing suspicion on to yourself by being paid an unreasonable salary for what your job appeared to be on the surface." The bottle of champagne had been finished when Cec ended his explanation, and Eve opened another bottle and refilled their glasses.

"Does Danny know of my relationship to Perrelli?" Maria asked.

"No," Cec replied.

"And Mrs. Dolansky?"

"No," Cec replied again, "Mr. Dolansky discovered that your father had changed his name but did not deduce that the Perrelli he was dealing with in New York was your uncle. Mrs. Dolansky's suspicion of you stems from her husband's death and our escape. She thought that it was too good; she trusted me; therefore she suspected you," Cec paused before continuing. "It appeared to me also that our escape was too pat. So my wife, Eve flew to New York, the night after Dolansky's death, to find out more about Perrelli, and she came up with the information that we had just discussed."

"When I took the job I was an innocent employee, then I became an observer, and now you are asking me to become an accomplice."

"You will be paid well, Maria, and you will be helping everyone concerned." Cec paused a moment, and went on. "In the negotiations with Perrelli's representative, I will not drive as hard a bargain as Dolansky, and I believe that your relationship with Danny and our friendship will influence the negotiations favorably with Perrelli."

Maria thought about her alternatives to working with Cec, if there was an alternative. She knew too much, although it was possible that Danny would provide the protection she would need if she decided to quit. She had a date with Tom for that evening when she finished her university class, and she had already decided to end her affair with him, as to incite Danny to jealousy or perhaps lose his love, was too dangerous. She could go back to Toronto; it would be nice to see her patents again and live at home, except that she would be back on the treadmill again with a nine to five job and poor wages, and there would still be the necessity of protection. The only viable alternative to accepting Cec's, offer was to quit and depend on Danny's continued love, for her protection. No one had spoken for a while as Cec and his wife waited. O Canada, was playing on the radio in the kitchen as a prelude to a sports broadcast, and Maria looked through the sliding glass doors and across the patio. A breeze rustled the leaves of the trees outside, and a leaf floated down onto the blue water of the swimming pool. "When do you want my decision" Maria asked, turning her eyes away from the pool and looking towards Cec.

"I was at the Lewes's last night," Cec said, "and we discussed a new approach to the situation. I will be getting in touch with Perrelli's representative tonight and I would like to be able to tell him that you are with us when I meet him."

Maria thought about the situation. There was no alternative. "Yes," she replied.

The red tile around the pool was bright in the sun, as Maria looked out to the swimming pool once more. The puddles of water that had been alongside the deck chairs before dinner had dried, and the pool appeared cool and inviting. Cec took his wallet from his pocket as he walked across the room, removed five one thousand dollar bills, and placed them on the coffee table before Maria. "You could consider this your first cash advance," he said as he replaced the wallet in his pocket.

"Okay," Maria replied, and there was just a trace of a smile on their faces, as she and Cec looked into each other's eyes. Maria picked the money up from the table and folded it carefully before putting it in her purse, and then standing, she solemnly shook hands with Cec across the coffee table.

"Thanks Maria," Eve said, and she breathed deeply with the easing of tension. "We appreciate what you are doing for us."

"Mrs. Dolansky could cause a problem?" Maria said looking to Cec.

" I will take care of it right away," Cec said, "Chatwell Marina, you said, was the name?"

"Yes," Maria replied.

"I will see if I can reach Mrs. Jonson on the telephone," Cec said as he stood up.

"Would you like to try out our swimming pool?" Eve asked, "I have a number of bathing suits from which you can choose."

"It sounds nice," Maria replied, and getting up the two women went into the bedroom wing of the house.

Cec was still on the telephone when Maria and Eve came back into the living room and went out to the pool.

When Cec hung up the telephone, he went to the sliding glass doors in the living room and watched Maria and his wife swim a few a lengths of the pool, then go to the deck chairs. The black bikini Maria wore showed off her beautiful figure, and he noticed her figure and the perfect bow of her lips, as tilting her head back, she took off the bathing cap and ruffled her hair, before she lay back on the chair. His wife, smaller than Maria, looked trim in her blue one-piece bathing suit as she lay down on a chair beside Maria. Cec went into a bedroom, put on his bathing suit, and then joined the women at the pool.

"Did you get in touch with Mrs. Jonson?" Maria asked, as she looked up shading her eyes from the sun with her hands.

"I talked with her for a while and, I feel that we have gained another ally" Cec, said, pleased with himself, and smiling.

Maria closed her eyes. The warmth of the sun caressed her body and she felt relaxed.

CHAPTER 22

It was ten to nine in the evening when Maria came out of the university building. The professor had let them out a little early - for good behavior he said, and the students, knowing that he would be the first one out of the parking lot and on the way home, all laughed in unison.

There were only a few students around as Maria came down the steps from the university entrance, and seeing Tom leaning against a bench a short distance away, she waved to him. They smiled to one another as they came together, and hand in hand, they walked across the lawn towards the truck. She hated to tell him that they were through; yet she would be courting disaster to go on the way they had been going. Tom stopped close to a clump of bushes.

"There is something that I have to tell you," Maria began, and sad herself, she watched Tom's reaction as she told him that she didn't want to see him for another month - she wanted time to think she said, time to collect her thoughts, and evaluate their relationship.

"I understand Maria," Tom said as they resumed their walk towards the truck. But it was obvious that he didn't, his face was set, his expression bordering on anger, and Maria noticed now that Tom was dressed up to go out. His new slacks were trim, and his hair was brushed and shining. She understood how he felt, as the pangs of sadness were tearing at her own heart. They reached the truck and not knowing what to say, they stood apart.

Maria glanced at her car that was parked just a few cars away, then back to Tom. "What had you planned for the evening, Tom?"

"I rented a motel and bought a bottle of champagne," Tom replied; his smile forced, sad, and ironic.

"Let us go there," Maria said, trying to put a note of pleasantness and enthusiasm into her voice.

"I think not, Maria. Now that you have made your decision, we will let the month go by and see what it will bring."

"I feel like a drink," Maria persisted, and taking his hand, she pulled him gently towards the truck.

The students were streaming out of the university as Tom helped Maria up into the cab, and going around to the front, he climbed in beside her.

* * *

Taking the tumbler of champagne that Tom offered her, Maria sat down on the bed in the motel Tom had rented, and Tom sat on the easy chair facing her, his champagne raised to a toast in his hand. "To our future," he said, and they drank a toast together.

"What have you been doing today?" Maria asked to make conversation, and Tom told her about his walk to the pasture in the morning. The water pump had been giving them some trouble recently, and he went to check to see that it was operating properly, and then on the way home he had fixed a fence that needed repair.

Maria told of Cec's promotion, and as they talked and drank their champagne, they became more at ease. She wanted Tom once more before they separated, and she hoped that they would part, lovers in waiting. Nevertheless, there was no excitement as they contemplated the cruelty of their separation.

Tom smoothed Maria's hair gently, and then they kissed just once, before drinking the remainder of the champagne. "For a month?" Tom said.

"For a month," Maria replied, while her heart ached with sadness, as they left the motel.

Tom watched Maria until she got in the car, and he waved goodbye before she drove away.

* * *

It was one-thirty in the morning when Maria, tired and sad arrived home at her apartment, although relieved that she had make the break with Tom. She let herself into the suite quietly, switched on the living room lamp, undressed in the living room, and put her clothes over a chair before turning off the light and going to the bedroom.

"You are late," Val said, as Maria slipped into bed beside her, "I couldn't sleep and I have been waiting for you to come home."

"I met Tom after class, and we went for a drink. Did anyone phone?" Maria asked in a whisper.

"Yes, Debbie phoned to say that she was not coming home tonight."

"Okay, I will see you in the morning," Maria said, before she turned her back on her friend, and within a few minutes she was asleep.

When Maria awoke, Val was putting the finishing touches to her hair, before going to work. "Are you still on payroll?" Maria asked, noting Val's ultra short skirt and form fitting blouse, which were sure to attract a lot of attention.

"Yes," Val replied, watching Maria through the mirror. "Mr. Evans has given me the job permanently now."

"How do you like it?"

"It's better than filing."

"And Mr. Evans?"

Val smiled. "He's a drag, but a girl has to earn a living."

A fleeting smile appeared on Maria's face; Val had changed a lot in the short time she had known her. Val's happy go lucky and naive approach to life was being eroded by her worries about maintaining her job and her desire to be popular with her peers. However, because of the method she was using to advance herself at work, the two were incompatible, and she was disliked by most of the girls in the office.

Val turned away from the mirror and waved to Maria. "I'm off," she said, as she looked back from the door. "I'll see you tonight," Maria smiled in reply, and then Val was gone.

The telephone rang as Maria, wearing her new blue housecoat, and with nothing else on other than her slippers, busied herself cooking breakfast. It was Cec; he wanted to pick Maria up at her home about ten o'clock. Maria went back to the kitchen and poured a cup of coffee. These were difficult times for Cec, and he was being more cautious than Dolansky.

CHAPTER 23

On Saturday, morning Maria and Val got up late, enjoyed a bacon and egg breakfast, and set their hair ready for Debbie's shower party that evening, which was to be held at Debbie's and Bill's apartment. Debbie had moved out to live with Bill in their apartment some days before. Maria was happy, and she helped Val with the breakfast dishes while her thoughts were of Danny. She had been with Danny at the Bay Tide Hotel just yesterday, and now they were to go sailing tomorrow. It was like old times again.

During the next several hours, the girls worked hard preparing for the shower party, shopping, getting Debbie's suite ready, and preparing the food. Phylis came directly to Debbie's suite from the store to help the girls, and shortly afterwards the guests started to arrive. Beautifully dressed in a wide variety of styles and colors, the young girls, happy and eager for life, placed their colorful wrapped gifts on the floor by the second hand television set that Bill had bought from a friend. Glad to be included in a close circle of friends, the girls took pleasure in fulfilling their social obligation. Some of the girls were married, but most were single and looked forward to their own wedding showers; hoping that, when their time came, their showers would be as successful as Debbie's. It was not for the gift per se, although they were often sorely needed, but for the feeling of self-esteem that comes with the knowledge that others wish you well and hold you in high regard. It was with happy abandonment, that the girls talked, played the games that Phylis organized, ate the cakes and fancy sandwiches that had been prepared, and drank the wine and beer.

However, beneath the happiness and laughter, there could be detected a distance between many of the girls and Val, and they spoke to her very little and were reluctant to choose her as a partner in the games. The girls resented Val for the way she played up to Mr. Evans, and noting Mr. Evans' eagerness to please Val, they knew the price that she had paid for the payroll job. Not easily discouraged, Val covered well; although her feelings were often hurt, and aided by Maria, Debbie, Glenda, and Phylis, she joined in the fun.

Debbie cried while giving her little speech to thank the girls for their kindness, and amid claps and cheers, unable to continue, she fell into Phylis' waiting arms. Then the party was over and it was time to go home. With

204   R<small>ON</small> L<small>EE</small>

the girls still spirited and merry as their husbands and boyfriends arrived, a hasty arrangement was made to continue the party at a private house. Everyone was invited to the party, and Maria, with about half the girls present, agreed to go, although Maria told Val that she would not stay late, as she wanted to be well rested for the sailing trip with Danny in the morning.

Val went on ahead with some girls from the house where the party was being held, and Maria, Phylis, and a number of girls stayed back to help Debbie clean up the suite. Bill had come in and was having a beer with another two chaps who had come to pick up their girlfriends and Maria while drying the dishes, smiled as she listened to their conversation. Boastful and loud with the other fellows, Bill was a wheel, and only a few minutes before, when seeing that Debbie was happy, he had almost cried

* * *

Alone in her car as she drove to the party, Maria watched the street signs carefully to find the house where the party was being held. None of the girls, besides Maria, who had stayed back to clean the suite, were going to the party; even Phylis and her husband had declined at the last minute; being tired, they decided to go home. Perhaps it was the darkness and the poverty of the neighborhood that made Maria feel uneasy, and she was sorry now that she had promised Val she would go. She turned the car off the main road and onto a side street in one of the older districts of the city. The houses were old, and many of them run-down; the owners failing to keep up the repairs, but charging all the rent the traffic would bear, while they waited to sell the land for large profits to a development company that was planning a new shopping center and an office complex in the area.

There were many cars parked on both sides of the street, and Maria, traveling slowly as she looked for a place to park, noticed that most of the houses were in darkness. She parked her car between a Cadillac and a Volkswagen near the far end of the street, and then glanced at her watch; the luminous dial showed it was ten after eleven. Maria locked the car and walked up the street; the trees on the boulevard casting dark shadows on the sidewalk and the houses, as she looked for the address that she had been given. A car door slammed somewhere up the street and she could hear the noise of the traffic on the main road she had just left. Maria stopped at the house, which appeared to be the house that had been described to her earlier. It was tall and narrow, and in the near darkness, she made out the address that was painted on the siding. The gate through the hedge squeaked noisily as she opened it, and clicked shut on a spring as she walked towards the house. There was a faint sound of music, as if from far away, and a dim light from the back of the house could be seen through the living room window. A dog barked in the house as she came to the steps, and one of the girls that Maria had seen at Debbie's party came to the door.

"Is that you, Maria?"

"Yes."

"Be careful on the third step. It is a little shaky."

The girl held the door open for Maria to enter, and in the dim light, Maria made out the old fashioned furniture. "Where is everyone?" Maria asked in a low voice as the girl closed the door behind them and the sound of the music became louder.

"Everyone is in the basement. Come, I will show you." Walking ahead, the girl led Maria through the living room and into the kitchen where the light from the stove was the only illumination. Then the girl opened a door, and they went down the wooden stairs into the basement.

The basement had been fixed up quite nicely, and near a bar at one end, a stereo record player was playing one of the latest hit tunes. The room was not large and the fifteen couples who were there made it appear full. About ten people were dancing, with the rest standing or sitting around the room on cushions close to the wall. A red and a blue light provided light, situated at opposite ends of the room, and a white light over the bar.

"A rye, Maria?" the girl asked, as Maria followed her around the edge of the room to the bar, where there were a number of cases of beer and several liquor bottles.

"A rye will be fine, thanks," Maria replied above the sound of music. She glanced around the room looking for Val. Some of the couples were strangers, and some of them she had seen at the shower party; Val was sitting cross-legged, on a cushion near a wall, between two other girls. There was a smell of marijuana in the air, and a weed was being passed along a group of people sitting against the wall. The cigarette lit up a youth's face as he inhaled, then he passed the cigarette on to the girl next to him as he picked up a bottle of beer from the floor with his other hand.

"Can I chip in for the bottle?" Maria asked taking the drink the girl was handing her.

The girl shook her head. "The boys bought it all," she said. The record changed as Maria took a sip from her drink, then she turned her eyes back to the group of people with whom Val was sitting. The liquor was strong and cheap, and the amount the girl had poured for her would make her high if she drank it too quickly. There was the buzz of talk, and loud laughter, and one of the girls, sitting alongside Val, was leaning heavily on her boyfriend, her blouse hanging open, and her eyes narrow as she fought to stay awake. Most of the couples, who were dancing, came back from the dance floor with the changing of the record, and one of the couples embraced and necked passionately at the edge of the floor. A boy and a girl began to gyrate wildly in the middle of the floor to the beat of the music, and a number of couples moved aside to give them more room. Maria took a drink from her glass and moved slowly around the room towards Val. A big man, wearing a brown suit and a matching shirt open at the neck, stood close to Val and looked down to where she was sitting. His neck was short and thick, and it almost appeared that his bullet like head sat directly on his broad shoulders. The man would be Glenda's friend Charlie and Val's old boyfriend, Maria thought, and she stopped for a moment to watch the couple on the floor as they continued to gyrate wildly in time to the loud music. A boy, standing nearby, passed her a marijuana cigarette. Maria smiled, took it from him, and passed it to the girl standing by her side. With her eyes smarting from the smoke, Maria moved on closer to Val, and she noticed that Charlie's long hair was slicked back and there was a serious expression on his face as he leaned forward talking to Val and the girl next to her while gesturing with his hands. The girl on the dance floor shrieked, and as she turned quickly to the fast tempo of the music, the hem of her skirt bellowed out and came up around her waist. Maria took another small drink from her glass as the record changed again, and the couple moved off the floor, hanging on to each other, laughing, and breathing heavily. Maria turned again to Val; her face was contorted as if expecting pain, and her arm was held out to another girl poised over her with a hypodermic syringe in her hand.

"Val!" Maria cried. As Val looked up towards her, she continued in a voice raised by the urgency of her appeal. "No!"

Maria's words were barely uttered when the back of a large hand struck her in the mouth. She had seen it coming a split second before, but not in time to save herself completely from the blow. She let her glass go, to fall and shatter on the floor, as she fell against a couple behind her.

"Get on with it," Charlie yelled, above the sound of the music, the voices, and the laughter in the room. Few people took notice as they continued to laugh, and talk or dance to the music.

The couple behind Maria, that had saved her from falling, pushed her back onto her feet, and there was the taste of blood in her mouth from where her teeth had cut the inside of her cheek. But there was no pain, and only the bruise at the corner of her mouth gave evidence of injury, while her face was expressionless to her all consuming anger of which the flash of her eyes were the only warning. Maria could feel the weight of the gun in her purse as she opened it carefully and put it in her hand.

"Come on," Charlie said impatiently, before his eyes followed the direction of Val's gaze to the girl he had struck.

"Wait," Val, cried, her voice on the verge of hysterics, as she lunged towards Maria. Then in a more placid voice, as she took hold of Maria's shoulder, she continued, "I'm sorry." Charlie looked on with a puzzled expression on his face as he watched the drama unfold before him.

"I almost did something foolish," Maria said, her voice unruffled by emotion, and there was a faint smile on her face as she released her hold on the gun and withdrew her hand from her purse. However, her anger was undiminished, and at a more opportune time, there would be a day of reckoning.

"Get out," Val shouted as she turned to Charlie, her voice tense and shaking with anger.

The room was quiet now, save for the music of the stereo, as the attention of its young occupants focused on the confrontation, and Charlie, angry and unsure of what to do, glanced at the people around him.

"Get out," Val shouted again.

"Bunch of bastards," Charlie muttered, as much to save face as to satisfy his anger. Then he walked away, climbed the basement stairs, and went out of the room while everyone watched him go. The door slammed behind him, the noise resounding through the room, and the people turned away, some couples began to dance; and someone lit up another joint, took a couple of puffs then passed it on, and the party resumed.

Minutes later with hardly anyone seeming to notice, Maria and Val went up out of the basement. They stopped at the top of the steps outside the front door, and looked down the gloomy street, where shadows moved back and forth on the sidewalk and the road, as the trees swayed in the breeze.

"Charlie hasn't left yet," Val whispered. "His car is still parked down the street."

"The Cadillac?" Maria asked in a low voice, as she looked to her friend. Val, her face shining with perspiration, nodded in reply.

Out of the corner of her eye, through the window in the front door, Maria could see the faint glow of a cigarette; Charlie was lying on the chesterfield, and he had watched them as they walked through the darkened living room. Maria touched Val's waist with her hand, and urged her to move. Then the two girls walked carefully down the steps, and there was the sound of music for a moment as someone opened and closed the door to the basement. On the street there was the noise of the traffic on the main road, and the rustle of the wind in the trees as Maria and Val glanced back to the house before they hurried away; someone was standing in the living room window watching them leave.

"Spooky," Val said, taking Maria's hand. However, Maria did not share her feelings; still angry, and with a slight taste of blood still in her mouth, it was only her reason and better judgment that prevented her from turning back to seek revenge. For revenge, she was determined there was going to be.

CHAPTER 24

Cec picked Maria up at 10.30 am. and told her that it wasn't necessary to go to the office this morning as one of the new detectives could type the reports.

Maria and Cec could go to the shooting range to practice. On the way back they stopped at the now familiar coffee shop with the checkered tablecloths. "I wish to discuss something very important with you Maria. Please bear with me until I am finished and I am sure that you will agree." Cec paused, took a drink of his coffee, while Maria watched him with some suspicion. "I spoke with the Leweses' this morning." Cec said. "They are worried about their daughter Irene, and she has gone to Edmonton after being in Paris. They fear that there could be an attempt on her life, and they would like you to go to Edmonton to be with her. The Leweses discussed this for some time and you were the only logical person to turn to. Even Danny had to agree that this was necessary."

Maria sipped her coffee, "Danny agrees to this?"

"Yes" Cecil, replied. "The only other person that could have gone was Mrs. Lewes herself, and no one agreed to that."

"Okay," Maria agreed reluctantly.

On the way back to the office their conversation continued. "You will be seeing Danny tonight," Cec said.

"Yes we plan on going to a party."

When Cec drove Maria back to the suite in the afternoon, it was with mixed feelings that Maria thought about Danny and the party in the evening.

* * *

The suite was dark and cool, compared to the outside, as Maria closed the door behind her. She opened the living room drapes, allowing more light into the room but she did not notice the cracks in the plaster, or the places where the paint was peeling from the wall, or the mark on the wall where the chesterfield had rubbed, or the worn spot on the carpet between the living room and the kitchen; this was home to her, and she felt sad to be leaving. Maria put her handbag down beside the chesterfield, kicked off her shoes, and lay down; she didn't want to be separated from Danny for a whole month. She could have refused to go to Edmonton. Danny's wife, the bitch was behind everything; she wants me out of the way while she is having her baby, Maria surmised. Debbie's wedding was next Saturday, everyone had been invited, and it seemed that none of the girls from the office would be able to go to Dawson Creek, where the wedding was to be held at her parent's home. One way or another she had intended to go, and now everything was finished and she would be in Edmonton, playing nursemaid to a spoiled brat. No, that was not true, from what she had heard about Irene. She was an adult and anything but spoiled, and a nice person. Damn it, I don't want to go, Maria thought, and there is no way out. However, there were other considerations, and she could not dwell on mere self pity.

* * *

Val closed the outside door of the suite noisily behind her, and noticing Maria lying on the chesterfield she crossed the living room quietly.

Maria awoke when Val closed the door, and she opened her eyes as her friend came towards her.

Val smiled and sat down on the chesterfield by Maria.

"You are home early."

"No, it is a quarter to six," Val said.

"I am leaving for Edmonton tomorrow."

Val looked tired and sad as she sat down on the easy chair, another reason why she shouldn't be leaving Maria thought, and while still lying down she put her hands behind her head, and told Val about her planned trip to Edmonton, emphasizing that she would only be gone for a month, when to herself it seemed like an eternity.

"The son of a bitch!" Val exclaimed, blaming Danny for Marie's impending absence.

"It is not his fault," Maria explained quickly, "his God damn wife wants me out of the way."

"There is no other reason for your going?" Val asked incredulously.

"Irene does need someone to be with her, but it didn't have to be me." Maria said, bitterness evident in her voice.

Getting up, Val started towards the kitchen, then stopped. "What about the apartment?" she said, her face tight with emotion.

Maria reached for her purse, took five hundred dollars from her wallet, and placed it onto the table. "Keep it, and use it for the rent. I will be back in a month."

"I don't want your money," Val said, and pressing her lips together, she fought to keep back the tears.

"I will move in with Glenda."

"Glenda won't have you," Maria said, her voice raised in anger. "She has already let everyone know that she wants to live alone, so shut you trap and take the money. I will want this apartment when I get back."

Her slim body taut and her teeth clenched, Val looked down at the money, and hesitated for a moment. "Okay," she said, and as she picked up the money, tears ran down her cheeks. Val put the money into her purse, while Maria, watched her every move. She didn't want to be angry with Val, but she had to make her understand that she wanted to return to the suite when she came back from Edmonton, and she knew that Val would not want her to pay while she was gone; although Val could not afford to keep the suite even for one month alone. There was the sound of the refrigerator opening and closing, the click of glass, and a popping sound as Val removed the caps from the bottles of beer.

"Thanks," Maria said, taking the bottle of beer from Val's outstretched hand, and refused the small yellow tranquilizer that Val offered, and then they touched their glasses together before sipping their beers. Their nerves were distraught and the beer would calm them down, and while Maria prepared to go out with Danny, Val got something ready to eat.

Danny arrived promptly at eight thirty, wearing a dark suit, edged with silk, and Maria dressed in a long blue gown, looking angelic, greeted him with a coy smile, before taking his arm. Then while looking into each other's eyes, talking enthusiastically about the new singer who was entertaining at the Bay Tide Hotel, they walked along the hallway to the elevator.

Closing the apartment door, Val went to the bedroom, and lay down. She had watched Maria and Danny until they had boarded the elevator, and they had gone without as much as a backward glance. Debbie had moved out to live with Bill, and she got to talk to her only during the dinner hour at work. She felt like she was being deserted. A whole month would be a long time to be alone, when even the thought of an evening without a friend was upsetting.

* * *

The nightclub was filled, and the music romantic and dreamy, as Maria and Danny, danced, and sipped their champagne at the table Danny had reserved. Together and happy once more, they commented on the excellence of the band and the female vocalist, who was the current sensation in the nightlife of Vancouver. Maria told Danny that she had informed Cec that she agreed to go to Edmonton. He smiled and said that he would pick her up and take her to the airport the following evening. Then they spoke no more of her departure, to forget, at least for a little while, their separation on the morrow, to drink in the full pleasure of their last evening together for a long time.

The dancers vacated the floor and the band struck a fast tune as an exotic dancer came on stage, twisting and turning to the tempo of the music and the claps of her audience. Then, the people were quiet as the dancer, a tall slim blond of no more than twenty, kicked off her shoes as she swayed to the music, and as the music thundered and rolled, dancing and writhing, in perfect coordination. Slowly, she removed her clothes, until completely exposed, her youthful breasts heaving and her hips turning with all her feminine charm, while smiling seductively, until with a sweep, she picked up her clothes, and ran off stage to the roll of the drum and the vigorous clapping of the audience.

The music began again after a short intermission, and once more, the patrons were on the floor, turning and swaying to soft lilting music made for love, as the vocalist, with closed eyes, sang from her heart. Maria and Danny raised their glasses, clicked them together and drank their champagne slowly, a silent salute to each other, and happiness.

The exotic dancer, dressed now in a long silver gown, entered the room and took her place alongside her escort, at a table not far away. He was a big man, well dressed and of powerful build, appropriate to the dancer's tall feminine figure. Maria and Danny recognized him together, he was Charlie. Instinctively, Maria touched the corner of her mouth lightly with a delicate hand, the bruise had gone, and only the memory and determination for revenge remained.

The light sparkled from the large glass chandelier that hung over the center of the room. The band stopped playing and the couples walked arm in arm around the floor, laughing and talking as they waited for the band to resume playing. Maria glanced again, to where Charlie was sitting, and there was a hint of a smile on Danny's face as he followed her eyes; a woman to reckon with when crossed, like none other, he had known before. The exotic dancer stood up and signaled to another couple who had just entered the room. She was very young, with shadows in her hollow cheeks, her face too thin to be beautiful, her bosom thrust forward beneath her silver dress as she raised her arm higher to attract the attention of their friends. Charlie looked towards his friends, and when he saw that they had located him, he glanced briefly to Maria.

The band started to play again, and the patrons stepped gracefully in time to the music. Maria turned back to Danny at the sound of his voice. "I haven't forgotten the incident," he said, a faint smile still on his face. "You really want revenge?"

Maria's smile broadened, her white teeth glistened between her red lips, and the nod of her head was barely perceptible.

A beautiful woman; Maria's eyes were wide and bright, her long black hair framing her face, resting on her shoulders and bosom; complimenting the blue of her dress. Danny took a drink of his champagne as he studied Maria, an angel any man would be proud to have by his side, beautiful and proud, every inch a woman, and programmed to raise hell.

Accepting Danny's invitation to dance, Maria took his extended hand as she arose from her chair, a picture of gentle unspoiled beauty. They moved gracefully onto the floor, swinging freely in time to the music, a well-matched couple, that drew the attention of many admiring eyes, acknowledging as Danny himself had done, that Maria was the most beautiful woman in the room. While Maria, her face radiant, read the message in her lover's eyes and she was happy.

Recognizing Maria as Val's friend, Charlie watched, Maria and Danny abandoning themselves to the music and each other, as they moved gracefully around the floor. The band stopped playing, and arm in arm, Maria and Danny promenaded the floor with a host of other couples, noticing as they walked, Charlie and the friends who had joined him and his girlfriend at the table. Dressed in a sheer black lace gown, Glenda sat along side Charlie, and following the direction of Charlie's eyes, she too had noticed Maria.

"Charlie and his company at his table are paying you a lot of attention," Danny said.

Maria smiled. "The other girl is Glenda. She works at the same store as my friends."

The music started up again, and Maria and Danny began to dance, as some words passed between the two couples at the table. Then Charlie's eyes searched the room, while his girlfriend looked at him with a puzzled expression on her face, and as Charlie stood up, Glenda rose quickly, said a few words, and grasping his arm she tried unsuccessfully to prevent him from moving onto the floor. Erect, broad shouldered, and with his head high, Charlie moved to meet Maria and Danny as they danced towards him. Standing close to the bar, Steve Bailey folded his arms, his hand close to the gun that hung in a shoulder holster beneath his coat, as he watched the drama unfold.

"Excuse me," Charlie said, as he cut into Maria's and Danny's dance, "I have an apology to make to Miss Petersen."

Maria looked up, calm and unmoved, "I'm sorry, we have never met," she said, and stepping aside, Maria and Danny resumed their dance, spinning away across the floor.

Puzzled and angry, Charlie went back to his table and sat down. Glenda said something to him by the way of appeasement, and he shook his head angrily. His girlfriend got up and walked briskly to the entrance, as a waiter moved to Charlie's side and spoke to him.

The dance finished, and Maria and Danny, hand in hand, went back to their table, as the waiter came towards them. "Please accept our apology for any intrusion of your privacy," the waiter said.

"Thank you," Danny said.

"If you would like us to remove this person from the hotel, Mr. Lewes," the waiter said, "we will be glad to oblige."

"It was just a little indiscretion on his part," Danny said with a smile. "I'm sure he didn't mean any harm."

The waiter nodded and moved away.

"Go to the washroom for a minute, Maria," Danny said, "I have a telephone call to make, and if you stay here alone, Charlie may be indiscreet once more."

"Okay." Then Danny watched Maria walk gracefully away, her dress clinging to her narrow waist and her hips swaying to the rhythm as she walked.

Danny went out to the hotel lobby, and Steve Bailey followed inconspicuously behind, hand in hand with a young lady. In the lobby Danny went to an easy chair well away from anyone, and using his cellular telephone he dialed a number, and after what appeared to be a one sided conversation, in which he did most of the talking, he ended the call.

The band was playing a lively tune as Danny skirted the edge of the floor, taking care not to jostle any of the dancers, returned to his table and poured a drink while he waited for Maria. Out of the corner of his eye Danny could see Charlie, Glenda, and her escort. A waiter had delivered another round of drinks to the table, and judging by the waiter's smile and deep bow, directed to Charlie, he had been tipped handsomely.

Slender and pretty in her long blue gown, and clutching her small handbag close against her side, Maria returned to the table, aware of the affluence of which she was a part. Danny returned her smile as she approached; Maria was as alert and eager, as her ready smile was contagious. Charlie's presence, their encounter, and the danger he represented, had merely quickened her pulse, and added a new dimension to the evening.

Rising to meet Maria, Danny offered his hand, and catching the tempo of the music, they danced forward to the front of the band. Maria closed her eyes; the music, the closeness of Danny, his strong arms about her were intoxicating, and for a time she forgot that with the coming day, she would be leaving Vancouver. Surrendering herself to the joy of the moment, she danced in a dream, a whirl of blue, as they spun to the rhythm of the music, and the sweet harmonious voice of the vocalist.

Seated at their table, Maria and Danny saw Rocky Devis enter the room and stand for a moment by the door looking about him. Tall and well built, he wore his clothes well, while his posture and ease of movement marked him as an athlete.

"Can I help you, Sir?" a waiter asked, noticing his penetrating blue eyes.

"No thanks," Rocky replied, with an easy smile. "Some friends are expecting me."

Rocky ran a large hand through his curly blond hair, and moved off between the tables. Moving forward slowly among the tables, a close observer would discern the agility of his walk, and the biceps of thick arms beneath his well fitting suit. A woman looked up and smiled as he approached, and unseeing, his eyes swept past to focus on Charlie a few tables away; sitting straight and erect, Charlie was unmistakably the largest man in the room. Rocky turned away, and made his way to the washroom.

With the stage set for revenge, Danny touched Maria's hand across the table. "We will leave now, dear," he said. Their glasses of champagne remained unfinished and a part bottle of champagne stood in a bucket of ice on a stand by the table, as Maria and Danny went out into the lobby and registered for a room in the hotel.

* * *

The band was playing a slow romantic tune when Rocky came out of the washroom. Many of the tables were empty, and the dance floor was almost filled with couples dancing close, while they listened to the band and the singer; as with the microphone close to her mouth and her slender body swaying, her voice rising and falling with emotion, she captured and expressed the mood of the love song.

Seated at their table, Charlie and his two companions conversed with one another. The two men deaf to the music and the mood of the song, with only Glenda, alert to what was going or around them, attune to the atmosphere created by the musicians and the singer. She had seen Maria and Danny leaving, but was unaware of Rocky, slowly threading his way among the tables towards them.

Turning to look at the singer as he passed by, Rocky, stumbled against Charlie, knocking the raised glass from his hand. The drink spread quickly over the table, and although Glenda pushed quickly away from the table and stood up, it was too late, the front of her black lace dress was soaked with liquor.

"I'm very sorry," Rocky said, with a look of concern on his face.

Charlie stood up abruptly his massive form dwarfing the people around him. "You rotten bastard," he hissed through clenched teeth as he pushed Rocky away.

Rocky stepped back rolling away from the push that had been intended to put him off balance, and then he came forward again swiftly, crouching slightly as his fist shot out and caught Charlie in the midriff. It had happened so fast that most of the people around didn't realize what was happening until Charlie was doubled up in pain, and Rocky was walking casually towards the door. Charlie straightened up, squared his shoulders and with his face contorted with rage, he followed Rocky towards the door. The band finished playing and the dancers made their way back to their tables, as Charlie in his haste ran headlong into a young man, then knocked down an old lady who happened to be in his way. His arms swinging, and not bothering to apologize or help the lady to her feet, he hurried on, to run into yet another person before he reached the door to the lobby.

Almost across the lobby and close to the door to the parking lot, Rocky, at the sound of hurried footsteps behind him, turned to face Charlie. Breathing heavily, Charlie stopped, and the two men faced each other only a few feet apart. Charlie breathed in deeply, a look of rage on his face, poised for action, and at a loss for words.

"I said I was sorry," Rocky said slowly and distinctly as he sized up his adversary, a little taller than himself, fifty pounds heavier, and a reach advantage. It was nothing new, he had floored the likes before, and he could do it again.

"Let's go outside," Charlie said in a raucous voice, and while the phrase had slipped off his tongue a thousand times before when he was a bouncer at the Dock Side Bar, never had he felt such hatred for a man as he did now.

"Okay," Rocky said with a shrug, and he stood aside as Charlie, looking back over his shoulder preceded him through the door.

"Charlie," Glenda called, a note of warning in her voice, as she hurried across the lobby, her black dress held up above her ankles. However, the two men disappeared through the door, and her warning went unheard. Turning, Glenda let her dress fall back, and putting a hand to her forehead, she walked slowly back to the dance hall, as the clerk and the few people in the lobby watched her with unconcealed interest.

High above in the hotel tower, Danny closed the door of the deluxe suite behind himself and Maria. Embracing with their eyes closed, their lips moist and apart, they kissed tenderly, and with a deft hand, Danny unzipped Maria's dress.

Outside in the parking lot, the dim streetlights shone from the rows of parked cars. The water of Burrard Inlet appeared black, and one could see the green and white light of a tug as it moved in cautiously from the sea; the chug, chug, chug, of its engine drifting across the water and mingling with the sound of the traffic on the busy, well lit street not far away. Charlie and Rocky faced each other in the dim light close to the lane, and the tall dark tower of the hotel with random squares of light, shining from its lofty windows, presided over them. Wary of each other and oblivious to all else, the two men stepped cautiously towards each other; animals in their own jungle.

Charlie attacked first, his big fist swinging around for Rock's head, to encounter nothing as Rocky ducked and moved in, smashing a heavy left into Charlie's mouth. With the taste of blood in his mouth, Charlie spit out a loose tooth, while knowing now that his opponent was no easy mark, he remained undaunted and confident of ultimate success; his strength had never failed him in a fistfight before. Lowering his head and feigning hurt worse than he was, Charlie took a glancing blow above the eye as Rocky set him up for his right, but Rocky's right hand was blocked by Charlie's left as Charlie straightened up and came forward, his right hand smashing into Rocky's chest, sending him sprawling across the hood of a parked car. Hurt and angry, Rocky rolled off the hood and away from Charlie, to regain his feet without falling. Cautiously, Charlie hung back when Rocky failed to go down; there was no hurry and he would make mincemeat of this upstart in his own good time.

Some passers-by stopped to watch the fight and the doorman of the hotel went to the telephone to alert the police of the trouble outside, as Rocky moved in, stuck a straight left into Charlie's face and moved out quickly again before Charlie could counter. The two men circled each other cautiously, and Rocky with the finesse gained from training and experience pumped a few sharp lefts into Charlie's face, and then backed away as his opponent came forward poised to hurl a killer punch. Charlie's right eye was closed and blood ran from his nose and mouth, while he looked a mess, he was still dangerous. Rocky knew this and that time was running out for him to finish the job that he had come to do. He stabbed Charlie with another left, clipped him with a right, and side stepped quickly, while the searing pain in his chest fanned the flames of anger within him.

A police car, its red and blue dome lights flashing and siren wailing, streaked across the bridge from West Vancouver. Meanwhile in a room, high in the hotel with its lights still burning, Maria sat over Danny, her slender and shapely legs forward, as Danny with his arms about her back, sat on the bed, a firm heaving breast gentle against his mouth as his lips drew on her red and sensitive nipple. The muscles of Maria's stomach, below her narrow waist alternately contracted and relaxed, while she moved upwards and downwards rhythmically, her pace quickening, as Danny responded with deep satisfying thrusts. Maria's head stretched back, her long hair hanging away from her shoulders as she clung to Danny, her eyes closed and, the delicate features of her face set in an expression of rapture.

In the parking lot far below, Rocky could hear the siren of the police car and with a new urgency he moved in, blocking a right swing thrown by Charlie, he ducked low and took a left on the side of the face before driving a hard right into Charlie's stomach below the belt. Charlie doubled up in agony, and Rocky stepping back pounded him in the face; left, right, left, right, like the rhythm of a march, until Charlie fell forward on his knees. Then Rocky turned and pushed his way through the group of people, who while complaining of his foul play, jeered and did nothing to stop him, and gaining the darkness of the lane, he broke into a run.

Moments later the police car turned sharply into the lane towards Rocky, its headlights throwing rays into the night sky, as it bounced over the sidewalk. However, Rocky had seen it coming and as the car's lights shone in the sky he dove for cover, concealing himself behind some garbage cans, as the light flooded the lane. Then after the car had sped past, he emerged from his hiding place and ran down the lane away from the hotel, and minutes later when a policeman shone his flashlight along the lane, Rocky had gone.

Danny finished dressing, and then zipped up Maria's dress as she brushed her hair before the mirror. A red and blue light flashing in their window attracted their attention, and switching off the room lights they went to the window, and looked down at the commotion in the parking lot. Danny smiled knowingly unaware that this night; he had planted the seed for his own demise.

A small group of people stood in the dim light, the red and blue lights from the ambulance and police car, flashing alternatively on and off in their faces, and only when the stretcher carrying Charlie had been pushed into the ambulance, did the people disperse, moving off in their separate ways as the police car and the ambulance, their lights still flashing, drove away.

Standing behind Maria, Danny pressed against her soft buttocks as she leaned forward looking through the window. The flashing lights disappeared as the cars turned around the front of the hotel, and Maria turned her attention to the inlet; its black waters illuminated by the occasional street light that stood close to the banks. The tug that had churned the waters a while before had gone, and the inlet was dark and quiet as they stood together and looked out over the calm waters

* * *

Ten after three in the morning, Maria let herself into her suite. The lights were still on, and Val lay asleep on the chesterfield, her breasts showing clearly through her sheer nightgown. A number of empty beer bottles stood on the floor close to her, a bottle of tranquilizers was on the table, and there was the sound of music from the radio in the bedroom.

Maria took off her shoes and tip-toed across the living room.

"What time is it?" Val asked, and sitting up she brushed her hair back from her face with her hand.

"Ten after three. What time did you go to sleep?"

"About one o'clock. I was hoping you would get home earlier."

Standing up, Val stretched and followed Maria into the bedroom, her nightgown doing little to hide her youthful figure. "Do you have a date with Danny in the morning?" Val asked as she sat down on the bed.

"No. He will be busy all day, and he will be picking me up at six to take me to the airport." Maria slipped out of her dress and hung it in the closet.

"I'm going to take the day off from work tomorrow, so that we can be together for a while before you leave" Val said, and she smiled in response to the questioning look on Maria's face. "You are concerned that I may lose my job?" Maria nodded in reply, and Val continued, "I will phone Mr. Evans in the morning and tell him that I'm sick."

CHAPTER 25

Putting her arms about Danny's neck, Maria stood on her toes and pressed her slender body close to him as they kissed good-bye at the airport. They would miss each other in the weeks that followed, and although Danny had promised to visit her in Edmonton as soon as possible, she had the feeling that this would not be until after his baby was born.

Stopping for a moment after passing through the security check, Maria turned and waved to Danny, who stood watching her leave, and looking trim and feminine in her new pant suit, her smile came easy, and her teeth shone white between her red lips.

Danny returned her wave, and disheartened, he watched as she walked gracefully away towards the departure lounge.

A mood of melancholy came over Maria as she settled back in her seat, awaiting the departure, and she was glad that Danny could not see her unhappy. She had conceded to the wishes of the Leweses, by going away, while Danny's wife gave birth to her baby, and while Danny's father had accepted her as Danny's mistress, and trusted her in her knowledge of the corporation's activities, she felt belittled and cheapened by his request for her to go to Edmonton.

On the observation deck, Danny with mixed feelings towards his father, watched the jet plane gather speed along the runway, become airborne, and climb steeply as it flew over the roof tops, its wheels folding back under the wings. Then still deep in thought, he joined the throng of people leaving the deck. By conceding to the wish of Perrelli and by his father's request that Maria go to Edmonton, his father was avoiding troublesome issues, that a few years before he would have met head on. After waiting his turn, Danny stepped onto the escalator, Steve Bailey following close behind. Danny gripped the handrail tight, his feelings for his father, included a mixture of anger, love, and pity.

Looking out of the window, Maria saw the buildings of the city get smaller as the plane climbed, although her thoughts were of other things. She had consented to going away to avoid causing a scene between Danny and his parents, and now feeling lonely and depressed, she questioned the wisdom of her decision. Her future during the next few weeks was uncertain; what was her status as companion and bodyguard to Irene and exactly what was expected of her? With Danny, it had been different, her role as detective had blended with her role as his lover, and as lovers, they honored and respected each other's wishes. However, with this new assignment, besides not knowing, exactly what was expected of her, she had doubts about the justification of her position. Was it merely an excuse to get her away from Vancouver, and how would Irene accept her? Maria swore under her breath; there was nothing she could do, and she should try to relax and see what would develop. Slowly Maria's melancholy mood lifted, and she began to see the aspect of adventure in her new assignment. She still wondered how Irene would receive her, only now come what may, she didn't give a damn.

Irene recognized Maria as soon as she entered the airport terminal and came forward to meet her. Tall and trim in her high heels, and brown flowered dress, her face too square to be pretty, she reminded Maria of Danny's father, although her skin was fair. Her blond hair was in disarray from the wind she had encountered in the parking lot, and the roots were darker than the light blond that her hair had been tinted, but her smile and look of pleasure were genuine, and Maria's response was warm and friendly.

"Maria?" Irene asked smiling.

"Yes," Maria replied happily, "and you are Irene?"

The two girls hugged each other warmly, their apprehensions relieved by what they saw in each other. "I would have known you anywhere. Danny has told me so much about you," Irene said, as they walked through the terminal building to the conveyor to retrieve Maria's baggage. "Danny phoned as soon as your plane left Vancouver and he described what you were wearing in detail, but I would have recognized you anyway from his previous descriptions."

Maria smiled, just what had Danny told his sister about her? "Danny talked a lot about you too."

"Nothing bad I hope," Irene said, still showing her pleasure of having made a new friend, and Maria smiled and shook her head, her long black hair turning about her shoulders.

The two girls stood by the conveyor, lined with people waiting for their baggage, and seeing her suitcase on the conveyor Maria stepped forward and waited for it to come around, unaware of Irene's close scrutiny. An extremely pretty girl Irene thought, not that Danny had not had pretty girl friends before, but there was something different about Maria, perhaps it was the ease with which Maria conducted herself, or perhaps it was the way Danny had spoken about her. She could make a fool of Danny if she desired, Irene concluded, and she wished that there was some way she could defend her brother from this danger.

Irene took one of Maria's suitcases, and the two girls, each carrying a suitcase, started walking towards the exit.

"Do you love Danny?" Irene asked abruptly.

Puzzled by the question, and the suddenness with which it was asked, Maria, looked at Irene, and saw the concern in her eyes as the two girls stopped and faced each other. "Yes, very much," Maria replied sincerely, and I am looking forward to having his baby - the thought she had tried to repress, surfaced in Maria's mind, but the words remained unuttered, and instead of confiding in Danny's sister, she merely smiled at the relief she saw in Irene's face.

"I'm sorry. It was a stupid question to ask," Irene said, with a smile in a renewed gesture of friendship, and the two girls continued walking towards the exit.

Irene stopped and put down the suitcase as a tall thin man in an open necked shirt approached them. "Ha, you made it after all," Irene, said smiling to the man who stopped before them. "Maria, I would like you to meet my fiancé, Ron Rahl," Irene continued.

"Pleased to meet you," Ron said, smiling as he put out his hand.

"I'm happy to meet you," Maria replied, returning his smile and extending her hand. His handshake was warm and his dark brown eyes were bright behind his horn rimmed glasses; his graying hair and receding hairline, giving him a distinguished appearance, in spite of his casual dress.

"I'm sorry I didn't make it on time," Ron said as he picked up the suitcases, and falling into step besides the two girls, he continued. "I got delayed by some students after class, and I knew that you would leave without me, so I wasn't too worried."

"Ron is a lecturer at the University of Alberta," Irene explained as they went out of the exit door. "My car is over here," Irene continued, pointing to the right in the parking lot.

"Yes, I saw it when I came in, and I'm parked just a few cars away."

"How was your class today?" Irene asked.

"It went wonderful. I started on quantum physics today, and the class response was tremendous."

"It sounds as if you enjoy your work," Maria said.

Ron smiled, "There are other things I would rather do sometimes but on the whole I like it, and it is quite challenging." Irene opened the trunk of her car, and Ron put in the suitcases as he went on. "Of course it helps to have Irene in Edmonton. It got rather dreary in the winter when Irene was in Paris."

"We will see you in my apartment, Ron," Irene said, as she opened the car door for Maria, and Ron walked further along the parking lot.

"Okay, but take it easy on the way back. There is a speed trap on the highway and I got a ticket on the way out."

The car was new and comfortable, and there were no tobacco fumes to mar the aroma of newness. The girls were at ease with each other and they talked freely as they drove from the airport to the city. Irene knew of Maria's involvement with Danny and of her knowledge of company business. She was inquisitive about the settlement with Perrelli, and happy that an agreement had been made and business was back to normal. Although, like Danny she knew nothing of Perrelli's relationship to Maria. Engaged to be married and in love, Ron and Irene planned to marry in the spring, even though her family might disapprove. Irene's parents and Danny had met Ron previously, and while they knew she had been seeing him, she had not told them about their engagement or the plans to be married. Ron was an intellectual, Irene explained, and although he was not unrealistic in the real world, he believed in principles and ideals, of which justice and honesty were cornerstones. Man should strive to achieve these ideals, so that eventually; perhaps not in our lifetime, the world would become a community based on law and order, where all men and women would prosper, and be free to develop their capabilities for the good of themselves and the community. Ron's work and his beliefs were almost a religion, and he believes that science, pursued with dedication and wisdom could prove to be man's salvation.

They passed the speed trap on the highway; traveling five kilometers an hour below the limit, then speeded up again and continued their conversation. Irene had taken a physics class from Ron two years ago and they had fallen in love that semester. Her parents were expecting her to marry someone who would fit into the family business, and eventually help Danny run the corporation as equal partners. Irene had put off the wedding as long as possible, and at one time she had even tried to forget Ron; breaking up their relationship, only to pick it again at a later date, and continue their correspondence and holidaying together whenever possible.

Maria sympathized with Irene and supported her in her determination to marry the man whom she loved, in spite of a possible family conflict.

Irene's apartment was a luxury penthouse suite in a high-rise, in the university area, and while it was evident Irene's parents spared no cost to satisfy her every whim, she was by no means spoiled or a snob. She insisted on doing her own cooking and often helped the girl who came in daily to do the housework.

During the next week, Danny telephoned Maria three times, and on one occasion they had talked for over an hour.

His father had not been feeling well it seemed, and loaded down with work, there was no opportunity for him to fly to Edmonton for a visit. Meanwhile, life in Edmonton went on as well as could be expected without Danny. Maria got along well with Irene, and together they experimented with new recipes, and tried them out on Ron, who dropped by every evening, sometimes staying for supper, and sometimes taking Irene out. In the daytime, Maria accompanied Irene to the university, where her professors, although recognizing her as a stranger in their classes, said nothing; probably Ron had made previous arrangements with them for her to be present.

With a lot of time on her hands, Maria tried to keep herself busy. She telephoned Val, and also her cousin's wife Alice, and spoke to them at some length; and in the class with Irene, she wrote an essay for her in one of her subjects, dropped a line to her Uncle Bert, and wrote a long letter to her parents. Still, during the evenings, when Irene was out, Maria had time to think about her parents, and have some misgiving on the kind of life she was living. She missed her parents tremendously. She would visit them at Christmas, and there would be presents under the tree and they would sing carols together. Things would be just as they always were, in the days before she ever dreamed that they would separate, and she would leave home to pursue a life of her own. She had considered telephoning, but decided to write the letter instead, not trusting conversation with her parents. There could be difficult questions, and she did not want to lie to them.

It was ten after nine in the morning, and dressed in their nightgowns, Maria and Irene were enjoying a cup of coffee in the living room of the suite, while talking and looking out over the city. After nearly two weeks together, they had become good friends, and they enjoyed each other's company, whether going to the university together, shopping, swimming, cooking, or just conversing with one another. There had been a thunderstorm and a heavy rain during the night, and the sun had only just broken through the heavy clouds that remained in the east, bathing the city in its golden light. The small pools of water on their roof top patio reflected the blue sky above, and shimmered with streaks of gold in the light breeze. Maria and Irene were in no hurry. Irene's first class was at eleven o'clock, and they would have time for a leisurely continental breakfast, before getting ready to go out.

When they finished their coffee, they continued their conversation, and busied themselves, making a shopping list for the things that they would need to prepare a steak dinner, which they planned for the evening. In the distance, there was the noise of the traffic in the busy streets far below.

The telephone began to ring on the coffee table by Irene's side, "Hello," Irene said, and then looked puzzled as the person on the line identified himself. "Sure, but give us about ten minutes to brush our hair." Irene put down the telephone, and pressed the button, that would release the catch on the front door of the apartment. "It's your Uncle Bert from Vancouver," she said.

"I received a letter from him a couple of days ago, and he never mentioned coming to Edmonton," Maria said, and like Irene, she was puzzled by what might be his reason for the visit.

The ten minutes were barely up, when the doorbell of the suite rang, and Maria pulling her purple dressing gown tight about her middle, went to answer the door. Maria swung the door open and smiled to her uncle. Dressed formally, in a suit, and a shirt and tie, the wisps of the little hair he had left had been brushed neatly into place, and his red face was serious. "Come on in," Maria said cheerfully, sensing his apprehension and stepping back to make way for him. However, the smile on her face vanished, when her uncle hesitated and she noticed that his lips were pressed together as he fought to control his emotions.

"It is your mother," he sobbed as he stepped forward, and took Maria in his arms. "She passed away last night."

Maria gasped and hung on to her uncle, and overcome by their grief, they clung to each other, the tears running down their cheeks. "Why?" Maria cried, drawing away from her uncle and holding him by the shoulders with her outstretched hands as she looked into his face; but she saw only his despair, and covering her face with her hands, she cried.

"Your mother has had cancer for a number of years, and she didn't want you to know," Bert said putting his hand lightly on Maria's shoulder.

Sobbing anew, Maria held onto her uncle for support, and as he held her gently in his arms, she could see again her father and mother, standing with their arms about each other as they waved goodbye to her at the railway station when she left home. Life for herself and her father, without her mother, seemed impossible. "My God," Maria cried. "What shall we do?" and she would have fallen, had her uncle not supported her in his arms.

There were tears in Irene's eyes as she closed the outside door, and led Maria and her uncle to the chesterfield. Sitting beside her uncle, Maria put her head back and cried anew, as her uncle controlling his emotions now, wiped the tears from his face.

Irene went to the kitchen, made some fresh coffee, and gave a cup to Maria and her uncle, before sitting opposite them on a chair. Maria and her uncle looked to each other in silence, grief written on their faces, the world seemed to be without reason and there was nothing to say.

"There is a plane leaving for Toronto in an hour and a half," Bert said, breaking the quiet that had come upon them. "Do you think you can make it?"

Maria nodded her head in reply, and then went to the bathroom to wash her face. Then with Irene's help she packed her suitcase and got ready to leave. Bert opened the door for them to go, as Irene held Maria close to her for a moment, and looked into her eyes; a silent communication of sympathy.

Sitting on the chesterfield, Irene heard the elevator door close behind Maria and Bert, and putting her head in her hands, she cried. She would skip classes that day, and get the lecture notes from a classmate another time.

Danny's secretary answered the telephone, when Irene called Vancouver. Danny had left for Edmonton that morning, and he would be arriving there soon. "Put me through to my father," Irene said.

"I'm sorry, Miss Lewes, your father has not come into the office this morning."

Then who is running the business? Irene was prompted to ask, but instead she thanked the secretary and hung up the telephone. Danny would arrive at her apartment shortly and she would ask him what was going on. It was unusual for both Danny and her father to be out of the office on the same day.

The door bell rang as Irene was putting the finishing touches to her make up. Dressed in a blue jump suit, she went out of the bedroom and closed the door behind her; the cleaning girl would not be coming in until the afternoon and the bed was still not made.

"You are getting prettier every time I see you," Danny said, after they had kissed, and when Irene smiled he went on, " are you surprised I'm here?"

"No, I phoned your office this morning and your secretary told me that you had left for Edmonton."

"Where's Maria?" Danny asked, as he sat on the chesterfield and looked around.

"Maria's mother passed away last night, and she left for Toronto this morning with her Uncle Bert," Irene said as she sat on the chesterfield by Danny.

Leaning forward, Danny put his hand under his chin and blew softly through his puckered lips. "Did she say when she would be getting back?" he asked after a time.

"No."

Irene went to the kitchen, leaving Danny to meditate alone. Her own questions about her father being away from the office would wait until she had explained to Danny what had happened that morning.

Taking a seat facing Danny after she had served him coffee, Irene talked of what had happened, and prompted by Danny's questions, she recounted how Maria had spent the past weeks, frankly admitting her admiration for Maria, and telling him about the good friends that they had become. Then in preparation for the time when she would break the news to Danny of her coming marriage to Ron, Irene deliberately made the implication that Maria was worthy of his love, and skillfully alluded to the fact of his unsatisfactory marriage. As Danny's sister, she had said more about his marriage than any other person would have dared, and being alert to his mood, she stopped short of arousing his ire to the point where he would vent his anger on her.

Going to the kitchen, Irene fetched the coffee pot and refilled their cups, adding the cream and sugar, as Danny stood by the window and looked out over the city, deep in thought and his expression grave.

"How are Father and Mother?" Irene asked.

"Not good," Danny replied, turning from the window to look at his sister as she sat on the chesterfield.

"What is the trouble?" Irene asked, putting her coffee down untouched, a note of concern in her voice.

"I don't know. I have been running my ass off between the warehouses and the office for the last week, and Dad hasn't come near the place."

"Is he ill?"

"The doctor has been in to see him, and Dad is getting some pills for his arthritis, but it seems to me that since we made the deal with Perrelli he has given up," and in a raised voice Danny continued. "He was all for it, when the agreement was signed, and I didn't like it then and I don't like it now."

"How is Mother?" Irene asked.

"Mother is, okay, but preoccupied with the happy event of becoming a grandmother, and she feels that it is time Father took a rest."

"Is the business doing well?" Irene asked her brow furrowed.

"Perrelli has brought us quite a bit of new business, and the business we had is returning to normal. We are doing better than ever, still I don't like the fact that outsiders are involved in the family business."

"It was bound to happen sooner or later." Irene took a drink of her coffee as Danny looked at her with disdain.

"Not you too," he replied forcefully. "I heard the same story from Mother and Father before we signed the agreement. However, you know who is doing all the work now? I am. At least Father asks about the business and discusses what is going on. However, Mother's only concerned about the grandchild she is going to have, and now to top it all, Maria has gone to Toronto."

Irene sympathized with her brother, she knew what he was going through, but she couldn't help him; he needed the support and understanding of the woman he loved. "How long will it be before Father gets back to work?"

"He is not coming back to work," Danny said emphatically. "Father is an old man." Then in a more conciliatory tone, a note of sorrow for the parents he loved in his voice, he continued. "They have passed the ball to us Irene, and it is up to us to carry it forward."

"You will be staying over night?"

Danny nodded his head; "I will telephone Maria from here this evening and I will fly back to Vancouver on the first plane in the morning. I would go to Maria and be with her at this time of sorrow, except it would be out of place."

"Would you like something else to drink?" Irene asked, noticing that Danny had not touched his second cup of coffee.

"Yes, a whisky."

Irene cleared away the cups and saucers, and brought Danny a whisky; mixed the way she knew he liked it. "Ron will be coming over for dinner this evening," she said, sitting down by Danny on the chesterfield.

" I thought you had broken off with Ron a year ago," Danny said, surprised.

"No, we never did break off completely, and we corresponded regularly when I was in Europe. We are going to be married in the spring." Irene got up and walked to the window, and looked out with her back to Danny.

"He won't fit into the business," Danny said angrily.

"That is not my concern," Irene said turning from the window, her eyes blazing with anger. "Regardless of the outcome, I don't intend to live my life separated from the man I love."

Lifting his glass slowly to his lips, Danny took a long drink of his whisky. Irene had turned her back to him and was looking out over the city, her eyes blind to the view, while in her mind she saw only Danny's matrimonial error - the error she had no intention of making herself. Her words had cut deep, as she knew they would. Danny had married Jean because of her beauty, and because she was well liked by Father and Mother and fitted well into the family. As he admired Jean for her beauty, their minds and hearts had never met, and the marriage was a disappointment to him, although Jean was quite content and happy, even with the knowledge that Danny often strayed from their matrimonial bed.

Neither spoke for a time and when Irene turned back from the window, she was still angry and determined to defend her decision, and if necessary reiterate her point.

"Oh, I guess Ron will fit in," Danny said, and after a pause he continued emphatically. "God knows I need someone to help me with the business." Silent and thoughtful, Irene watched Danny, her eyes as cold as ice, he had been hurt and it wasn't like him to let the matter drop; he took another drink from his whisky, placed the glass carefully back on the table, then put his hand to his forehead. "But god damn it Irene," he said, seemingly out of distress. "If he wasn't such a fucking egghead."

"Danny," Irene began slowly and purposefully. "When Ron comes here tonight watch your lip, he doesn't take crap from anyone, and if you get into a fight, I will help him beat the shit out of you."

Danny laughed. "It is nice to know, that I am loved," he said, and smiling he continued. "Don't worry, Ron and I will get along okay."

"I have some grocery shopping to do," Irene said.

"Very much?"

"No, it will only take a few minutes."

"Okay," Danny said, getting up and leaving his unfinished drink on the table, "I will come along with you, and we can go somewhere and have a bite to eat." Irene smiled, took the car keys from her purse, and threw them to Danny.

CHAPTER 26

The rain fell in showers, at times hard and then soft, but without really letting up, while overhead, driven by a brisk wind, the clouds moved quickly across the sky. The trees and grass between the monuments were a dark green, and pools of water shone black on the cemetery road, alongside the line of cars parked behind the hearse. A small group of people, not more than twenty, stood on sheets of plywood, huddling under umbrellas around the open grave and the coffin as the priest prayed. The priest and the mourners crossed themselves, and some of the people started to move away, as Maria stood with her father, both somber and erect, their dark clothes pressed neatly, and new for the occasion. Maria's Uncle Bert stood on her other side and held an umbrella over her head as the family looked down at the coffin being lowered into the grave. At the side of Maria's father her uncle, Mario Perrelli, stood with his young and pretty wife and held an umbrella to shelter his brother from the rain. Perrelli, as Maria had learned to refer to him, was older than her father and not quite as tall, although they were clearly brothers from the close similarity of their features, their bearing, and the way they walked.

Andrew Peterson's small circle of close friends had observed his brother and his pretty wife with interest and curiosity, and although later they would whisper among themselves of these strangers of whom they had never heard Andrew speak, and the inevitable rumors would flourish; they would make no mention of these things to Andrew.

Maria put her arm about her father's waist as she felt his arm, gentle about her shoulders, and while tears ran freely down their cheeks no sound escaped their set lips as they turned their heads away from the grave. Holding each other closely they walked slowly back to the car, the rain washing the tears from their faces, and a small group of people, their heads bent, followed, treading carefully through the wet grass.

Amid the noise of starting cars, the swish of windshield wipers, and the wind in the trees, Maria and her father looked back to the freshly dug grave, deserted now among the many flowers; they both knew that they were leaving something of themselves behind, and this knowledge passed between them as Maria looked into her father's eyes before he helped her into the car. Something good, steadfast, and beautiful had passed out of their lives.

With the rear seat of the car cushioning her head, Maria leaned back and closed her eyes, and her father, sitting by her side, looked ahead between her Uncle Bert and a friend from the warehouse where he worked. Maria's mind swept back over her life; no paragon of virtue, she had strayed from the path that her parents had diligently prepared her to follow. Nevertheless, the presence of her mother, her love, and the awareness of the good that she tried to pass on, served to suppress, albeit not always with complete success, the vicious trait in her personality that Maria believed to be innate, and her transgressions had been accompanied by perturbations, so that she never lost sight of the straight and narrow path that her mother held as an ideal that one should attempt to follow. In the past, while she was growing up, the influence of her family and home had helped guide her endeavors, and it was through her parents' eyes, as well as her own, that she judged her accomplishments. Maria's more recent actions had been motivated primarily to achieve only her own gratifications; nevertheless; in the long run she had known that, her affairs would have to be set straight, so that they would bear favorable judgment in the eyes of her family as well as her own.

A week ago this had not seemed an impossible task. Although geographically separated from her immediate family they were still united, and the stability and morality the family espoused would sustain and help her to overcome the purely hedonistic and materialistic aspects of her character that strived for immediate gratification. She would cut away the immoral and unsavory loose ends that had developed in her life, and bring the other parts together into a whole that was more consistent with the norms of her family. But now she was unsure and afraid that this goal could not be achieved.

No one spoke as they drove back to the house, and Maria felt more alone than she had ever felt in her life. It was almost inconceivable, that, at least on earth, she would never see her mother again, and deep within her, mixed with other emotions, there was anger. Death had cheated her of the happy reunion with her family of which she dreamed and planned; the future was empty, and she was afraid not only for herself, but for her father too.

Maria's Uncle Bert, her Uncle Mario and his wife, and some friends and neighbors came back to the house after the funeral; where some neighbors, whom she had known all her life, with the help of Uncle Mario's wife, served a light lunch and some drinks. Now although distressed, Maria talked with her family and friends, while the dampness and darkness outside seemed to penetrate the house, and the lights, some only bare bulbs, failed to brighten the rooms and cut through the gloom.

"Do you like your job?" Uncle Mario asked. Maria nodded, not knowing how else to reply, and she forced a smile in appreciation of his concern. "There are some things that I wish to discuss with you," her uncle went on. "Although there is no hurry, and I will phone you in three or four weeks."

The immediate neighbor asked Maria to drop in for coffee the following day, and then she left to prepare supper for her husband coming home from work. Everywhere the house screamed the absence of Andrew Petersen's pretty and charming wife, and Maria, unable to bear it any longer, retired to her room, where she cried herself to sleep.

* * *

It was daylight when Maria awoke. The sun had emerged from the clouds, and the small bedroom, which had been hers since childhood, was bright as she began to dress. Then alternatively the room darkened and brightened again as clouds drifted before the sun. There was the sound of her father moving around downstairs, and the aroma of freshly brewed coffee met her as she descended the stairs.

"Good morning," Maria said.

"Good morning," her father replied, turning from the kitchen window, where he had watched the birds singing shrilly in the bushes along the fence, as if greeting the return of the sun which glistened from the beads of water on the trees and the grass. Unable to forget their common tragedy, father and daughter smiled weakly. "Our friends insisted on washing the dishes and tidying up the rooms," Andrew continued, by way of explanation of the absence of dirty dishes, as Maria looked around the sunlit kitchen.

The pretty and colorful aprons were in the drawer, clean and pressed, the way her mother had left them. Maria took out a favorite, slipped it over her head, and from force of habit turned her back to her father, who took up the strings, pulled the apron into place, and tied a bow at her back. She would cook bacon and eggs, and fry some bread in the fat, as her father liked it.

"Have a cup of coffee first," Andrew said, as he arranged the bow he tied in the strings.

"Okay," Maria replied quietly, and then sat at the table, while her father poured the coffee and brought it to the table. Maria helped herself to the cream and sugar, her actions seeming to be reflections of the past. Many times they had sat down to have coffee before breakfast, when there had been three of them, starting a new day with hope and happiness, and now the chair at her father's side was empty. Maria took a drink of her coffee; her father, always healthy and handsome, was sad, and the events of the past days had put lines in his face that she had never seen before.

"When do you go back to work?" Maria asked.

"I don't intend to go back to work at the warehouse," Andrew replied, giving careful consideration to his words and speaking slowly lest he would alarm his daughter. Maria smiled, giving approval to his decision, and Andrew continued. "Your mother and I had planned that I would quit the job as soon as we had enough money put together to tide us over while I attended a technical school to learn a trade."

Content to drink their coffee in each other's company, they said nothing for a time. Then Maria got up, and bringing the coffee pot to the table, she poured a second cup for herself and her father. She was worried that her father had quit his job, although as a child, not knowing the economics of their lives; she had urged him to quit when she learned that he was not happy with his work. Her father was skilled; he knew the warehouse business inside out; inventories, cost, sale price, turn over, and under what market conditions merchandise should be held or sold to gain the most from appreciation, and avoid depreciation or spoilage. The transportation of goods, the management of personnel, the office work required, the government regulations to be followed, and many other aspects required to run an efficient merchandising warehouse; he had learned it all, and his advice was actively sought and followed by the young relatives of the owner of the business where he worked, who held the important managerial positions. Yet, his expertise went unappreciated and unpaid for in the minor managerial position he had worked his way up to over the years. He had a trade and knew it well nevertheless; he would have to start at the bottom and attend a technical school, as the piece of paper he would get on graduation was necessary to make a new beginning. She knew he could do well at technical school; he had helped her with her homework all through school, and in high school, where the material had gone beyond his education, he studied her books and kept pace with her every step of the way. They had joked about it at her graduation, and Mother had given him a graduation gift too. For a man in his forties, who had a trade and knew it well, but lacked that piece of paper, which was a passport to a new job, to go back to school, to start afresh, seemed such a waste. He would get discouraged, and if Mother was alive she would give him the necessary moral support and encouragement to see it through. However, he would be all alone, and she was worried.

"Did you make an application to attend a technical school?"

"No, I intend to go to Italy to see my parents. They are getting old, and I find that it is something that one cannot put off."

Maria nodded her head with understanding. Oh, if only she could have seen her mother just one more time before she died.

"When I get back from Italy?" Andrew shrugged. "I don't know I haven't made any plans. I will probably find another job, and take night school to learn a trade."

Getting up from the table, Maria went to the refrigerator to start on their breakfast. "What about the house while you are away?" she asked, as she put a carton of eggs on the kitchen counter.

"I don't want to live in this house any longer, and it is yours if you want it, Maria."

Surprised, Maria said nothing for a time as she took the bacon from the refrigerator and laid the strips carefully in the pan. She put the pan on the stove and turned to her father. "Thanks, but I can't take it. I will stay for a few days then go back West." Maria turned the bacon in the pan as Andrew cracked the eggs into a dish, then taking two pieces of bread from the loaf, he moistened them a little, ready for Maria to fry in the bacon fat.

The sky was clear, and the sun shone warm through the kitchen window as they ate their breakfast. A neighbor, passing in the lane, waved, and Maria glad that the woman was far enough away not to see the tears in her eyes, returned the wave - her world was coming apart at the seams. Andrew came around the table and squeezed her shoulders affectionately, and looking up, reassured by the warmth and confidence she read in her father's eyes, she smiled. They washed and dried the dishes together, and she listened with interest as he told about her grandparents whom he had left behind in Italy many years before, although he said nothing about his brother, Perrelli.

Maria told him about her work in Vancouver, and she lied; an office and selling job for the Plastick Utensil Company, she said, and quickly changed the subject to tell him about Vancouver and the west coast. There were no questions, which was unusual for him, and she was suspicious that he knew that she had lied.

With the dishes stacked neatly on the counter top, Maria sat down at the kitchen table and watched her father as he put the dishes away in the cupboard. His cotton shirt pulled at the belt around his narrow waist and stretched across his wide muscular shoulders, as using both hands he placed the plates gently into the cupboard. His barbell and weights would be sold with the house and furniture; still, he could join the Y.M.C.A. when he got back. She wanted him to be fit, and fuss with his physique as he always had while Mother was alive.

Finished with the dishes, Andrew went into the small living room. Maria felt the warmth of the sun on her arms, and she heard the rustle of yesterday's newspaper as her father picked it up. She was glad now that her father had quit his job, the master servant relationship had been all too obvious at the warehouse, the owner and his relatives the masters, and the likes of her father, who had inherited nothing and worked for a living, the servants. The master and servant definition, for employer and employee, was still in the law books, at this day and age when men had fought and died to get and retain what? The respect and freedom they had, as long as they did as they were told and were careful not to sass the boss, or were wealthy enough to buy respect and freedom. Wealth, influence, and power; the vicious circle, if you were in, you had it made; otherwise you would work hard and be bled white by taxes and inflation. It was little wonder that there was a growing disrespect for the laws - even the people on welfare laid claim to more respect than the servant. If Father could learn a trade, he could go into business for himself and gain the respect his work deserved, and there could be no sudden laying off of the aging employees, or a paper sale and a change of name to save the company the cost of paying retirement pensions to which the employees had contributed. Maria looked up; her father was standing in the door; how long had he been there? She didn't know, but she knew that she was pale; she had seen a ghost - the ghost of poverty.

"Have you changed your mind about wanting the house?"

"No, and I think you are doing the right thing to sell. Perhaps when you come back from your trip you could come to Vancouver, and we could make a fresh start in the West." Maria got up from the table and ran some water into the kettle. "Would you like a cup of tea?"

"Please," Andrew replied, sitting down at the table, and while Maria put the kettle on the stove and brought out the teapot and the cups, he went on. "We could look around and see what we want to keep and, put in storage, and I will phone the real estate after dinner and get things started."

"Okay." Maria sat down at the table and leaned on her elbows while she waited for the kettle to boil, and the trace of a smile crossed her face; the barbell and weights would be put in storage.

Three days later, when most of the furniture had been sold and some items put in storage, they moved into a motel. The real estate company had received a number of offers on the house, and after a couple of day's deliberation they accepted an offer, and the house was sold.

"No tears," her father said, before they parted at the airport to begin his journey to Italy. "I will come West to see you when I get back," he promised. They kissed, and she let her tears flow freely, then he picked up his suitcase and walked away. She watched him as he walked towards the security check and the departure lounge. Tall and graceful, he looked youthful; the distance hiding his graying hair. Maria had toyed with the idea of whether she should warn her father of the illegal drugs trade, and the drug lords, and their schemes; yet, she had said nothing.

She waved her white glove when he looked back, and she also worried that in his innocence he would become victim of some scheming woman. This was nonsense, he was an older man and her father, she reasoned. But however inappropriate, her concern, mixed with a sense of loneliness, was real, and turning away she walked through the terminal building to a telephone. Perhaps she should have told him about Danny and the baby she was expecting. She would have told him the day before, after visiting a gynecologist, except for her concern that it would spoil his holiday if she burdened him with her problems.

CHAPTER 27

Ron answered the telephone when Maria telephoned Irene, and he sounded disappointed when she told him that she was in Toronto, and not at the airport in Edmonton.

"Who is it?" Irene called from another room, and after some silence, she was on the line bursting with enthusiasm. They had been expecting her to arrive for days; there was some good news that Irene wanted to tell, and she would save it until they picked her up at the airport in Edmonton that evening.

Maria hung up the telephone still thinking about what Irene had said; was she expecting a baby too? It would be a happy event, with no confusion about the identity of the father, and no barrier to prevent their marriage and future happiness.

The big plane moved slowly along the runway, until gathering speed it lifted slowly into the air. Maria sitting alongside the window, saw the sun shining from the tops of buildings as the plane gained altitude, then they were over farms; a checkered pattern of fields far below. The noise of the engines lessened, and Maria felt herself drifting involuntarily off into sleep, as the elderly man at her side shifted his position to make her more comfortable.

Maria awoke, moved, and realized that her head was resting on the shoulder of the man by her side. Lifting her head she rubbed her eyes, and brushed her hair back with her hands. "I'm sorry," she apologized, looking up into the face of the man on whose shoulder her head had rested for the past three quarters of an hour.

"I have been the envy of every man on the plane," the man replied cheerfully; while Maria's unusual beauty, her expensive clothes, and the dark circles around her eyes sparked interest and curiosity. "Will you join me in a drink?" he asked good-naturedly.

"It will be a pleasure," Maria replied, smiling as she imagined the picture they had presented to the other passengers.

The man was a retired traveling salesman and on his way to visit his son who lived near Edmonton, Maria learned in the enjoyable conversation that followed. He was a gentleman and very interesting, and like ships passing in the night they took pleasure in each other's company knowing that they would probably never see one another again.

Entering the terminal building at the International Airport at Edmonton, Maria was again intrigued by the good news that Irene was saving to tell her, and she wondered whether her summation that Irene was pregnant was correct. She looked around for Irene and Ron, and then the riddle was answered. Irene, Ron, and Danny were coming forward to meet her; and in moments she was in Danny's arms, with her arms about his neck, experiencing again the thrill of his kisses, her breasts crushed against him by the embrace for which they hungered.

Dusk was falling when they arrived back at the penthouse, and the aroma of the dinner, the young maid had prepared, greeted them as they entered the door. Maria's spirits rebounded with the presence of Danny, and she was happy again as they lingered over the dinner, eating with delicacy, relishing every portion of the well-prepared food, and talking quietly while the flickering candlelight reflected from youthful faces.

As had been prearranged, Irene telephoned Danny immediately after Maria telephoned from Toronto, and he had flown into Edmonton to be on hand when Maria arrived. The thrill of her reunion, and the excitement of being with friends one could appreciate and respect was still present, when after dinner, the two couples retired to the living room. Dressed in a black and white uniform with an appropriate bonnet, the maid served the champagne while, in a dimmed light and a background of stereo music, the lovers conversed happily, the lights of the city bright through the patio doors, was a fitting background to the young people with the world at their feet.

Later, in the bathroom when the two girls talked in private while they retouched their make-up, Maria learned from Irene that Danny's wife had given birth to a boy, and it was with happiness and joy that Irene confided that she and Ron had advanced their wedding date and they would be married during the summer. Ron had resigned his position with the university, and after the wedding at the Lewes' home and a short honeymoon in the Caribbean, Ron would go to work for the L. W. C. Import and Export Corporation. Irene touched up her lips and Maria straightened the belt about her waist, and looked at Irene in the mirror. This had been the good news that Irene had saved to tell her, and she had been presumptuous in thinking that Irene's happiness was for Danny and herself. Was Irene's preoccupation with herself the mark of a true aristocrat or just human nature? Whatever, at that moment a new ruthless determination to be wealthy was born in Maria, and a silent prayer to God went out for herself and her father. She would say nothing to Irene about her own pregnancy, and while Irene fussed with her make-up, Maria ran a brush through her hair, and giving no thought to the problems that could arise in the future, she basked in the warm glow of the knowledge that deep within her life had kindled anew. There was a click as the front door to the suite closed; the maid, finished with her work in the kitchen and dining room was going home. Maria put the hairbrush down as Irene studied herself in the mirror; she had taken pains with her make-up and she looked pretty. Pleased with herself, Irene took her eyes away from the mirror and glanced at her watch to keep track of the overtime she would pay the girl.

The stereo played softly as Irene and Maria emerged from the bathroom, and they laughed together when they found Danny and Ron doing push ups on the living room carpet, their empty champagne glasses on a coffee table as a recording of a popular tune played on.

"A few more drinks and you two will be twisting wrists," Irene said, as she and Maria curled up on the floor next to the two men.

"We have tried it already," Ron said, still gasping for breath, "and I'm no match for Danny. He says it is the champagne, that keeps him in shape."

Kneeling, Maria arranged her dress, and sat on a chesterfield beside the stereo, Danny was on the way to the kitchen to bring another bottle of champagne, and when he returned he bent down and smoothed her head lightly with his hand, and looking into each other's faces, they smiled the smile of lovers immemorial.

"I didn't know, I was so out of shape," Ron said, as Irene, lay down on the carpet by his side. His work did not give him a lot of time for sports or exercise and he was still exhausted from his exertion.

"You have worked too long at a desk, Ron, and we will change that when we are married," Irene said, reassuringly - Danny knew that Ron was not in shape and he had led him on deliberately. The bastard, Irene thought, but her anger dissipated as Ron's breathing returned to normal. When Danny got up to go to the bar, Irene helped him pour the drinks. She was conscious of her sudden forgiveness and she mused over the possible reasons as she filled the glasses with champagne; was it because of brotherly love or was she unconsciously competing with Maria? Danny carried the drinks to the tables as Ron got up from the floor and sat on the chesterfield.

With her shoes kicked to the side Maria had laid on her back in front of the stereo, her colorful patterned dress, pulled down as far as it would go, hiding little of her long shapely legs and the belt about her waist giving emphasis to her full breasts, as with her hands under her head and her shining black hair falling around her pretty face, she looked at the ceiling with clear brown eyes. Irene put the champagne bottle back into the bucket of ice; she wasn't jealous of Maria and she liked her far more than her sister-in-law. Danny took a drink to Maria, and sitting up she took it from his hand, drank a little so that it would not spill, then stood up and followed Danny to the love seat as Irene sat close to Ron on the chesterfield.

The evening passed by quickly, as the two couples drank the champagne, talked happily, and danced in their stocking feet twisting and swaying to the beat of the music; while outside, the moon round and large, bathed the city in its silver light.

Afterwards, in the privacy of their own bedrooms, the lovers held each other in their arms and satisfied the desires, which fanned by the sensuous movements of their dancing, had been raised to a pitch before they retired.

"Did you miss me?" Danny whispered.

"Yes. Why do you ask?"

"I wanted to know."

Maria put her lips to Danny's their passions spent, the kiss a communication of their hearts. From the other room there was the faint sound of Irene and Ron talking.

"I will return to Vancouver with you tomorrow," Maria whispered. "I believe Ron has moved in, and it is of little use for me to stay."

"Okay," Danny replied. "It will be fun traveling together. I will telephone Cec in the morning and tell him what we are doing, in case he wants to make further arrangements. The recent wave of kidnappings has us worried."

* * *

Sunny Alberta, lived up to its reputation the following day and the blue sky stretched endlessly over the prairie when late in the morning the two couples, well rested and happy, arose from their beds to cook and enjoy a good breakfast, and took pleasure in the new comradeship that had developed between them. After breakfast, they toasted their future happiness with coffee before Maria and Danny left for the airport and their trip to Vancouver.

Happy to be together, Maria and Danny enjoyed the short trip back to Vancouver, and even when they parted at the airport, there was satisfaction in the knowledge that their love was strong. Interwoven in common experiences, the fabric of their lives was durable and beautiful.

Leaning back in the taxi, Maria watched with interest the people on the street as the car splashed through the puddles left on the street by a heavy shower five minutes before. Danny in the company of Cec Banas, drove back to his office and the work that awaited him. Things would be better when Ron and Irene were married and back from their honeymoon, and they would have more time to spend together, Maria thought.

"Are you in a hurry, Miss?" the taxi driver asked, looking at Maria in the rearview mirror when he stopped the car for a red light.

"No," Maria replied. It felt good to be back and she was enjoying the drive.

"Good," the driver responded cheerfully. "It has been especially busy today for some reason, and everyone has been in one hell of a hurry. I took a pregnant woman to the hospital on my last trip, and was she ever in a hurry; still, I think I was the more scared." The taxi started forward again and the driver, with his eyes on the road ahead began to whistle a popular tune.

CHAPTER 28

A waft of stale air met Maria as she opened the door of the suite, and she wrinkled her nose with displeasure as she put her suitcases down inside the door. She closed the door quietly, and threw her raincoat on a chair as she walked through the living room; the air smelled dank as if the suite had not been lived in for some time. Debbie's bed had been stripped of bedclothes, while in her own and Val's bedroom, the bed was unmade and some of Val's clothes still hung across the back of a chair. In the kitchen, dirty breakfast dishes littered the sink; there was an open box of cornflakes on the table, and the refrigerator was empty, except for a part bottle of sour milk and a moldy piece of cheese.

The suite had not been lived in for sometime and there was no indication of what had happened to Val. A breeze ruffled the kitchen curtains as Maria opened the kitchen window, and the sound of the traffic in the street below, was welcome to her ears after the eerie stillness of the suite. She would get in touch with Val at work, before she went somewhere else for the night again. While it was against company policy for the employees to take private calls, the girl on the switchboard usually ignored this and set her own rules.

Rita answered Maria's call to the switchboard, and after talking for a little while, Maria asked to speak to Val.

"I'm sorry," Rita, replied, "Val was fired almost a week ago and I haven't seen her since. Hold the line for a minute Maria, I have a couple more calls on the board and I will put them through then get back to you."

The line went dead as Rita disconnected, and Maria sat down on the chair by the telephone to puzzle about Val. What could have happened to her she thought? while she waited for Rita to come back on the line.

"I'm sorry to keep you waiting," Rita said, when she reconnected the line. "Val had a little trouble with old man Evans. She missed a few days from work after you went away, which resulted in her having a set to with Mr. Evans one morning, and she was fired on the spot." Rita chuckled, before continuing, "I have got to hand it to Val; she blasted Evans, right, left and center, and he has been as white as a sheet ever since."

"Have you any idea where Val might be working now?" Maria asked.

"No, the girls around here have been wondering what happened to her, as no one has heard from her since she left."

"Thanks Rita," Maria said, and she returned the telephone slowly to its cradle. It wasn't like Val to be tardy with her work or to fly off the handle at her boss. Perhaps Debbie and Bill are back from their honeymoon? Maria picked up the telephone and dialed Debbie's number, but the telephone went on ringing and ringing in an empty suite, and she hung up the telephone with the question of what had happened to Val still unresolved.

There was the sound of someone running water into the bathtub in the suite above. She had never formally met any of the other tenants in the apartment; she recognized a few faces, although who it was that lived above them, she had no idea, and it could be Val up there for all she knew. Maria took her hand off the telephone and leaned back in the chair. It had been well over a week ago since she had telephoned Val from Edmonton, and Val would have no way of knowing that she was back in town. Maria walked slowly back through the suite, looking more carefully now, than she had previously. Val had not taken all her clothes, and some of her good clothes still remained in the dresser drawers and the bedroom closet, suggesting that Val planned to return. The rooms, for the most part were clean but there were some rings left by drinking classes, on the television top and on the coffee table in front of the chesterfield. Also, a large mark on the kitchen floor, where the polish had been removed, indicated that an alcoholic drink had been spilled, and there was a small fragment of glass in one corner. It appeared that Val had thrown a party, and a cigarette burn on the table by the side of the bed hinted that someone had stayed over night with Val. From all indications, the party seemed like a repeat of the party that Val and Debbie had thrown during the time she had been away overnight with Danny. Who were the people who attended the party? Most of the girls at the office shunned Val, after she became the payroll clerk, and Debbie, Phylis and Glenda, were the only girls from the department store who befriended her.

The suite was empty without Val, and Maria was disturbed and lonely as she sat at the kitchen table to make a shopping list for groceries. She would drop into the store tomorrow and talk with Phylis; perhaps she could shed some light on who had been at the party and where Val was staying.

* * *

"Good morning," Cec said cheerfully, as soon as Maria entered the office in the morning. It was nine o'clock, and while there was no need for her to be at the office this early, after spending an evening alone, Maria had hurried to the office to be once again among people.

"Come into my office," Cec said, and he stood aside for Maria to precede him through the door, then he waited for her to be seated before sitting down on his swivel chair behind the desk.

More formally dressed than before, Cec looked like a successful executive, who had spent all his life behind a desk, issuing orders and being waited on hand and foot. His crew neck sweater had been replaced by a shirt and tie, and a stylish new jacket hung on the coat rack. Maria smiled - Cec fitted the role even better than Dolansky.

"I was very sorry to hear about your mother," Cec said with concern written on his face. "Everyone on our staff was grieved by your loss and wishes me to express theirs and my deepest condolences."

"Thank you," Maria replied, while experiencing again the pain of her loss.

"We have missed you, Maria, and it is good to have you back," Cec said sincerely, and pushing his chair away from the desk, he leaned back and smiled. Maria was pretty, and sitting in his full view, her long legs crossed, her short dress cinched about her slim waist, and the dimples in her cheeks deepening as she returned his smile, she was a vision worthwhile in any man's office. Besides, except for his wife, she was the only person with whom he could confide and trust to type his correspondence that was falling behind.

"Who has been doing your typing while I have been away?" Maria asked, and she smiled knowingly as if reading his mind.

"My correspondence, it is a disaster," Cec said throwing up his hands. "My wife came in for a couple of days to help out, but she is so tied up with the house, and the charity work that she has undertaken, that she really doesn't have the time to spare, and Eve asks me every day without fail, if you are back."

"It feels good to be needed," Maria said, although she was aware that both Cec and his wife, were more interested in her for her relationship with Danny and her family connection with Perrelli, than for any other reasons.
.

"The Lewes' with the help of your uncle have been doing exceptionally well. Perhaps you saw him while you were in Toronto," Cec said, giving the bait and fishing for information.

"He was at the funeral, and I talked with him for a little while," and having nothing to hide, Maria continued, "he promised to telephone in three or four weeks, as there are some things that he wishes to discuss with me."

"Your uncle wants to send a man out here to take a position with the corporation, and help you represent his interests," Cec said, while turning a pencil in his hand and studying Maria's face for her reaction.

Maria nodded her head slowly in acknowledgement of the statement and waited for Cec to go on. It seemed like a logical extension to the agreement, as she knew nothing of the details of the corporation's business transactions and Danny could certainly use some help in dealing with the increased business.

"Bill Lewes has accepted the idea, but Danny is balking because he likes to choose his own men."

Did Cec expect her to persuade Perrelli that she could look after his interests, and thus change his mind about sending a man to join the company, or did he want her to influence Danny into accepting Perrelli's representative with the corporation? The situation placed her in an awkward position, and she felt uneasy. "How determined is Perrelli to sending his representative here?"

"He has made up his mind, and his representative will be coming."

"And Danny?"

"He doesn't have any choice," Cec said, putting the pencil down and leaning forward over the desk. "The idea is quite reasonable really and it is Danny alone who doesn't agree. Nevertheless, if Danny and Perrelli's representative do not get along, it could result in a serious rift between Perrelli and the Leweses."

"You want me to attempt to influence Danny to cooperate with Perrelli?"

"It would be better for us all if they would cooperate," Cec replied. "Danny knows nothing of your relationship to Perrelli, and he will have to know sooner or later."

It was just a matter of time before Danny learned that Perrelli was her uncle; Maria was aware of this and the fact that it was better she tell him herself, than he learn of it from his father or Cec, although she wasn't sure how he would accept this knowledge.

"For you to tell him now, would be as good a time as any," Cec said. "Business is doing very well, and his wife has recently given birth to a son."

The statement had been made matter of fact; as if Danny's wife and son were of no concern to her - to some things Cec was blind. He didn't realize that she and Danny were in love, and that there was no love between Danny and his wife. Maria put her head back and brushed a lock of shining black hair from her forehead, the gesture somewhat more than was required to remove the offending lock, was a manifestation of her pride. It was true that Danny's wife had given him a son, but what of the baby she carried; it was not only wives that were blessed with the capacity to bear children, and no matter what society thought, it was no lesser a child.

"You are a beautiful woman," Cec said, after a prolonged pause. He was shrewdly aware that something of what he had said previously had touched a nerve, and he would give it some thought later, in an attempt to discern the weakness in Maria's defenses. "Danny will accept the fact that you are Perrelli's niece, and slowly you can influence him to take a more reasonable attitude towards your uncle's representative, who will be coming to assume a position with the L. W. C. Import and Export Corporation."

"How would you assess my chances for success?"

Cec rubbed his chin with his hand, and narrowing his eyes, and surveyed Maria with an exaggerated expression of deep contemplation. "You won't have any trouble at all," he replied.

"You are a blackguard!" Maria exclaimed good-naturedly, and they both laughed together.

Still smiling, Cec took a wallet from his pocket and placed five thousand dollars on the desk. The appeal to Maria's sense of humor had helped, and now by exploiting her weakness for money, he would insure her cooperation.

Without a word, Maria got up, took the money from the desk and placed it in her purse. Then, when she sat down again, she and Cec looked into each other's eyes and smiled - they understood one another perfectly.

"There is a new brown mercury in the parking lot," Cec said as he threw a set of car keys to Maria. "My wife's idea, and an expression of appreciation."

"Thanks, and give your wife my regards," Maria said, and getting up she placed the keys to the car on the desk alongside a sheaf of sketched letters, written in long hand.

"Those are the letters I was referring to," Cec said, indicating the letters by a gesture with his open hand. "You can read them and make any changes you think necessary, and we can go over them together before you do the typing."

"Okay," Maria replied cheerfully, placed the car key in her purse, and taking the letters and her purse, she went to her desk by the window.

During the next month, Maria became the personal secretary to Cec and almost a daily companion to Danny, who picked her up almost every noon for lunch, Monday to Friday. It was an exciting life, having the freedom to come and go as she pleased in the office, seeing Danny in the privacy of her apartment, enjoying the luxury of the club, where they played tennis, went swimming, and talked and drank with Danny's friends. They went sailing in the yacht as often a possible and occasionally they danced until the early hours of the morning at the Bay Tide Hotel. They were in love and living life to the full. Danny had been angry at first when she told him that she was Perrelli's niece, and he was hurt by the thought that perhaps Maria had deliberately courted him to help her uncle advance his ambitions. However, as time went on they came to understand one another better, their love deepened, and nothing more was said about her family relationship to Perrelli or his representative, who was still to arrive.

Meanwhile, negotiations between Perrelli and the Leweses had proceeded, and an agreement was transacted for Perrelli's representative to arrive in the near future and take a senior position with the company. Maria discussed the matter with Cec and learned that although Danny's attitude had mellowed to the situation, he had attempted without success, to have Perrelli's representative take a minor position with the company; arguing that Maria could in the main look after the interests of the mole. This knowledge bothered Maria as the Lewes' association with Perrelli had brought them more business and greater profits, and she would have discussed the matter with Danny, if Cec had not cautioned her against it and advised her to wait until her uncle's representative arrived; reasoning that perhaps things would work out well and her intervention would be unnecessary. Still she wasn't convinced, and she was suspicious that Danny's continued opposition was due to his juggling of the books to the benefit of himself and his family. Nevertheless, with another five thousand dollars more in her purse, and a growing Swiss bank account, she agreed to wait and see what would happen.

A telephone call from her uncle in New York one morning was a pleasant surprise; he talked with Cec for a few minutes then spoke with Maria for some time. He was in good spirits and happy, and he promised to come West for a visit as soon as business permitted. Maria discussed frankly her position with the Plastick Utensil Company, her relationship with Danny, and Danny's opposition to the appointment of his representative, even while she was aware that Cec was taping the conversation on the extension line. She told her uncle too, of the talk she had with Cec, and his advice not to attempt to influence Danny to taking a more reasonable approach at this time. Perrelli agreed with this advice and like Cec, he believed that things would work out all right, in spite of the fact that he was certain that some profitable transactions had not shown up on the financial statements he received from the corporation. Still, Maria said nothing of her own suspicions in this matter, lest she endanger Danny.

The new car was large and luxurious, and while Maria enjoyed the prestige that it gave her, there were few friends now with whom she could associate and be proud. She spoke to Debbie on the telephone on a number of occasions, and whereas they met a couple of times and had coffee together downtown, Maria was never invited to her home. Maria hadn't seen Phylis, since she had gone to see her at the store and enquired without success, about what had happened to Val. Danny bought her a large diamond ring, the cost of which she couldn't begin to estimate; and like the car, although she found personal gratification in its possession, it was in the eyes of strangers that she saw admiration and sometimes envy. She talked with Alice and her Uncle Bert occasionally on the telephone, and avoided seeing these members of her family, where her many new clothes and other material possessions might arouse suspicion, rather than praise.

During the evenings without Danny, Maria was lonely, and she had time to ponder her way of life and the future. Danny's love for her was as strong as ever, and where for the most part they confided in each other and discussed all aspects of their lives, there was a deliberate avoidance of anything about her uncle's representative, which to Maria marred unnecessarily their otherwise beautiful relationship. Val's disappearance too, bothered Maria, and while some of Val's clothes were still in the suite, there had been no word or hint of where she had gone. She might have become the victim of foul play, and there was a growing pressure within Maria to actively search for her friend. She had received a number of letters from her father in Italy, long letters, digging into their past, involving her mother, discussing his parents and friends whom he had left behind, and the many changes he saw around him. Her replies, written during the long evenings, were equally long, and through it all there was a note of loneliness for one another and a longing to be reunited. It was certain now that he would be coming to visit her, and there was a problem of how he would accept her new way of life? Maria found herself drinking too much, and she cut it out entirely while she was alone; the last thing she wanted was to become a lush, drinking, in an attempt to escape her problems and loneliness. Instead she read profusely, improving her knowledge of current events so that she could discuss intelligently with Danny the happenings in the rapidly changing world, and she exercised diligently to preserve the health and suppleness of her youthful body. That Danny was the father of her baby to be, she was convinced, and she would move into a new and luxurious apartment before her baby was born. He would want for none of the things that she lacked as a child, and Danny would be proud and spend more time with her and the baby. He? Why in her thoughts did she anticipate a boy; no matter, boy or girl, the baby would be loved and well cared for. However, there were doubts about the future and she hoped that one day Danny would divorce his wife to marry her.

One morning, Tom Balant stopped ahead of her in his pick-up truck at the lights close to the office building where she worked, and she watched his eyes in the truck's rear view mirror, but he did not recognize her in the new car; or at least he made no indication of recognition - whatever, perhaps it was better that way.

A ring on her apartment doorbell startled her, and because it was in the evening she thought that it might be Tom, or perhaps Val had returned. Maria opened the door cautiously, and smiled when she saw her cousin, Ted.

"Come in Ted," she said, genuinely happy to see him. She had read a few days ago in the newspaper of some minor drug seizures in the city and a roundup of more than a hundred people; most of them teenagers who were arrested for possession or trafficking in drugs. The newspapers had made a big thing of the arrests, applauding the police force for the crackdown on drug traffickers and suggesting that more money should be made available to the department. As one editorial put it. "Our police are our front line of defense, cleansing the city of those, who in their greed for money, would defile our youth and threaten our very way of life." On the same page the writer urged the city fathers to accept a proposal by a large development company, to build a massive hotel and convention center in a rundown area of the city in return for a liquor license, tax concessions, and a land grant.

"I thought I'd drop in to see how you are getting along." Ted sat down on the easy chair, as Maria walked to the chesterfield after closing the door. "We haven't seen you since you arrived back in the city."

"I have been very busy," Maria excused herself.

Ted looked down at the floor, and back to Maria, weighing what he had to say, "I made time to come and see you, Maria."

A smile spread across Maria's face; he was being frank, and he was right, her excuse was hollow.

"Your father has told me quite a lot about your baby, and I would like to see him. Will it be all right if I drop in and visit, some evening during the week?"

"Is that a promise?" Ted asked by way of a reply.

Maria nodded her head. Not a thing had been said about the passing of her mother; perhaps Ted thought it best not to revive painful memories. "Can I get you a drink?"

"No thanks. I have to go back to the police station in a little while. I'm sorry about your mother."

"You knew that she was ill when you visited with my parents in Toronto?" Maria felt her eyes moisten, and she fought and controlled her tears.

"Yes. They asked me not to tell you about it. They didn't think that it was going to end this way."

"I understand," Maria replied, forcing a smile. "Perhaps it was better that way," she said with a fleeting smile, while she wished that she could have seen her mother alive, one more time.

"Have you heard from your father?"

"He has written quite a lot since Mother passed away, She always did the writing before. He will be coming to Vancouver for a visit when he gets back from visiting his parents in Italy."

"I will be looking forward to seeing him again, and there is room at my place if he would like to stay with us, Maria."

"Thanks," Maria replied, and she smiled in appreciation, before continuing, "there is room for myself and father to stay here now. One of my friends got married and moved in with her husband, and my other friend Val; I think you met her." Ted nodded, and Maria went on. "She disappeared. She was gone when I got back from Edmonton, and everyone that I have asked about her, doesn't know what happened to her."

"Check with the missing persons department," Ted suggested, "but don't be too concerned if they have nothing on her for awhile. There are dozens of young people go missing every day, and they usually turn up after a time quite hale and hearty." Ted glanced at his watch. "I have to run," and as he got up he continued, "we will be looking forward to seeing you soon."

"Okay," Maria replied and followed her cousin to the door.

"Phone me if you should need anything."

The newspaper had made a big thing of the drug arrests made by Ted's department. Maria smiled as she closed the door; he didn't seem to be elated by the apparent success, or perhaps he was modest. Anyway, he had not bothered mentioning it.

A police car pulled away from the front of the apartment, and amid the busy traffic and the flashing neon lights, it stopped for the traffic lights on the corner on the way back to the city center. Ted wasn't pleased with the latest round of arrests. The police had known most of the kids arrested for months, and they had been watched carefully, as the police gathered the evidence necessary to convict them. However, their surveillances had not led to any important persons in the criminal hierarchy, and the hours spent questioning those arrested had turned up nothing new. Once again they had acted too hastily, and destroyed many potential leads in order to satisfy the public, and newspaper's clamor for action on the drug problem. The public would be happy for a while again, and if re-elected, the mayor would make good his promise to increase the police department budget.

Coming away from the kitchen window, from where she had watched the police car drive away, Maria poured herself a cup of coffee, and sat down at the table to reflect on the visit that Irene had paid her one evening a few days before. There was the thump, thump of a high-fi from somewhere in the apartment as Maria took a drink of the coffee, then pushed the cup away from her and leaned on her elbows. Irene had come alone, as Ron had been busy with her father making arrangements for the wedding and their honeymoon. Irene had been enthralled with the coming event, and while she explained in detail the design of her wedding dress, the plans for the reception, and the islands in the Caribbean where they would spend their honeymoon; there was no invitation to the wedding. Maria knew that she was supposed to understand; and she did, still, it didn't lessen the pain. Maria reached for her coffee cup and raised it to her lips. It would have been better if she was invited and they trusted her not to show up. To hell with Irene, Maria thought on the way to the living room, where she sat in the easy chair by the telephone.

Debbie picked up the telephone after the first ring. She was happy and looking forward to their baby. Bill was working nights and she was expecting him to call from the shop, when he got his time off to eat. Big with her baby Debbie stayed at home for the most part; even so, she was bubbling with enthusiasm, and Maria smiled when Debbie explained that she had gone to see Mr. Evans at the store; she wanted her job back after the baby was born, so she and Bill could save for the down payment on a house.

"Mr. Evans promised you a job?" Maria asked.

"He said I should come and see him after the baby was born and if there was an opening, I would be hired."

"Will it be worth your while to hire a baby sitter for you to go to work?"

"Yes," Debbie replied laughing, "Bill is working nights, and we will be able to get by without a sitter. We figure that we will have enough money for a down payment in about two years and be on easy street."

"Then you will quit working?" Maria asked.

"Yep. Bill is quite set against me working, but we don't have much choice for the first two years. We will need three bedrooms as we plan to have four children. What do you think?"

"About the bedrooms or the children."

"The children," Debbie replied happily, and with hardly a pause, "how many do you plan on having?"

"At least one," Maria replied, the significance of what she had said going unnoticed, and to change the subject, Maria continued. "Did you hear from Val yet?"

"No, and I am beginning to get worried about her," Debbie replied with concern. "It has been a long time now since she went away and I'm afraid that we may never see her again."

"I told my cousin about her being missing, and he doesn't think there is anything to worry about, although he advised me to check with the missing persons department at the police station."

"Mm," Debbie replied, "I phoned Phylis last night, and I asked if her brother had seen Val since she went missing."

"Her brother!" Maria exclaimed.

"Yes, you know him, his name is Charlie."

"I have met him, although I didn't know that he was Phylis' brother, and I even talked to Phylis about him and she never mentioned that he was her brother."

"Well, I'm not surprised, as she is none too proud of him - he is involved with drugs and he tends to be a bully."

"That is the impression of him that I got too," Maria agreed, "and I thought it would be more likely that he was related to Glenda than Phylis."

"No, he is not related to Glenda and she wouldn't have anything to do with him, if it wasn't that she is involved with him in business. Knowing Charlie, it is uncanny the respect he has for Glenda, but he probably knows that she would cut his throat just as soon as look at him if he ever stepped out of line. Glenda is as cold as ice and as lazy as they come. She and I never got along when she lived at the suite and we would have come to blows a number of times if it hadn't been for Val coming between us." Debbie paused then continued. "Oh, that reminds me, Charlie got beat up by someone just about the time you were to leave for Edmonton. He was really in bad shape for a while, and except for Val, everyone I spoke to was glad that he finally met his match."

"What did Val have to say about it?"

"Nothing much really. She felt sorry for him and visited him in the hospital."

"I had better let you go and give Bill a chance to talk to you." Maria said.

"Okay," Debbie said cheerfully, "and if you hear from Val, let me know."

"I will," Maria replied.

Putting the telephone down, Maria leaned back in the chair as her pensive mood returned. Debbie was as happy as a lark, while as big as a mountain and living in a crummy little suite in the dog end of town. With inflation the way it was, Debbie and Bill would never have a pot to piss in, let alone a house of their own. A woman screamed at her children or her husband, close to the apartment and Maria shivered; she should have moved into a nicer apartment, instead of hanging on where she was in case Val came back and she would not be able to find her.

Standing by the window in the kitchen, Maria looked down on the street bustling with life. the apartment was quiet and Maria listened; on a number of occasions after a similar outburst, she had heard the woman crying, now there wasn't a sound. The traffic was heavy on the street and the neon signs at the theater flashed on and off over the heads of the people waiting to go in; everyone seemed to be going somewhere.

Maria closed the drapes, poured herself a glass of milk, and going to the living room she sat on the chesterfield with the drink in her hand to wonder what Danny would be doing at that moment. She had a date to go sailing with him in the morning if the weather was good, otherwise they would stay at the club. Lonely and pensive, Maria longed for the companionship of someone close with whom she could talk and be herself. Tom Balant would be fixing his machinery, or sitting at the kitchen table making entries in his account books, or perhaps he was lonely too, sitting in his pickup truck on the hill overlooking the farm, seeing the lights of his home, hearing the cattle in the pasture, and smelling the scent of the earth which was his; yet his thoughts would be of her.

Raising her drink to her lips, Maria tasted the milk, cool and sweet, and she checked the fierceness which had accompanied her thoughts of Tom - she would be jealous if he was with another woman. Her emotions seemed to be inexplicable and she frowned as she put down the glass and stood up to begin her exercise routine. She extended her arms above her head, stretched, then leaned sideways as far as she could, feeling her stomach muscles pull before she brought herself back, and leaned over on the other side, repeating the exercise in a steady rhythm, her shoulders well back and her breasts pushed forward, her long black hair swinging to and fro across her back. Had Val gone away with Charlie? It would have been an unlikely thing for her to do just a month to go, Val had been alone for some time and virtually without friends, she would have spent many a day and evening alone in the suite with no one to turn to. Maria got down on the rug, lay on her back with her hands under her head, stretched her legs out straight and raised them slowly about fifteen inches from the floor then lowered them slowly; repeating the exercise as she looked at the textured cream colored ceiling. She could feel her panties tight in her crotch and stopping for a moment she took off her pants, and continued with the exercises. If Val had gone away with Charlie, Phylis would know about it, and probably know where they were. Lying on her back, Maria rested for a time before doing some sit up exercises. She had talked to Phylis since Val had disappeared and she had disclaimed any knowledge of what had happened to Val - it wasn't like Phylis to be deceitful. Standing, Maria put her hands on her hips and did some knee bending exercises. The young couple living next door turned on their stereo and the sound of the music vibrated through the suite. My God, how long will they leave it playing, Maria thought as breathing heavily after finishing her exercise routine, she slipped out of her dress and readied herself for bed. She was going to bed early so as to be well rested for the sailing trip with Danny in the morning. She drank the rest of the milk and swallowed a sleeping pill from the bottle that a doctor had prescribed for Val. Her long hair shone as she brushed it with long clean strokes, keeping count of the number as she admired her nude body in the mirror. Someone had turned the volume on the stereo down and the music was barely audible, when Maria put out the light and lay down in bed.

CHAPTER 29

At eight o'clock in the morning it was already warm, seventy-five degrees and hardly a breath of wind. It was quiet at the yachting club, few members were around this early, and the two employees who had come on shift at seven were busy cleaning the leaves from the surface of the swimming pool. Down at the wharf the yachts rolled lazily on their moorings, in the wash from a cabin cruiser that had left a few minutes before.

On the deck of the Bliss-In, Danny relaxed in a deck chair with a long drink of juice in his hand, as he watched the steps leading down to the wharf. Maria looked as delicate as a daffodil in spring as she waved from the top of the steps, her white and yellow flowered dress, short and trim, giving emphasis to her slender legs. Three seagulls took off noisily from the water as she hurried down the steps, holding her sunhat in one hand and grasping the rail with the other. Danny remained seated, watching Maria as she descended the steps and walked gracefully along the wharf, the skirt of her dress moving rhythmically with the swing of her hips; she was happy and it showed on her face and the carefree swing of her body as she walked.

"Good morning," Maria called from a distance, and while smiling; Danny came to the rail of the boat to meet her.

"Good morning," Danny replied, and with an outstretched hand he helped Maria aboard, and kissed her lightly on the lips before giving her a juice drink he had prepared for her.

"I listened to the weather forecast on the way over in the car, and they are predicting temperatures in the nineties today," Maria said, still holding the glass of juice in her hand.

"There isn't enough wind for sailing," Danny said, as he took off his shirt, exposing his bronzed body to the sun, "so we will use the motor to cross the strait, then cruise the Gulf Islands." Danny smiled as he threw his shirt onto the chair, and the muscles of his body rippled with the movement. He was happy now, although only a little while before, for seemingly no reason at all, he had been apprehensive about Maria showing up for their date.

"There are not many people around this morning," Maria said, and she looked up as with a flutter of wings a seagull landed on a mast, "I suppose most of the members will be in church."

"It is more likely that they are still in bed," Danny said with a broad smile. "There was a dance at the club last night, that went on until early this morning."

"Were you at the dance?" Maria asked, and while watching Danny, she took another sip of her juice.

"No. My father and mother went. They don't dance much anymore, still they like to get together with their friends and live it up once in a while."

Maria's white teeth shone and her eyes sparkled as she smiled. She didn't know whether to believe Danny or not; in any event, his mother attending the dance would have excluded herself as a guest. "I am going below to change and I will be back in a jiffy," Maria said, handing the glass to Danny, and she smiled back to him, as he followed her down the steps into the cabin.

Things were different now, she had a locker of her own where she kept her sailing clothes and the boat was familiar; like an old friend. She knew the place of every cup and spoon, and where the guns were kept; it was here on the yacht that she felt at home. She undressed slowly as Danny sat on the chesterfield, and when she had shed her last piece of clothing she took the hand Danny offered and allowed herself to be pulled gently down onto the chesterfield beside him. Her firm nipples tingled at the touch of his lips, while his hands followed the smooth outline of her body. Then with her eyes closed, her knees bent, and her nipples red and tender, she waited for Danny to undress and come to her. Kneeling before her open thighs he eased his weight down on her, and Maria drew in her breath with relief and raised herself to meet him; the toned muscles of her stomach and legs, responding to her desire, giving force to her thrust, and hastening their union.

The Bliss-In slipped smoothly out of the harbor and the few people on the lawn before the club house, directed their gaze to the yacht with the young man and the girl at the helm, as the sleek white ketch with its tall masts, glided through the blue calm water of the sea, an example of man's harmony with nature.

A large ferry, out from Nanaimo, going in the opposite direction passed the Bliss-In as they approached Gabriola Island, and they turned to go north. Looking back over back over the stern, they returned the waves of the passengers lining the rails, as the Bliss-In cut a white path through the water. Ahead, the sea lay calm, and like a sheet of glass it reflected the blue of the sky, and an island on the horizon shimmered in the haze. Later in the morning they dropped the anchor off Qualicum and watched the crowds of people as they played on the sandy beach and swam in the sea. Moved by the revelry of the people on the shore they too went swimming, diving from the deck of the yacht and, playing in the warm water with a colorful beach ball that they had brought with them.

The small pools of water left on the deck as thy climbed back onto the boat, dried in the sun as they ate their lunch sitting cross legged on deck. Watching the movements of the people and boats around them, they were gratified to be a part of the happy scene. In the afternoon they pulled up the anchor and cruised slowly up the coast, drinking in the ever-changing view of beaches, forests, and island, and waving to the people on the other boats that passed their bow.

Trusting Maria now, Danny confided in her of the difficulties and dangers of importing drugs, as still dressed in their bathing suits and, with an arm about each other's waists they stood together at the helm of the boat in the warmth of the afternoon sun. The main problem was to have people you could trust; police agents were everywhere, although when drugs were seized the corporation claimed no knowledge of what their facilities were being used for, and the employees accompanying the cargos took the rap, unaware that the L. W. C. Import and Export Corporation was a party to their crime. On occasions, illegal, shipments, not authorized by the company had been reported to the police by the Leweses, themselves, and when arrests were made and drugs seized the Leweses had been given credit for being outstanding and concerned citizens. This device served their purpose well, by eliminating competition, winning recognition and prestige, and placing them above suspicion in cases where their own shipments fell into the hands of the police. However, the enterprise was not without dangers; that the relentless investigation by the police would uncover some damning evidence, and also that the few employees who by reason of necessity, knew of the Leweses involvement, would become a menace by injudicious actions. Of course the Leweses were not helpless and when imminent danger was suspected, such as was the case with Doc Ellis, action was taken to nullify the threat. Maria did not question Danny for details; she wanted no knowledge that would increase her present involvement and feelings of guilt, lest it would somehow mar the pleasure she gained from her new found wealth, but there was something else too, the more depth her knowledge of the sin, which to the Leweses was a way of life, the greater was the likelihood that one day she might be considered an unwarranted risk. Deny it as she may, Maria was aware that the mere mention to her of Doc Ellis, was in itself a subtle threat.

Nonsense, she and Danny were in love, and her mind without reason gave life to imaginings, which were unreal. Maria laughed as with one hand on the wheel and an arm about her waist, Danny pulled her closer and told her about a group of entertainers who were coming to the city with a fantastic act, which they would see together, and with happy, abandonment they projected their plans far into the future. They would sail the Bliss-In to Hawaii; if not next year, then the year after, when Irene's husband would have sufficient experience to run the business during Danny's absence.

The year after next she thought; her baby would be going on two years of age. Danny never spoke of a divorce, which Maria hoped would one day come about, and she did not believe that Danny would do nothing while his baby, which she carried within her, would be brought up without the benefit of a father. She would keep the baby a secret for a while as their love for each other matured, becoming stronger, day by day. They passed close to a sand bar where a number of people were fishing from a variety of small boats, and standing together an arm about each other they smiled when they saw a fisherman bring a salmon into his boat, and hold it up for everyone to see as he grinned from ear to ear. They dropped anchor in a sandy bay off an island, and still dressed in their bathing costumes they went below for a cool drink of gin. Taking off the top of her bathing suit she hung it over the back of a chair, before raising her firm breasts lightly with her hands, appreciating her new freedom while Danny poured the drinks. Handing Maria her drink, Danny raised his glass to proclaim a toast while he admired Maria's beauty in the flower of her youth.

"To our love and happiness," Danny said, as they clicked glasses together. To which Maria added a silent prayer for the future as they drank the toast; then they stood before bringing their lips together, the warmth of their bodies mingling in the cool of the cabin, rekindling their desires.

On the bed, Maria knelt over Danny, her mouth full, her lips and tongue moving gently, feeling the throb of her lover's pulse, as Danny lay with his head between her open legs, his arms embracing her buttocks, while his tongue aroused her to orgasm - happy together, as their love was uninhibited.

* * *

Tired and happy after her day on the yacht with Danny, Maria opened the door of her suite, and then bent down to pick up the note that someone slipped under the door during her absence. She closed the door behind her, switched on the light, and turned the note over in her hands. "Val is staying at 1982 Kastor Avenue." The note was typed and there was no signature. Maria walked on to the bedroom and lay the note on the dresser as she rummaged through the top drawer among the magazines, novels, bills, and assorted things which belonged to both herself and Val, that had been put in the drawer to clean off the top of the dresser. She found the map of Vancouver and lying on the bed she studied it for a while. Kastor Avenue was a small street off Fraser, she had driven through the area, and finding it would be no trouble. It was strange, Maria thought as she put the note in her purse, that if Val really was in Vancouver, why had she not contacted her, and who was the author of the note?

In bed, Maria attempted to concentrate her thoughts, to unravel the mystery of who might have delivered the note, and the reasons Val had not gotten in touch with her, yet sleep was irresistible and for a while, in the twilight between wakefulness and sleep, fantasy reigned, and she was a princess in a large ballroom, her two escorts competing for her favor, while an orchestra played and the couples, formally dressed, waltzed in time to the music. When the orchestra stopped playing and the floor cleared of the dancers she could see Val across the room, aged, poorly dressed, and all alone, grasping a large marble pillar for support, and in spite of her efforts her hands slipped on the smooth surface and she toppled awkwardly onto the floor, while the people around her seeming not to notice continued laughing and talking. Debbie and Phylis stood with their husbands and watched Maria as if trying to tell her something, while on the other side of the room, formally dressed, their clothes new and expensive, Glenda and Charlie, like a lady and a gentleman clicked their glasses and drank a toast. On a balcony above them all, her father and Ted, tall figures in dark suits, stood stern faced, surveying the scene. Maria gasped when she saw Val fall, and deserting her escorts, holding her long gown above her ankles, she hurried across the floor towards her friend, while a soft blue mist, swirled around the floor and her ankles, then rose to engulf the figures in the room, and Maria was asleep.

A door slammed noisily in the hallway as the young couple in the suite next door left for work. "Ssh," the young mother said to her sleepy baby, as she hurried to overtake her husband, already pressing the elevator button, his lunch pail and a plastic bag of the things the baby sitter needed for the baby clutched in his other hand, and outside the gray light of dawn slanted over the mountains. Maria's eyes flickered; she heard the baby crying as the girl went by the door and she turned and tried to go back to sleep, haunted now by the fantasy of the night before.

* * *

At two-thirty in the afternoon, Maria sat in her car across the road from 1982 Kastor Avenue. The house was in an older section of town and like the others on the street, it was set well back from the road. The houses were large, and although old, were well kept. The trees on the boulevard helped shield the car from the sun, which shone warm through the haze, and while it was not as warm as the day before, the humidity had increased, and Maria was glad that she had worn her green and white flowered dress, which was light and comfortable. She had thought about Val a lot during the day as she worked with Cec at the office and later when she and Danny had dinner together, but she said nothing of the note, or her plan to visit the mentioned address.

Two girls came out of the house and walked towards Fraser; wearing bright colors, their bust lines low, and their dresses short and tight, they swung their hips provocatively. Prostitutes; they stopped on the corner of Kastor and Fraser by the delicatessen; the dark girl with kinky hair swung her purse, and the blond with long straight white hair hanging down her back put a hand on her hip, as they looked up and down Fraser. Then they sauntered around the corner and disappeared.

A curtain moved on one of the bay windows as someone standing in its shadow, drew it aside to get a better view of Maria and the car she was driving. A policeman was coming down the street and tagging the cars where the meters showed a violation, as Maria pulled the strap of her handbag over her shoulder, slipped out of the car on the driver's side and jay walked across the road to the house. The policeman pushed his cap back on his head as he watched Maria cross the road. He had noticed her sitting in the car and the violation on the meter, and now with the jay walking infraction too, he shook his head. He tore a ticket out of his book and placed it on the windshield of a car and continued walking along the street; there was one more car with a violation before he would get to Maria's.

Looking back, Maria saw the policeman stop by her car before she walked up the wide wooden steps of the house and rang the doorbell. The door was sturdy and solid; not the kind that a man might kick in with his feet, Maria noted as she waited for her ring to be answered. A tall woman of about thirty-five neatly dressed and wearing dark rimmed spectacles, opened the door.

"Yes?" the woman said quietly.

"I have come to see a friend of mine, Valerie."

The woman hesitated, and looked past Maria, across the street to the policeman who was putting a ticket on her car. "I'm not sure you have the right address, but do come in," the woman said as she moved aside for Maria to enter into a wide hallway, and while the woman closed the door, Maria looked about her. The doors and woodwork were of oak, and an oaken coat rack stood in one corner close to the door. On her left, there was a large living room, with expensive furniture; lovely paintings hung on the walls, and a beautiful glass chandelier was hanging from the center of the high ceiling. The sound of women's voices came from behind a closed door at the end of the hallway, possibly the kitchen, a pack of cards was being shuffled noisily. "I will raise you," a girl said, her voice sounding muffled through the door.

"I am Maria Petersen," Maria introduced herself, "Val was in touch with me yesterday and she is expecting me to call."

"God damn you," a man said in a loud voice from behind the door, and a girl giggled.

The husky voice of the man was unmistakably Charlie's; and while Maria drew in her breath, she gave no other sign of recognition.

The woman smiled, "Val didn't feel well after dinner and she has gone to her room to lay down. It is the first room at the top of the stairs," she said, indicating with her hand the wide staircase partway along the hallway on their right.

"Thank you," Maria replied, before she turned away and walked towards the stairs.

The woman touched her horn rimmed glasses with her hand and watched Maria ascend the staircase. She could use a girl like her, still she was wary of Maria's presence. She had recognized Maria from across the street as the girl whom Glenda had warned her to be careful with, and she would have preferred not to let her in the house. However, she had been told to handle her with kid gloves and avoid trouble, and the policeman across the street had seemed to suggest just that. She watched Maria until she turned the corner at the top of the stairs, then she went to the kitchen, where Charlie and three girls were playing cards.

" I told you she was pretty," Charlie said, his smile ugly. Charlie's smile had always been ugly, and his face showed little evidence of the beating he had received at the hands of Rocky. Inside it was different, his vicious nature had become even more vicious, and while incensed by a desire for revenge, he was more cautious now than he was previously. He realized that he had been set up and the man whom he had fought was a trained boxer who had probably been hired to do the job. Even so his plans for revenge were frustrated, he had crossed with hundreds of people in his career and he had no way of knowing whom it was he should attack. It was this frustration that left the deepest scars in Charlie. He had trouble sleeping at night for the first time in his life and his dreams of revenge left him sweating and shaking with anger, but worse, Charlie had started to sample his wares in an attempt to escape.

"I could use a girl like her," the woman said thoughtfully.

"Forget it," Charlie replied emphatically. "She hobnobs with big shots and she's loaded."

The front door bell rang interrupting their conversation, and as the woman went to answer it the three girls and Charlie resumed playing cards.

"There is someone to see you Candice," the woman called from the hallway, and Candice adjusting the bodice of her dress to reveal more of her breasts got up from the table and went to meet her guest.

The madam went into the living room as Candice entered the hallway, "Hello," she said shyly.

"Hello," the man replied, returning her smile, and Candice took his large hand and led him up the stairs.

Back in the kitchen, the madam ordered the other two girls to clean some vegetables, and then beckoned to Charlie to follow her to the living room. "I shouldn't have let this Petersen girl into the house," she said, and her brow was furrowed with concern as she sat on an easy chair.

"You don't have to trouble yourself about her, Mary," Charlie said, and sitting on a chair opposite her, he hooked the fingers of his hands together and pulled until the muscles of his back and arms were taut.

"She could talk in the wrong circles," Mary replied. "Her cousin is a detective on the police force."

"She won't talk," Charlie said, while he continued his exercise, "my sister said that she has been wise to Glenda's game for weeks, and nothing has come of that."

Mary smiled, and getting up from her chair, she walked across the room, to slip between Charlie's open legs and sit on his knee. Charlie put his arm about her narrow waist and felt her warm breath on his face. "Even so we should be more careful, with the drugs, and drop them altogether for a time," Mary said, and holding her, body close against Charlie she kissed him lightly on the lips.

"Okay," Charlie replied, and she was soft and warm as he leaned back and pulled her close, to lie between his legs with her bosom upon his chest.

* * *

Although impatient to see Val, Maria climbed the stairs slowly, fully aware that the madam was watching her. The woman was pretty, her figure trim and she had taken pains with her dress and make-up, and it was only the lines on her face, which betrayed her age. She had deliberately not introduced herself, but otherwise she seemed pleasant and too refined for the role she filled. It would not be easy to run such an establishment, even with the help of Charlie; the girls would be rebellious, customers disagreeable, and on occasions, Charlie too would have to be made to toe the line. Then, in cases where Charlie was ineffective, negotiations and pay offs would have to be made to those who might otherwise close her house. The woman's outward appearance was deceptive, a facade that covered a personality that was hard and tough.

Upstairs the decor was elaborate, and there was the sound of music, as Maria walked along the passageway, her feet sinking into the plush blue broadloom. Stopping at the door where Val's name was written in gold lettering, Maria knocked lightly, and after trying again with no response, she opened the door and stepped inside.

Dressed only in a sheer slip, Val lay on the bed, her breasts cleanly visible, rising and falling as she breathed deeply in a peaceful sleep. The room was carpeted entirely in a cream broadloom and furnished as a bed sitting room, and besides the modern bed, there was a sofa, two easy chairs, and a bar with a good assortment of liquor, and glasses clean and shining. The walls were done in a light blue, and the drapes on the large window matched the broadloom. An open door led to a bathroom, and visible to Maria, there was a wall length mirror and a vanity with double sinks. Another door which appeared to lead to a clothes closet, was closed and Val's dress, nylons, and under clothes, were folded neatly on a chair beside the bed. Youthful; Val looked innocent and peaceful in her sleep, although the dark rings under her eyes, the marks left by tears on her cheeks, and the loss of weight since Maria saw her last indicated that all was not well.

Val's eyes fluttered open, as Maria sat on the bed beside her, and as if experiencing a dream, she lay still for a time, until her mind focused on reality, and sitting up she smiled to Maria before laying down again.

"You sent me a note?" Maria asked.

"No, I knew that you would find me."

How naive, Maria thought as she looked down on Val's young and innocent face, where the stresses she had experienced since leaving home were beginning to show. She was still very appealing to men - but for how long? Val wasn't hard enough to withstand for long the mental anguish that accompanied her career as a prostitute, and the scars from a hypodermic needle in the crooks of her arms showed that she was already buckling and resorting to drugs. "What happened after I left for Edmonton?" Maria asked.

"I got fired from my job and I needed money, so I came here."

It was a lie. She had given Val enough money to pay for the rent, and she could have easily managed for the two weeks before she started to receive unemployment insurance. "You could have hung on for a while longer?"

"Yes," Val replied, "It wasn't just the money. I was lonely too. None of our friends came to see me or wanted anything to do with me. Charlie was the only one who came around, and he was all racked up, from a beating he took when someone set him up outside a hotel. Did you have anything to do with it?"

Maria shook her head, easily concealing her surprise, behind her calm and unmoved composure. "You threw a party in the suite before you left?"

"That was Charlie's idea. He invited some people and I invited the girls I knew from the office. Not one of my friends showed up to the party," Val laughed to conceal her hurt, then continued, "I didn't know anyone besides Charlie, and I made friends with a couple of girls from this house who came the party. I decided then that I would go home to my parents as soon as I had a thousand dollars in the bank and some new clothes. I will shake the dust of the city off my feet. But I can't go home looking like a tramp." Val bit her lip, a tramp that is just what she was. "There is a boy back home and I will take up with him again," Val said with tears in her eyes when she finished.

"It won't work, Val quit here and come back to the suite, and look for a decent job."

Val shook her head. "It won't take me long now, and I will be able to go home."

Anger welled up in Maria as she listened to Val; she was refusing the outstretched hand of a friend, for a dream of going back in time, which was impossible. "You are hooked on drugs and a prostitute," Maria said, her voice rising in crescendo. "If you don't leave this place, in six months you won't be fit material to flush down the toilet." Maria stopped abruptly and got up to leave.

"Wait," Val cried, and when Maria hesitated she continued, "are you in that big a hurry?" Val sat up in bed and swung herself off the bed. "Sit down for a minute and we will have a drink."

Sitting erect on an easy chair, Maria looked at Val as she poured two drinks of vodka, and her anger ebbed away as Val, unsure of herself, and her hand quivering, added some soda water mix and ice to the drinks.

" No Thanks," Maria said, just soda water please. Val shrugged and taking another glass poured a straight soda water, and added ice. Maria took the drink and put it on the small table by her side. Val sat on the sofa, her drink in her hand.

"I'm glad you came," Val said, after taking a drink from her glass, "things are really not as bad as they appear."

"You have a drug problem."

"It is not that bad any more," Val, said, her smile forced and weak, "Mrs. Lenard; the woman you met downstairs, is doing a lot to help me and I will have it licked in a little while."

"Don't be too confident, Val and although you haven't gone too far yet, to come away and make a clean break would be a better solution."

"I appreciate your offer to help, Maria, but I'm only going to be here a short time anyway."

"There must be better ways of making money," Maria said.

More at ease now, Val laughed and took another drink. "If there are, I don't know of any." Then becoming serious. "Once I have this drug thing licked, everything will be okay and I will be on easy street. Some of the girls here are nice and they are doing what they can to help."

Listening to her friend, Maria felt sorry for her, yet there seemed little she could do to help. Val was actually afraid to come back - afraid that she would be left alone again, to relive the loneliness that she had found unbearable. While hiding the feeling of dismay that she felt for her, Maria told Val about what had happened during the past weeks, and Val expressed her condolence. Still their conversation lacked enthusiasm and candor, as Val avoided discussion of her problems and spoke only of her plans for the future. Going back home, marriage, children, and a home of her own! Maria was aware that Val's projections into the future were dreams and not a plan based on a rational assessment of her situation. The two girls embraced warmly before parting, and as good friends, they promised to keep in touch with one another. Maria never told Val of her baby, and Val had her own secret of Tom Balant, who had never returned after he recognized her.

Descending the stairs, Maria felt unhappy, and her mood was of anger, an anger for which she could find no expression. She saw Mrs. Lenard waiting at the bottom of the stairs and it was no surprise. She hadn't expected to walk away without anything being said.

"Can I speak with you for a moment, Miss Petersen," Mrs. Lenard said indicating the way to the living room.

"Certainly," Maria replied, and thinking about Charlie, she followed the madam into the living room. She didn't want any trouble with Charlie, although she wasn't afraid of him, and she would shoot to kill if necessary.

Maria sat on the sofa and turned to face Mrs. Lenard alongside her, their knees only inches apart. Mrs. Lenard smiled, and then began; her voice low and confidential. "Your friend Val is a nice girl; the men find her very appealing, and I like her. I don't deny that I would hate for her to leave, nevertheless, I will not try to persuade her to stay if she wishes to go. All my girls are free to leave any time they choose and they can take with them every cent they have earned."

The two women looked into each other's eyes steadily, perhaps attempting to read each others thoughts, or discover some hidden strengths or weaknesses. From what Val had told her, the madam was telling the truth, and on the surface at least she appeared to be reasonable. "I asked Val to come away, but she doesn't want to leave," Maria said. "She is not suited to this way of life and she has developed a drug problem since I saw her last."

"She does tend to be refined, and I think this is what the men find appealing. The drug problem," Mrs. Lenard sighed, and threw up her hands, "I'm doing my best. A customer was giving the drugs to Val, and she was hooked before we realized it. I have forbidden this fellow to come here any more, and some of the girls and myself, are doing all we can to help Val. She was ten times worse a couple of weeks ago and she seems to be coming along all right now. Still, I can't promise you anything, Miss Petersen, because I don't know."

Maria stood up. Mrs. Lenard showed more concern for her girls than she thought a madam would. "A quality service," the words from a book she had read recently, echoed in her mind. Mrs. Lenard was courteous and there was no threat, to persuade her not to take further action.

"1 will get Val to phone you and keep in touch," Mrs. Lenard said at the door, and her warm handshake was a plea for understanding and silence.

"Thank you," Maria replied.

The door closed quietly behind Maria, and as she went down the steps Mrs. Lenard took a position at the window and watched Marie cross the street to her car, take the ticket off the windshield, throw it onto the passenger seat, and drive away.

The two prostitutes who Maria had seen leave the house earlier, were window-shopping on Fraser when Maria passed in the car. Bending low, they looked into a jewelry store window, and Maria grimaced, both were heavy duty-it was no wonder the madam wished to hang on to Val. Pondering the events of the afternoon, Maria wended her way home through the heavy traffic. Mrs. Lenard had behaved like a lady, yet to run a brothel successfully, she would have to be as hard as nails, and she wasn't everything she appeared to be an the surface. Who had it been that felt concerned enough about Val, to have written the note? Not Mrs. Lenard, by a long chalk. Perhaps one of the prostitutes with whom Val was friendly? Then it came to Maria as she stopped the car in the parking lot outside the apartment; Phylis had written and delivered the note herself. She had known where Val was all the time and she had lied to protect her brother.

CHAPTER 30

The following morning, Maria spent alone in the inner office, catching up on Cec's typing, filing, and answering the telephone. Cec had gone to the airport to meet her uncle's representative, who was arriving from New York. She had learned from Cec, a week ago, that Perrelli's representative would arrive this day, but Danny had not mentioned a word. She had tried in the beginning, with no apparent success, to persuade Danny to accept the new conditions to which the corporation had evolved. Now sitting alone she paused in her work and prayed that Danny would not be embittered by the new situation.

At noon, Steve Bailey came into the office. He had just left Mr. and Mrs. Lewes, Danny, Cec, and her uncle's representative, at the Bay Tide Hotel where they were to have dinner. Steve had brought his lunch with him and Maria took the opportunity to go down to the main floor cafeteria to eat. The restaurant was crowded and she waited twenty minutes in the line up for her hamburger and chips, before she took a table with two of the girls who worked as typists for the Plastick Utensil Company. The girls liked Maria, and while their conversation was casual and pleasant, she was something of a mystery to them, aware as they were that she carried a gun and knew how to use it.

In the office after lunch, the afternoon dragged. Steve Bailey had gone out, and alone in the inner office, Maria looked out of the window; it was a beautiful day, a little cooler than it had been on the weekend, and there were a few clouds, thin and streaky, floating high in the predominantly blue sky. The light breeze would have made it an ideal day for sailing and exploring the Gulf Islands. The clock in the office showed three thirty; it had been a day in her life wasted. Cec had asked her to stay until he returned; perhaps if he would just telephone the waiting would be more bearable. A multitude of boats plied the waters of the strait, and now a large freighter, its decks lined with large crates, dominated the scene as it moved slowly towards Vancouver.

The intercom buzzed in Cec's private office and Maria ran quickly to answer it.

"Mr. Banas is here," Betty said, when Maria opened the switch.

"Thanks," Maria replied, and after scanning the closed circuit television she opened the door. Cec had returned with another man, tall and square shouldered, his back to the camera; he reminded her of someone she knew well, and her heart beat a little faster. Maria switched off the monitor and waited, was it possible? She was right when Cec opened the door and stood to the side, it was her father who entered, smiling and walking towards her while Cec stepped inside and closed the door behind them.

"Father!" The word escaped Maria's lips and she ran forward to meet him, throwing her arms about his neck as he lifted her off her feet, and kissed her tenderly.

Questions raced through Maria's mind as with her father, she followed Cec to his office. How had her father met Cec? Why hadn't he written to say that he was coming? Did he have a place to stay? Was he on holiday or had he come to Vancouver to live?

"Your father is Perrelli's new representative with the Lewes' corporation." Cec said as soon as they had sat down. Then he went on to explain that the appointment had been made only a couple of days before, and they had kept the news as a pleasant surprise.

Happy for their reunion, Maria hid her misgivings that her father was to become party to the dirty business of trafficking in illegal drugs. Her father's involvement compounded the misgivings, of her own involvement, which after seeing the plight of Val, tugged at her conscience.

They had supper with Cec and his wife at their home, and after cocktails and a friendly chat, Cec drove Maria and her father to a lavish apartment, which he had rented for Andrew Petersen. A penthouse overlooking English Bay, the kind of a home that Danny had urged Maria to rent, to be more in keeping with her position and taste for life, but which until now she had declined as she waited to hear from Val.

* * *

Andrew Petersen started work as the warehouse supervisor for the L. W. C. Import and Export Corporation the following morning, and during the next few days he went over the books with his secretary, quickly bringing himself up to date with the warehouse procedures, and visited every warehouse a number of times to become acquainted with the foremen, and the men with whom he was to work. The men took to Andrew immediately, appreciating him for the willingness and pleasure he took to sit down with them in their lunchrooms, and talk with them over lunch; where they recognized his ability and knowledge of the work.

In the weeks that followed, as Andrew became acquainted with his new position, he changed a number of procedures in the warehouses, making them more efficient, and paid special attention to security, to insure that the drug traffic flowed smoothly with a minimum of risk. Slowly, Danny Lewes relinquished the responsibility of running the warehouses, and though he spent most of his time at the office attending to the work that had once been his father's, he still found time to occasionally visit the warehouses, where as always, he was extremely popular with the men. Meanwhile Danny introduced his brother-in-law, Ron Rahl to some of the office procedures, and with a view to him learning the business, he encouraged Ron to visit the warehouses and get to know the men and the work.

It was during his visits to the warehouses that Andrew came to know Ron Rahl, and with prior knowledge of each other, by way of Maria, they quickly became friends. Andrew appreciated Ron's eagerness to learn, although it was apparent that he knew nothing about the illegal nature of the business, and Ron respected Andrew for the wide knowledge that he possessed, and the efficiency with which he did his work.

Meanwhile, the relationship between Danny Lewes and Andrew Peterson was less than cordial. Danny resented the intrusion of Perrelli's brother into the family business, and his very efficiency was a thorn in his side, giving him no justification by which he could seek Andrew's removal. He resented too, Andrew's involvement with Maria, and he was afraid that Andrew might interfere in his private life, with him coming between himself and Maria to spoil their relationship; a relationship that he considered sacred. In the beginning, Maria attempted by persuasion to bring Danny and her father together; but, when after a time no progress had been made, she resigned herself to living with the situation as best she could.

For his part, Andrew was aware of Danny's resentment and suspicion, and preferring that their relationship remain cool, he said nothing to allay his fears. At the same time Andrew avoided, as far as possible, open antagonism, subtly negating Danny's attempts to discredit him in the eyes of the other employees, and judiciously honoring the individuality of Maria and the privacy of her personal life, saying nothing that would mar their strong family ties. Had Andrew been an ordinary employee, his tenure would have short lived, but the situation called for some delicacy, and Danny could do little to interfere seriously with his work. This frustrated Danny, and while his resentment remained, he came to acknowledge Andrew's ability and the efficiency with which he ran the warehouses, and he sensed a cold ruthlessness in the tall, athletic, and unsmiling man, which bid him use caution in his plans to be rid of him. Danny cared nothing that Andrew was the father of his lover; Andrew Petersen was a thorn in his side, that eventually would have to be removed, and in the interim a way must be found to circumvent his efficiency that had prevented him from bringing in the shipments of drugs that would exclude Perrelli from his share of the profit. While the regular shipments were going through unimpeded, under the watchful eyes of Andrew, the drugs that Danny intended for the personal profit of the Leweses were collecting in Montreal and awaiting shipment.

A rift had developed in the Lewes family, as Danny's parents and Irene, noting Andrew's efficiency and the smooth operation of the warehouses, apposed the idea of bringing in drugs contrary to the agreement, while Danny had no wish to honor the agreement, which he felt had been forced upon them. Outvoted by the other members of his family, Danny agreed that at least for a time the company would go straight with Perrelli, although first a plan must be devised that would enable them to bring secretly to Vancouver the illegal drug shipments that had been stored in Montreal.

The community swimming pool was almost deserted at eight o'clock in the evening, as Maria, young and feminine in her two-piece bathing suit, sprung lightly on her toes as she tested the spring of the high diving board before diving. There were a few people in the water, children and adults, and fewer people watching in the bleachers. A number of people were paying attention to Maria as she prepared to dive, and the lifeguard, a college undergraduate who worked part time to finance his education, smiled from his seat overlooking the pool. Slender and attractive, Maria sprung high from the board, graceful in every movement from years of practice, her body arched and turned, and with her hands stretched before her, she cut the water like a knife, surfacing in seconds, then turned and watched her father, as he prepared to follow in a dive from the spring board.

Tall, muscular, and beautifully proportioned, he catapulted high from the board, jackknifed, straightened and cut the water clean in a perfect dive. A narrow waist and agile, only the lines on his face and his graying hair, betrayed his age, that was more evident since her mother's death. A feeling of sadness swept over Maria as treading water, she watched her father swim easily beneath the water. Perhaps, because she knew Danny better than she would to herself admit, she felt responsible for her father's involvement in the illegal drug trade, and concern that some harm would befall him.

Since he had come to Vancouver, Maria visited her father in his swank apartment, almost every evening. They enjoyed each other's company, whether it be cooking, watching television or exercising, when she was thrilled to see her father lift the heavy barbells with ease. Physical fitness conscious, they visited the swimming pool twice a week, but they liked going out on the town too and they enjoyed many an evening in the sumptuous and tranquil atmospheres of Anne's Lounge. Maria was happy to observe her father and her uncle become good friends. They had met Ted and Alice at the lounge on a number of occasions also, and although they enjoyed the evenings together, Andrew never visited them in their home or invited them to his apartment. "A policeman is always on duty," her father explained, "and it is better, at least for the time being, that we stay away."

Maria's life with Danny remained unchanged; they had dinner together at noon daily, and he visited her regularly in the new apartment she had rented and furnished elaborately. On the weekends they went yachting or dancing, and on one Sunday, she and Danny made a foursome with Irene and her husband for tennis. Yet for all this and her new found wealth, Maria was unhappy. Her concern for her father's safety had grown; Danny no longer discussed with her the problems he encountered with his work and she was suspicious that something was afoot, that would in some way harm her father. Also, she had seen Val on the street with another girl, and parking opposite at a meter, she had watched them without being seen. Val's addiction to drugs and her decline in health were all too apparent and this too bothered Maria.

Coming home after a pleasant evening with her father, Maria washed her hair then took a bath in the large round bathtub that she had installed in her suite. The tub had not been available in Vancouver, in the shade of blue, which she liked, and the interior designer who furnished her apartment, had it brought in from San Francisco. Maria switched on the ceiling sun lamp, as she stood nude before the full-length mirror and brushed her long hair. The strained relationship that existed between Danny and her father since the day he arrived in Vancouver had not lessened, and her father noticed a new boldness and lack of respect from Rocky Devis. Andrew had confided in Maria that the bastard was up to something. Maria poured a glass of water and took a sleeping pill from a bottle in a drawer in the vanity, then she changed her mind and put it back in the bottle; she was taking too many tranquilizers and sleeping pills lately, and she lay awake thinking about the future; it was murky. In bed, Maria read for a time, before switching off the light and closing her eyes, only to question the worth of giving up; for wealth and Danny's love, the values of honesty, justice, and charity, which her mother had exemplified, and which for reasons of expedience, she had all but abandoned.

Also, Danny had become fascinated with his son, and he showed her pictures of him, in the crib, in the bathtub, and beside the swimming pool. Did he expect her to understand and accept his other life without a qualm? She couldn't. It disturbed her and she delayed telling Danny about her own baby, realizing that his son had cemented a bond between himself and his wife, stronger than their marriage vows. Soon she would have to tell him of her baby and there would be a showdown. She could insist that he sue for a divorce to marry her, but Danny, happy with the present arrangement, would blame her father as the instigator, and he would see the retribution would come swift and with good measure. But then again, Danny didn't know her father.

Restless and afraid, Maria drifted off into an uneasy sleep, to awake again in a little while, and with a curse she got up to take the sleeping pill that she had tried to do without.

* * *

Parking her car outside her father's apartment, Maria turned off the ignition, and father and daughter sat quietly for a time, pensive after a relaxing evening at Anne's Lounge, as a steady stream of people passed by on the sidewalk, their faces and clothing, reflecting the colors of the vapor lamps and neon signs along the street.

"Are you coming up for coffee?" Andrew asked.

"Sure," Maria replied, turning to her father and smiling.

Andrew laughed as he opened the car door. "Since when do you need an invitation?" he asked.

It was true, she had always been made welcome, and her father's apartment was like a second home, yet she had waited for the invitation and her father had been aware of it. She needed her father and perhaps he needed her, still she felt she was imposing on him and restricting his way of life. Mother had kept him on a tight leash, not the he would do wrong, but that he would do the right thing, he would have kicked his boss' ass.

Andrew closed the door of the penthouse apartment behind them, and in the darkness they went to the large windows overlooking the bay. The moon shone yellow off the water, dotted here and there by dark moving shadows of the patchy clouds that drifted in the sky. There were the scattered lights of ships that plied the waters. A passenger liner, ablaze with lights from stem to stern, looking like a small city in the water, was moving dead slow, her course outward bound.

"It is beautiful," Maria said, putting her arm about her father's waist, "but is it worth it?" And there was a note of sadness in her voice.

"Is it?" Andrew said, tousling his daughter's hair and switching on the lights. "Coffee?"

Maria shook her head. "Mix me a double vodka and lemon."

"Do you need it?"

"No." Maria, replied, and almost laughed. She was still his little girl.

The telephone rang as Maria closed the drapes, and she listened as her father answered it.

A young woman's voice came over the line, "I have been in touch with Montreal, Mr. Petersen, and the truck that you asked me to inquire about has a problem with the rear end. It will only be in the garage at most one day, and the garage owner thinks that he might be able to get the truck fixed overnight, so that it will be ready to roll in the morning."

" Thanks, Lois," her father replied, "I will take care of it."

"Okay, Mr. Peterson, and good night."

"Good night."

Her father hung up the telephone and came to sit by Maria on the chesterfield. It was unusual for even a private secretary to telephone her boss at ten o'clock at night, Maria thought, and she experienced a pang of jealousy. She was being unreasonable, and it was unthinkable that her father would not eventually remarry?

"We had a memo on a truck that was to be tied up in Montreal for six days." Andrew explained. "It would have delayed some of our shipments, so I had Lois check on it. Evidently it was an error, and the truck will be available."

"You are efficient, father. You let nothing escape you."

Andrew shrugged, and Maria got up to go to the kitchen. "Coffee, Dad?"

"Please," Andrew replied.

Returning from the kitchen, Maria served her father with coffee, and sat on an easy chair opposite him. Should she tell him or not she thought. "I'm pregnant," she said quietly.

"I know Maria," Andrew said with understanding, as he put his cup down.

"You knew," Maria, said surprised. Although she should not have been surprised. Her father had done or known the unexpected many times before; it was a part of his character, which she loved, and she would have laughed had she not seen the hurt in his eyes.

"I was concerned when you visited our doctor in Toronto; because of a headache, you said at the time. I talked to him later that day." Maria raised her eyebrows? "He's our friend," Andrew said.

"I know Dad, I just thought it would be cruel to tell you," Maria said, as she leaned on the arm of the chair. "But you are the only one with whom I can talk." Andrew forced a smile, and Maria continued. "The baby's father could be Danny or Tom Balant. Did you meet Tom?"

"No," Andrew replied, " I have heard a lot about him from your Uncle Bert, and I saw him once at Anne's Lounge," and after a pause, Andrew continued. "He seems to be a nice fellow; even so I didn't want to be introduced as I don't like the image I would present, with you being Danny's mistress, and my acquiring a good job in his warehouses."

"I'm sorry," Maria said, and she noticed that the lines on her father's face appeared deeper and his sadness so profound. She was not sorry for having affairs with men, or being pregnant out of wedlock. She was sorry that she had been the cause of sadness for her father, whom she loved very much. "I am not ashamed, Father. The baby will be a Petersen, and I will bring him or her up with all the love and understanding that you and Mother showed me."

"Don't be mistaken Maria. I am sad that your baby may not have a father in its life; however, I am not ashamed, and as surely as you will be a good mother, I will be a proud grandfather. You are a pretty woman, Maria life is yours for the taking, and you will have many opportunities of marriage."

Maria crossed the room to sit once again by her father. In a subtle way she was being reproached for her conduct, but she knew he meant well and wished to impart to her some of the wisdom, which he had gained over the years.

"When your mother and I met, we saw life's fulfillment in each other and were happy, although not always satisfied with our lot in life, and we tried to better ourselves. When you were born, it was a godsend, but I wished that I could have provided you and your mother with more of the material things of life. But now I know that wasn't necessary."

"I know what you mean, Dad, and I am beginning to get the picture," father and daughter both laughed.

With riches and material things they now possessed they were less happy, and as they looked into each other's eyes they smiled now, a smile of understanding. Then both becoming serious, they looked deep into each other's souls.

"It isn't the baby that is bothering you, Maria it is something else."

"I saw Val on the street yesterday," Maria began thoughtfully, as she recalled the events of the previous day, "I parked and watched for quite a while. She and another girl, younger than herself, were hustling on the street. They looked ill and were not very successful, but they were making enough to pay for drugs and satisfy somebody's purse. I telephoned the madam at the house where she worked from, when I saw her last, and she told me that Val had left and she didn't know where she had gone. It was a dirty lie, Father," Maria said, her voice rising. "She sold Val to some pimp, when her quality slipped below the standard she had set for her house. Glenda, Charlie and now some unknown pimp, like Judas, they are betraying what is good and clean in humanity, selling their souls and the well-being of others, for a few shekels. Even worse, with drugs and the addiction to drugs, they have corrupted the minds of the innocent; the filthy tentacles of vice, spreading through society like an open cancer." Stopping abruptly, Maria covered her face with her hands and cried quietly.

"Perrelli, the Leweses, Cec Banas, and now us; are we any better?" Andrew said viciously, his face a mask of pent up anger.

"No," Maria cried, in anguish, "That is why I want us to be out of it. We will run away and be free."

"It is impossible, Maria. With our knowledge we are a threat to everyone else involved. Everyone is afraid, watching, and being watched, and to make a sudden break with the organization or even cause a hint of suspicion that we would disclose our knowledge, would bring us disaster."

Nodding her head, Maria reluctantly agreed. She had known this to be true, and her outburst was in anguish of the helplessness of their position. Maria looked at her father steadily, his face was cold and ruthless, and she prayed to God that he felt the same way as she. "You must help me to do something for Val," she said, her voice rising in crescendo, a plea to her father. "She is a kook, but not deserving of the fate that has befallen her."

"Let us have a bite to eat," her father interrupted abruptly.

Pressing her lips firmly together, Maria nodded, then got up and went to the kitchen. There was no need to plead with her father, he would help in every way he could. Her father followed her into the kitchen and as she tied an apron about her waist, she watched him go to the refrigerator for a beer. They ate their sandwiches in silence, and while Maria drank her tea, her father drank his beer from the bottle.

"Your friend is beyond voluntary help, Maria. She has to be picked up by the police for prostitution and trafficking; it is about the best help she can get now."

"It won't work. She has been picked up before. They have lawyers, witnesses, and alibis, that make it difficult for the charges to stick."

"Then it will be up to you, to collect the evidence that will convict her, and her associates. If you are good enough, and collect the evidence without bringing suspicion of your own involvement, you could make a deal with Ted to keep your name entirely out of the records, obtain special privileges for your friend, and unknowing to Ted, establish some credit for your own future use."

"It is worth a try," Maria said after some deliberation, and the realization that there was no other way. Perhaps the credit earned would also apply to her father. Maria glanced at her watch. "It is too late to go back to my apartment. Is there anything special that you would like for breakfast?"

"I have had a craving for pancakes for days, and no one to cook them," Andrew replied, and father and daughter smiled together.

"Okay, pancakes it will be," Maria said, as she retired to the bedroom that her father had prepared for her when he first occupied the suite.

Andrew cleared away the plates and glasses from the kitchen before sitting down again to finish his beer, his brow furrowed as he contemplated their future. The poverty that had dogged him all his life was gone; replaced by more worrisome problems. The steady breathing from the bedroom told him that his daughter was asleep. If his wife could have lived to share the luxury of their new surroundings - he smiled, living in memories, and knowing her reaction; she would have been even more worried than either himself or Maria.

The alarm clock was ringing in her father's room when Maria awoke; the first sound sleep she had in a week. Her father was letting the alarm ring to make sure she was awake, and she smiled as she slipped out of bed to cook the bacon and pancakes that her father enjoyed.

Andrew was dressed and ready for work by the time breakfast was ready. They had got up early, and it was only six-thirty when they finished their breakfast. He wanted to be at A depot when the first trucks arrived; an important shipment was going through that morning, her father explained. Maria knew what he meant; the drugs would be in and out of the warehouse in a matter of hours, and the shipment would not be out of his sight until it was through. The truck that had been delayed in Montreal; he would delve into the matter further as soon as he was free.

"Take good care of yourself," Maria said, after kissing Andrew good-bye at the door.

"You bet," he said, with a reassuring smile, and then he closed the door, and walked to the elevator, tall and straight, his footsteps silent in the heavy carpet, while he thought about the task before him that morning.

CHAPTER 31

Taking a second cup of coffee, and leaving the dishes for the maid to clean, Maria went into the living room and sat in one of the large easy chairs where she could see through the sliding glass doors. Teeming with rain outside, the droplets bounced on the roof top patio and splashed in the small pools of water in the hollows. Beyond, on the windswept waters of the bay, a small fishing fleet raced for the open sea; heading for Juan De Fuca Strait, and the fishing grounds off the west coast of Vancouver Island, and North until their holds were filled. The water around the little vessels was white with foam as they ploughed on in defiance of the rough sea. Maria imagined she could hear the steady throb, throb, throb, of the boats' engines above the roar of the wind, and see the men at their helms; dogged in their determination to make good time to the fishing grounds, resolved to do their work well, ready to laugh in the face of danger, and carry on until their task was complete. She would need some of this same spirit and determination herself, in the coming days, if she was to save Val from the clutches of the creeping death to which she had abandoned herself.

A fierce anger gripped Maria. While out on the sea, the lead boat, fighting to keep its position, smashed its bow into an oncoming wave and shuddered in hesitation, then, with a burst of spray, it was through and racing forward once more. She would help Val, come what may, and free her father and herself from their involvement in the drug trade. Certain of her father's support, Maria resolved to work diligently and cautiously to save Val, and prayed for her father's and her own deliverance; knowing that one false move would bring them to an untimely death, which would be neither their own or any other's salvation.

Slowly Maria's anger ebbed, and her mind sought to give reason for their participation in an enterprise that was contrary to their morals and the morals of a healthy and vibrant society.

Weary and discouraged from trying unsuccessfully, within the constraints of their position in society, to win the goals of wealth and the good life which society holds to be success, they like many others, stepped outside the bounds of the law to achieve the goals to which they rightfully aspired. They had been weak; lured by wealth and the promise of quick success, they had heeded the advice of unscrupulous persons. By forsaking the values and convictions by which they had lived, they had become parasites in the society to which, although imperfect, they were indebted for everything they cherished and held dear.

"The bastards," Maria muttered, seeking scapegoats for her own human imperfections. Then standing up, she pulled her finely embroidered dressing gown about her and went to her bedroom to brush her hair before dressing.

* * *

In spite of the rain and the dreariness of the day, Maria and Danny enjoyed their lunch together at the club, and they laughed and talked happily while they drove to her apartment to spend an hour or so, before Danny returned to his work. There was something akin to worship in her love for Danny; it was impossible to be unhappy in his presence, and her fears evaporated like a mist in the August sun.

However, when Danny had left, Maria thought again of Val and her father, and the reality of their situation returned. Although she hadn't mentioned staying overnight at her father's place, Danny had known. He had divulged it in his conversation, and she had ignored it at the time and said nothing. But she realized now its full implications; she and her father were under close surveillance. Had Danny divulged it by the slip of the tongue or had it been uttered as a warning, or a threat. She had no way of knowing.

Maria had skillfully, she thought, broached the delicate subject of divorce, but Danny had changed the subject abruptly; he was happy and content with the present arrangement, and she recalled Tom Balant's warning. To Danny and his wife, this type of arrangement was a way of life, taken for granted, and not allowed to interfere with their marriage. Maria had taken Tom's warning lightly then, but now she was finding it increasingly difficult to accept what Danny considered to be a comfortable arrangement. She might have accepted this without qualm, to live for the present, and to hell with the future. But now there was her baby, her increasing involvement and commitment to the drug scene, and the rift between her father and Danny necessitated she live in two separate worlds, which she couldn't bring together.

However, there was something else too, slow but relentless, the moral standards she had internalized in her childhood and thrust aside in the exuberance of youth were resurfacing in her mind. Her conscience was bothering her for things that she would have not given thought just six months before, and coupled with this was her uncontrollable love for Danny, whom, although with perturbation, she would follow like a child the Pied Piper. Even now as she prepared to find Val, she looked forward to the morrow when she would see Danny once more.

More appropriate to her purpose of searching for Val, Maria changed from her mini dress into a pair of slacks and a sweater, and then she took the gun from her purse and checked it to make sure it was loaded. Only a short time ago, she had carried the gun for the sole protection of Danny, and now it was an instrument for her own defense in a world she recognized to be deceptively hostile.

It was still raining, when Maria parked her car in a neighborhood near the docks, which she knew Val worked. Lifting the collar of her raincoat, Maria gathered it about her neck and hurried to the doorway of a cafe, where she stood for a moment looking at the rain and pools of water on the street being splashed up by the passing traffic. Then turning her head, she let her eyes search the cafe through the glass door; besides the girl behind the counter, two young men, and an elderly couple were its only occupants. Maria hurried along the street to the doorway of a hotel, where she waited for a while thinking that perhaps Val was inside, then she changed her mind; the proprietor could lose his license if it was known that girls worked the hotel, and Val's profession was obvious.

"I'll buy you a drink," a man said, stopping in the doorway and waiting for Maria to reply.

Maria shook her head, and hurried on in the rain to the doorway of another cafe. Val was sitting at the counter with another girl younger than herself, but with the same stunned expression on her face. Opening the door, Maria stepped inside, and the two girls looked around briefly, before turning back to look at themselves in the mirror behind the counter as Maria passed behind them to sit at a booth and order a coffee. Val and her friend were talking and giggling, their coffee cups empty before them, as Maria waited and studied the situation. An older man entered the cafe, and after a few words with the girls, Val's friend got up to accompany her escort, leaving five dollars on the counter for her coffee. Even the cafe owner took his cut.

"Hi," Maria said, as she sat down beside Val and put her cup of coffee on the counter.

There was a puzzled expression on Val's face for a moment before she smiled. "I hardly recognized you with your hair tied back and your new coat."

"I have the afternoon off," Maria said, returning Val's smile. "So I thought I would drop around and look you up."

Expressionless, Val abruptly turned on her seat as someone entered the cafe. A man went by them and sat in a booth, and Val turned her attention once again to her friend.

"Let's go to the hotel for a juice," Maria said.

Val shook her head. "Clive would be put out, if I just took off while I was supposed to be working."

Maria put one hundred dollars into Val's purse. "Come on," Maria said, turning on the stool to get up. "Clive will feel less put out with some money in his pocket."

"Okay," Val replied with a worried expression on her face, "but I can't stay long."

Fishing in her purse, Maria took some money out, and put it on the counter to pay for her coffee as Val left a toonie by the side of her cup.

* * *

The hotel bar, half a block along the street, was dirty and run down. Occupied mostly by men gaffing over their beer, they looked up as Maria and Val entered the dimly lit room, and returned to their conversations when the two girls sat down at a table some distance away. Maria put up her hand, two fingers, to order their drinks, and the waiter hesitated and looked back to the man behind the bar, who looked the girls over and rubbed his chin thoughtfully before nodding his head.

The waiter was about to say something as he put down the beer that Val had ordered, and an apple juice for Maria, but after looking into Maria's delicate and pretty face, and expensive clothes, he changed his mind. Her appearance commanded respect, and it was best he leave unsaid the warning he had prepared to give the girls.

A tall man entered the bar, and stood close to the door looking around, letting his eyes become accustomed to the light, as he shook the rain from his open coat.

"Is the policeman following you or me?" Maria asked.

Val glanced towards the door and shrugged. "I don't take notice of the them any more."

The plain-clothes policeman sat down at a table next to theirs, and ordered a beer. Val and Maria conferred quietly, took a drink, and on a signal from Maria they got up and carried their drinks to another table a good distance away. The waiter watched them move, and said something to the man behind the bar.

The barman in his early thirties, drew a glass of beer, and walked over to the policeman with it in his hand. He set the beer down on the table and looked steadily into the eyes of the policeman. "If you annoy the girls any further, you will have to leave."

The policeman made as if to protest, then changed his mind, and with a resigned look on his face, he nodded his head. But as the policeman watched the barman return to the bar, his large behind swaying as he walked, the expression on the policeman's face changed to one of extreme disdain, and his mind rebelled against the injustice he had been subjected to. Yet, there was nothing he could do, his assignment was far too important to blow it by chewing the ass out of the barman.

Out of earshot, Maria and Val, their heads close together, talked earnestly in low voices. Maria took Val's hand in her own across the table as her friend related her experiences. Val was emaciated, a mere shadow of her former self, still, Maria's friendship had brought life to Val's eyes, and they glowed like coals from the dark hollows from which they had sunk. She had trusted Charlie, Mrs. Lenard, and some of the girls from the former house, only to be betrayed and forced to leave when her customers had become few. She still hoped that she could go it alone, and she didn't know that she had been sold to Clive, for a pittance, that he may ring the last dollar from her body until she would be cast aside as human garbage for which there was no use or hope. Devoid of friendship, Val had no one with whom she could confide, unburden her troubles, seek advice, or reach out for help. Now close to Maria, feeling the warmth of her hand and the unwavering bond of friendship between them, she poured out her troubles, and the dream of her own resurrection was rekindled. She had two hundred dollars in credit with Clive; just a couple more hundred, and she would break away and go home to her parents to start a new life. Val ordered another beer, and over Maria's protests she insisted on paying for it. "Do you think I'm sort of a fucking bum?" she said, and laughing aloud, the two girls attracted the attention of some of the people in the bar. Then they lowered their voices and continued their conversation as Maria, slowly and skillfully, maneuvered her friend to talk about drugs and how she obtained them.

Val could obtain drugs, for herself and her customers, at the flophouse where she worked, or the hotel, as the bastard who runs it prefers to call it. There was no money involved; she got what she ordered as long as it was within reason, and the owner settled later with Clive.

"I'm going to a party on the weekend, and I'm supposed to bring some hashish and cocaine," Maria said, squeezing Val's hand affectionately. "Do you think I could get some?"

"Yes," Val replied. After taking a long draft from her beer, she continued, "Clive would skin me alive, if he knew I was selling it outside the hotel."

"I don't want to get you into trouble," Maria said with concern. "How about Charlie, perhaps 1 could get some through him?"

"Yes," Val said, nodding her head in agreement, "Charlie would be your best bet, as the stuff I get is piss poor quality anyway. Ah! But Charlie's a pain and I hate to give him the business."

"A pain?" Maria questioned in surprise.

"Yes, he polices the whore house. If there is any trouble, they call Charlie, and he takes care of it for a price. Besides that, he gets a rake off on all the drugs that are sold." Val paused and took a deep breath. "The guy is worth a mint," she went on, disgust evident in her voice. "However, if you want good quality stuff that is where you will get it."

"If possible, I don't want him to know that I am doing the buying."

"I understand," Val said knowingly. "Charlie only deals with regular customers anyway, and he wouldn't sell to you." Taking a piece of paper and a pencil from her purse, Val wrote down the name of a person trusted by Charlie and gave the paper to Maria. "Phone this girl and tell her that you are a friend of mine. You will mail in the money and she will let you know where to pick the stuff up a few days later. Although if something goes wrong and Charlie gets suspicious you will lose your money," Val added, not wanting to be responsible in case Maria was taken.

"I will take that chance," Maria replied, nodding her head in a gesture of understanding. She had learned what she had wanted, and she changed the subject back to Val. "I want to see you again before you leave to go back home," Maria said. "Perhaps we can arrange a party with Debbie and some of your old friends."

A smile appeared on Val's face and for a moment she was carefree again, until she glanced at her watch. "I have to be going," she said, getting up from the chair. "Let me know how your weekend goes?"

"Sure," Maria said, smiling as she stood up.

Leaning with his elbows on the table in the semi darkness, the policeman watched the two girls leave.

"I will get in touch with you in the beginning of the week, and maybe we can have lunch together."

"Okay," Val replied, experiencing a happiness which she had not known for many a long day.

Out on the street, they pulled the collars of their raincoats up about their necks, and Maria waited for a moment close to the door of the hotel and watched Val hurry back to the cafe; her thin ankles splashing in the puddles of water on the sidewalk. Then turning away, Maria walked slowly back to her car, oblivious of the rain that beat on her face.

The parkade of the Bay Store was nearly full, when Maria parked her car and stood in the shadows until the green car drove by, then she walked to the store entrance. Glancing back as she entered the store, Maria saw the tall gray suited policeman getting out of his car, and she grimaced; they were giving her priority over Val. Maria shopped in the lingerie department for a few minutes, and asked the sales girl if she could use the telephone. "The public telephone is busy and I will only be a minute," she explained with a smile.

"Dial nine for an outside line first," the girl said returning Maria's smile.

"Thanks," Maria picked up the telephone as the girl moved to another counter.

"I have to see you right away, Ted," Maria said, after her cousin had identified himself.

"Okay, I will wait for you in my office."

"No, I have to see you in private and make sure no one sees us together." Maria looked around the lingerie department, and Ted waited for her to continue. "You have a policeman following me."

"Yes, that is right," Ted, replied, in a matter of fact tone. "He has been with you for quite a while."

"Tall, gray suit, and a receding hair line?"

"That will be Ken," Ted's voice came over the telephone.

"There may be someone else following me too, and that makes it a little more difficult for me to see you in private. Can you help me to get rid of the tail?"

"Sure. Where are you now."

"In the Bay Store."

"I will meet you in the lobby of the Coronation Hotel as soon as possible.

Now go back to your car and drive out of the parkade. Ken will follow you and I will be able to get in touch with him on the radio. Park again on the street a few blocks away, and give Ken a few minutes to make sure that no one is following you."

"Okay," Maria replied, putting the telephone down as the sales girl came back to the counter with a customer.

Browsing in a music store, near where she had parked her car, about a mile away from the Bay Store, Maria pretended to examine the records in a rack close to the window, while she watched Ken apprehend a young blond man as he got out of his small car. The policeman flashed his badge, and skillfully and quickly removed a pistol from a shoulder holster under the young man's coat, as the man, protesting, claiming possession of a permit.

"If you have a permit, you will get it back," Ken said, his voice calm as he slipped the pistol into his pocket. "My car is parked behind yours," and with a gesture, Ken invited the man to walk ahead of him. "I will want to examine your papers," he continued. The passers-by, hurrying through the rain, intent on their own concerns, didn't notice the incident.

Leaving the store Maria saw Ken hustle the young man along the street, as she got into her car and drove away. Ken, taking his own sweet time, examined the man's credentials to discover that he was hired as a detective by the Plastick Utensil Company, and he was assigned to protect Miss Petersen for an insurance company as a condition in their life policy. After a few questions, and a check on the radio with the police station to verify the permit to carry the gun, Ken apologized for the inconvenience he had caused and returned the pistol to the man. While some miles away, Maria entered the high vaulted lobby of the Coronation Hotel.

* * *

There were a good number of people sitting in the plush lounge of the lobby, as Maria paused, removed her raincoat, and looked around; Ted hadn't arrived. A bellhop, dressed in a red uniform with black trim, smiled as he passed by on the way to the desk. Folding her coat, Maria put it over her arm, and walked to the washroom to comb her hair and freshen her lipstick.

Ted was waiting for her when she returned to the lobby, and they smiled in greeting as they came together. "I will treat you to a drink." Maria smiled in response to the invitation, and slipped her arm through Ted's as they walked to the Gas Light Lounge. She felt comfortable with her cousin, and she was relieved now that she was doing something positive to help Val.

The dark wood panel walls of the room shone dully in the dim light cast by the gas lights, as Maria and Ted sat in the large velvet upholstered chairs; their voices muffled by the heavy decor as they conversed.

"Did you know the man who was following you?" Ted enquired, after disclosing what Ken had discovered.

Maria shook her head and frowned with concern. Cec would be aware of her meeting with Val and she might have aroused some suspicion.

"Do you want to tell me about it?" Ted asked.

"Not now." Maria forced a smile. "I have other things more important to say."

A waitress placed two glasses of apple juice on the low table between them, and they were quiet until she had gone. "Do you mind if I tape our conversation?" Ted asked as soon as the girl was out of earshot.

"It will be all right." But Maria was apprehensive, and sad as she thought about Val. She could not chicken out for Val's sake. "I am concerned about a friend of mine. She is a drug addict, and if something is not done for her soon, she will die." Then Maria paused while her mind went back in time.

Saddened by the concerned look on the pretty face of his young cousin, Ted leaned back in the plush chair, the small tape recorder concealed beneath his jacket ready to catch everything that was said, and seeing the distant look in Maria's eyes he waited patiently for her to continue.

Val was putting down a beer case in the suite, a pretty girl, happy, and exuberant. Then she sprawled on the chesterfield, a youthful figure, full of life and hope, she laughed as she complained jokingly about the weight of the case. Abruptly Maria's mind focused on the present, and she saw Val, as she would see her now, sitting at the cafe, an empty coffee cup before her, emaciated, a mere shadow of her former self. Her face hardened by experience, exposing her as crude and embittered, as a cruel life had made her; waiting to be picked up, by some poor gaffer or a bum, so that she could escape the wrath of Clive, pay for another fix, and perhaps add to the little money she had saved. "Pride goethe before the fall." This was not true of Val. Even now her pride inspired her to dream that she could go it alone and provide for her own deliverance.

"I want you to promise, Ted, that you will go easy on my friend, and as far as possible give her preferential treatment."

"I will do everything I can for her," Ted replied sincerely.

"There is one more thing. I want my own name to be kept entirely out of the records. I can give you information that will enable you to collect evidence for yourself, so it will not be necessary for me to appear as a witness."

Ted nodded his head, and Maria began her story, stopping only occasionally to take a sip from her glass, as Ted leaned forward; his face a mask as he concentrated on what was being said. "Thanks, Maria," he said, when she had finished. "Your information will be of immense help, and I will do what I can for your friend," and putting his hand in the inside pocket of his coat, he switched off the tape recorder.

"The policeman will continue following you for a while." Ted smiled before continuing. "I guess you realized he was following you some time ago; we didn't try to keep it a secret."

Feeling tired and sad, Maria smiled weakly in reply and lifting her drink to her lips she finished it. "Shall I give your regards to my father?"

"Sure," Ted replied. "Did he know that you were going to meet me?"

"It was his idea."

When Ted had gone, Maria leaned back in the large easy chair. She had made her pitch for her friend and her father, and now she was exhausted. The mental ordeal of what she had undertaken had sapped her strength, and she closed her eyes, and prayed. She prayed for the deliverance of Val and her father, and maybe herself too, from the clutches of the drugs that hung over them like a curse, dogging their footsteps, through torment and anguish, towards an early grave.

CHAPTER 32

The sun streaming in through Maria's bedroom windows, penetrated the gold-flecked curtains, and flooded the room with morning light. Turning on her side, Maria glanced at the clock radio on the table by the bed. It was ten to eight and she had been awake for over an hour, her mind going back over the events of the past day.

She had dinner with her father in the evening at the Wharf Restaurant. It was a swanky place, where the cooking, was superb, and they had thoroughly enjoyed their food while listening to the band. Her father had brought her home and come in for a drink, and they had sat talking until about ten o'clock when he went back to his own apartment. Maria cherished these hours with her father when she could relax and be herself, as she could with no other person, not even Danny.

With the arrival of her father, these experiences had been relegated to the back of her mind; revived only by the occasional dream, when she would wake up feeling afraid; afraid of being alone and poor in a harsh and bitter world, and understanding better, if not fully, why Val had succumbed to drugs and a life that was repugnant. Still, she was having second thoughts about the talk she had with her cousin the afternoon before. She was afraid that her communication to the police would be discovered, and some terrible revenge would befall her father and herself.

Maria turned on the radio and listened to the eight o' clock news, and she was glad when there was no news of sweeping drug arrests by the police. She switched off the radio and slipped out of bed, and feeling the warmth of the soft carpet under her bare feet, she brushed her hair before the full-length mirror, while admiring the femininity of her figure. The telephone jarred Maria's nerves when it rang, and full of apprehension, she waited for it to ring four times before she lifted the receiver.

"Good morning," her Uncle Bert's voice came over the line, and she felt better.

"Good morning," Maria replied.

"Alice telephoned me a few minutes ago," her uncle continued enthusiastically. "The police with whom Ted is working," Maria sucked in her breath, "they intercepted a truck in Alberta, on the way to British Columbia with twenty-five million dollars worth of illegal drugs."

"Wow!" Maria exclaimed, knowing that it was expected of her, but having no feeling for the impression it conveyed. "That is the biggest haul I have ever heard of, were there any arrests?"

"There was the driver of course, and probably other than that I don't know. I thought I would give you a ring and let you know. It will probably be on the news at nine o'clock, with more details."

Maria and her uncle chatted for a while longer about unrelated events, and when her uncle hung up, Maria put the telephone receiver slowly back into its cradle, and sat down on the bed. The truck was the same one that her father's secretary had telephoned about late at night, just a couple of days before. She saw it all now; the Leweses had connived to make it appear that the truck was laid up in Montreal for repairs, so that it would be available to them to haul a huge shipment of drugs, that was to by-pass the agreement with Perrelli. Her father had been suspicious that night, and he had tipped off the police.

With her mind troubled, Maria got up from the bed and from a bottle on her dressing table, she shook a tranquilizer into her hand; all hell would break loose if Cec and the Leweses had any inclination that her father was involved. She put the pill back in the bottle; she didn't need it with Father around; however, she was trembling as she raised the glass of water to her lips. Her father would have taken precautions to avoid suspicion falling on himself. Cec and the Leweses would be angry and looking for clues, and she would have to be careful to act as natural as possible so as not to draw attention to her father.

The drug seizure was reported on the nine o'clock news, with new details to what her uncle had told her. Maria switched off the radio and continued getting herself ready to go to the office, taking more care with dressing than usual. The sun that had been so bright earlier in the morning disappeared in a haze, and she drew back the drapes to lighten the room. Her nerves were steady now as she inspected herself in the mirror, her red dress suited her complexion and long black hair, and she was satisfied with her appearance. She checked the gun in her purse, and with her raincoat over her arm she left the suite for the office.

It was unusually quiet in the inner office, as Maria checked the mail and did some filing, all the time worrying and wondering what was going on. Cec had not come to the office, and Danny had left a message with Betty to say that he would be busy at noon, and he would get in touch with her later in the day. Maria considered telephoning her father, and decided against it, there was nothing she could do, but keep calm. She left the office to go to A Depot, as soon as Steve Bailey arrived at eleven-thirty; she would have dinner with her father, as she did on occasions when Danny was tied up with business at noon.

It was almost noon when Maria entered the busy depot and amid the noise of trucks and men talking loudly, she walked towards her father's office. "Back her into the dock and leave it until after lunch," a man shouted on the loading platform, and after a man driving a loaded forklift had driven by, she noted that her father was busy talking with two men in his office. Plain clothes policemen, Maria, knew it immediately, and her heart beat a little faster, while the warehouse that had been a beehive of activity moments before, suddenly became relatively quiet, and the men, in groups walked towards their lunchroom for dinner.

Her father saw her coming, and when he raised his hand in greeting, her smile came easy. The two men stood up as Maria entered the office, and while one of the men turned to appraise her, the other man thanked her father for his cooperation. Maria sat behind the secretary's desk, while Andrew showed the men to the door, and when he closed the door behind them and turned towards her, Maria stood up ready to leave. "You are not busy today?" Andrew said, smiling with pleasure.

Maria shook her head, "I thought we might have dinner together," and she was happy to see her father was all right and in good humor.

"That will be nice," Andrew said, and with a change of expression as they walked towards the door. He went on. "It has been one hell of a busy morning, but everything has been taken care of now."

"I have been worrying about you," Maria said, and Andrew smiled.

"Just a minute," Andrew said, when coming out of the office, he saw Lois, his private secretary, walking towards them.

Smaller than Maria and about three or four years older, Lois smiled to Maria and said hello, before turning to her boss and raising her eyes to meet his.

"I will be out for the rest of the day," Andrew said. "Make a note of anything that needs my attention, and I will look after it tomorrow."

"Okay," the girl said with a smile, as Maria noted her unconcealed admiration for her father, and the contrast of her father's swarthy complexion to the girl's light skin. She liked Lois, and according to her father she was an efficient secretary.

"Any place special, where you would like to dine?" Andrew asked, cutting into Maria's observations and thoughts.

"Not really," Maria replied, and they walked across the cement floor of the warehouse to the large overhead doors, while Lois entered the office. "I'm not even sure, that I want to eat," Maria went on, crooking her arm through her father's; an unconscious gesture of possession and love, observed by Lois in the glass walled office.

* * *

"Would you like to dine at the Hotel Royale?" Andrew asked, as they made themselves comfortable in his new silver gray Cadillac.

"Okay," Maria replied, returning her father's smile, while a look of understanding passed between them. Exclusive and expensive, the Hotel Royale was reputed to have one of the best restaurants in the city - they might just as well enjoy life while they could.

"The truck the police seized in Alberta, with twenty-five million dollars worth of illegal drugs; is that the truck Lois telephoned you about the other night?"

"Yes," Andrew replied as he started the car, and while he drove leisurely out of the parking lot, Maria studied him carefully, a trace of a smile on his face.

"You tipped off the police?" Maria asked.

Andrew nodded his head in reply and drove the car into the stream of traffic on the main road.

"Do the Leweses suspect you?"

"Not yet."

"Bring me up to date on what is going on," Maria said. Perhaps they were not as alike as she thought; she had been worried sick about him while he seemed to be enjoying himself.

Andrew glanced at his daughter and smiled, and with his eyes on the road and the traffic, he related what had taken place.

Cec Banas had visited him last night, shortly after he arrived home. Cec was disturbed to say the least, and evidently the Leweses were all up tight too. Danny Lewes was worried that something was amiss with a truck that had been dispatched from Montreal and at that time should be in Alberta, but a routine telephone call that should have been made by the driver an hour before, had not been received. It was a company truck, carrying drugs, and if the police had intercepted it, they would be sure to follow through with their investigation, searching the warehouses and questioning the employees in Vancouver, where the truck was bound. Danny, Cec, Rocky Devis, and himself, had worked through the night to clear the warehouses of drugs, and store them in a safe location. The police questioned the employees and searched the warehouses that morning as Cec predicted, and they found nothing. As Andrew came to the end of his account of what had happened he paused, and with laughter in his voice, he said. "You should have seen those three guys sweat. They never worked so hard in their lives."

When her father had finished, Maria closed her eyes and thought about her father's part in the whole affair. After tipping off the police that the truck was carrying drugs, he had waited with a cool devil may care attitude, for the Leweses to become suspicious that something had gone wrong and organize the necessary action to cover their involvement. The drug shipment would have circumvented the agreement with Perrelli, but as her father explained, there would be no suspicion of his involvement. The Leweses and Cec would make a judgment in the light of their own characters. First, no one was supposed to know of the shipment outside of the Leweses; not even the shipper at the warehouse in Montreal, not even the truck driver knew the true nature of the cargo, and besides if Andrew Petersen had somehow found out, then it was inconceivable that he would inform the police, when he and his brother, Perrelli, could have arranged to have had the truck hijacked for themselves and reap the benefits of the valuable cargo.

After driving in silence for a time, Andrew glanced at his daughter; with her eyes closed and her face ashen, she looked ill. Slowing Andrew pulled the car over to the curb and stopped.

"Are you all right, Maria?"

Opening her eyes, Maria turned to Andrew, "Father," she said sharply, her eyes blazing with anger. "With even a part of that money, we could have made a break from this whole dirty business. We could have escaped to another country, changed our identities, and started life anew."

Andrew looked at his daughter, forgiving, as one would look at a child who had erred. His very expression annoyed her, and with clenched fists she could have struck him; however, instead she closed her eyes and bent her head, her lips set firmly together, as she waited for her anger to subside.

there was no relief from the torment of having missed an opportunity of being rich and free, an opportunity, which would never reoccur.

"And you would have left Danny behind?" Her father said in a soft and quiet voice.

The question had been answered even before it was uttered, although it was only then that Maria became aware of the answer, and the realization left her feeling empty and worthless. She leaned close to her father, put her head on his chest and covered her face with her hands. For richer or poorer, the words ran through her mind, part of the vows, she dreamt, she would one day take with Danny, she could never accept with honesty. Then after a while, with her emotions spent and calmed by the reassuring arms of her father, Maria sat up, and as passers-by in the street watched them, then turning around and looking back, they wondered what was going on. The older man, the young girl, and the Cadillac, stirred their imaginations, and after Andrew put the car into gear, and drove away as the people walking by, watched the car glide slowly from the curb and into the stream of traffic.

* * *

Sitting across the table from her father in the exclusive restaurant of the Hotel Royale, Maria sipped her juice and Andrew took a drink from his beer, while their menus remained unopened on the table set for dinner. They had ordered the drinks and told the waiter that it would be some time before they decided what they would have for dinner. The waiter smiled agreeably, delivered their drinks, and retired to serve his other customers and await their convenience.

Recovered now from her outburst of emotions in the car, Maria told Andrew of her meeting with Ted and his promise that he would do everything he could to see that Val received preferential treatment. Her father nodded his head in agreement and they smiled together, even though they both realized that the two events coming together, would throw some suspicion on them and make their lives more dangerous.

Maria took a sip from her juice and examined her menu, and her father sipped his beer, while his menu remained unopened.

"Are you going to order, Dad?" Maria asked, closing the menu and looking up to her father.

"Whatever you order will suit me too," he replied smiling. "I'm not that particular."

The waiter took their order, and while they waited for their dinners to be served they leaned back in their chairs, Maria savoring her juice while her father drank his beer slowly, both enjoying the luxury of the restaurant, where only the wealthy could dine.

As they expected, their meals were delicious; however, being in pensive moods they ate little, and Maria's thoughts involuntarily returned to thinking about the twenty-five million dollars that had slipped through their fingers. They might have been on easy street for the rest of their lives, and she wondered what was running through her father's mind, as she observed the thoughtful expression on his face.

After dinner they drove to Stanley Park, and with only a few people about, they went for a walk on the grass close to the sea. The sun was still hidden in the haze, and as they walked they buttoned up their raincoats to protect themselves from the cold wind that was blowing off the sea. They walked slowly, while the pensive mood that they experienced in the restaurant continued. Ken, the undercover policeman, was parked along side the curb, and when Maria pointed him out to her father, he went to the car, introduced himself to him, and thanked him for protecting his daughter.

Continuing their walk, Andrew thought about his life with his wife and his daughter in Toronto. They had not been carefree days; but he never would have a good job in the front office of the warehouse, and he had been wild at the injustice of the situation.

He could have changed all that in one sweep if he had wished - he had been tempted to hijack the truck, as Maria had wished he had done, although it would have not been easy. The truck was already on the way by the time he had realized its contents, and there wasn't much time to think and plan the operation. The truck would have been in Alberta before his brother could have intercepted it, then it would have been necessary to hide the drugs, and ship them secretly to some center for sale. His brother might have been able to pull it off, and he would have paid him handsomely for the information. However, he and Maria would have had to take cover immediately from both the underworld and the police, as the word would have gone out for them everywhere - twenty-five million dollars worth of drugs, he had never dreamed there would have been that much; still in the hands of the police it was twenty-five million dollars worth of misery, from which some people had been spared.

The turf was soft under their feet, and Maria's long hair blew free in the wind. "Did you decide not to take the twenty-five million dollars, because you thought that I wouldn't leave Danny and go away with you?" Maria asked.

Andrew looked straight ahead, over the grass to the sea, where the white-capped waves rolled and broke. "No," he confessed, still looking out over the troubled water. "I didn't think of it until you became angry, and I searched for an excuse."

Maria breathed in deeply, stopped, and looked into her father's eyes as he paused and turned to her, a faint smile on his face. "Andrew Petersen, you're a blackguard," she exploded.

An old woman standing by a tree with a dog on a leash, looked at them disapprovingly, while Andrew threw back his head and laughed heartily, then arm in arm, close to each other, the wind in their faces, father and daughter walked on.

"Another thing, Andrew said, "both the police and Cec are having our telephones tapped, and we are being followed."

"What! Maria exclaimed. "They must feel that we are both a threat."

"It's okay." Andrew replied. "My brother is keeping tabs on Cec too." Then turning to each other they both laughed.

CHAPTER 33

The following week, Maria lived in dread that the twenty-five million dollar drug seizure by the police would be linked to her father, while every day she listened to the news for word that Val and the other persons she had implicated in her talk with her cousin, had been picked up by the police, but the days went by with no other arrests being made.

Danny was furious about his twenty-five million dollars loss, although the police had not found any evidence to link the Leweses to the drugs, and when Maria suggested a week later, that perhaps someone had tipped off the police, he had said that no one but the Leweses knew about it, and besides, if someone had known, who would have been that stupid, to let twenty-five million go dollars go down the drain. Maria agreed, and Danny mistook the hurt expression on her face as sympathy for his loss. While Maria was thinking of the one person, who for some trivial matter of principle, had as far as she knew, did just that - let the whole goddamn works go down the drain.

"The truck was stopped by the R.C.M.P. in Alberta at a check stop to take drinking drivers off the road. It was just a routine stop," Danny said, gritting his teeth, and putting his hand to his forehead, he continued "and twenty-five million dollars was lost. It boggles the mind."

However, it was not only the twenty-five million dollars. The police investigation had drawn closer to the L.W.C. Import and Export Corporation and besides the police searches of the warehouses, they had personally interviewed Danny and his father at their home, and warned them that it was possible that unknown to them, some of their employees were using their facilities to smuggle drugs. Danny and his father had thanked the police for the information and promised that they would tighten their own security, to apprehend and prevent anyone from using the company facilities as a vehicle to contravene the law.

The flow of drugs did slow down for a few days, and security was tightened to insure that there were no more costly seizures by the police, but within a week, things were back to normal. And there had even been a slight increase in the shipments, to make up for the drugs that were lost.

It was about another week later, in the wee hours of Sunday morning, when the police made sweeping arrests in the city, picking up seventy-five persons on suspicion of trafficking in illegal drugs. Many of those arrested were caught with drugs in their possession, while some were on a trip and didn't know that they had been arrested until later on Sunday.

Danny was furious; a number of their most profitable outlets in the city had been closed, and, it would take weeks to replace them. Meanwhile a shortage of drugs had hit the city, and users of drugs found difficulty in replenishing their supplies. With conditions ripe for profiteering, the law of supply and demand, sent even the price of the cheapest drugs skyrocketing, and the rash of crimes in the city was unprecedented in history, as the drug addicts worked harder in an attempt to try to overcome the inflation.

An outcry by concerned citizens, demanded better protection and more efficiency in the police force, while the chief of police and the commissioners protested about being under staffed, with policemen being required to work double shifts. The city fathers were caught in between and their attempts to appease both groups resulted in an internal conflict, which virtually paralyzed city council.

The drug arrests made by the police were much wider than Maria had anticipated, and many persons were being tried for a variety of offenses of which she had no previous knowledge. Some of the persons arrested early that Sunday morning had been released after questioning, and Phylis and Glenda were among these persons.

Maria was pleased to hear from Ted, that Val had been placed in a sanatorium immediately after her arrest and was undergoing treatment, and she followed the trial in the newspaper with interest, although, she thought it wise not to visit the court, not even to see Val. Then the trials were over, without any acquittals, with sentences ranging from one year to ten for the most serious crimes. Charlie got ten years, Mrs. Lenard seven years, and Clive five years; bastards in that order, Maria thought; and their sentences less than they deserved. While at the same time she was angered by the seemingly harsh sentence of two years, which Val had drawn.

Attempting to appease her anger for the harsh sentence Val had received, Maria rationalized that it would take at least two years for Val to fully recover from her drug addiction, and in the long run, the sentence was to her advantage. However, when a few days later, Maria met with Irene for a morning's swim at the club, before making it a foursome with Irene, Ron, and Danny for dinner, she was still angry.

It was a beautiful morning for a swim, warm, and a gentle breeze rippled the surface of the pool, when Maria and Irene came out of the dressing room to join the few people at the pool. Dressed in a scanty red bikini, Maria stood at the edge of the pool, her hair hidden in a bathing cap. Irene dressed in a one piece blue swim suit, dived into the water and swam gracefully the length of the pool and back while Maria remained standing at the edge of the pool, her face set as she contrasted Val's imprisonment to the freedom and leisure which she and the others at the pool were enjoying. Six months, or perhaps a year, but two years seemed so cruel.

"Come on in, the water is beautiful," Irene called, and Maria, dived into the water to join her.

The two girls, side by side, doing the crawl, swam the length of the pool, and then back again. Meanwhile Maria was thinking of Val; and venting anger on the water, she gradually gained speed. Irene kept pace for five lengths, and then swam to the side to watch Maria as the other bathers had done. Length after length Maria's lithe body cut quickly through the water, while her audience was amazed by the speed and stamina of this slim and seemingly delicate girl. Then after twenty lengths, amid the applause of the group watching, Maria abruptly pulled herself from the water, and breathing heavily, lay down on a towel close to where Irene sat watching her.

"You're angry about something," Irene said, lying down by Maria's side, with the warm sun on their backs.

Maria nodded her head in reply, and after she had rested she turned on her side and told Irene about Val, and the seemingly harsh treatment that she had received from the law. Irene readily agreed and feigned sympathy for Val, but unknown to Maria, a seed of suspicion had been implanted in her mind. In the opinion of Irene, drug addicts were the victims of their own stupidity and in her mind there was no place for sympathy for Val's predicament.

It was sometime ago that Irene, even with Maria being her friend and her brother's mistress, had complained to her father and Danny that Maria knew far too much about their drug trade, and as far as possible there should be a curtailing of information to her. Also, it had been on Irene's suggestions that Cec Banas had one of his men follow Maria to check on her activities, and for a different reason, Danny agreed; Maria was to be protected to make sure that she came to no harm.

It was the day after their swimming date, that Irene confronted her father and Danny in the privacy of her father's office with her suspicion that, Maria had leaked information to the police, and should be investigated thoroughly by Cec Banas.

Both her father and Danny brushed her suspicions aside, and she accepted their decision, knowing that it was not by logic, but it was by these two men's mentalities by which she had been over ruled. Maria's feminine, appeal and mystique, as nature intended, glossed over the faults, which to another woman were obvious. Maria possessed that fresh look of youthful innocence that put her above suspicion, even though logic would suggest the contrary. Rather they would look for a man, who had deceived the girl and committed the crime. The twenty-five million dollar loss and the round up of drug traffickers in Vancouver had alerted her father and Danny to a possible leak of information, still, as far as they were concerned, Maria was an angel, created by God, and above suspicion.

Irene might have consulted with Ron on the matter; if it had not been that he was still unaware of the corporation's illegal activities. However, even had it been otherwise, Irene had the distinct feeling her efforts would have been futile. To discuss her feelings with her mother would be too dangerous, as her mother was unaware of Danny's relationship with Maria. In addition, it would have violated her understanding with Danny and her father concerning these affairs, and besides, since she was not innocent, the mud she would stir up would engulf her too, and cloud her own marital relationship.

Did Andrew Petersen have something to do with the loss of the twenty-five million-dollar shipment, and the sweeping drug arrests by the police in Vancouver? Danny and Bill Lewes didn't know, but they were suspicious that something was wrong. Certainly, since Andrew Petersen had come on the scene, they had an unusual amount of bad luck, if that is what it was. They conferred with Cec Banas on the matter, and Danny suggested getting rid of Andrew Petersen immediately. While Cec, recalling what had happened to Dolansky at the hands of Perrelli for a much lesser matter than killing his brother, advised caution.

Eventually after some argument, it was decided much against the wishes of Danny, that because of the threat represented by Perrelli they would wait, and give more study to the situation before getting rid of Andrew Petersen. In the meantime they would watch him carefully to see that he got as little opportunity as possible to betray the trust that they had placed in him, and they would investigate him fully to determine positively, whether or not he was responsible for the corporation's past misfortunes. To these things the three men agreed, and because immediate decisive action would have been preferable; they added a proviso, for Cec to begin planning immediately to devise some method to permanently remove Andrew Petersen in some way that would not implicate the Leweses.

Of course, Perrelli would insist on another representative; still no one could be as bad as Andrew Petersen; he was incorruptible and too efficient in preventing Danny Lewes from circumventing the agreement they had made with Perrelli. Also, a new man would be given a lesser position with the corporation, to insure that he would not have access to information that would be a threat to the Leweses.

Life for Maria and Danny went on with little apparent change, they went sailing at every opportunity, dined at expensive restaurants, danced at the most exclusive night clubs, enjoyed swimming, and played tennis, or just relaxed in the lounge at the yachting club overlooking the sea. Danny taught Maria to golf; a sport which she had never participated in previously, and on one occasion they went horseback riding with a group of friends, and meanwhile their love and lust for each other remained unquenchable.

Nevertheless, something had changed, from the day Maria had realized that her love for Danny was not for better or for worse, and her dream of marriage to him faded and disappeared; lost forever in the passing of time. She loved Danny as he was, handsome, healthy, rich, influential, and with time and money to squander on her every whim. For Danny's part, he was as ardent a lover as ever, becoming more possessive of Maria as time went on, and even becoming jealous at times when other men paid her special attention.

The future with Danny, that to Maria had once seemed predestined and bright, was now clouded by misgivings of how he would accept her baby. However, she still looked forward to giving birth to her baby, and in the mornings, Maria spread both her hands over her stomach and looked at herself in the mirror, for the first signs in her figure that would reveal the presence of her baby. During these mornings, when new life stirred within her, she thought about Tom. It had been over a month, since they had last been together; they had parted good friends, satisfied, and thoughtful of each other. Their agreement to get in touch with each other after a month had been a gesture on her part, an attempt as far as possible to avoid injuring Tom's pride. Had he thought of her while that month went by, and since? Had he met someone new?

These questions arose from the recesses of Maria's mind that she had once thought closed. She might have telephoned Tom, but she still loved Danny, and now there was her baby too, which in spite of her happiness to bear, complicated her life. Reasons enough, and besides there was also her pride and a reluctance to involve Tom, in a part of her life that, although profitable, was dangerous and repugnant.

CHAPTER 34

It was a Monday morning, after an exciting weekend with Danny and a pleasant Sunday evening with her father, that Maria visited Val for the first time at the sanitarium where she had been confined. Maria walked to the information desk to inquire about Val. The waiting room was like that of any other hospital, patients who were well enough sat with their friends on the sofas and easy chairs in the room, and Maria realized that it was an ordinary hospital, and there were no iron bars or guards to keep Val under detention. The girl at the desk looked up Val's name in the computer, "Room 310," she said with a smile; looking up to Maria. "Please call at the nurses' station before you go to the room."

Happy now that she knew Val was in an ordinary hospital, Maria smiled pleasantly, thanked the girl, then went to the elevator and ascended to the third floor. She walked quietly along the wide polished hallway, glancing at the room numbers and into the rooms that she went by. Some patients were sitting up in bed or moving about their rooms, while others were lying down. Maria noticed too the flowers and the cards on the tables, and she thought about returning to the lobby, where she could buy a bouquet for her friend. The girl at the nurses' station interrupted her thoughts.

"Can I help you, miss?" she asked, her voice soft and pleasant.

"I have a friend in room 310," Maria said, and she smiled in response to the girl's pleasant manner.

"Oh yes!" the nurse said. "You must be Miss Petersen." Maria looked puzzled, and the girl continued, "Val has talked about you every day since she has been here." The nurse pointed along the hallway. "Just a little way down the hallway, and the room is on your right."

"Thank you," Maria replied, before she walked along the hallway towards Val's room. Val would be feeling a lot better now; she had been in the hospital for two weeks, and receiving treatment.

Maria looked down on the thin figure on the bed; except for her lips, and her cheeks where she had applied a touch of makeup, and the black rings around her eyes, Val's face was chalk white. The tresses of her blond hair streaked with dark, longer than she had worn previously, lay soft on the pillow alongside her face. Even so, Val's dark brown eyes sparkled and her lips parted in a smile as she recognized Maria and in attempting to sit up she would have fallen, had Maria not given her a hand before bolstering her head and back with the pillows.

The two girls chatted for a while; Val was full of hope, she would be well again in a little while, and she would be paroled in a year. In the meantime, she would learn another trade, perhaps a dental assistant or a laboratory technician

Her heart tied in a knot, Maria forced a comforting smile, Val's condition had deteriorated; however, she seemed happy to see her. Maria looked around the; room at the two bouquets of fresh flowers, and the bouquet of roses she had sent a week ago, wilting between them. She examined the cards as Val looked on with a smile on her face; and she failed to see the surprise on Maria's face; both bouquets were from Alice and Ted.

"Is there anything I can bring?" Maria asked preparing to leave, knowing that while Val appreciated her company, she was too ill to be subjected to a prolonged visit.

"I have everything I need," Val replied smiling, "Ted and Alice brought me a new night gown and that beautiful dressing gown," Val said, pointing to a blue and white gown draped over a chair. "Alice told me that your father had moved to Vancouver and that you were busy getting him settled," Val continued. Maria realized that she had neglected to tell Val about her father coming to Vancouver, though it had been over a month since he arrived.

Alice or Ted had come to visit Val every day since she had been admitted to the hospital, Maria had learned in the ensuing conversation, and she felt guilty; Val had needed friends, and she had been afraid to visit her, lest she draw more suspicion to herself and her father.

"Your cousin Ted," Val continued, her voice becoming weak. "He's too good to be a policeman."

Maria smiled, and getting up she tousled Val's hair lightly. "All policeman are not mean, you know."

"I know," Val said smiling and wrinkling her nose. "I guess I have known it all the time, but there were times when I just wasn't in the mood to admit it."

Maria took Val's thin and cold hand in her own, and squeezed it lightly as she looked into Val's eyes, shining and alert, with just the faint trace of a tear wetting their surfaces. "I will be able to come and see you more often now," Maria said.

Smiling, Val nodded, she could feel, the warmth of Maria's hand creeping into her own. Then Maria took the pillows from behind Val's shoulders and head, and helped her lay gently back onto the bed.

"Your hair looks pretty," Val said.

"You are teasing me," Maria replied smiling, and Val shook her head slowly, indicating the sincerity of her words. Maria bent over her friend and kissed her gently on the cheek, and then with a backward glance and a wave of her hand, she walked from the room.

In the hallway, Maria took a handkerchief from her handbag and bending her shoulders, she stifled her sobs. Then stopping at the nurses' station, she wiped the tears from her face and eyes, as the nurse watched her sympathetically. "I thought she would be a lot better by now," Maria said.

"Perhaps you would like to speak to the doctor."

Maria nodded her head in reply and once again put her handkerchief to her eyes.

"There is a waiting room across the hall, if you would like to sit there for a while, I will get the doctor to come up and see you."

Looking through the window in the waiting room, Maria watched the cars coming and going in the crowded parking lot below. The sun came through the clouds, shining from the tops of the cars, as people hurried to and from the hospital. Nurses, walked with their patients in a garden across from the hospital, while Maria fought to control her need to cry. She turned slowly, when she heard the doctor approach; clad in a white coat, his hands thrust firmly into the pockets; he stood before Maria, his face stern.

"Take a seat, Miss Petersen," he said, gesturing to a chair. He waited for her to be seated, then sat on the edge of a chair close by, and leaning forward, his face still serious, he began. "We are doing everything we can for Valerie and she is a fine person, with lots of spirit," and he paused to contemplate how he would continue. "But I am afraid that her chances are not good."

"Why?" Maria asked, her voice coming out as barely a whisper.

"Your friend is a heroin addict, and while we have her on methadone treatment, she has used a wide variety of drugs; experimenting, and perhaps some persons have used her to find out the effects of new drugs or mixtures of drugs before they put them on the market, and as a result her liver is diseased."

In full control of herself now, with only the redness of her eyes to show that she had been crying, Maria nodded her head, understanding fully, only now, the kind of persons, that Val, while lonely for friends, she had associated with.

The doctor pressed his lips together, and looked at Maria almost in despair. "Your friend also has syphilis. We will do whatever we can for her."

Maria bit her lip and tensed her muscles to control her emotions.

The doctor turned his head away and looked out of the window, his face set and angry. "The filthy bastards," he said emphatically. "That would defile a young girl like Valerie." Then he turned to Maria, "I'm sorry," he said.

"No," Maria said, shaking her head. "There is no need to apologize."

"Come and see her as often as you can." the doctor said. "There will be no need for you to pay attention to the visiting hours." He paused, and continued, "Valerie's parents and a boy from her home town, came to see her yesterday. It was very upsetting, not the kind of thing that Valerie can bear very much of. Your visit was different; I dropped in to see her before I came here to see you, and she was fast asleep."

"Thanks doctor," Maria said, standing up, "I will be in to see her again tomorrow."

The doctor stood up and smiled. "Good."

A doctor was being paged on the intercom as Maria walked away, along the wide white hallway with its polished floor, her heart heavy as she thought about Val.

That same evening, not being able to bear staying alone any longer, Maria moved in to her father's suite, keeping her own suite only for the convenience of herself and Danny. Her father was happy that she had come home to stay, and the next days, throwing caution to the wind, father and daughter together visited Val.

In the days that followed, Maria visited Val daily, making certain there were fresh flowers and a warm smile to cheer Val in what Maria hoped would be a recovery to health. But Val, although her spirit and will to live were strong, remained gravely ill, and her slow deterioration, in spite of the doctor's warning, was a shock to Maria. Then less than a week after she had visited the hospital, Alice telephoned early one morning, before Maria's father had gone to work, to say that Val had passed away in her sleep.

Grief stricken, and hiding it from the world, Maria and Andrew went about their daily routines as usual; although, from that day on a new determination had been born, and they vowed that day, that they would not only extricate themselves from the drug trade, but also sabotage the importation of drugs, and hopefully bring it to an end.

On the offensive now, and with a positive goal to pursue they felt better; however, they would be cautious, and Maria requested that Danny too would somehow be protected. Andrew did not protest, although he despised Danny Lewes, and would have liked nothing better than to see him in jail.

Both Andrew and Maria were aware that they had attracted suspicion, and their surveillance by Cec Banas was, both annoying and extremely dangerous now that they had embarked on their new careers.

With dedication born by Val's death, Maria and her father, in the luxury of their penthouse apartment examined in detail, the various options that were open to them to sabotage the drug trade. Every avenue they examined was fraught with danger, still, their determination to do something did not diminish; gone was the ambivalence they had experienced earlier; weighing the advantages of their new found wealth and luxury, against the perversion of the society in which they lived, and which, although far from perfect, they held dear. It was in the light of Val's suffering and death, that they saw their own transgression from the moral, ethical, and spiritual values, which were the foundation of their own lives and country. Wealth and luxury that their money could buy were no longer as important; they could see clearly now, the suffering, humiliation, and death, on the other side of the coin.

Nevertheless, even in the face of their convictions, self-preservation within them was strong, and they recoiled from going directly to the police, for fear of retribution from the underworld.

CHAPTER 35

Wearing a blond wig and with her hips padded with a towel underneath her slacks, Maria turned in front of the appraising eyes of her father, who nodded his head in approval. "It will do," he said, his face a mask of concern, "but if you think that you have been recognized when you leave the building, abandon our plans and return immediately."

"It will be all right, Dad," Maria said, forcing a reassuring smile, as she noticed the concern on her father's face and in his voice. Maria put on a raincoat, and after one final look in the mirror, she slipped out of the apartment door to begin their task of destroying the drug trade in Vancouver.

As an extra safety precaution, Maria went down five flights of stairs, and on a lower floor, she joined a number of people to take the elevator to the lobby. When she stepped out of the elevator with three other occupants, the young blond man in the employment of Cec Banas, looked them over from where he was sitting with another man, on a sofa near a large potted plant. Then he returned to reading the paper, and Maria breathed a sigh of relief.

Outside, Maria turned and glanced back, the man who had been sitting with the blond young man, was walking toward the entrance, while across the street a plain clothes policeman was watching the people an they left the apartment, and Maria noted as she stood at the bus stop, that his attention had turned towards her. She frowned, was her disguise insufficient? The man who it appeared might have followed her from the apartment, had disappeared, and she wished now that she had paid more attention to him and knew where he had gone.

The policeman in the parked car narrowed his eyes and rubbed his forehead. There was something familiar about the blond girl who had come out of the apartment, and he just couldn't put his finger on her identity. He shrugged, and turned his attention once again towards the apartment door.

It was only five minutes before the bus arrived, and to Maria fearful that she was being watched it seemed like an eternity. Five people had joined her at the bus stop, and any one of them could have been following her.

Downtown, Maria alighted from the bus in front of a department store, and went inside. There she casually walked around in the store for a few minutes, tried on a pair of gloves, and looked at some handbags, before leaving by another door. A block away, on the main thoroughfare, she entered a telephone booth, and dialed the police number. She ignored the policeman's request for her identity, and speaking slowly and distinctively, while disguising her voice, she said, "this is the same source of information, as the tip you received regarding the twenty-five million dollar drug seizure in Alberta. Check Cass' Intercontinental Fruit and Vegetable Company Premises, and the home of Cec Banas."

Knowing the police would be busy tracing the call, in an attempt to apprehend her, Maria did as her father had advised, and ignored the policeman, when he asked her to repeat, what she had said, and instead, gave him the telephone number of the box from where she was calling. Maria hung up the telephone, and after making sure that she had left her fingerprints on the telephone and the booth, she walked quickly away.

The sound of a police siren came to Maria as she drew near the department store, and glancing back before she entered, she saw the red and blue flashing dome lights of the police car and heard the squeal of its tires as it braked before the telephone booth. Maria's heart beat faster now, as she walked through the store, While the policemen went to work questioning the people who stood near the booth about its last occupant and preventing anyone using the telephone until the finger print experts arrived.

Boarding a bus a couple of blocks away, to take her back to the apartment, Maria took a seat in the rear, and looked out at the people in the street. Keyed up and alert to possible danger, Maria was glad the job had been done, and while still tense from the risks it had involved and not knowing for sure whether she had been followed and observed placing the call, she felt satisfaction and relief in what she was doing. It was as if, after rebelling against her hedonistic drive, she had succumbed to what was a dream, and her actions were being propelled by an unknown force, which was in accord with her nature. She felt a desire for a glass of wine as a celebration more than a need to calm her nerves, but she would settle for the cup of tea her father would make when she arrived back at the apartment. The champagne and beer that they once enjoyed, had been nearly abandoned in order that their faculties, in these times of danger, would be unmarred by the effects of alcohol.

At Cass' Warehouse the police would find the marijuana that had been shipped from the L.W.C. Import and Export Corporation's warehouse just a day before, while at Cec's place they would find nothing, Cec was too crafty to have anything on his premises that would incriminate him. Still, the police would be suspicious, their source of information, although unknown, had proved to be reliable, and Cec would be thoroughly investigated and kept under observation for some time. Thus, Maria and Andrew hoped, at least partly, to nullify the threat of Cec Banas, and to give them a margin of safety. Danny Lewes, the other person whom Andrew regarded as a threat to himself and his daughter; by a special request from Maria had escaped involvement in their plot.

In the apartment, Maria and Andrew listened to the late news. It had been as they had predicted; a large quantity of marijuana had been seized. from Cass' Fruit and Vegetable Company, and Cass himself, along with some of his employees had been arrested. No mention was made of a raid on the home of Cec Banas.

The latest round, of activities by the police, caused the Leweses and Cec great anxiety. Cec learned of the arrests and seizure of marijuana at Cass' Intercontinental Fruit and Vegetable Company, almost as soon as he had heard about the raid on his own home. He telephoned the Leweses immediately and a meeting was hastily arranged to assess the implications of the renewed police activities and determine what should be done. Some line of defense was necessary now, as the assault by the police on the drug trade in Vancouver, drew ever closer to the Leweses themselves. Because of the recent assault by the police, they reasoned, that one or more undercover agents had infiltrated their organization and were supplying the police with vital information. There would be a careful check of all new employees and anyone who possessed the necessary information that had enabled the police investigation to draw ever closer to the Leweses, and where any evidence of betrayal by an individual was uncovered, his or her removal by death would be mandatory. Even the Lewes' new son-in-law was held in suspicion, and Irene would keep a careful watch on his movements. Still when Irene once again brought Maria's name into the picture, Danny protested; Maria lacked the necessary information that was used to implicate Cass' Intercontinental Fruit and Vegetable Company, and besides Cec had her under careful surveillance. Cec nodded in agreement, as much in his own defense as in the defense of Danny's reasoning. Andrew Peterson, Cec suggested, was in the possession of the necessary information, which passed along to the police, could have resulted in the recent raids and arrests. It was still only a suspicion, but with the police investigation, drawing ever closer, his permanent removal became a necessary precaution in their defense. However, his death would necessarily have to appear an accident, both to the police and his brother

Perrelli, the latter of whom would reap immediate revenge, if he felt otherwise. Perhaps a traffic accident, as had happened to Doc Ellis, or a fatal accident in the warehouse. It was the responsibility of Cec to devise a suitable plan, and the Lewes family too, would give it thought and consideration to expedite the necessary action.

For Maria and Andrew, life went on much as usual, as they deliberately kept to old routines in an attempt to divert suspicion from themselves, and on the surface at least, it appeared that their relationships with the Leweses and Cec had not changed. Maria still served as a private secretary to Cec, dated Danny regularly, and occasionally went to the club with Irene, to swim or play tennis. With Maria and Danny, there was no pretence; they loved each other and while they took genuine pleasure in each other's company, to Maria at least, the future was clouded.

For their part, with the intention of killing Andrew in mind, the Leweses and Cec played the same game, to have it appear that good relations existed. As an added precaution Bill Lewes and his wife Emily, went on holiday to a country in the Caribbean, where they held substantial investments.

Nevertheless, Andrew was aware that something was amiss. The arrests by the police at, Cass' Fruit and Vegetable Company, had not been discussed with him though it was, pertinent to his position. Also, the flow of drugs through the company warehouses, had slowed to a trickle, with only the most profitable, and easy to conceal drugs, being shipped. Andrew was aware that some action would be taken against him, and although he was not afraid for himself, he was deeply concerned for the safety of Maria. At night he kept, a loaded doubled barreled shotgun on the floor by his bed, in case that on pretext of a burglary, an attempt would be made on their lives.

Cec might have found some way to quickly dispatch Andrew himself, but the constant police surveillance, since his home had been raided, made this almost impossible, but damn it, the job would somehow have to be done, and done with finesse.

The agency, from whom Andrew had hired the cleaning girl, telephoned one evening to say that the girl was sick, and another lady would take her place in the morning. Andrew listened politely while the woman at the agency explained and expressed her regret for the inconvenience, then he cancelled the service until the original girl would be well enough to return to work. It was just possible that a plan involving a new cleaning lady was being evolved, and Maria took over the cleaning of the suite.

The tranquil days that followed, might have lulled Maria's senses to the danger to which they were exposed, had it not been for the presence of the shotgun by her father's bed when she cleaned his room; loaded and ready for action, it served to remind her of the necessity of remaining alert.

* * *

It was Wednesday morning. Andrew pressed the button that would draw back the drapes in the living room of their penthouse suite. It was raining a slow drizzle, the sea was calm, and a fog shrouded the horizon, hiding the ship that sent the lonesome sound of a foghorn drifting over the water. Andrew stood for a moment, lost in thought; his brother-in-law, Bert O'Brien had invited Maria and himself to Anne's Lounge in the evening, to help him celebrate his birthday, and keeping it as a pleasant surprise, Andrew had not mentioned it to Maria.

"Are you going to take a lunch this morning Dad?" Maria called from the kitchen, as she pulled her dressing gown around her.

"'Yes," Andrew replied, turning away from the window. He had been up for some time, and he was already dressed ready to go to work, with only his tie still loose about his neck for comfort, until the last moment before he would leave the suite. He had made the coffee before Maria got up, and poured two cups after calling her. Andrew sat down at the kitchen table and took a drink of his coffee as he watched Maria shuffle around in her loose bedroom slippers, her dressing gown tight about her slim waist, and her long black hair hanging down her back; she reminded him of her mother, not long ago.

"Cheese Dad?" Maria asked, turning from the kitchen counter, where she had placed some bread, ready to make the sandwiches. "We ate the last of the ham last night."

"Cheese is okay." Andrew replied. "Your sandwiches are ten times better than the meals they serve at the greasy spoon."

Maria took the cheese from the refrigerator, and then came to the table, and while still standing, she took a drink of her coffee, before returning to finish Andrew's lunch and put the porridge and eggs on for their breakfast.

"I promised your uncle that we would come to the lounge this evening to help him celebrate his birthday," Andrew said, watching his daughter carefully, and taking pleasure in seeing her eyes sparkle and her face brighten in a smile.

"I'm glad to see that you and Uncle Bert have become good friends. He's a nice guy and I wouldn't miss his birthday for anything," Maria said happily, and turning back to the counter she finished buttering a slice of toast.

"I sent him a card a couple of days ago, he should get it today."

"How did you know when it was going to be his birthday?" Maria asked, as she looked up and studied her father whimsically.

Andrew smiled, "I have a complete record of relative's birthdays and other such important events as anniversaries and even the first time you started to walk, and a long list of addresses and telephone numbers." Then taking a small address book from the kitchen table, he handed it to his daughter.

"Oh yes, now I remember, it belonged to Mother," Maria said, while she thumbed through the pages and for a time her mind dwelled in the past.

Andrew took the book from his daughter's outstretched hand and put it back on the table. "We will keep it in the top drawer of the desk, where we can find it easily, so that you will not forget my birthday," Andrew said, smiling.

"Is this something new?" Maria asked, matching her father's mood, "you always told us when your birthday was coming up." Maria and Andrew laughed heartily together.

"What do you think I should wear tonight?" Maria asked, becoming thoughtful, as she went to the stove to take off the porridge.

"Wear something really nice; Alice and Ted are going to be there too, and I want you to look your best."

During breakfast, Maria and Andrew talked happily about Bert and the birthday celebration until it was time for Andrew to leave, and while still in her dressing gown, Maria said. "Take care Dad." Andrew smiled, and with her hands on her hips, Maria watched her father as he left the suite. He was tall and muscular, and if it had not been for his graying hair, he could have passed for a man of thirty.

* * *

Anne's Lounge was busy for the middle of the week. The band was playing a romantic tune and five or six couples moved gracefully on the floor, swaying rhythmically in time to the music. The waitresses moved about in the dim light, some of them keeping time to the music as they walked to and fro, serving food and drinks to the patrons. Maria wondered about her father, he seemed to be enjoying himself, but for how long? Drinking his beer slowly, and talking across the table to Bert and Ted, as she and Alice chatted with each other over their glasses of champagne. She and her father would pay close attention to the menu, as had become their habit, depending on the delicacy of the food to tickle their palates, rather than indulging heavily in the brain dulling booze. They were alert, and needed to be.

Ted took Maria to dance, and Andrew watched them for a time, Maria's black hair swinging away from her bare shoulders, and her low cut, white and gold gown accenting her feminine figure, as they turned, carefree to the beat of the music. Then Alice and the two men continued their conversation until Maria and Ted, hand in hand, and laughing returned to the table. The next dance was a tango, and Andrew took Alice to dance while the others watched. Maria smiled to see her father leading Alice in perfect time to the dance and music he loved.

After the dance, when they were all seated once again at the table, a waitress brought the menus, and Maria pointed out a dish to her father that she had tried before and found delicious. Then her uncle Bert was standing, beckoning to someone across the floor - and Tom looking brawny and healthy, as Maria always remembered him, was coming towards them, seeming a little uncomfortable in his finely tailored suit. Maria was happy when she saw that he was alone, and she smiled as he approached the table, his eyes brushing over the others and resting on Maria. Happy to see him, she realized more than ever, how much she had missed him in the two months that they had been apart, and the smile of welcome on her face was an expression from her heart.

Bert went forward to meet Tom and stood by his side as Tom nodded to the others at the table in a gesture of greeting.

"Tom, I would like to introduce you to Maria's father," her uncle said.

Andrew pushed his chair away from the table, stood up, and stepped forward to meet Tom.

"Tom Balant, I would like you to meet Andrew Petersen," Bert said, and the two men shook hands, and after formally expressing their pleasure in meeting each other, there was a moment of silence, until Bert continued. "Right this way, Tom," he said, the proprietor now in his own establishment, as well as a friend. "I will make room for you, here by Maria," and with a chair brought from another table, Tom sat down alongside Maria, and then they looked briefly into each other's eyes, before a waitress brought another menu to the table, and took Tom's order for a beer.

The conversation at the table continued, with everyone enjoying themselves, conversing amicably on a wide range of topics, and whether by accident or design the subject of drugs which was of great concern to some of them, was never mentioned. The meal was superb, and Bert graciously accepted the compliments from his friends, and asked the waitress to convey the compliments to the chef.

Andrew rose, and raising his glass, be proposed a toast to Bert, and everyone at the table stood up and with raised glasses, they wished Bert many happy returns of the day, and then drank to his health, continued success, and happiness.

"Thank you," Bert said smiling broadly, his eyes moist with tears. Touched by the good wishes of family and friends, he was both happy and sad at this time of rejoicing, while he recalled to mind his wife, who might have shared in his good fortune.

"Would you like to dance?" Tom asked.

"I would love to," Maria replied, and taking Tom's hand, she smiled in response to his invitation, and together they walked onto the dance floor, were entranced by each other and the music to which they danced rhythmically, and whispering to each other, they confided in the events of the past days, their lithe and youthful bodies swaying in time to the quick tempo of the music. When the dance was over, out of breath and with an arm about each other, they returned to the table to excuse themselves from their company. Tom had purchased a new car and he wished to show it to Maria.

Huddled together for a moment, in the shelter of the doorway to the parking lot, Maria and Tom peered out into the rain, as above their heads, the neon sign flashed on and off, bathing them and their surroundings in its warm red glow. A sudden squall, swept the parking lot with rain, and the tops of the many cars shone wet, beneath the arc lamps.

"There it is," Tom, said pointing a distance along the parking lot, to where a light blue two tone Chevrolet, shone new in the dim light. Dressed only as they had been for the dance, they raced across the parking lot to the car.

Opening the door quickly, Tom allowed Maria to slip behind the wheel, before running around to the other side to sit beside her.

"It is beautiful," Maria said, taking the steering wheel in her hands, and she caught the fragrant aroma of newness, as she examined the dash and the upholstery of the seats.

Taking Maria's hands, Tom pulled her close to him and kissed her tenderly on the lips, as she responded warmly to his touch, their wet faces pressed together. Another couple, their raincoats tight about them, ran across the parking lot to their car, as Maria and Tom separated from their embrace.

"Will this be goodbye once again?" Tom asked seriously.

"Not if you don't want it to be," Maria replied, and her long hair swept back and forth across her back as she shook her head slowly, adding emphasis to her words.

"I waited for you to telephone, and I thought perhaps you wanted to forget about our bargain."

"I'm sorry Tom. I missed you and thought about you a lot, and I wanted to phone, but for a time life was too complicated." Maria looked into Tom's eyes, while the rain ran down over the windshield and splashed on to the hood, where it stood in shining beads before it ran away.

"Your uncle told me about your mother passing away, and I wanted to be close to you."

"It was sad, and my father and I miss her so much. However, there were other things too." Tom nodded his head, thinking about Danny, and Maria continued. "I am going to have a baby."

Tom closed his eyes for a moment, and on opening them, he looked steadfastly across the rainswept parking lot. A car's lights went on, a little way along the row, and it moved out and drove in front of them, its windshield wipers swishing back and forth, then there was just the red glow of its tail lights before it left the parking lot. "Is Danny the father?" Tom asked, without turning his head.

"I don't know, it will be either yours or Danny's. I tried to work out the date, but I still don't know."

"What does Danny say, about this?" Tom asked, turning to face Maria.

Maria shrugged her face serious and pained at the hurt she saw in Tom's eyes. "I haven't told him." Then, she took Tom's hands in hers, "I'm sorry Tom," she said, her voice almost a whisper. "It was foolish of me not to be more careful. But now that I am with the baby, I intend to go through with it and bring the baby up in much the same way as my parents raised me."

They sat close together, quietly and alone with their thoughts, Maria let go of Tom's hands. He was deeply hurt and there was nothing now that she could do to ease his torment. Time passed slowly for them both and the only sound was that of the rain beating down on the roof of the car. Then without a word, Tom took the car keys from his pocket and handed them to Maria.

The car started with a roar, before settling down to a quiet purr. "Take her for a trip around the block," Tom said. Maria shook her head. "She's not a Cadillac, but she has lots of pep just the same."

"A V-8 motor, I bet," Maria said, smiling and looking into Tom's eyes.

"Do you want to see it?" Tom asked, and he laughed, "a girl to look at a motor, and in the rain? She'd be crazy."

"Perhaps," Maria replied, then she continued. "I would really like to see it," and then she released the hood, opening the car door, stepped out into the rain, and walked to the front of the car with Tom following.

Sheltered from the rain by the raised hood, they admired the engine. "A four barrel carburetor, automatic transmission, power steering, power brakes." Tom discontinued his explanation abruptly. "You must be cold, Maria." He closed down the hood, and they ran back to the side of the car, where Tom opened the rear door for Maria to get in first.

A sudden shower of rain beat down onto the roof of the car, as Maria and Tom embraced and kissed. The headlights of a car shone through the back window, as it pulled out into the lane behind them, and Maria and Tom lay down on the seat.

They kissed passionately, and slowly Tom slipped Maria's dress above her waist, her slim legs and flat stomach, a pale white in the dim light of the arc lamps as he removed her pants. Breathing deeply and aware only of her desire, Maria with closed eyes and mouth open to Tom's lips, spread her legs, put her arms about him, and sighed with relief and gratification as they became one.

The sudden downpour of rain had abated when Maria and Tom combed their hair and straightened their clothes. "Will I see you tomorrow?" Tom asked, noting Maria's beauty as she ran a comb through her long hair.

Pausing before replying, Maria gave thought to Tom's words and planned ahead. She wanted to see Tom tomorrow, and the next day, and the day after, without end; and with caution bidding her wait, she continued. " I'm going to be busy tomorrow, Tom. Although, I will be home at my father's place in the evening, if you would like to give me a ring." Tomorrow would be Thursday she thought, and then there was the weekend when Danny wanted her to be free. "How about Sunday evening?" Maria asked.

"Okay," Tom replied, understanding the reason for the delay over the weekend.

Inwardly Maria cringed that she was hurting Tom again, yet she was thinking of Danny too; torn between two loves, wanting to hurt neither.

Still, with Tom there would be a future for herself and her baby – if there would be a future. "Will you give me a little time, Tom?"

"I waited two months Maria, not knowing if I would ever see you again. A few more days will be bearable, and we will have supper together on Sunday evening."

"It's a date," Maria said, and putting her arms around Tom's neck, they kissed once more, her tears wetting his cheeks.

"I want you to come, to my home for supper on Sunday, and meet my mother."

"I would like that," Maria said, smiling as she dried the tears from her eyes and cheeks.

CHAPTER 36

It was still raining lightly next morning, when Cec Banas telephoned Danny and told him about the party that Maria and her father had enjoyed the night before at Anne's Lounge. Danny thanked Cec for the information and hung up the telephone. He was furious, and his first inclination was to be angry with Tom. He got up from behind his desk, slammed his office door closed, and paced the soft plush carpet in front of his desk, letting his anger subside and rethink the situation. It was Maria's father who was responsible for Maria's renewed interest in Tom.

"The bastard," Danny muttered aloud; his voice giving vent to the malice in his heart. Cec was as much to blame as anyone. They should have got rid of Andrew Petersen long before, and wait had always been his advice; one couldn't wait, wait, wait, forever wait, while everything that you had ever worked for comes tumbling about your head. Danny picked up the telephone receiver and dialed a number.

"Rocky Devis," the voice came over the line.

"I want you to do something for me today," Danny said.

"Sure," Rocky Devis replied cheerfully, although the urgency in Danny's voice made him feel uneasy.

"I want you to give Andrew Petersen a good working over, and make it appear that the fight was unplanned."

"That shouldn't be difficult," Rocky replied.

"I want you to kill him," Danny said quietly. Rocky drew in his breath, and his eyes narrowed as he contemplated what Danny was asking him to do. After a pause, Danny went on in the same quiet voice. "You may get a couple of years for manslaughter; however, you will be five hundred thousand dollars richer when you get out." Rocky said nothing, and only his heavy breathing told that he was still on the line. "I will give you an hour to think it over," Danny said.

"Hold the line for a moment," Rocky said hastily. Five hundred thousand dollars was a lot of hay. He visualized the home he could buy for his wife and the places that he could take her for holidays, and he had no love for Andrew Petersen anyway. Andrew Petersen was a pain in the ass. He could take a few punches, and make it look like a real fight; he was willing to bleed a little for five hundred thousand dollars, and two years would be the maximum he would get. "Okay, I will do it," Rocky said, through pursed lips.

Rocky's decision had not been easy; he was crabby with the workmen all the morning, and at noon he had no appetite to eat. The ham sandwiches with lettuce and relish, that his wife had packed for him, remained untouched, and the cake his wife had baked especially for him was started and unfinished. By the afternoon, Rocky was hoping that Danny would telephone and call the whole thing off, but there was no telephone call, and Rocky planned for what he felt he must do.

* * *

The whistle sounded in A Depot to indicate the end of the shift. Andrew Petersen looked up from the papers that he had been studying, and the young secretary at a desk by his side looked up the same time. She put the invoice she had been checking into a basket on the desk. "Is there anything else that you would like done tonight, Mr. Petersen?"

"No thanks, Lois," Andrew replied. Through the glass walled office he could see the workmen filing into the lunchroom to pick up their coats and lunch buckets before going home.

Lois smoothed down her dress. Then taking a mirror and lipstick from her purse, she refreshed her lipstick. "I have a dance date tonight, but with the weather as it is I would prefer to stay at home."

"You will enjoy the dance," Andrew said, turning his attention to Lois and smiling.

"A friend of mine says that she saw you at the swimming pool a few days ago."

"Yes," Andrew said, "my daughter and I go there about, twice a week." Lois pulled the belt snug around the narrow waist of her short dress . "Do you like swimming?" Lois had nice legs, and she was well made, everything in the right places. "I enjoy swimming, and it is good exercise." Andrew turned his attention back to the warehouse. The men were going out of the large overhead doors in groups, their lunch buckets swinging in their hands, and a couple of the younger men were pushing each other and laughing as they went through the door.

"Does your daughter stay with you?" Lois asked.

"She has a suite of her own, although she visits me quite often."

Two truck drivers were locking the rear doors of their trucks which were partly unloaded at the bays, and Rocky Devis was there with them.

"Good night, Mr. Petersen," Lois said, as she put on her raincoat near the door of the office.

"Good night," Andrew said, turning back to Lois and smiling. Then Lois was gone, and pulling the belt of her raincoat tight about her, she followed the men through the overhead doors.

The night watchman came out of the lunchroom with one of the day workers; his heavy flashlight stuck in the back pocket of his trousers. The two men seemed to be arguing as they walked side by side, then at the door of the warehouse, where the watchman stopped, the two men said good night. The watchman stood in the door for a moment and waved to his departing friend, before he walked towards the bays stroking the gray stubble of his beard.

"Fuck off, you old bastard. You only get in the way around here." Andrew heard Rocky Devis' voice ring out, with a viciousness that even for him was uncommon, chastising the old man for something that was not true.

The two drivers had locked up their trucks and were standing at the back of a truck talking, and not wanting to be involved in any quarrel between the foreman and the night watchman, they started to leave. One of the drivers touched his friend lightly on the arm and nodded his head just a little in the direction of the warehouse supervisor, walking towards Rocky across the now deserted warehouse, and they waited to see what would happen.

"You have no right to say that," the watchman said, hesitantly.

"You heard me. Now fuck off," Rocky said, as Andrew came up to them.

The whole thing didn't ring true. Rocky usually got along well with the watchman. Andrew glanced to the old man; he was puzzled and hurt and he looked to Andrew for support. "What is the problem?" Andrew asked, addressing himself to Rocky Devis.

"It is none of your business," Rocky Devis replied, with viciousness still in his voice. "When it is any of your business I will let you know."

Unperturbed, Andrew said nothing for a time, and looked carefully at Rocky, he seemed poised for a fight. The two drivers went back to a truck on a pretext of making sure that a door was locked. Andrew had expected this for a long time; Rocky Devis had got the word to beat him up. "You are fired, Devis," Andrew said, his voice calm and cold.

"I think you had better see Mr. Danny Lewes about that," Rocky retorted, through clenched teeth.

"Fired," Andrew repeated. "If your friend wants to rehire you later that will be up to him, now get out."

Rocky lunged for Andrew; his big fist aimed for Andrew's chin, but Andrew's arms came up quickly in his defense, and the punch landed on his forehead and sent him reeling backwards. The watchman had his flashlight in his hand, and he would have attacked Rocky had Andrew not cut in to forestall his action. "Keep out of it," he said his voice harsh and as cutting as Rock's had been a minute before.

The two drivers came away from the truck; it didn't appear they were a part of the plan, Andrew thought. Still, he would keep them before him just to be sure that they weren't.

The drivers grimaced with imagined pain as Andrew staggered backward from Rocky's first punch. Rocky's reputation as a fighter had spread through the warehouses. He was known as a hard hitter and dangerous when crossed, and, rather than risk a confrontation, men shied away from him when a disagreement arose. Maybe, if the supervisor was twenty-five years younger; there would be a match, one of the drivers thought as he noted Andrew, tall and athletic, poised and waiting for an attack. However, the graying hair at Andrews's temples and his wrinkled brow foretold his age, and the driver shook his head, and wondered.

Rocky, with his years of boxing experience, thought differently as he watched his man with cold eyes. His sudden and vicious attack had been designed to cripple Andrew at the start, but Andrew had deflected the punch and reeled back with the blow. And although there was blood on Andrew's face from a cut on his forehead, Rocky knew well that his opponent was not badly hurt. Andrew's stance too was a puzzle, and leaning forward with his big arms outstretched and his hands open, he was obviously aggressive. Nevertheless, Rocky was still confident of success, and inwardly he laughed; Andrew Petersen would put up a fight, and thus give him the alibi he needed to land only one solid blow, then he would take his time and with a few well-placed punches, kill Andrew.

Rocky shot out a left between Andrew's outstretched arms. As quick as a viper's tongue it struck Andrew in the corner of the mouth, then recoiled, but for a moment, Rocky felt Andrew's hands close on his arm until he wrenched it free, and staggering back to the drivers, he watched a thin trickle of blood running from the corner of Andrew's mouth.

Coming forward again, his fists raised before him, Rocky flexed his left arm to relieve the ache in his shoulder, damn near dislocated after his last punch. He was wary of Andrew now, the man was a Samson, and he would have to be careful. Rocky feigned with his left, and suddenly moving forward, he lashed out with his right. Andrew stepped back quickly, and the blow losing its force, fell harmless on the taut muscles of his stomach.

Rocky retreated as Andrew, standing erect with his arms stretched before him, came forward quickly, then Rocky winced with pain as Andrew's heavy shoe struck him in the left hip.

The watchman, with his heavy flashlight still clutched in his hand, came around and stood by the two drivers. Except for the sound of the heavy breathing of the two antagonists, as they faced each other, their eyes ablaze with hate, the warehouse was quiet. The two men circled each other warily, and Rocky, like lightning, struck Andrew twice again on the head. Rocky jabbed with his left, then swung wide with his right, and Andrew side-stepped clear of the killer punch, clutched Rocky by the hair, and pulled him forward. Rocky fell forward on his hands and knees, and rolled clear of Andrew as the watchman's laugh peeled through the lofty ceiling of the warehouse. Still, Rocky regained his feet unhurt and a little wiser for his mistake. Coming forward warily, Rocky pressed his attack only when it seemed safe, and while his left leg felt numb from the injury to his hip, he smiled grimly; he was landing punches to Andrew's head, and slowly he was wearing him down.

Moving back as Rocky came forward, Andrew tripped over a piece of two by four that lay on the floor behind him. Rocky sprang forward, and raising his foot to kick Andrew; but he lost his balance as his left leg, still numb, buckled beneath him. They were on their feet in a second, and Andrew moving in before Rocky was completely in balance, grasped Rocky tightly about his waist, lifted him bodily, and threw him backwards to smash against a wall of the shipping office. The big glass windows set in a metal frame, shattered, and glass fragments spewed across the floor, leaving the frame wall standing with jagged pieces of glass hanging from the metal.

Still on his feet, Rocky stumbled forward, and with blood streaming from a large cut in the back of his head, he regained his balance. For a moment Rocky's brain fogged, then it cleared, and from a nearby shelf he grabbed a hand hook that the men used to handle sacks of produce. Bounding forward, Rocky swung the hook cruelly as Andrew jumped away and lowered his arms to protect his body. The hook slashed into Andrew's left arm, making a deep wrench in the flesh and leaving his tattered shirtsleeve red with blood.

Moving forward as Rocky swung again, Andrew felt the hook pierce the flesh at the side of his waist, and with the pain searing in his side, he smashed his right fist into Rocky's face. Stumbling back, Rocky left the bloody hook dangling in Andrew's side, and ignoring the pain; Andrew pursued his opponent, to strike him with a mighty right hook to the jaw. Rocky's eyes clouded, and with his feet clear of the floor, he slammed once again into what remained of the shipping office wall, then with all consciousness gone, he fell forward on his face into the glass that lay shattered on the floor.

Leaning against a stack of boxes of canned milk, Andrew gasped for breath as the two truck drivers, amid the noise of crunching glass beneath their feet, went to the aid of Rocky. Andrew steadied himself with one hand against the boxes, and while the night watchman grimaced, Andrew, using his free hand, slowly removed the hook from his flesh and threw it clattering to the floor close to the shelf from where it had been taken.

The two truck drivers half carried and half pulled Rocky clear of the broken glass, his head hanging back covered with blood and his nose twisted awkwardly to one side, as he lay limp between them. Laying Rocky down on his back clear of the glass, one of the drivers propped Rocky's head up with a bundle of empty sacks, and the other looked to Andrew.

"Phone for an ambulance," Andrew said, before turning away. Then with his shoulders hunched and a hand pressed firmly against his side, he walked slowly back across the floor of the warehouse to his office.

* * *

"I have been in an accident, Maria," Andrew said over the telephone, "and I will need a doctor."

"Where are you?" Maria asked hurriedly.

"I'm at A Depot. But hold it for a minute and let me finish. I am not badly hurt and I am able to drive. I don't want to go into the hospital emergency, so get in touch with your Uncle Bert; he will know a number of good doctors and he will be able to get someone out to our place. I will be there in about a half hour."

"Are you sure you are able to drive, Dad?"

"There are just a few minor cuts, and I will be at home directly."

The night watchman hurried into Andrews's office with the first aid kit as Andrew put down the telephone, and there was the sound of an ambulance siren, in the distance, growing louder as it approached.

"Are you going with the ambulance, Sir?" the night watchman asked. Andrew shook his head in reply.

The ambulance drove into the warehouse, its red lights still flashing, as the night watchman helped Andrew apply wads of bandages to his wounds. The ambulance driver and the attendant put Rocky onto a stretcher pushed it into the ambulance, and after a few words with the truck drivers they got into the ambulance and drove out of the warehouse.

When his wounds had been dressed, Andrew thanked the night watchman, put his coat over his arm, and walked towards the door. Then turning back as he walked away, he said. "Get in touch with Mrs. Devis, and break the news easy."

"Okay," the watchman replied, and the frown on his face told of the displeasure of his task.

Slipping painfully behind the wheel of his car, Andrew rested for a moment before starting the engine and driving away slowly. The wounds in his side and arm bled profusely, and although he grit his teeth from the pain in his side, his mind was clear and alert - there would be hell to pay for what happened to him that day.

A doctor and Bert O'Brien were already at his apartment when Andrew arrived home, and he smiled briefly to Maria before the doctor began treating his wounds. The cuts on his forehead and the inside of his mouth were not serious, but the gashes in his arm and side required stitches. While the doctor worked on his wounds, Andrew told them what had happened. Although Bert's inquisitiveness as to why Rocky Devis had attacked him remained unexplained, and Maria, pale from anxiety, was quiet, asking nothing of her father, only listening, knowing that Andrew would discuss the incident with her when the doctor and her uncle had gone.

Later, Andrew confided in Maria that he believed the fight had been an attempt on his life. The heavy punches that Rocky threw at the outset were intended to stun him and make him an easy victim to his lethal fists, and had he not been prepared and expecting trouble it is likely that Rocky would have been successful.

There was no doubt in Andrew's mind that Danny Lewes was responsible for the attack, and Rocky had been corrupted by money and used to do his dirty work. Nevertheless, Andrew let Maria draw her own conclusions about who was responsible, and although Maria was thoughtful, she chose to make no comment on this aspect. There weren't many to choose from; the two senior Leweses were abroad; which left, Cec Banas, Irene, and Danny. However, in spite of the evidence, Maria clung tenaciously to the belief that Danny could not plan such an act against her father.

During the night, Maria was awakened by her father calling her name. Haunted by a nightmare that her conscious mind would not accept, she had been crying in her sleep. Lying awake for a long time afterwards, Maria worried about her father; he was hurt more seriously than he would admit, and if the plan was to kill him, the persons responsible would try again. Even in the night, when fear and suspicion were rampant, by neglecting the irrationality and fury of human emotions, and suppressing her subconscious mind, Maria, reasoned that Danny could not be involved.

In the morning, Maria fussed over Andrew, prepared an especially good breakfast, and implored him to stay away from work for a while as the doctor had advised. Andrew, while enjoying the fuss Maria was making of him, laughed off her advice. He was okay; he wasn't expected to do much work anyway, and in a few days he would be as good as new. At the door, Maria kissed her father goodbye, and with gestures that expressed her love and concern, she held his hand and looked into his eyes for longer than usual.

"Take good care of yourself," Andrew said - his last words before he closed the door.

Leaning back on the door when her father was gone, Maria closed her eyes; she had a premonition that something ominous would happen. "Mother," the word escaped her lips, and as tears welled up in her eyes, a silent prayer went out for Andrew's deliverance. She wanted to be with him; however, they were bound to carry through with their original plans, and would trust in providence to show them the way. She knew Andrew would not let what had happened to him slide, and when the time was opportune, if there would be a time, he would strike back with a vengeance.

Chapter 37

When Andrew arrived at the warehouse, Rocky Devis' wife was waiting for him. A nice figure, tall and attractive, a beautiful woman, except for the blemishes on her face and the dark rings around her eyes, which even the heavy makeup failed to hide.

Lois made the introductions. "Please take a chair, Mrs. Devis," Andrew said.

"There is a detective Roche from the police force, to see you too, sir," Lois said.

Andrew had noticed the man some minutes before, and surmised that he was a detective. "Do you mind if I ask Mr. Roche to come in too?" Andrew asked, turning to Mrs. Devis. "He will want to hear what happened also."

"I don't mind," Mrs. Devis replied, looking steadily into Andrew's eyes.

The woman had experienced a rough night; it was written on her face, and Andrew felt sorry for her, even when at that moment he realized that she believed it was he, and not her husband who was responsible for the fight. "Ask Mr. Roche to come in Lois, and please get the night watchman to come to the office."

Mrs. Devis put the purse she had been holding on her lap onto the floor, as Lois left on her errand. "I'm sorry this happened," Andrew said, to Mrs. Devis, and then he got up to meet the detective as he entered the office.

The detective had met Mrs. Devis earlier, and he nodded his head solemnly in a gesture of recognition and respect.

Lois arrived back in the office with the night watchman almost as soon as the detective was seated. "Shall I leave, Sir?" she asked, after she had seen the watchman to a chair.

"No, that won't be necessary," Andrew, replied, and Lois was glad. Rumors had been going around the warehouse about the fight, since she had arrived fifteen minutes before, and now as the whistle sounded to start the morning shift, Rocky Devis was still absent.

Starting at where Rocky Devis had words with the night watchman, Andrew told Mrs. Devis and the policeman, what had happened, while the watchman confirmed his story.

"Would you say that you were being a little heavy handed when you fired Mr. Devis?" the policeman asked when Andrew had finished.

"I don't think so," Andrew replied, with a shrug, "Rocky had been crabby all day, and he was very insulting when I spoke to him. He didn't give me any choice other than to act as I did." Andrew stopped and looked steadily at the policeman; he was probing for another motive for the fight. Had his talk with Mrs. Devis, and perhaps Rocky, brought to light some other motive? Mrs. Devis was expressionless as Andrew continued. "The firing wasn't really that serious, Rocky is a friend of one of the owners of the corporation and he would have been back to work today anyway."

"Wouldn't that have bothered you, Mr. Petersen?" the policeman asked, continuing to probe.

"No," Andrew replied, shaking his head slowly, "Rocky is a good man. One of the best foremen we have, and if Mr. Lewes didn't rehire him, I would have. One bad day doesn't warrant the permanent dismissal of a good man."

Mrs. Devis looked at the floor; Andrew's last statement bothered her, and she was visibly upset.

"Have you ever been a professional boxer, or a wrestler?" the policeman asked, his notebook and pencil still in his hands.

Andrew merely shook his head.

"Then you have some training in self defense?"

There was silence in the room for a time as Andrew reflected on the past, recalling his boyhood years to memory, as the others waited for his reply. Andrew looked hard at the policeman. "My family lived in the slums of an Italian city."

The policeman nodded his head with understanding. "Do you wish to lay any charges?"

"No," Andrew replied.

The policeman closed his notebook slowly, a thoughtful look on his face. "We may want to talk with you further, Mr. Petersen."

"Feel free to come and see me anytime you think I can be of assistance," Andrew replied.

The policeman stood up, and Mrs. Devis and the watchman, followed his lead. "My apologies, Mrs. Devis," Andrew said, and she opened her mouth to say something, then changed hear mind, her eyes shining with tears.

The watchman went back to the lunchroom to get his coat and lunch bucket before going home, as Mrs. Devis and the policeman walked slowly towards the large overhead doors, where the morning sun, streaming through, cut a brilliant path of light into the warehouse.

Andrew turned his attention to the floor of the warehouse, already a beehive of activity, three freight cars were being unloaded at the doors by the track, and at the bays on the other side of the warehouse, two trucks were being loaded with canned food for distribution in the city. "The trucks that had been in the bays the night before had already been unloaded and were gone. Feeling a stab of renewed pain in his side, Andrew stepped out into the warehouse and closed the office door behind him. A good portion of his life had been spent under the lofty ceilings of a warehouse. The bustle, the smell of dust, the clang of freight cars banging together, the clarion sound of truck horns, the hard manual work, and the shouts of the men and their comradeship were in his blood. A strange sadness came over Andrew as he crossed the floor of the warehouse towards a gang of men unloading a freight car. He had wanted to be free of the warehouse, and now with his career uncertain, he was sad. A man went by driving a forklift loaded with a flat of produce; and Andrew raised his hand to return his wave, before he stopped before the boxcar.

"Jack," Andrew called.

A man came out of the boxcar and stood on the ramp. "Yes, Mr. Petersen?" the man answered.

"Take over for Rocky today."

"Okay."

The man came down the ramp taking off his work gloves, and walked quickly towards the shipping officer, as Andrew, deep in thought, returned to his office.

Things wouldn't rest as they were; people who were afraid or angry would not remain still. Andrew put his hand on his side where his wound was bothering him as he walked - thank God, Maria was unhurt.

CHAPTER 38

Deeply troubled by what had happened, Marj Devis said nothing to the policeman as they walked together from the warehouse. There seemed to be no grounds now for the complaint, which she had made with the police against Andrew Petersen. She hadn't believed that only one man had fought with Rocky, and now hearing Andrew Peterson's story; substantiated as it was by the night watchman, with two other witnesses who could be brought in if necessary, there was nothing for it, but to accept what had happened. Andrew Petersen was hurt too, he favored one arm and he walked and sat with care to avoid rupturing the wound in his side. He appeared to be a gentleman; not the sort of man with whom her Rocky would quarrel. By her car, Marj Devis thanked the policeman and tried to smile.

The policeman opened the car door. "Get some sleep, Mrs. Devis, you are bushed," he said sympathetically.

Marj Devis watched the policeman walk to his car, before she put the key into the old Mercury, and it started right away. She backed the car carefully out of the parking place, and then drove back to the hospital. It wasn't like Rocky to have been crabby all day and pick a fight with his boss. He had been cheerful when he had left for work in the morning. Something must have happened to upset him; Rocky had been really crabby when he was hired to beat up Charlie. Was this a similar situation? She had quarreled with Rocky then, for degrading himself. She loved Rocky with all her heart and soul; he was so handsome and strong, and he took such pleasure in buying her things, she had accepted the fur coat he had bought her, he wanted nothing more than to please her. He didn't know that she would love him, even if he could never afford to buy her anything, and the fancy coat, the rings, and the flowers, weren't necessary.

Rocky was propped up in bed when Marj arrived back at the hospital. A big piece of tape covered the back of his head where he had hit the shipping office wall, one of his arms was wrenched at the shoulder and in a sling, and there was a bruise on his hip, the size of a plate. These things would heal, and it was the scars left in their minds and Rocky's face that Marj worried about. His nose was broken and twisted to one side, and the glass he had fallen into, had cut his face to ribbons. Also, there was a big wad of bandage over his left eye, where the glass had done the most serious damage, and the doctor had warned that the vision in the left eye would always be impaired. Grim reminders, for years to come, of things that need never have occurred.

Rocky smiled sheepishly when he saw his wife - man she was beautiful, and he felt like an ass. He didn't hate Andrew for what he had done, he hated himself.

But what Marj saw was ugly; Rocky had been so handsome, and now he was a mess and she was angry.

"I told you not to go and see Petersen," Rocky said.

Marj nodded, her lips drawn tight and her eyes mere slits. "You are right Rocky," she said, "he wasn't to blame. Then why? Tell me why?"

"I was crabby. I had a bad day," Rocky replied.

"A bad fucking day," Marj cried, and the tears ran down her cheeks.

Rocky bent his head and his own eyes filled with tears as he saw the hurt he had caused his wife.

" Yes, you can be sorry," Marj said, and near to hysteria she continued. "Who is going to pay the fucking bills while you are laid up here?"

"Don't worry about the bills. They will be taken care of."

Marj tossed her head back and sniffed as she reached for a tissue in her purse, "I suppose they will give you sick pay for getting into a fight?" she said sarcastically.

"I told you not to worry. Danny Lewes will take care of the bills."

A look of contempt crossed Marj's face, as she realized that her suspicion of what had actually happened was correct. She wiped the tears from her eyes and cheeks. She had stopped crying. She didn't feel sorry for Rocky or herself anymore, she felt helpless and empty that Rocky had degraded himself.

Rocky saw the change in Marj, she was beautiful, and he reached out to touch her and be forgiven, but she turned away in despair and walked out of the room.

Unhappy and dejected, Marj walked along the hallway, as Danny Lewes, handsome and tanned, dressed in a brown checked sports suit and white shoes, the very latest of fashion, enquired about Rocky at the nurses' station. He turned his face to Marj when he saw her approach, his thick brown hair, wavy and soft, and his hands that had never done an honest day's work in their life, brown from the sun - she despised him.

Danny had heard from Cec, of Rocky's bungling of the job he had asked him to do, and he had been angry; fit to be tied, you couldn't trust anyone these days. If a job was to be done right, then you pretty well had to do it yourself. Rethinking the situation during the night, Danny realized that it would be dangerous to go and see Rocky half cocked, Rocky knew too much, and it was better, he was sympathetic and kind, for the time being at least.

Leaving the nurses' station, Danny walked towards Mrs. Devis, her blond hair was in disarray and she was as white as a sheet; like death warmed up. A few kind words to reassure her and show his friendship would be in order. Rocky would be all right in a few days and back to work. He was a good man, and they needed him at the warehouse. If there was anything he could do to help in the meantime, she should get in touch with him, and he would be glad to be of assistance. Danny prepared his little speech as he and Marj walked towards each other, but his smile of greeting froze on his face, as Marj took a small pistol from her purse, and leveled it. Danny dived for the cover of a doorway as four shots rang out, echoing along the hallway and Danny Lewes lay in a crumpled heap in the doorway.

A nurse grabbed Marj's hand and forced it high above her head, although there was no resistance, and Marj let the gun fall from her hand and clatter to the floor. A male ward aid took over from the nurse, and led Marj to a bench opposite the nurses' station, where she sat down and covered her face with her slender hands. A large diamond, sparkled from a ring next to her wedding band, and her red fingernails contrasted with the white of her skin, as the ward aid remained standing and looked down on her.

A crowd of patients and visitors quickly gathered in the hallway, as a doctor knelt by Danny's side, while a pool of blood spread across the floor, then the doctor stood up and shook his head slowly.

Dressed only in his pajamas, Rocky Devis limped out of his room, and looked over the heads of the people before him. " Oh, my God," he gasped, and then pushed roughly through the crowd, to sit by his wife's side. "It will be all right Marj," he said, putting an arm around her. Although she loved him with all her heart, she didn't answer or move as she tried to shut out all consciousness.

* * *

With his hands thrust into the pockets of his windbreaker, Steve Bailey elbowed his way to the outside edge of the crowd of people standing around Danny and the Devis'. Some new arrivals on the scene asked Steve, what had happened, as he emerged from the crowd wiping a large hand through his thick red hair, and wrapped up in his own troubles, he didn't hear or pay any attention to the people around him. He had fallen down on his job of protecting Danny Lewes. He had not been expecting any trouble, and he didn't have a chance. Steve had walked ahead, when Danny stopped at the nurses' station to enquire about Rocky, and when he turned to come back along the corridor, Mrs. Devis had her back to him and was approaching Danny. There wasn't the slightest indication that there was anything wrong, until Danny dived for cover in the doorway, and by that time it was too late; Mrs. Devis had already started shooting. There was no percentage in him shooting Mrs. Devis.

Troubled, Steve walked away from the scene to a telephone booth at the end of the hallway. He glanced at his watch, as he kicked the door of the telephone booth closed behind him; it was ten-thirty. Steve stood for a moment and looked at the telephone, while he bit his lip and cursed; he was up shit creek without a paddle, and he didn't even know what the hell had gone wrong. Still cursing, Steve picked up the receiver, and dialed Cec's number.

Cec was furious, as Steve expected, and there was a cold sweat on his forehead as he hung up the telephone, and kicked open the door of the booth. He would do as Cec advised; take it on the lam, and keep his big mouth shut about anything concerning the Leweses. There was no alternative, but to keep out of sight, or Cec would put a bullet in his head. He might even get a bullet in the head anyway, for falling down on his job and just knowing too much. There was no sense in sticking around to find out.

* * *

Thoughtful, his face grave with concern and anger, Cec Banas put down the telephone after talking to Steve Bailey, and looked across the room to Maria typing at her desk by the window. A shaft of sunlight came over her shoulders, bathing her in its light, almost like a halo. How could anyone as angelic as Maria, have a bastard like Andrew Petersen for a father. Rocky Devis and his wife would probably tell the police all they knew. It wouldn't be enough to convict anyone as influential as the Leweses, still, it would be enough for the police to pick up Andrew Petersen, who in his position as warehouse supervisor, possessed the knowledge and the access to documentary evidence, that could convict the Leweses and himself; and Andrew Petersen would sing like a bird to save his own skin.

Andrew Petersen would have to be killed and right now. Cec came to the only conclusion that appeared open to him - without Andrew Petersen the police investigation would run into a brick wall. He knew of a person who would do the job for a fee, and because this person had no connection to Andrew Petersen, the police would, find it impossible to solve. Cec smiled, the job would be done while he remained in the office with Maria, a perfect alibi. The smile on Cec's face was short lived; there was Perrelli to consider too, and unlike the police, he didn't need proof, just a suspicion, and he would kill to revenge his brother. Cec got up from behind his desk and paced his office while he considered his position. He had no choice; he had to get rid of Andrew Petersen, however he didn't have a snowball's chance in hell, of escaping the wrath of Perrelli - unless he dropped out of sight. Cec's calm composure had gone, and beads of sweat appeared on his forehead; the only chance he had was to run away. He and his wife had long since devised a plan in case of such an emergency, and they could stay out of sight indefinitely. They would pack a suitcase and disappear, and with more than enough money in off shore bank accounts they would abandon their families, friends and home, to start a new life, with different identities, in a place which they had prepared in advance. It was a hard decision to make; and while he and his wife would never be happy away from their families and home, there were no alternatives. The only bright spot in the whole abortive situation was that Andrew Petersen would be dead. Suppressing a chain of oaths, that fought, to be uttered, Cec picked up the telephone and dialed a number. The conversation was brief and to the point. Andrew Petersen was to be knocked off immediately, and the method - it didn't matter, anyway it pleased the person with whom he spoke, as long as the job was efficient.

Feeling better now that the die had been cast, Cec telephoned the outer office and had a girl bring coffee for himself and Maria. He drank the coffee slowly while he cleaned out his files and placed the papers into his briefcase. Maria was still typing by the window, stopping now and then to drink her coffee, and Cec noticed that it was eleven thirty, and she was on the telephone for a little while; although it couldn't have been important, as she continued with the typing, and be wondered how she would take Danny's and her father's deaths, then he picked up his briefcase and left.

CHAPTER 39

The shipper poked his head into Andrew Petersen's office. "That truck from Edmonton, still isn't in," he said. "The god damn driver, probably shacked up with some broad over night, and we will be lucky if he is here before we close."

"I will check into it," Andrew replied, before he glanced towards Lois. She continued working at her desk as if she hadn't heard a thing. If the truck had broken down, the driver might have telephoned the office and the message had not been relayed to the warehouse. However, it was more likely that the shipper's explanation was correct. He would check it out with the office and see if they had got word from the driver. Andrew picked up the telephone, dialed a number, and asked for Danny Lewes.

"I'm sorry, Mr. Petersen," the telephone operator said, recognizing his voice, "but Mr. Lewes is not in. Perhaps you would like to talk to Mr. Rahl?"

"Put me through to him please."

"Hello, Andrew. I was getting ready to go home," Ron paused before continuing. "I have some bad news. Danny was killed at ten-thirty this morning," he said, his voice choking with emotion, and then he went on more slowly, his voice sincere. "Danny went to the hospital to visit an employee who is sick; Rocky Devis, you will know him, Andrew?"

"Yes."

"Danny was just going to go into the room to visit with Rocky, when Mrs. Devis came out and shot him." Ron mistook Andrew's silence for grief, and he went on, "I am going home to break the news to Danny's wife and Irene, and I was going to telephone Maria, though it would be better if you would break the news, Andrew."

"Sure," Andrew replied, his voice flat, and Ron understood.

When Andrew hung up the telephone, his face was serious and thoughtful as he digested what had happened, and thought ahead to what would probably occur. The Devis' would tell all they knew, and the police would come to the warehouse to pick him up. Andrew looked at his watch; it was eleven-thirty.

"Andrew," Lois said, and looking up from her desk, she pushed her glasses back from her young and pretty face.

"Yes," Andrew replied.

"What happened to the truck?"

Andrew laughed, "I don't know," he replied, "I forgot to ask." Then before Lois had time to reply, Andrew continued, "Will you bring me a cup of coffee from the lunchroom?"

Lois smiled, and getting up from her desk, she walked out of the office, to get the coffee, her hips swinging just a little more than usual.

Picking up the telephone, Andrew watched Lois walk away, before he dialed Maria's number at the Plastick Utensil Company.

"Hello," Maria said pleasantly.

"Hello," Andrew replied. "Is Cec Banas there?"

"Yes, although he appears to be getting ready to leave. Why are you asking, Dad?"

"Something has happened. The whole set up is falling apart and I want to see you. I can't tell you more, or we will attract the attention of Cec," Andrew paused to give emphasis to his warning. "Be damn careful from here on in, and as soon as Cec has left, I want you to leave. Shake the policeman and whoever else may be following you, pick up some chicken and chips, and meet me in Stanley Park, at the place where we went for a walk the other day."

"Okay, Dad, I will see you."

Wondering what it was that was going on, Maria hung up the telephone. Cec had his back to her, cleaning out the filing cabinet; fortunately he was far enough away to be out of eat-shot, and thinking about her father's advice, to be damn careful from here on in, Maria opened her purse and made sure her pistol was handy and ready for action, took a drink of her coffee, and continued typing.

It was a few minutes after eleven-thirty and Danny was supposed to pick her up at twelve, Maria grimaced, meeting her father was more important now. To Maria, waiting impatiently. She was glad he didn't take the time to say goodbye - no doubt he was in as big a hurry as she was, and she wondered what he was up to. The whole set up is falling apart. Maria recalled her father's words. It was apparent by the way Cec behaved, that he knew what was happening. Toying with her cellular telephone, while she waited to give Cec a chance to clear the building, Maria gave thought to what he was up to; it was evident that he was not coming back, as he had even taken the picture of his wife and family off his desk - if Cec and his wife were making a run for it, what would they do?

In the reception room, Betty was troubled by the way Cec had left. His usual smile was conspicuously absent and he was obviously preoccupied and in a hurry. Cec had not even noticed her as he passed through the office, and Betty was still frowning with concern, when in the inner office, Maria put the telephone into her purse, and got up to leave.

The blond young man in the employment of Cec, followed Maria out of the building, and passed as she got into her car, his blond hair almost to his shoulders; a menace if there ever was one, and she was glad to feel the comforting weight of the pistol in her purse. Glancing back and across the street, to the policeman in the gray suit, Maria smiled and he raised his hand just slightly; if he followed her much longer, they would be on a first name basis in no time. It was obvious he hadn't learned that the set up was falling apart, or he would be showing his badge. Whether the blond young man knew or not, there was no way to tell, and perhaps he was biding his time to put a bullet in her back. Whatever, she would lose no time in losing them both, and meanwhile the rod in her purse would comfort her as she drove between the tall buildings; like a valley, with pillars of granite on either side casting shadows across her path.

In the dim light of the Bay Store parkade, Maria stopped her car, and waited while the policeman preceded her into the store. The blond young man waited in his car, and Maria was part way to the store entrance before he followed, and the back of her neck tingled when she heard the hollow sound of his foot steps behind her. Inside the store, Maria felt better again as she mingled with the many shoppers.

The policeman was looking at some get well cards when Maria purchased some items she needed from the cosmetics counter, before she went to the ladies' clothing department to wander among the racks of dresses. Then Maria casually stepped out onto the busy street, and under this hot sun, amid the bustle of people and the noise of the traffic, her short blue dress tight about her thighs and waist, she examined some dresses on display in the window. A crowd of people was boarding a bus behind her, and when the bus was about to pull away, Maria abruptly turned, and hurried to the closing door of the bus, smiling to the driver as he opened the door and she stepped inside. The blond young man was at the door in seconds, but the door closed, and occupied by his driving and the attention of Maria, the driver wheeled the bus away from the curb, leaving an angry blond young man on the sidewalk, and the policeman in the gray suit frowning near the store entrance.

Getting off the bus at the next stop, Maria took a taxi to a restaurant off the main street. There she picked up two orders of chicken and chips to go. Then after waiting in the restaurant while a police cruiser drove by, she went out onto the street and hailed a taxi to take her to Stanley Park.

THE

Grand

OKANAGAN

LAKEFRONT RESORT AND CONFERENCE CENTRE

86   warmth on her slim legs.

92   expensive china

95   cream colored skirt down her slender legs.

100   - Pretty.

001   pink flowered mini skirt that emphasized
       her long slim legs.
       lights outlined the soft curves of her
   breasts through the sheer dress.

102   lamps cast shadows on the teak wall & shone
     from movies black hair

103   Shining black hair

104   Soft warm body

107   pretty legs

108   long dark hair shining in the sun

111   long black hair   her long shapely legs.

The Grand Okanagan Lakefront Resort and Conference Centre
1310 Water Street, Kelowna, B.C., Canada V1Y 9P3
Telephone (250) 763-4500   Facsimile (250) 763-4565
Resort Toll Free 1-800-465-4651

310 after making sure she left her
finger prints on the telephone   } she
                                      did.
hedonistic drive

314   white & gold gown

333   brown checked sports suit and
      white shoes, the very latest of
            fashion

335   There was no percentage
      in him shooleng mrs. Davis
      He was up Shit crack without a
            paddle

CHAPTER 40

A tall man in a dark suit entered the warehouse as Andrew hung up the telephone after talking to Maria. The man stopped momentarily in the doorway and looked around, then walked slowly towards the office. Andrew took his coat off the back of the chair and carefully put it on over the heavy bandages on his arm. The bulge under the man's coat suggested a revolver - a policeman? Andrew decided not, a fallen angel perhaps - an emissary of a legion lost. Lois was still not back with the coffee as Andrew closed the door of the office behind him and walked towards the stranger. They met near the middle of the warehouse floor.

"I'm looking for a Mr. Petersen," the man said, addressing Andrew in a husky voice.

"He is probably in the lunchroom," Andrew replied, pointing to the door at the far end of the warehouse.

"Thanks."

The man walked towards the lunchroom as Lois emerged through the door carrying two cups of coffee, and Andrew continued on his way to the large overhead doors. Once outside Andrew hurried to his car; it started right away, and silently he thanked the Lord. Andrew put the car into gear as the stranger in the warehouse stopped to speak to Lois. When the stranger, with a puzzled expression on his face, looked towards the door, Andrew was driving away.

A police car turned into the parking lot, and Andrew stopped at the entrance to let it go by as the mournful sound of its siren died. Then, as Andrew pulled his car onto the street, the police car, its red and blue dome lights flashing, swept through the large overhead doors into the warehouse, and while the two uniformed policemen quickly got out of the car, Andrew drove across the street to the shopping center to park his car and take a taxi to Stanley Park.

* * *

It was warm and sunny with just a few puffy white clouds dotting the blue sky, and many people in the park, enjoying the beauty of the day, were sitting on the benches that looked out to sea, walking, or relaxing on the grass. A man wearing a trench coat stopped on the path, and looked out to sea, and then turning slowly; he looked at Andrew before walking on.

My God would they ever leave them alone! Removing his tie and coat to be more comfortable, Andrew hung them over his arm and walked slowly over the grass looking for Maria; the man in the trench coat had disappeared. Young men and women were coming into the park from the surrounding offices to eat their lunches; emerging from their cars full of enthusiasm, and laughing and talking as they took their sandwiches from the brown paper bags. Maria was nowhere in sight, and Andrew, apprehensive that something evil may have befallen her, sat down on the grass near the point to await her arrival, while behind him a group of children were playing with a ball on the grass close to the trees. Then after only a short while, Maria was walking towards him, fresh and youthful in her blue mini dress, swinging a brown paper bag, and laughing when she caught his eye.

* * *

"Have you been waiting long?" she asked, taking the bag of chicken and chips, and putting it down on the grass.

"Just a little while."

"Hungry?"

"No, we are not alone here, there appears to be a man stalking us."

"Interesting, but we are prepared for just about anything. Tell me about what has happened," Maria said, and she opened her handbag containing her gun.

A girl sitting on the grass a few yards away, who had been watching them since Maria arrived, returned to eating her lunch and reading the book that she held open in her hand.

"Well?" Maria asked enquiringly, and her father seemed reluctant to begin shifting his position on the grass, Andrew looked intently at Maria as she waited, appearing almost unconcerned, for his explanation. Then noting the concerned expression on her father's face and his prolonged hesitation to tell her what he had to say, Maria's calmness and feeling of ease faded and was lost.

"Danny is dead," Andrew said slowly and quietly.

"No!" Maria cried, and the girl sitting on the grass nearby once again gave them her attention.

Putting his arm around his daughter's shoulders, Andrew held her close as bending forward she sobbed, her shoulders heaving under the gentle pressure of her father's arm. Slowly, Maria's grief subsided and she dried her eyes and lay back on the grass with her hands under her head, her eyes closed, and the warm sun on her face.

"How did it happen?" Maria asked, after opening her eyes.

Andrew looked down to his daughter as she looked far away into the blue of the sky, and as tactfully as possible, he told Maria what had happened. Then, when he had finished, Andrew folded his coat and placed it under Maria's head. Maria closed her eyes and rested; the expression of sadness on her face slowly relaxing, as above their heads, seagulls soared and dived in the wind, and behind them in the trees, birds sang.

The young people were going back to their work in the offices, and there was the sound of cars starting and driving away. Maria moved her foot until it touched her father's, and Andrew turned his head to look once more at his daughter; her eyes closed, and her face beautiful and serene, bathed in the light of the sun. The sounds of the wind in the trees and the wash of the sea mingled with the songs of the birds, and the raucous call of a crow. Maria opened her eyes, and looked again far away into the blue of the sky - it was hard to say goodbye.

"What will we do now?" Maria asked after some time.

"I'm not sure. It seems that we have come to a turning point in time," Andrew said, his voice quiet and pensive. "We could move on and try to elude Cec Banas and the police, or..." Andrew's voice trailed off.

"Or we could give ourselves up to the police," Maria said, sitting up and looking into her father's eyes.

"Yes," Andrew agreed. "We can stay here together in the sun for a while." Andrew saw the man in the trench coat standing close against the trees and said nothing; he could see the gun in Maria's open purse and he was ready.

Maria smiled in agreement. They would make the most of their freedom and the warm summer day, and while neither knew what the morrow might bring, they were relieved that their involvement in the trafficking of drugs had come to an end.

"If we give ourselves up, do you think we will be in jail for long?" Maria asked; her eyes on the sea, where a yacht, with her red striped sails full with the breeze, was making her way down the coast.

"No," Andrew replied, as he studied Maria and contemplated the possibility of her going to jail. She was beautiful - a woman who was intended to be happy and free. "The help that we have given the police will show that we were unwilling participants in the drug trade and worked to prevent its success. This should help us in any trial, and we could ask that it be kept confidential to avoid reprisals from the underworld."

"What will happen to Cec, Irene, and her parents?"

Laying back on the grass, Andrew put his hands under his head; his dark brown eyes seeing the small white clouds, drifting through the endless blue of the sky. "The police will pick up Irene easily enough, but her parents will give them a more difficult time. Extradition proceedings will have to be taken to bring them back to Canada from the Caribbean for trial. They have a lot of money invested there and it will be difficult; although, I believe that eventually justice will be served." Andrew rose up on one elbow in response to the sharp cry of a seagull. The man in the trench coat had retreated into the shelter of the trees, and Andrew considered going and flushing him out.

"What about Cec?" Maria asked.

Andrew sat up, and looked to Maria now sitting by his side. "He is our biggest problem. Cec will have some place, prepared in advance, where he can hide and unless the police apprehend him on the way there, he will be gone. Perhaps not very far, and out of anger and frustration he may strike back at us when he finds out that he has been tricked."

"Tricked!" Maria exclaimed, with a puzzled expression on her face.

"Yes, my brother died of a heart attack just a few days before Val. His lawyer was in contact with me regarding his estate, and he left me his thirty percent share that he owned in the L.W.C. Import and Export Corporation. I explained to the lawyer that the corporation was going through a crisis, and I asked him to keep my brother's death a secret. When the time was right, I said I would tell the Leweses about it."

"Dad, do you know what this means?"

"Yes, we may be able to prevent the company from dealing in illegal drugs" Andrew replied. Then father and daughter looked to each other and laughed.

"Weren't you tempted to throw in with the Leweses when you found out that you were part owner in the corporation, Dad?"

"No," Andrew replied. Then after a pause when his mind went back in time, he continued, "Val was our savior."

Val's death had been a decisive factor in their lives, and Maria was sad as she recalled to memory the young girl who had been her friend. Her death had been tragic, although as long as they would remember, her life and death will not have been in vain.

"Do you know, Maria, that Cec is one slimy bastard; a credit to the devil himself," Andrew said, with a note of concern in his voice. "He could do us a lot of harm if he is on the loose, and it would take a miracle for the police to catch him."

The patch of red on her father's side grew as the blood soaked through the dressing on his wound, evidence enough of the close call to another world, and silently, Maria prayed; she couldn't imagine life without him, and she wanted him, to live, to be a grandfather to her child.

Out on the sea, a blue and white ferry churned through the water, and the yacht with the red striped sails had disappeared from view. Maria turned back to her father, intending to tell him something concerning Cec, but his eyes were directed towards the trees, and quietly she picked up the lunch bag from the grass. The chicken tasted good, and she ate slowly, while behind them, a short distance away, the children played and shouted with glee when one of them scored a goal. Maria wiped her hands with a serviette, placed the remains of their lunch back into the bag, and took it to a refuse container a short way off, and then she returned to sit on the grass by her father.

A cloud passed before the sun, and its dark shadow traveled over the grass and the edge of the water. Maria thought about Tom; she had promised to see him on the weekend and she had looked forward to their date, and now with the future uncertain this didn't seem possible. Tormented by the thought of once again hurting Tom, Maria closed her eyes; she wanted to see him, to hear his voice, and feel his arms about her. The shadow passed from before the sun and once more they were bathed in its warm light. She would telephone Tom at the first opportunity. Maria looked to her father. His eyes were open, and he was watching her. "Do you like Tom?" she asked.

"Yes," Andrew replied, "he seems to be a very nice boy."

"I'm glad you like him. He comes from a good family."

"His mother is a very well spoken woman," Andrew said, with just the hint of a smile on his face. "She was very pleasant when I spoke to her on the telephone Wednesday afternoon."

"Why did you talk to Tom's mother?" Maria asked emphatically, her eyes narrow with suspicion.

"We chatted for a time while we waited for Tom to come to the telephone."

Maria sighed. "Then our meeting with Tom at Anne's Lounge wasn't by chance?"

345

"No. I talked to him that afternoon. I just caught him in time; he was to leave for Europe in an hour or so to attend a livestock show and a meeting involving cattle."

Maria's jaw set, and she drew in a deep breath, as Andrew closed his eyes. "Father!" she exclaimed.

A gust of wind rippled the surface of the sea and caused the trees behind them to bend and murmur, while all around there were the sounds of life; children playing, adults talking, and birds singing. Even Tom had said nothing about the invitation her father had extended. Still, she was glad he had come.

Maria turned her attention back to her father lying on the grass, his hands beneath his head, his eyes open, a faint smile on his face, and the patch of blood on the side of his shirt ugly and larger. Bending over him, Maria kissed him lightly on a cheek, then, with his coat under her head, she lay down by his side. Andrew sat up to keep an eye on the bushes behind them.

With her eyes closed, Maria relaxed and while experiencing the warmth of the sun on her face and legs, and hearing the sounds of people, of birds, the occasional car passing by, and the sea washing on the rocks, she thought again about Tom. She wouldn't meet his mother on Sunday, and have dinner with them as they had planned; still, there was a lifetime ahead of them, to be lived and enjoyed. She was unaware that Andrew's eyes were open and of the thoughtful expression on his face.

Putting his thoughts of Cec Banas aside for a time, Andrew's dark eyes peered into the heavens above while his mind retraced his life. A life full and happy, although not always contented; there were just a few things he would change, and a lot he would give for his wife to be with them this day.

There was the noise of cars braking on the road as the sounds of people around them ceased; then even the birds were still, and there was only the relentless sound of the wash of the waves on the rocks. Andrew knew what was happening, and he had hoped that it would not happen this way.

The policemen surrounded them as Andrew stood up and called Maria's name. Maria opened her eyes as the shadow of a policeman passed before the sun; the detective in the gray suit stood by her father, and snapped a handcuff on his wrist, then with his free hand, Andrew bent down and helped Maria to her feet.

"You are both under arrest," the policeman said quietly, as the people around them watched in silence.

The man in the trench coat emerged from the bushes, and joined the other policemen; with whom he had been in contact on his cellular telephone.

Andrew picked up his coat and tie from the grass as the people came closer and began to whisper. The policemen didn't handcuff Maria, and Andrew appreciated the gesture. Then in the company of six policemen they walked towards the two police cars parked on the side of the road, with their doors still open. Turning to each other, Maria and Andrew smiled; in the back of the police car behind the one to which they were being led, Cec Banas, morose and with Danny's yachting cap still on his head, sat in the company of a police officer.

"I was suspicious of Cec," Maria said, "When he left the office with his briefcase full of papers, I had the feeling he was on the lam." Then as Maria bent her head to get into the front seat of the police car, and the policeman in the gray suit went before her father into the back seat, she continued. "It was a shot in the dark, but I telephoned Ted and asked him to keep his eye on the yacht." Andrew laughed, and with laughter in her eyes, Maria went on. "After all, the yacht is company property."

"I will get a lawyer for both of us," Andrew said, as a policeman closed the door of the car. "Perhaps, there is someone else whom you would like to telephone."

"Thanks, Dad," Maria said, knowing her father understood. She wanted Tom to know that she would be late for dinner before he read about them in the newspaper.

The children laughing and playing with the ball ran over the place that Maria and Andrew had just left, and the people that had gathered dispersed when the two police cars drove away, and the waves washed up on the beach.

EPILOGUE

But the story did not end there, Andrew received two years less a day in jail for his part in the whole affair, and Maria was put on probation for two years with a $10,000 fine. In jail, Andrew continued his education, and there are a lot of the kids who needed counseling, and he is doing what he can. Ron Rahl is running the L.W.C. Import and Export Company. With the help of Andrew, the company is doing well, and the handling of illegal drugs was discontinued. Irene for the part she played got ten years behind bars, but with good behavior she could be out in five.

Ron and Irene owned twenty-one percent each of the company, and with Andrew's thirty percent they are running the company as they wish.

Ron comes to see Andrew once a week for advice, and when Andrew is released they will manage the company together.

But not before Maria had her say on their ill-gotten gains; they bought a gravestone for Mother's grave, and gave the rest of their money to charity. Andrew is paying for his university education with scholarships and student loans, which he will repay with company profits. Remember Lois, Andrew is still seeing her, and I will leave the rest of this affair to your imagination.

Maria married Tom, and they have a boy and a girl and another baby on the way. Tom is the father of them all, and what can you say, they are happy.

Some of Perrelli's henchmen got caught dealing drugs, and got 25 years in jail, but they are still in the racket even from within jail, but they are more cautious than ever, and one of them told Andrew that he was taking a course in counseling, which he is, and then he laughed. When they are bad they are bad.

The Leweses are still in the Caribbean on the run from the police and the drug lords; evidently they still owed money on the last shipment, and they would be safer in jail. And Cec, he will be in jail for a long time.

ISBN 141201824-2

9 781412 018241